Memory and Medievalism in George R. R. Martin and *Game of Thrones*

Memory and Medievalism in George R. R. Martin and *Game of Thrones*

The Keeper of All Our Memories

Edited by
Anna Czarnowus and Carolyne Larrington

BLOOMSBURY ACADEMIC
LONDON • NEW YORK • OXFORD • NEW DELHI • SYDNEY

BLOOMSBURY ACADEMIC
Bloomsbury Publishing Plc
50 Bedford Square, London, WC1B 3DP, UK
1385 Broadway, New York, NY 10018, USA
29 Earlsfort Terrace, Dublin 2, Ireland

BLOOMSBURY, BLOOMSBURY ACADEMIC and the Diana logo are trademarks of
Bloomsbury Publishing Plc

First published in Great Britain 2022
Paperback edition first published in 2024

Copyright © Anna Czarnowus and Carolyne Larrington, 2022

Anna Czarnowus and Carolyne Larrington have asserted their right under the Copyright,
Designs and Patents Act, 1988, to be identified as Editors of this work.

Cover image: Deutsch-Ostafrika, Reise Bernhard Dernburg (© Das Bundesarchive)

All rights reserved. No part of this publication may be reproduced or transmitted
in any form or by any means, electronic or mechanical, including photocopying,
recording, or any information storage or retrieval system, without prior
permission in writing from the publishers.

Bloomsbury Publishing Plc does not have any control over, or responsibility for, any
third-party websites referred to or in this book. All internet addresses given in this
book were correct at the time of going to press. The author and publisher regret any
inconvenience caused if addresses have changed or sites have ceased to exist,
but can accept no responsibility for any such changes.

A catalogue record for this book is available from the British Library.

A catalog record for this book is available from the Library of Congress.

ISBN: HB: 978-1-3502-6959-0
PB: 978-1-3502-6963-7
ePDF: 978-1-3502-6960-6
eBook: 978-1-3502-6961-3

Typeset by Deanta Global Publishing Services, Chennai, India

To find out more about our authors and books visit www.bloomsbury.com and
sign up for our newsletters.

Contents

List of Figures — vii
List of Abbreviations — viii
Show episodes — ix
Acknowledgements — xi
List of Contributors — xii

Introduction *Anna Czarnowus and Carolyne Larrington* — 1

Part I Reimagining history — 9

1 George R. R. Martin's *A Song of Ice and Fire* and Maurice Druon's *Les Rois Maudits* (*The Accursed Kings*) *Carolyne Larrington* — 11
2 Broken bodies, broken kingdoms, broken promises: The revolutionary failure of *Game of Thrones* *Robert Rouse and Cory James Rushton* — 24

Part II Key institutions — 35

3 The Citadel and the ivory tower: Academia and education in Westeros *Mikayla Hunter* — 37
4 'The Iron Bank will have its due': Trade and economics in *Game of Thrones* *Caroline R. Batten* — 50

Part III Faith and salvation — 65

5 The dog, the cynic and the saint: The case of Sandor Clegane *Thomas Honegger* — 67
6 The figure of George R. R. Martin's Septon Meribald and the Franciscan legacy *Maria Błaszkiewicz* — 80

Part IV Chivalry: Theory and practice — 93

7 The warrior(s) in crisis: The knights of Westeros and the process of civilization *Anja Müller* — 95
8 Tournaments and judicial duels in George R. R. Martin's *The World of Ice and Fire* and *A Song of Ice and Fire* *Przemysław Grabowski-Górniak* — 108

Part V Memory   117

9   On medieval dream tradition in George R. R. Martin's *A Song of Ice and Fire* Bartłomiej Błaszkiewicz   119
10 The medievalist emotional economy in George R. R. Martin's *A Song of Ice and Fire* Anna Czarnowus   137

Part VI The 'HBO effect': Violence and misogyny   147

11 From romance to rape: The portrayal of masculine sexuality in *Game of Thrones* Kristina Hildebrand   149
12 The Rise and Fall of Cersei Lannister: Neomedievalist misogyny in George R. R. Martin's *A Song of Ice and Fire* Sylwia Borowska-Szerszun   161

Postscript *Carolyne Larrington*   173

Notes   175
Bibliography   204
Index   216

Figures

1	Sandor Clegane enters Winterfell	68
2	Sallet in the shape of a lion's head (Italy, c.1475–80)	68
3	Sandor Clegane's helmet	69
4	The loyal greyhound at his (dead) master's feet	70
5	King Garamantes, being rescued by his dogs	70
6	Sigil (or coat of arms) of the Clegane family	72
7	Direwolf, lion and crowned stag attacking the dragon	73
8	A dog-headed *cynocephalus*, one of the Plinian races	76
9	Fourteenth-century manuscript illustration to Marco Polo's *Il Milione* showing the dog-headed inhabitants of the Andaman Islands	77
10	Saint Christopher Kynokephalos (Doghead)	77
11	Saint Christopher carrying Christ	78
12	Saint Christopher with a dog's head carrying Christ	79

Abbreviations

Books in *A Song of Ice and Fire* series

GT	*A Game of Thrones*
CK	*A Clash of Kings*
SS	*A Storm of Swords*
FC	*A Feast for Crows*
DD	*A Dance of Dragons: Dreams and Dust*
AF	*A Dance of Dragons: After the Feast*

Other works by Martin

KSK	*A Knight of the Seven Kingdoms*
HK	'The Hedge Knight'
DE	'Dunk and Egg'
FB	*Fire and Blood*
WIF	*The World of Ice and Fire*

Citations are by page number or, for some electronic editions, location number.

Show episodes

Season One (HBO, 2011)

Ep. 1 Winter Is Coming
Ep. 2 The Kingsroad
Ep. 3 Lord Snow
Ep. 4 Cripples, Bastards and Broken Things
Ep. 5 The Wolf and the Lion
Ep. 6 A Golden Crown
Ep. 7 You Win or You Die
Ep. 8 The Pointy End
Ep. 9 Baelor
Ep. 10 Fire and Blood

Season Two (HBO, 2012)

Ep. 1 The North Remembers
Ep. 2 The Night Lands
Ep. 3 What Is Dead May Never Die
Ep. 4 Garden of Bones
Ep. 5 The Ghost of Harrenhal
Ep. 6 The Old Gods and the New
Ep. 7 A Man without Honor
Ep. 8 The Prince of Winterfell
Ep. 9 Blackwater
Ep. 10 Valar Morghulis

Season Three (HBO, 2013)

Ep. 1 Valar Dohaeris
Ep. 2 Dark Wings, Dark Words
Ep. 3 Walk of Punishment
Ep. 4 And Now His Watch Is Ended
Ep. 5 Kissed by Fire
Ep. 6 The Climb
Ep. 7 The Bear and the Maiden Fair

Ep. 8 Second Sons
Ep. 9 The Rains of Castamere
Ep. 10 Mhysa

Season Four (HBO, 2014)

Ep. 1 Two Swords
Ep. 2 The Lion and the Rose
Ep. 3 Breaker of Chains
Ep. 4 Oathkeeper
Ep. 5 First of His Name
Ep. 6 The Laws of Gods and Men
Ep. 7 Mockingbird
Ep. 8 The Mountain and the Viper
Ep. 9 The Watchers on the Wall
Ep. 10 The Children

Season Five (HBO, 2015)

Ep. 1 The Wars to Come
Ep. 2 The House of Black and White
Ep. 3 High Sparrow
Ep. 4 Sons of the Harpy
Ep. 5 Kill the Boy
Ep. 6 Unbowed, Unbent, Unbroken
Ep. 7 The Gift
Ep. 8 Hardhome
Ep. 9 Dance of Dragons
Ep. 10 Mother's Mercy

Season Six (HBO, 2016)

Ep. 1 The Red Woman
Ep. 2 Home
Ep. 3 Oathbreaker
Ep. 4 Book of the Stranger
Ep. 5 The Door
Ep. 6 Blood of My Blood
Ep. 7 The Broken Man
Ep. 8 No One
Ep. 9 Battle of the Bastards

Acknowledgements

This book was first conceived at the Medieval Fantasy Symposium, organized by Dr Łukasz Neubauer and Dr Izabela Dixon of Koszalin University of Technology, held in Unieście in May 2016. The editors offer their grateful thanks to both these scholars for bringing together the core group of contributors to this volume. The editors would also like to thank all at Bloomsbury, in particular Rhodri Mogford and Laura Reeves, as well as the anonymous reviewers of the book in manuscript form. We would also like to thank Dr Felix Taylor and Will Brockbank for their invaluable assistance with the text.

Professor Czarnowus would like to dedicate this volume to the memory of her aunt Anna Lipińska (1924–2021), who always supported her research.

Contributors

Caroline R. Batten has been an Icelandic Research Fund postdoctoral Fellow at the University of Iceland and is now Assistant Professor of Medieval English Literature at the University of Pennsylvania. She received her DPhil from the University of Oxford. Her work on medieval magic, science and gender has appeared in the *Journal of English and Germanic Philology*, *Medium Ævum*, *Scandinavian Studies*, and the *Review of English Studies*, among others.

Bartłomiej Błaszkiewicz is Professor of Medieval Literature at the Department of English Studies, University of Warsaw. He has published extensively on literature and culture of the Middle Ages and the Renaissance and the continuation of these traditions, on medievalism and various aspects of oral culture in the Middle Ages, medieval versification, romance and folk ballad, as well as modern fantasy literature. His book publications include *Oral-Formulaic Diction in the Middle English Verse Romance* (2009), *George R. R. Martin's A Song of Ice and Fire and the Medieval Literary Tradition* (editor, 2014) and *Medieval Contexts in Modern Fantasy Fiction* (2021).

Maria Błaszkiewicz is Associate Professor at the Department of English Studies, University of Warsaw. Her academic interests focus on the fantastic in literature, the diachronic study of the epic, literature as *locus theologicus*, the libretto and the Victorian novel. Her publications include articles and chapters on Tolkien, Milton, Handel, Martin and Pratchett.

Sylwia Borowska-Szerszun is Assistant Professor in the Faculty of Philology at the University of Białystok (Poland). She has published on medieval and early Tudor drama, cultural memory, medievalism and fantasy literature. She has recently co-edited *Images of the Anthropocene in Speculative Fiction: Narrating the Future* (2021).

Anna Czarnowus is Associate Professor in the Faculty of Humanities at the University of Silesia, Katowice (Poland). She has published monographs and articles on monstrous children in Middle English literature, Middle English Oriental romance and medievalism. She has co-edited (with M. J. Toswell) *Medievalism in English Canadian Literature: From Richardson to Atwood* (2020).

Kristina Hildebrand is a lecturer in English at the School of Education, Humanities and Social Sciences at Halmstad University, Sweden. Her work on gender, sexuality and disability, especially in medieval and modern Arthurian texts, has appeared in *Arthuriana* and *Journal of the International Arthurian Society*, among others.

Przemysław Grabowski-Górniak has received his PhD from the University of Warsaw. He has published on the martial aspects of Arthurian literature, medieval heroic epic, medievalist and religious symbolism in superhero comic books. His major focus is the literary heritage of Robert E. Howard, including articles such as 'Robert E. Howard's Conan Cycle as Modern Epic' (2014) and 'The Age Undreamed of: Reality and History in Robert E. Howard's Fantasy' (2020).

Thomas Honegger is Professor of Medieval English Language and Literature at the Friedrich-Schiller-University Jena (Germany). He has published widely on animals in medieval literature, historical pragmatics and medievalism (esp. J. R. R. Tolkien). His latest monograph is *Introducing the Medieval Dragon* (2019).

Mikayla Hunter wrote her DPhil on themes of disguise and deception in medieval English romance and Robin Hood ballads at the University of Oxford. She has published articles on Arthurian literature in *Journal of Arthurian Studies* and *Arthuriana*, and she also works on Robin Hood studies and medievalism, in particular *Game of Thrones*. Her research primarily focuses on disguise and perception, memory, history of emotions and socio-historical contexts of literary works.

Carolyne Larrington is Professor of Medieval European Literature at the University of Oxford and Official Fellow in Medieval English Literature at St John's College. She has published widely on Old Norse and Arthurian literature, emotions and family relationships in medieval literature and medievalism. Her monographs from Bloomsbury on *Game of Thrones* are *Winter Is Coming* (2015) and *All Men Must Die* (2021).

Anja Müller is Professor of English Literature and Culture at the University of Siegen (Germany). She has published on eighteenth-century literature and culture, childhood concepts and children's literature (e.g. *Framing Childhood in Eighteenth-Century English Periodicals and Prints, 1689–1789*, 2009), identity construction, intertextuality and adaptation, fantasy and role play, and is co-editing the series *Studies in European Children's Literature*. A co-edited essay collection on pre-modern masculinities is forthcoming with Universitätsverlag Winter, Heidelberg (*Zwischen Ehre und Schande: Praktiken und Narrative vormoderner Männlichkeiten*, eds. Anja Müller, Hans Rudolf Velten and Rebecca Weber, 2021).

Robert Rouse is Associate Professor of Medieval Literature at the University of British Columbia, Vancouver. He has published widely on medieval romance and Arthurian literature, spatial humanities, the erotic in medieval literature and contemporary medievalism. He has most recently co-edited (with Siân Echard) the *Wiley-Blackwell Encyclopedia of Medieval Literature in Britain* (2017).

Cory James Rushton is Associate Professor of English at St Francis Xavier University in Nova Scotia (Canada). He is most recently the co-editor of *A New Companion to Malory* (2019) and has published work on Arthurian literature and film, medieval romance, modern fantasy and zombies.

Introduction

Anna Czarnowus and Carolyne Larrington

Bran the Broken, First of His Name, becomes king of the Six Kingdoms of Westeros in the final episode of the HBO TV series, *Game of Thrones* (2011–19). His qualifications for kingship reside partly in the fact that he is almost the last surviving male from any of the Great Houses of Westeros and partly in his all-encompassing knowledge of past, present and quite possibly future. For Bran, as Tyrion Lannister claims in that final episode at the Great Council, is 'our memory, the keeper of all our stories' (8.6). Memory and story, history and narrative are more important than military power, physical prowess or messianic vision for the future of the survivors of the Massacre of King's Landing: they will teach how to prevent the recurrence of the past with its civil wars, violence and horror with a wiser, more altruistic statecraft. It is from Tyrion's persuasive rhetoric in that key speech that seeks to bring resolution amidst the ruins of King's Landing that we take our subtitle. For *Game of Thrones*, and George R. R. Martin's still unfinished novel series *A Song of Ice and Fire*, with which it exists in symbiosis, Martin himself and the showrunners are indeed memory keepers, reshaping, reinterpreting and remediating many versions of the medieval past to make meaning in our present.

The novels and show diverged at different points along the storylines of particular characters but, broadly speaking, after Season Five the showrunners, David Benioff and Daniel Weiss, developed the plot themselves with some reference to notes given them by Martin. These often varied in detail from the narratives that are still underway in the books. The TV show lays claim to being the most-watched show in TV history, broadcast in 207 countries, in 194 of them on simulcast: that is, at the same time as the US East Coast broadcast. Its huge success depends on a number of factors: its interest in large and still relevant political questions, its exploration of the dynamics of the family, not to mention its reputation for nudity, explicit sex and bloody violence. Crucial however is the believability and coherence of the secondary world, in which the show was set, a universe that takes its inspiration from medieval history, literature and culture, the building blocks for Martin's world creation. The books and show (hereafter referred to as the 'series') then are fundamentally *medievalist* in their vision; their setting is a medievalized universe, their cultures are calqued upon a range of global medieval societies and their imaginary is one that takes the medieval supernatural as its starting point.

Medievalism and *Game of Thrones* studies

The universe in question is inspired by the Middle Ages and – according to Martin and the showrunners – it purports to reflect the historical Middle Ages in varying ways. Helen Young notes of *A Song of Ice and Fire* (and her observations also hold good for the TV show) that the series falls within 'the realm of Gritty Fantasy . . . which claim[s] to represent the medieval period as it really was'.[1] Young defines Gritty Fantasy as 'marked by low levels of magic, high levels of violence, in-depth character development, and medievalist words that are [characterized by] rain, blood, and mud'.[2] It is a dark and brutal world in which Whiteness dominates; Gritty Fantasy is not intended for children but is rather a dark and often pessimistic vision created for adults.[3] While this kind of world preserves some features of the Middle Ages, its inscenation is partly driven by the Renaissance conception of the period as the Dark Ages and the twentieth-century reaction against the 'romantic Middle Ages' (to use David Matthews's influential terminology).[4] Martin's world is indeed medievalist in the sense of returning to and rescripting the always imaginary Middle Ages. However, as Shiloh Carroll notes, both Martin and the showrunners tend alternately to 'pass the buck' in response to criticism of their depictions of a medievalized world.[5] Thus they claim either that the series depicts violence (particularly sexualized violence) because this accurately reflects the medieval period or, when medieval experts dissent from this vision, fall back on the argument that the series is a fantasy work and thus makes no claim to medieval historical authenticity.

Medievalism, as first formulated by Leslie J. Workman, has always been understood as including creative reworkings of the historical period: the '*process* of creating the Middle Ages, and a scholarly, but also artistic recreation of it, the study not of the Middle Ages themselves, but of the scholars, artists, and writers who . . . constructed the idea of the Middle Ages that we inherited'.[6] Tison Pugh and Angela Jane Weisl indeed have posited that the entire construction of the Middle Ages is itself a fantasy; hence it is unsurprising that literary fantasy as a genre should participate enthusiastically in this type of construction.[7] Pugh and Weisl extend their definition of medievalism more broadly, to encompass along with art, literature and scholarship, those leisure activities that can be understood as entertainment and culture. At the same time as taking the Middle Ages for their subject or inspiration, they necessarily engage with the artist or creator's contemporary sociocultural milieu.[8] Any attempt to enter into dialogue with the Middle Ages is thus itself a form of medievalism.

Contemporary medievalist cultural products tend to incorporate other kinds of medievalisms, producing what Carol L. Robinson and Pamela Clements have called 'a post-postmodernist medievalism: fragmentary, fluid, attempting to encompass all truths, yet also brazenly fictionalizing these apparent truths . . . a medievalism . . . fully aware and celebratory of the constructed nature of its world(s)'.[9] Such postmodernism, or *neomedievalism*, is typical of the representations of the medieval in Martin's novel cycle and the TV show; this form of medievalism reworks the historical Middle Ages, mediating them via or in reaction to other medievalist conceptions in order to 'engage alternative realities of the Middle Ages'.[10] As we shall see below, *A Song of Ice and Fire/Game of Thrones* draws widely on pre-existing iterations of medieval history, historical fiction and post-medieval reimaginings of the medieval. Thus, its depiction of the Ironborn derives both from the Vikings as historical phenomenon and as they have been imagined by twentieth-century Hollywood films, such as the 1958 Kirk Douglas film *The Vikings*. This eclecticism has made the series a key text for many canonical studies of medievalism.[11] David Matthews's *Medievalism: A Critical History* starts with a reference to the TV show as a medievalist fantasy where 'dark-age power struggles are played out'.[12] And yet, since the series is also read as gesturing towards real-world, contemporary issues, those apparently distant power struggles are also highly relevant to the present. Simultaneously medievalist and neomedievalist, the *A Song of Ice and Fire/Game of Thrones* series has attracted a sizeable and diverse fandom that includes medieval and medievalist scholars as well as ordinary enthusiasts. Thomas A. Prendergast and Stephanie Trigg identify the show as the most conspicuous example of a fantasy work that 'regularly brings scholars and fans into the immediacy of online debate and discussion. Medievalism here generates a global community of historical scholarship, critical analysis and enthusiastic play'.[13] So too, this volume reaches out to and participates in that global community, bringing together a historical understanding of the Middle Ages that offers parallels, analogues and sources for the series, literary- and media-critical analysis of Martin's books and the TV show and taking up Prendergast and Trigg's idea of 'enthusiastic play': scholarly knowledge, literary imagination and fan interest are brought into juxtaposition by contributors who are both medieval experts and fans of *Game of Thrones*.

The relationship between medieval studies and medievalism has always been complicated, as Matthews's discussion shows. These parallel domains emerged in the 1850s when scholars, artists and interested amateurs in Britain, Germany and France began systematically to investigate the period from the perspective of the newly formalized disciplines of history and literary studies.[14] The result was the emergence of 'professional' medievalism – an academic interest in the medieval – alongside a 'non-professional' medievalism that inspired writers, artists and the general public.[15] The two fields developed in parallel in the academy; while medievalism at first took a back seat to medieval studies within the domains of history and literature, by the early twenty-first century the situation seems to be reversed. Medieval history and literary studies are no longer central to university humanities curricula; yet medievalism studies flourishes.[16] Consequently, one aim of this book is to place medieval studies and medievalism in creative contiguity: to compare structural developments and concepts across two distinctly imagined worlds in order to argue that we can treat medieval history and imaginative literature as offering a series of analogies to the world created by Martin and the showrunners in the novels and TV show. The essays collected here aim both to lead the enthusiast for medievalist fantasy to investigate the institutions and concepts of the medieval world and to invite scholars to the medieval period to discover how medievalism illuminates, reimagines and remediates the ways in which we have come to understand the material realities, textual constructions and ideological functions of that past.

Medievalist fantasy

The medieval, thanks very largely to Tolkien, has become a conventional setting for fantasy, offering the benefits of intertextual allusion and an assumed pre-existing familiarity with medieval or pseudo-medieval cultures. It is of course possible to write fantasy set elsewhere, whether in the future (at which point it becomes science fiction) or in a different past period. Yet the time and space within which the story is set will not be totally unfamiliar if the author's worldbuilding task is not to be exhausting. Thus, the medieval functions as both recognizable and estranged, in part because of its fragmentary survival in our own culture: audiences both know what a medieval world should look like and yet have insufficient detailed knowledge to critique individual manifestations of such a world.[17] The 'Known World' of Martin's fantasy epic, as fan communities like to call this universe, is a medievalist creation. It draws some inspiration from, but as much reacts against, Tolkien's Middle Earth which itself was inspired by nineteenth-century medievalism. Martin comments in an important interview:

> Ruling is hard. This was maybe my answer to Tolkien, whom, as much as I admire him, I do quibble with. *Lord of the Rings* had a very medieval philosophy: that if the king was a good man, the land would prosper. We look at real history and it's not that simple. Tolkien can say that Aragorn became king and reigned for a hundred years, and he was wise and good. But Tolkien doesn't ask the question: What was Aragorn's tax policy? Did he maintain a standing army? What did he do in times of flood and famine? And what about all these orcs?[18]

Martin took a minor in history in college, and he is interested in such questions as Aragorn's tax policy: namely, the organization and finance of military expeditions, international credit and, importantly, how monopolies on literacy and the separation of learning and religion affect the development of cultures. He is of course not writing history, or anything like it. And since Martin is notoriously cagey about his sources and research, repeatedly taking the line that the late medieval English 'Wars of the Roses' provided the primary inspiration for the War of the Five Kings, we cannot, of course, claim a one-to-one relationship between real-world historical phenomena and the institutions of Martin's societies. Nevertheless, the building blocks of the series' storyworld are largely medieval institutions, beliefs, stories and cultural practices, utilized, not always with a deliberate historicized intention, by the author. As noted above, Martin also draws on popular medievalism: his dragons are descended directly from Tolkien's Smaug, with some influence from Ursula Le Guin's dragons in the Earthsea series.[19] While the various essays in this volume investigate many of the elements employed within the storyworld and use medieval concepts to illuminate their function within that storyworld, they also reflect back on the cultures of the actual medieval world.

The TV show ended in 2019, leaving some fans highly dissatisfied, while others accepted that it had run its course. The story arcs of those particular characters thus came to their conclusion. However, HBO and other media companies have sought to capitalize on the show's success; a number of prequels and spin-offs are either in production or being commissioned. The 'Thrones' universe then has the potential to expand into a medievalized equivalent of the Marvel Comic Universe: an imaginative space in which the series' larger themes can be revisited, new characters developed and new dilemmas explored. *Game of Thrones* has become a transmedia franchise, equivalent to Tolkien's 'Lord of the Rings' in its global appeal and – so we argue – in the moral seriousness of the questions that it raises about contemporary preoccupations: changing constructions of masculinity and femininity, faith and ethics, education and capitalism, and the ways in which we remember and remediated the past.

Like Tolkien's writings too, *A Song of Ice and Fire/Game of Thrones* has functioned as a kind of 'gateway drug'; the interest that it has awakened in the 'real' medieval past, alongside the phenomenon of medievalism, has attracted thousands of new enthusiasts to the study of medieval history and literature. It functions, particularly in North America, but equally in Europe, as an introduction to medieval historical events and cultural phenomena. This is one of the primary aims of this volume: to open up and examine the ways in which the series both introduces and interrogates medieval history and culture, capturing the imaginations of ordinary viewers and students alongside academic researchers.

Medievalism and Martin studies

A Song of Ice and Fire/Game of Thrones studies is now an important subfield in contemporary medievalism. Martin's importance in medieval fantasy is powerfully asserted in Shiloh Carroll's magisterial monograph *Medievalism in A Song of Ice and Fire and Game of Thrones*. Here she argues that Martin is 'the "American" Tolkien', where, as she astutely observes, '"American" carries with it many connotations, among them power, imperialism, individualism, and a level of cynicism'.[20] Carroll's study focuses on the series' antithetical attitude to conventional romance, alongside issues of gender and sexuality, postcolonialism and Whiteness and the relation of the TV adaptation (up to the end of season six) to the novels, along with its critical and fan reception. Earlier collections of essays on Martin's books and the show including Anne Gjelsvik and Rikke Schubart's *Women of Ice and Fire: Gender, Game of Thrones, and Multiple Media Engagements* (2014) are devoted to the female characters in a transmedia context, while Zita Rohr and Lisa Benz's 2020 collection *Queenship and the Women of Westeros: Female Agency and Advice in Game of Thrones and A Song of Ice and Fire* locates those characters in the context of queenship studies.[21] In the United States, McFarland Books has published a series of monographs which typically do not deal with the complete TV show as they address particular topics in the *Game of Thrones* universe. These include Valerie Estelle Frankel's 2014 *Women in Game of Thrones: Power, Conformity and Resistance*, Ken Mondschein's 2017 *Game of Thrones and the Medieval Art of War*, and Carol Parrish Jamison's 2018 *Chivalry in Westeros: The Knightly Code of A Song of Ice and Fire*.[22] Previous essay collections in the field include the seminal volume *Mastering the Game of Thrones: Essays on George R. R. Martin's A Song of Ice and Fire*, edited by Jes Battis and Susan Johnston from 2015 and the forthcoming volume, *Power and Subversion in Game of Thrones*, edited by A. Keith Kelly.[23] *George R. R. Martin's A Song of Ice and Fire and the Medieval Literary Tradition* from 2014, edited by Bartłomiej Błaszkiewicz, was one of the earliest publications in the field; significantly, like the present volume, it included contributions by a good number of European scholars.[24] One of this book's editors has also made a significant contribution to Martin/*Game of Thrones* studies with *Winter Is Coming* from 2015, a study of the medieval building blocks of Martin's world, and the 2021 *All Men Must Die*, one of the first readings of the complete TV show.

About this book

The chapters in this volume set out to investigate Martin's imagined world, the different ways in which it relates to the medieval past and the ways in which that world was mediated in the TV show. The collection originated in a Medieval Fantasy Symposium, organized by Łukasz Neubauer, in Poland in 2016. A range of European non-Anglophone scholars, whose voices are not always amplified in English-language medievalism studies, gave papers on Martin and *Game of Thrones* there. Subsequent invitations to contribute to the volume were extended to scholars who could not attend the original workshop, among them well-established academics and early career researchers. Their uniquely individual perspectives have generated a wide-ranging conspectus of the series world and its relation to the medieval world: essays set in dialogue with one another. The book begins with Carolyne Larrington's discussion of how history is reimagined in exploring Martin's considerable debt to *Les Rois Maudits* (The Accursed Kings), a hugely popular French historical novel series written by Maurice Druon in the 1950s and completed in 1977. Martin often mentions his admiration for Druon's series and cites it as key to his decision to write in the medieval high fantasy genre rather than imitating Druon with his own historical novel series. Martin's dialogue with Druon's work demonstrates precisely the American author's 'neomedievalism': his appropriation of other medievalist works, in addition to his own immersion in actual medieval history and culture. Robert Rouse and Cory James Rushton focus on the series' treatment of disability, masculinity and their relation to the body politic, arguing that the TV show loses its nerve in reimagining large-scale possibilities for reform. While the book series seems to herald social and political change in Westeros, the show ends with a feel-good narrative, promoting Bran's story, that of a disabled nonmartial man, as the most interesting and representative narrative arc and mocking Sam's tentative ideas about democratic reform. The show's failure to envisage substantial change within Westeros's political system suggests that high fantasy is incompatible with democratic innovation; its emphasis on realism gradually mutes the fantasy elements.

The next group of essays focuses on approaches to faith and salvation. This starts with Thomas Honegger's consideration of Sandor Clegane's deceptive appearance. He wears a hound helmet, reflecting his identity as both man and dog. In medieval tradition the dog symbolizes faithfulness and yet is also an ignoble animal, invoked in insults: both aspects that are present in Martin's saga. Sandor Clegane is also a cynical (etymologically therefore dog-like) observer of the chivalric establishment. In the course of the novel series, he undergoes religious conversion, a condition that is close to sainthood, although this plot line remains unfinished in the novel cycle to date. Maria Błaszkiewicz expands the discussion of the concept of salvation by placing the character of Septon Meribald in the wider context of the Franciscan tradition, especially in comparison with the figure of St Francis of Assisi. Starting from the medieval biographies and *florilegia* she studies the impact of contemporary reception of both St Francis and the *Fioretti* on the presentation of Meribald, foregrounding the septon's attitude towards the natural world and the series' comparative neglect of Franciscanism's deeper spiritual context.

The following two chapters analyse key institutions within Martin's and the showrunners' worlds. Mikayla Hunter discusses academic and scholarly activities in Westeros, examining the structure of the Westerosi educational system alongside historical medieval systems, with a particular focus on the subject areas of formal education such as medicine, jurisprudence and theology. In the television version of Westeros, education is completely secularized; in the books, the study of prophecies and portents still (nominally) falls under the maesters' jurisdiction. Hunter also considers the class-influenced and gendered aspects of the Citadel's university system. Caroline Batten investigates the economic systems of the Known World, contrasting the differences in the depths in treatment offered by the books and show. She focuses in particular on the Iron Bank of Braavos as a political actor in Westeros and the economic realities of Meereen as they shape and challenge Daenerys's developing understanding of rulership. Batten shows how, unlike the well-imagined political economy of King's Landing, the neomedieval fantasy economy of the Ironborn is not viable, while the Dothraki's ambitions, in contrast to the Mongols, on whom they are largely based, are limited by their political and economic systems.

The theory and practice of chivalry are addressed by, respectively, Anja Müller and Przemysław Grabowski-Górniak. According to Müller, knighthood is key to our reading of the novels, but less important in the show. She uses Norbert Elias's 'process of civilization' theory to interpret knighthood in the novels; chivalry in Westeros functions as an ideal or myth, demonstrated by Bran and Sansa's individual perspectives on the world they live in. Martin's crisis of knighthood is a key driver of the plot, unpacking and critiquing the concept of 'courtly knighthood'. Grabowski-Górniak's essay presents an appreciation and explanation of the intricacies of medieval martial culture as reflected in Martin's saga. As in Sir Walter Scott's medievalist fiction, the tournaments in the cycle are central and of critical importance. The tourney at Ashford Meadow, the Tourney at Harrenhal and the Tourney of the Hand illustrate are discussed in relation to key aspects of medieval tournaments. These ultimately derived from Roman and Carolingian war games; the principles of judicial duels are illustrated by the Trial of Seven in *The Hedge Knight* and by the duel between Prince Oberyn and Ser Gregor Clegane in both books and show.

Next come two essays that consider how medieval psychological, cognitive and emotional phenomena are remembered, reimagined and utilized in the series. Bartłomiej Błaszkiewicz's essay studies the connections between medieval philosophy of dreams and Martin's novel cycle. His chapter refers to key classical and medieval commentaries on dreams, establishing the nature of medieval dream theory, and he reads the characters' dreams as situated at the intersection of medievalist fascination with dreams signifying possibility and the expression of the modern condition: the dreams underpinned by a Jungian view of the collective unconscious. Next, Anna Czarnowus focuses on and distinguishes between medieval and medievalist emotions in Martin's fantasy cycle and the TV adaptation. Drawing on the 'history of emotions' field her critical perspectives interpret the presentation of love, honour (and the emotions of shame and sympathy that accompany it) and anger across the series. The essay considers how emotions, in particular Cersei's anger, are 'spent' and 'distributed' across the cycle.

Game of Thrones is notorious for the debates its violence and misogyny provoked. Kristina Hildebrand analyses sexual, and sexualized, violence, especially as aimed against women. Where the novel *A Game of Thrones* presents Daenerys and Khal Drogo's wedding night as seduction, the TV show converts the encounter into a rape, exemplifying ideas about violence as evoking 'gritty' medieval 'realism' and endorsing contemporary views of sexuality and masculinity in its naturalization of violent male sexuality. In the novel Daenerys develops from a passive victim to a powerful actor, seizing agency and power. In the show she is subject to a voyeuristic gaze, and we lose access to her interiority. Sylwia Borowska-Szerszun identifies Martin's saga as a powerful instance of 'muscular medievalism', to use Amy S. Kaufman's term.[25] Martin justifies the misogyny of the world he creates by claiming it is 'medieval', but both the novel cycle and the TV show rather, so Borowska-Szerszun argues, draw on neomedievalist conceptions about medieval women. While Cersei Lannister defies clearly defined boundaries of gender in the books' patriarchal world, she also embodies medievalist and neomedievalist misogyny. As the plot of the novel cycle progresses, she loses the looks she has been proud of, takes to drink and becomes sexually involved with men of increasingly lower status; in the TV show she uses violence and cruelty to assert her agency, trying and disastrously failing, to regain influence over her son Tommen and refusing to negotiate with the *force majeure* that Daenerys represents.

Our postscript glances at the future of *A Song of Ice and Fire/Game of Thrones*. We catch up with the latest TV prequel and Martin's continuing expansion of his universe and note the emerging preoccupations of this kind of medievalist fantasy in the current decade. The medieval is an active constitutent in the present, and fantasy is a key mode of keeping cultural memory alive.

Part I

Reimagining history

1

George R. R. Martin's *A Song of Ice and Fire* and Maurice Druon's *Les Rois Maudits* (*The Accursed Kings*)

Carolyne Larrington

George R. R. Martin often points to the fifteenth-century English Wars of the Roses as the chief historical inspiration for his unfinished novel series, *A Song of Ice and Fire*. Indeed, the chime between the names Stark and York and Lannister and Lancaster is suggestive, echoing the names of the principal magnate houses involved in the protracted civil war that saw the throne of England change hands backwards and forwards between Henry VI of the Lancastrians and Edward IV of the House of York. Both men were descended from the sons of Edward III. Henry VI ascended the throne as an infant in 1422, following the death of his father, Henry V, but proved, on reaching his majority, an unsatisfactory king. Critics have largely accepted Martin's assertion that the Wars of the Roses were central to his vision of the main storyline set in the western continent of Westeros; Alex Gendler has produced an informative ED-TED video which charts some of the parallels, though he has to range rather widely across the generations to make his case.[1] In gesturing towards the fifteenth century as providing some of the source material for the imagined world of Westeros however, Martin distracts attention from his very real debt to the twentieth-century French author, Maurice Druon, and his seven-novel sequence, set in the fourteenth century, *Les Rois Maudits* (translated into English as *The Accursed Kings*, the name by which I shall refer to it in what follows). Martin is open about his regard for the French author – writing the preface to the reissued English translations that appeared between 2013 and 2015 and penning an accompanying article that explored the ways in which Druon's exemplar had shaped his thinking, in particular about genre.[2]

> *The Accursed Kings* has it all: iron kings and strangled queens, battles and betrayals, lies and lust, deception, family rivalries, the curse of the Templars, babies switched at birth, she-wolves, sin and swords, the doom of a great dynasty and all of it (or most of it) straight from the pages of history. And believe me, the Starks and the Lannisters have nothing on the Capets and Plantagenets. Whether you're a history buff or a fantasy fan, Druon's epic will keep you turning pages: it is the original game of thrones.[3]

In this essay, I examine the relationship between Martin's novel sequence and that of Druon. I shall argue that Martin's historical vision is more firmly rooted in the fourteenth than the fifteenth century, and that Martin borrowed a number of narrative techniques, themes and even some details from the French historical novelist, reworking his material to fit his chosen genre of epic fantasy. It is vital to remember that Martin studied history as a minor when he was an undergraduate at Northwestern University, Evanston, Illinois, in the late 1960s (his major was journalism). *A Song of Ice and Fire* shows, at almost every level, the fruits of a good deal of historical research, but also, and perhaps more importantly, it bears witness to profound, thoroughgoing thinking about the structures of medieval society and culture. Martin himself calls attention to his fascination with history in the long and significant interview he gave to *Rolling Stone* magazine in 2014. In this he takes gentle issue with J. R. R. Tolkien; his comments point up the differences between the earlier writer's essentially linguistic and mythic imagination and his own historian's sensibility:

> Ruling is hard. This was maybe my answer to Tolkien, whom, as much as I admire him, I do quibble with. *Lord of the Rings* had a very medieval philosophy: that if the king was a good man, the land would prosper. We look at real history and it's not that simple. Tolkien can say that Aragorn became king and reigned for a hundred years, and he was wise and good. But Tolkien doesn't ask the question: What was Aragorn's tax policy? Did he maintain a standing army? What did he do in times of flood and famine? And what about all these orcs?[4]

Thanks in part to that early training as a historian, Martin is interested precisely in the real nuts and bolts of rule. He thinks about how crown expenditure is financed and how constant warfare revitalizes popular religion and fuels urban unrest. And so too did Maurice Druon.

Maurice Druon and his novels

Maurice Druon was a remarkable figure: he was born in 1918 and died as recently as 2009. During the Second World War he was active in the resistance, and he spent the latter part of the war in Paris. After the war he became a man of letters, writing the *Rois Maudits* series between 1955 and 1977; the first six novels appeared in quick succession between 1955 and 1960 and the final novel, *Quand un roi perd la France* ('When a King Loses France', but translated into English as *The King without a Kingdom*), thus seems to represent something of an afterthought. Druon was elected to the Academie Française in 1966 at the age of forty-eight, and he became very well known in France when *Les Rois Maudits* was adapted for TV in 1972; the series was remade in 2005. The novels were translated into English during the period from 1956 to 1961 by Humphrey Hare; the final book was translated by Andrew Simpkin in 2015. This completed the set when the earlier translations were reissued in 2013. Hare's translations were originally published by Rupert Hart-Davis and were periodically reprinted in the United Kingdom and the United States up to the 1980s. Martin does not read French, so these translations were the means by which he encountered Druon (and, it will be important to note, he could not have read the seventh and final novel before publishing *A Song of Ice and Fire*). HarperCollins, which is also George R. R. Martin's UK publisher, acquired the rights and republished Hare's translations, commissioning Simpkin's new translation at the same time. Martin was asked to provide a foreword, which, as we saw earlier, includes the cover blurb, 'This is the original Game of Thrones.'[5]

The novel sequence relates the history of King Philip (Philippe) 'le Bel' (the Fair) IV of France (1268–1314) and his immediate descendants, including his daughter Isabella, queen of Edward II of England (*c*.1295–1358). It also foregrounds an intense feud for the possession of the county of Artois between Count Robert of Artois and his aunt Mahaut and has a secondary narrative thread featuring the fortunes of a certain Guccio Baglioni, the nephew of an important Tuscan banker based in Paris. The narrative begins in March 1314 as the Grand Master of the Order of Templars is burned at the stake in Paris. As he dies, he pronounces a curse on the king, Guillaume de Nogaret (chief councillor and Keeper of the Seal) and Pope Clement, predicting that they will all die within the year. Before this execution takes place, however, Robert of Artois makes a visit to England to see his cousin, Queen Isabella.[6] Here they hatch a plan to reveal to King Philip the behaviour of his three daughters-in-law. Two of these are involved in extramarital affairs with two young knights, the third is party to the adultery, but has not taken a lover herself. Marguerite and Blanche, the two adulteresses, are daughter and niece of Mahaut of Artois, so it is very much in Robert's interest to precipitate this revelation; Jeanne, Mahaut's second daughter and wife of the later King Philip V of France, ends up placed under house arrest. The scandal was known as *l'affaire des brus* (the daughters-in-law affair) and was to have extraordinary repercussions on fourteenth-century French and English political history.

Martin may well have taken over the important narrative technique of varying point-of-view (POV) chapters from Druon. There are speedy changes of focus, particularly in Druon's later novels, between different characters whose stories run in parallel; this so-called narrative interlace structure, used in, for example, the French Vulgate prose romances about Arthur, was a tried and tested medieval technique.[7] Druon is a more intrusive narrator than Martin; he often opines about the ramifications of the actions he recounts, and he grants many of his characters a complex interiority. Yet he also holds back some important facts so that it is not until rather late in the sequence that we gain some access to some of the essential beliefs which shape the thinking of Beatrice Hirson, Mahaut's lady-in-waiting and a skilled poisoner, as discussed later.[8] Insight is given into the motivations and thoughts of most of the major characters, from Robert d'Artois to Roger Mortimer, from Beatrice to the obdurate Cressay brothers, deadly enemies – and brothers-in-law – of Guccio Baglioni. Martin, in contrast, maintains a strict rota of characters to whom he grants POV status; it would be quite wearisome to access the minds of every one of his multiple protagonists, while Joffrey's mind, for example, might well prove a rather uncomfortable place to be.[9]

Such switching between POV facilitates one of Martin's other key narrative habits: the cliffhanger. This creates suspense of course, particularly when a character – very often Davos Seaworth – appears to be doomed to death.[10] This becomes a slightly tiresome trick in Martin's repertoire, to the point that once it looks as if a character is about to die, the death can in fact be discounted until – as in the cases of Ned and Robb Stark – we see the blow actually struck. Druon is less addicted to effects of suspense, for he is given to portentous narratorial remarks such as 'If this husband and wife, these two lovers, had known that they would only see each other once again in the whole of their lives . . . they would probably have killed themselves on the spot.'[11] This produces a momentary narrative shock, one which is indeed immediately effective but which, in the longer run, militates against page-turning suspense.

Druon's princes and potentates, his kings, counts and bishops, are generally preoccupied with power and status. Few of them have any interest in the ordinary folk of the realm, or even the longer-term well-being of the kingdom. Robert is solely and obsessively concerned with recovering his paternal inheritance from his aunt; Charles de Valois, brother of Philip le Bel, a deeply stupid and unthinking man, seeks at every turn to try to restore the privileges of the aristocracy and the operations of local customs which Philip, a strongly centralizing king, had abolished. Druon admires Philip for his coolness, for his keen administrative brain and his decisiveness; the many improvements that he has made in the running of the kingdom are detailed and praised.[12] Philip's sons are distinctly less impressive as ruler than their father. Louis IX 'le Hutin' ('the Quarreller') has been compared with Joffrey, but Joffrey's psychopathic tendencies and impetuosity are rather different from le Hutin's casual cruelty and his incapacity to make up his mind.[13] Druon does not shrink from gruesome description in places: when Philip's daughters-in-law are forced to witness their two knightly lovers tortured, broken on the wheel, partly flayed and castrated before finally being beheaded, Druon vividly describes the process for his readers.[14] The death of Oberyn Martell seems both speedy and merciful in comparison.

As venal and cunning, for the most part, as the nobility, the high churchmen of *The Accursed Kings* broadly lack any vestige of Christian ideals. Druon writes some strong comedy for them, in particular in his descriptions of the cardinals attempting to find some kind of agreement to elect the next pope, while trying to evade being put under pressure by the French king.[15] The papacy is of course in exile in Avignon at this time, and Druon draws a clear picture of how the factionalism of the Italian, French and German cardinals effects a stalemate. He is less interested in popular religious movements than in high church politics; extremist sects, in particular those involved in the second Shepherds' Crusade of 1320 (the *pastoureaux*), are covered in a couple of pages, and he has little interest in exploring ecclesiastical reform movements.[16] Martin shares Druon's scepticism about organized religion; his treatment of the Faith of the Seven is largely cynical, and he avoids endorsing any of the gods in his imagined world as truly transcendental.[17] However, he does have a sharp sense of the pressures which lead to grassroots religious enthusiasm taking hold of hearts and minds, as demonstrated in his detailed delineation of the Sparrows. In particular, the shrewdness with which the seemingly harmless new High Sparrow negotiates with Cersei is key to the political developments in *A Feast for Crows*.[18] Druon affords credence to the operation of the Grand Master's curse (mentioned above) among the characters who heard it, although it is clear from his historical treatment of his material that there are many other good reasons for the deaths of the men upon whom the curse falls. Just so, Melisandre's blood magic with the leeches containing the blood of Gendry/Edric

Storm may not cause the deaths of three of the contenders in the War of the Five Kings, yet her ritual is darkly suggestive.[19] Nevertheless, in keeping with the historical novel genre, Druon neither elaborates on nor endorses the overtly supernatural: there are no dragons for him.

Martin's primary debts to Druon

In this section I examine five very strong points of comparison between the novel series of the two authors. The first occurs in the opening chapter of the first book, *The Iron King* (*Le Roi de Fer*). After discussing the plan to reveal Isabella's sisters-in-law's adultery, the two cousins experience a sudden moment of powerful desire. Although he has fathered four children, Isabella's husband, the homosexual Edward II, no longer shares her bed, as she complains to her cousin. Robert is moved by her golden beauty: 'he desired her with a sort of robust immediacy he did not know how to express.'[20] Robert has to compete with the courtly love poetry of Isabella's grandfather, William IX of Aquitaine, for she has just been listening to a recital of his verses about both love and exile, and he does his best: 'Can it be true that those lips are never kissed? That your arms . . . your body . . . Oh! take a man, Isabella, and let that man be me!'[21] Isabella gazes at her huge red-haired cousin, who smells of the forest, of leather, of horse and of armour:

> He had neither the voice nor the appearance of a seducer, yet, she was charmed. He was a man, a real man, a rugged and violent male, who breathed deep . . . Isabella felt her will-power dissolve, and had but one desire: to rest her head upon that leathern chest and to abandon herself to him . . . slake her great thirst. She was trembling a little. Suddenly she broke away from him.[22]

Isabella has more sense than to do exactly what she is accusing her sisters-in-law of doing, but, Druon adds, 'the moment just gone would never vanish from their memories'. Isabella's tenderness for Robert remains; he supports her in her later machinations against her husband, and he owes his later welcome as a refugee at Edward III's court in part to the long association between them.

This moment of suppressed passion is not incest of course, though the two cousins are closely enough related for it to count as such in medieval terms. Robert shares his name, his bluffness, his fondness for low-born women, his size and his appetite for life with Cersei's husband, rather than with her brother. Nevertheless, the sexual attraction between the golden-haired queen (the she-wolf of France rather than the golden Lannister lioness) and her relative is clear enough. Although, as mentioned earlier, the comparisons of the War of the Five Kings and the Wars of the Roses are telling, and often cited, they are also in some ways superficial. For Cersei has a much closer kinship with the ruthless Isabella than with Henry VI's loyal queen, Margaret of Anjou. Both queens are instrumental in the deaths of their hated husbands and both take lovers. Isabella openly allies herself with the charismatic Roger Mortimer in order to increase her power while her son is a minor, and both women struggle to find a role when that son grows up and marries – a point to which I return below. In *The She-Wolf*, Isabella becomes estranged from her husband, Edward II, because of his sexual preference for young men (rather like Renly Baratheon), and she travels to France to her brother Charles to seek his aid. She is meant to help broker an arrangement whereby the young Prince of Wales, the future Edward III, will do homage to the French crown for Anjou, a ceremony in which Edward II does not wish to involve himself. Once she is in Paris, and Prince Edward joins her, Isabella takes the exiled Lord Roger Mortimer as her lover and from there she plots her next move.

Second, Robert's arch-enemy, the redoubtable Mahaut, has much in common with Olenna Tyrell, the Queen of Thorns. Olenna, as we know, was behind the poisoning of Joffrey at the Purple Wedding, though Sansa and Tyrion are held responsible for it.[23] Mahaut has a dark-haired lady in waiting called Beatrice Hirson, introduced earlier. Beatrice has strong connections with the Paris underworld, with apothecaries and magic practitioners who can provide spells and potions for a certain price, and it is she who obtains the materials for Mahaut to carry out her plans.[24] Mahaut in part blames the chancellor of the realm, Guillaume de Nogaret, for the downfall of her daughters, and she conspires with Beatrice to kill him with a mysterious candle: whether it is poisonous or enchanted – or both – is hard to say. Mahaut's action helps thus to fulfil the second part of the Grand Master's dying curse. Later in the novel sequence Mahaut becomes even bolder in her interventions. Again with Beatrice's assistance, she is instrumental in killing King Louis X, Philip's successor and the former husband of her daughter Marguerite.[25] Marguerite (the strangled queen who gives the second novel its title) died mysteriously in prison, just in time for Louis to be able to marry again when he succeeded to the kingdom. Not content with murdering her former son-in-law (in order to help his altogether smarter brother, Philip, married to her other daughter, to the throne), Mahaut also poisons Louis's posthumously born child.[26] There has not been quite so much poisoning in *A Song of Ice and Fire*. Nevertheless, in addition to Joffrey's death through 'the strangler', a poison produced in Lys, Jon Arryn had also succumbed to 'tears of Lys' before the events of *A Game of Thrones* began; Daenerys has survived more than one attempted poisoning, and so too has Melisandre. Oberyn's poisoned spear eventually slew the Mountain; and plenty of poison is used eastwards in Essos.

Late in *The Accursed Kings*, in a rather surprising move, Beatrice abandons her service to Mahaut and takes up with her lady's arch-enemy, Robert, whose mistress she becomes.[27] At his behest, she poisons both her former mistress and her daughter, Jeanne, the dowager queen, in hopes of entering Robert's household and perhaps displacing his wife. She aids him in forging certain important documents, previously destroyed by Mahaut, which he needs to prove his claim to Artois. Quite unbidden, Beatrice delivers a brief lecture to Robert on her beliefs, which she claims to have derived from the Templars, in order to explain why she has never married:

> You see, Monseigneur, that the priests and the popes of Rome and Avignon don't teach the truth. There is not one God; there are two, the god of light and the god of darkness, the prince of Good and the prince of Evil. Before the creation of the world, the inhabitants of darkness rebelled against the inhabitants of light, and the vassals of Evil, in order to exist – for Evil is death and annihilation, devoured

part of the principles of Good. And then, since the two forces of Good and Evil were in them, they were able to create the world and engender mankind, in whom the two principles are not only mingled, but in perpetual conflict, though Evil is predominant, because it is the natural element of their origin. And it is evident that these two principles, since man and woman exist, diversely made, like you and me, ... and it is Evil that arouses our lust and draws us together. And therefore people who have a stronger disposition towards Evil than towards Good must honour Satan and make a pact with him, if they are to be happy and successful. For them the Lord of Good is the enemy.[28]

Druon characterizes Beatrice's credo as something that stinks of hellish sulphur, as an amalgam of 'ill-digested scraps of Manichaeism and corrupt elements, ill-transmitted and ill-understood, of the doctrines of the Cathars'; and Robert himself is condescendingly amused to hear his mistress talking about philosophy.[29] Yet here we have, it seems, the core of the religion of R'hllor, the Lord of Light, a figure locked in eternal combat with the Great Other; just like Beatrice's credo the faith of the Red God is fundamentally Manichaean. So too is the religion of the Ironborn; this centres on the Drowned God whose dark adversary is the Storm-God.[30] Although Martin has clearly fleshed out his imagining of these two religions – which are among the more clearly conceived faiths of the Known World – with other research, it seems likely that the kernel of these two faiths derives from Beatrice's confused understanding of the kinds of popular beliefs that were attributed to the Templars. These are rooted in the propaganda employed by Philip le Bel, enabling him to confiscate their wealth when he proscribed the order. The burning of Jacques de Molay, the Grand Master of the Order, along with Geoffroy de Charnay, is vividly described in *The Iron King*, the first of *The Accursed Kings* books, and the parallels with the various victims sacrificed to the Red God by Melisandre, Selyse and Stannis are clear.[31] Neither Manichaeism, nor Catharism, nor Zoroastrianism (the real-world belief systems which most resemble the religion of the Red God) called for punitive or sacrificial burning of the kind that Melisandre demands.[32] Indeed, almost a century earlier than the setting of the novels, the Cathars had been the *victims* of judicial burning: two hundred Cathar *perfecti* were burned in 1244 at Montségur castle in Languedoc.

Along with Robert d'Artois, the other hero of *The Accursed Kings* is the Sienese Guccio Baglioni, the nephew of Spinello Tolomei, head of one of the most influential Italian banking houses in Paris. Spinello recognizes his young nephew's potential and trusts him with various confidential missions – in which he is accompanied by, or coincidentally meets up with, Giovanni Boccaccio, the Italian author of *The Decameron* and other texts in Latin and the vernacular. The Tolomei banking house is emblematic of the numerous Lombard bankers whose operations enabled the free flow of trade between countries, and who offered current account and overdraft facilities to hard-pressed kings, whether of England or of France.[33] Edward II borrowed heavily from Lombards, to the extent that at one stage he was forced to yield the monopoly of the wool trade – England's most valuable export – to them. By the end of his reign, he had effectively outsourced the financial management of the kingdom to Italian banking interests. In France, the Lombards lent extensively to the royal exchequer and the aristocracy. Philip le Bel cast covetous eyes on their wealth once he had spent the gains from the Templar resources; the bankers swiftly closed up their grand mansions in Paris and returned to Italy, but they soon struck a deal with the king and his counsellors and were allowed to return. Nevertheless, Philip's successors periodically threatened them with expulsion in order to extort further loans from them.

Lombard finance is key to enabling Isabella and Roger Mortimer to invade England when they have made a new ally in Flanders. The couple had been living on credit in Paris and eventually that credit ran out. Spinello Tolomei, head of the Tolomei banking house, spells out the situation:

> But we Lombards, who can no longer face the prospect of supporting your exile, could still face the prospect of supporting your army, if Lord Mortimer, whose valour is known to all, would undertake to lead it, and, if, of course, we had your guarantee that you would take over Messire Edward's debts and liquidate them on your success.[34]

The Flemings provide troops and supplies, since the future Edward III has agreed to marry Philippa, daughter of the Duke of Hainault, but it is the Lombards who put up the money. The Italian banks of *The Accursed Kings* were well advised to take a strategic view of the queen's chances; in supporting Isabella and her son against her husband they backed the winning side. History shows that Edward III would, like his father and grandfather before him, rely on Italian bankers for immediate cash and overdraft facilities. Druon mentions briefly how Edward III actually visited the king of France in disguise in order to negotiate a crucial trade deal for English wool to be exported to Flanders.[35]

There is a clear echo of the Iron Bank of Braavos in Druon's depiction of the Lombards and their operations. We recall how, as a result of Cersei's refusal to pay the Crown's debts until the rebellions against Tommen are quashed, Tycho Nestoris sets out to find Stannis at the Wall and strikes an agreement to back him, in return for a promise to take on the Iron Throne's fiscal responsibilities.[36] Meanwhile, Ser Kevan Lannister has been trying unsuccessfully to raise credit from other Free Cities banks in Pentos and Myr, just as the other Italian banking houses held together when Isabella's credit began to run out in Paris. The Iron Bank's mode of operating is similarly imagined in the show; the powerful arguments made by Davos and Stannis at the Bank's headquarters in Braavos result in the Bank offering them support. Tycho Nestoris recognizes the force of Davos's question, 'When Tywin's gone, who will you back?' and the argument that Stannis represents 'your best chance of getting back the money you've sunk into Westeros, which is a lot, I imagine'. By financing Stannis's campaign, the Bank aims to hedge its bets.[37] Mace Tyrell went to Braavos to negotiate a rescheduling of debts in 'Dance of Dragons' (5.9), but the outcome of that mission remained rather unclear.[38] The Iron Bank is not seen again in the show, but Cersei is able to use the gold taken from the attack on Highgarden to pay off some of the Crown's debts to the Bank – despite Daenerys's attack on Lannister forces – and uses the new loans from the Bank to fund her employment of the notable mercenary company, the Golden Company, led by Harry Strickland, in 'The Spoils of War' (7.3).[39]

Another important motif which Martin found in *The Accursed Kings* – as well of course as widely elsewhere in medieval history and romance – is that of the lost heir. From Bran and Rickon – apparently dead as far as the court in King's Landing is concerned, but, in fact, alive (at least in the books) and likely to offer different kinds of leadership in restoring the fortunes of the Starks – to the lost Targaryen child or children, the idea that the true heir has survived attempts to destroy him and that he may try in adulthood to reassert his rights is recurrent in the series.[40] The show briefly explores the motif in the final season, as the secret of Jon Snow's true birth and legitimacy is shared among his supposed siblings, and then with Varys and Tyrion.[41] Varys in particular sees him as a more acceptable and viable candidate for the succession than his aunt Daenerys, once Cersei is overcome; Daenerys too fears that her lover will command more support among the Great Houses than she can as an invading foreigner.[42] Nevertheless, Jon does not press his claim to the Iron Throne – quite the contrary – and his murder of Daenerys disqualifies him from further consideration as a viable candidate to occupy the Iron Throne.

So too in *The Accursed Kings*. Guccio, the lively young nephew of the head of the Tolomei banking house, becomes involved in a romance with, and finally secretly marries, Marie de Cressay, the daughter of a highly impoverished but proud, noble family. Marie's brothers deplore the idea that their sister might marry a man in the banking trade, even one who has saved them from starvation. They refuse to recognize the marriage and threaten to kill Guccio. The young man has to flee to Paris, where his uncle thinks it expedient to send him to Italy, out of harm's way. Meanwhile, the pregnant Marie is installed in a convent, away from her brothers.

On the larger political stage, the realm is in stasis. Mahaut of Artois has secretly poisoned King Louis X who has died; the kingdom awaits the outcome of the pregnancy of his queen Clémence of Hungary. Clémence and Marie give birth around the same time; Clémence's son is sickly while Marie's boy is robust, and Marie is asked to wet-nurse the little king Jean. The royal chamberlain, Bouville, fears that Mahaut may make an attempt on the life of the royal baby during the baptism ceremony; as a peer of France she is entitled to receive the child at the font. Hence he exchanges the two babies in advance of the christening. Mahaut indeed takes the baby once the ritual is over, wipes its lips with a poisoned handkerchief, and moments afterwards the child, who had formerly appeared quite strong and healthy, dies. Mahaut's daughter, Jeanne, married to Louis X's brother Philip, is now queen of France.[43]

In the world of the novel, it is of course Marie's baby that has died; consequently, she is left to nurse and later to raise the true king of France. Chamberlain Bouville swears her to secrecy, threatening to murder her beloved Guccio if she ever breathes a word of the baby swap. Like Ned Stark, also protecting a child whose life would be at terrible risk if his true parentage were known, Marie keeps the secret until her dying day, although Bouville later confesses the imposture to the pope.[44] Guccio, meanwhile, takes charge of the boy when he is aged around nine and brings him to Italy to train up in the banking business. It is only at the very end of *The Lily and the Lion* (for years the final book in the series) that we learn how, after Guccio's death, the now-adult son arrives in France and announces his true parentage.[45] However, it is now far too late for his candidacy for the throne to gather any support and his bid fails.

The poisoning subplot, laid at Mahaut's door, is fantastical but, in fact, decades after the death of the real Jean I, whose five-day life ended in 1316, an Italian called Giannino Baglioni did indeed come forward, asserting his right as the lost son of Louis X to sit on the throne of France. In 1360, Baglioni was to be found in Avignon, where he was trying to convince the pope (Innocent VI) in Avignon of his claim; the pope refused to see him. Baglioni continued to press his claim, but he was subsequently imprisoned in Naples (where Clémence of Hungary's family ruled) and he died in prison.

These, then, are the major parallels between Druon's series and Martin's: the figures of Robert d'Artois and Isabella of France who shadow Robert Baratheon and Cersei; the importance of poison, particularly as an instrument employed by an ambitious and powerful old woman who seeks her female descendants' well-being; Manichaean religious beliefs; the crucial role of the Lombard bankers and the theme of the lost heir. A number of minor details may well have been adopted by Martin from the French author. When the unhappy Edward II has been deposed, he is imprisoned in several different locations. One of these is Kenilworth Castle in Warwickshire, whose 'red keep', we are told, can be seen from many miles away.[46] More striking, however, is the cell in which Edward is imprisoned in Berkeley Castle, the place where he meets his agonizing death. Edward's captors, following Mortimer's orders, aim to bring about the king's death without actually doing detectable violence to him. The king is kept in a small cell in the castle; in the middle of this is a deep, but now disused well: 'One false step and the prisoner would fall into the deep hole. Edward had to be constantly on his guard.'[47] The jailers throw stinking dead animals into the well, in hopes the miasma that comes up from it will make Edward fatally ill. Significantly, the floor of the cell slopes towards the open hole of the well so that 'whenever he fell asleep, he would wake again at once in a sweat afraid he had moved nearer to the well'.[48] Here we can see the origin both of the Eyrie's terrifyingly vertiginous Sky-Cells, where Tyrion is imprisoned in *A Game of Thrones*, and of the Moon Door, the trapdoor in the floor of the throne room in the Eyrie, through which Lysa Arryn will eventually be pushed by her beloved Littlefinger.

The Accursed Kings makes much of the apparent reimposition of Salic law in France, specifically its provision that a woman may not inherit the throne. In the novels (and indeed in real life) Louis X died leaving a young daughter, Jeanne of Navarre, by his first wife Marguerite, as well as his pregnant second wife, Queen Clémence. Louis himself and his advisers, aware of the scandal surrounding Marguerite's affair, suspected that Jeanne might not in fact Louis's daughter at all, but might rather have been fathered by Philippe d'Aunay, Marguerite's lover. Jeanne is thus usurped of her rights (though she is allowed to retain Navarre), and her line is thereafter excluded from inheriting the French throne.[49] The sidelining of Jeanne functioned greatly to the benefit of her paternal uncles who successively took the throne after Louis's death, though none of their children lived to inherit from them. The concept of Salic law was invoked only retrospectively by lawyers and historians to explain the outcome of the succession crises of 1316 – when Louis X died – and a similar one of 1328 (when the last of Philip IV's sons died without a male heir). The principle of excluding the female line became the more important in 1328, given that Philip IV's only daughter, Isabella of France, did have surviving sons: Edward III and his brothers. Edward's claim to the French throne via his mother, as transmitted to his descendants, remained the driving force behind the prolongation of the Hundred Years' War.

The books' manoeuvring around male versus female inheritance laws reminds us of the importance (in the books, if not in the show) of the differential inheritance customs in Dorne. Not only does Arianne Martell assume that she will inherit from her father, but her consequent perception that Myrcella's right to the Iron Throne is stronger than Tommen's and that supporting it will strengthen Arianne's own claim to succeed her father in Dorne is what drives the botched conspiracy in *A Feast for Crows*.[50] The political situation in Dorne diverges considerably in the show; Arianne does not exist in the show world, and thus the issues raised by varying inheritance rights for men and women die with Myrcella, particularly as the show radically curtails the Dorne storyline in its race to the finish.[51] Other parallels could also be mentioned: for example, when stripped of his blazon and expelled from France, Robert d'Artois falls, like Arya Stark, into the habit of tallying up his foes: 'he added more names to the list of his enemies, his sister of Namur, his brother-in-law of Hainaut, John of Luxembourg and the Duke of Brabant.'[52] Similarly, Druon's account of the Battle of Sluys (L'Eclus) in 1340, in which Philip VI's fleet was 'annihilated', sets the scene for the Battle of Blackwater Bay.[53]

The seventh novel

The final novel of the *The Accursed Kings* sequence was written nearly twenty years after the others and is very different in tone and style. It is narrated in the first person by Cardinal Hélie Talleyrand de Périgord, a self-important churchman who is travelling in his litter all the way from Périgueux in the south-west of France north to Metz, to the court of the Holy Roman Empire. During the journey he is accompanied in the litter by his young nephew, Archambaud, the future count of Périgord, and Hélie recounts to him the history of the past twenty or so years, including the catastrophe of the French defeat at Crécy. Celibate, highly political, intelligent and Machiavellian, Hélie is strongly reminiscent of Lord Varys; his analyses of the disastrous politics of the two previous French kings and, in contrast, the superior military strategy of Edward III of England are worthy of the eunuch mastermind. Hélie notes, for example, how maintaining a standing army is key to Edward III's successes, just as the Lannisters benefit from being able to deploy tens of thousands of men at a few days' notice, rather than, like Robb, having to wait to summon and negotiate with his bannermen in order to get an army into the field.

Hélie's perception of what is best for France is relatively disinterested: 'I call a traitor he who betrays the higher interests of the kingdom', he says, echoing, or so it might seem, Varys's smooth rejoinder to Ned's question, 'Who do you serve, Lord Varys?', with 'The realm, my lord, someone must'.[54] The long monologue from Hélie, delivered to the uncomplaining Archambaud, also recalls the intense discussions between Varys and Tyrion in Illyrio Mopatis's carriage as they travel east from Pentos in *A Dance with Dragons*. Yet Martin could not have read this final novel in Druon's series before the five novels currently published appeared, and thus we must explain away these similarities as coincidence.

Conclusion

Martin has gone on record as saying:

> I did consider at a very early stage – going all the way back to 1991 – whether to include overt fantasy elements, and at one point thought of writing a Wars of the Roses novel. But the problem with straight historical fiction is you know what's going to happen. If you know anything about the Wars of the Roses, you know that the princes in the tower aren't going to escape. I wanted to make it more unexpected, bring in some more twists and turns. The main question was the dragons: Do I include dragons? . . . I was discussing this with a friend, writer Phyllis Eisenstein – I dedicated the third book to her – and she said, 'George, it's a fantasy – you've got to put in the dragons.' She convinced me, and it was the right decision.[55]

His reading of Druon persuaded Martin that he could write at the kind of length that he intended for his series, that questions of power, control and effectiveness in rule were central to the kind of epic he had in mind, but that, in order to include his dragons, to write in the infinitely more popular genre of fantasy, he had to abandon the idea of writing a straightforward historical novel sequence. Martin learned a great deal from Druon in terms of managing a complex interweaving of personal narratives and in setting out large-scale historical changes and political conspiracies, ubiquitous hunger for power and effective models of rule; he also adopted his hero's cynicism about religion. Both authors successfully imitate the medieval narrative technique of interlace; this affords them both a series of changing perspectives and a kind of heteroglossia, the creation of distinctive internal voices for different characters. Martin found in Druon a basis for the characterization of some of his most important protagonists – Robert and Cersei in particular – but also inspiration for some of the figures on the Small Council: Mace Tyrell is reminiscent of the bumbling Bouville, whose baby swap works out so impractically in *The Accursed Kings*. More importantly, Martin learned what not to do from Druon; he is able to maintain suspense from strand to strand, rather than writing for a readership who know already from history – the ultimate spoiler – what is going to happen, and he avoids prolepsis, in particular, such portentous prophetic remarks as the one cited above about Guccio's hopes for a reunion and happy family life with his beloved Marie. In that same *Rolling Stone* interview, Martin remarks:

> History was my minor in college. I don't pretend to be a historian. Modern historians are interested in sociopolitical trends. I'm not interested in that. I'm interested in

the stories. History is written in blood, a gold mine – the kings, the princes, the generals and the whores, and all the betrayals and wars and confidences. It's better than 90 percent of what the fantasists do make up.[56]

And there we may give Martin the final word. It is, as he argues, the narratives, not the geopolitics that seize our imaginations in the first instance. Yet at the level of world building, it *is* precisely the seriousness and detail with which the blood, the gold, the wars, the taxes and the trade policies are treated by its creator which make us believe so powerfully in the world of Ice and Fire.

2

Broken bodies, broken kingdoms, broken promises

The revolutionary failure of *Game of Thrones*

Robert Rouse and Cory James Rushton

When the *Song of Ice and Fire* phenomenon first began to attract significant and sustained scholarly attention – just as its HBO adaptation *Game of Thrones* appeared – one primary focus was on the relationship between masculinity and disability. In varied and complex ways, both George R. R. Martin's novel series and the HBO TV adaptation appeared to be about broken bodies and the broken body politic. The figures of Tyrion, Bran, Jaime and the Hound all interrogated what it meant to be a man in Westeros. With so many claimants contending for the Iron Throne, and the rise of apolitical and even vaguely 'democratic' groups like the Brotherhood without Banners, the series seemed to promise a vision of social and political change. Now that the television show has ended, this promise does not seem to have come to fruition. Instead, Westeros and its monarchical system seem relatively intact: Starks, Lannisters, Tullys and others mostly rule where their families ruled before. Disability is reduced to a feel-good narrative about Bran's story having been the most interesting one, while the possibility of democratic reform is roundly mocked when Samwell Tarly suggests it in even a limited form. At the same time, the narrative does not want to contend at all with who has paid for the survival of the aristocratic system in Westeros: it was Essos, whose few surviving representatives simply sail away again, having shed their blood to maintain the political status quo in a foreign land. In other words, what appeared to be a radical reinvention of the fantasy genre ends with a remarkably conservative political finale. While there are other elements playing a role in the widespread negative reception of the HBO series' conclusion, this chapter will concentrate on the striking failure of the promise of political and social reform in the show.

The seeds of this perceived failure are already contained in the narrative's structure itself; the competition for the Iron Throne prompted most immediately by the execution of Eddard Stark, in a show of political theatre intended to end in a pardon before Joffrey's act of impulsive cruelty. The HBO show must present a winner of this competition, and to do so it necessarily starts stripping away characters and plots (even as Martin is busy adding ever more tangential storylines in *A Dance with Dragons*).

This was always going to be necessary in the TV retelling, despite the narrative (both book and TV) requiring a multiplicity of characters to achieve its sprawling, unpredictable effect. Some of this process of paring down begins earlier in the TV show – the absence of Lady Stoneheart, for example, or Jeyne Poole – but it accelerates in Season 6, at the same moment that the show's vaunted, perceived realpolitik begins to be subsumed in standard fantasy tropes. High fantasy, with which the HBO show has a fraught and paradoxical relationship, ultimately seems incompatible with the promise of progressive political and social change.

This problem is largely one of the show's own creation, albeit abetted by journalistic observers and Martin himself, who has famously said that his publishers considered the books 'fantasy for people who hate fantasy'. The TV show's survival was believed to depend on it being perceived as more Sopranos than Narnia.[1] As Adam Debosscher observes, the show early on chose to emphasize the 'perceived medievalist realism of the fiction over its traditional fantasy elements', a choice which included changing the series name: *Game of Thrones* signalling politics over the literal elements, and their associated creatures and gods, of the original title, which in turn necessitates that the battle with the Night King not be the climax of the show.[2] The books, in turn, embrace this realism, replacing the standard 'bright (almost garish)' early covers with 'covers one might expect on books of historical fiction: the pommel of a sword, a crown, a knight's helmet, a chalice'.[3] Fantasy elements were initially muted in promotional materials for the show, with fantasy elements being played down from Season 3 and only openly embraced from Season 7, when 'the fantasy elements, such as the dragons and exploding wildfire, swallowed up large portions of the budget with CGI renderings and became central to the plot of the show'.[4] This early marketing worked to such an extent that fantasy elements were a perpetual caveat in discussion of the books, let alone the new series: 'For all its high fantasy flourishes, its medievalising historical trills, its zombie horror subtext, the series is a work driven by power politics of a particularly amoral, even immoral kind,' a Machiavellian narrative.[5]

The final episode of Season 6, 'The Battle of the Bastards', is the last time the show would nod towards radical or alternative political and social ideas in any but the most perfunctory ways; the seventh episode of that season, 'The Broken Man', reminds viewers of the show's previous interest in broken bodies and minds, particularly male ones, which had seemed to promise a connection between those broken selves and an equally broken royal politics, ripe for replacement, or – indeed – possibly revolution. The show initially followed the books in this: 'Victims of signifying mutilation can be found throughout the cycle,' notes Charles Lambert, who points to Jaime Lannister and Davos Seaworth as examples.[6] Let us begin then, with the theme of the broken body.

The theme that was promised

Martin's use of disability, both genetic and inflicted, seems to represent an attempt to interrogate the primary model of masculinity that dominates the medievalesque world of the Seven Kingdoms: the image of the chivalric knight.[7] That an ideal conception of knighthood exists in the world of *A Song of Ice and Fire* is evident from heroic tales and cultural fantasies favoured by young women such as Sansa Stark and idealistic young men like Bran Stark. However, we soon see that such ideal figures no longer walk the earth, as they discover through cruel experience. The state of chivalry in the Seven Kingdoms is succinctly summed up by Sandor Clegane when he attempts to convince Sansa to flee King's Landing with him during its unsuccessful siege by Stannis Baratheon: 'There are no true knights, no more than there are gods. If you can't protect yourself, die and get out of the way of those who can. Sharp steel and strong arms rule this world, don't ever believe anything different' (*CK*, ch. 52). True knights have become the *rara avis* of the Westeros of the novels.

As the novels develop, this sense of nostalgia for a lost age of chivalry, and thus for a refined masculinity and for the knightly embodiments of that age – most often in the form of previous legendary members of the Kingsguard – becomes an oft-repeated lament. Characters such as Barristan Selmy articulate this nostalgia in the spirit of an *ubi sunt* complaint: where now are the great knights of yore, where now is honour, truth and justice? This is, of course, a characteristic medieval mode of addressing the past, inherited largely from the Christian trope of the fallen and ever-declining world of mankind, but it also has clear parallels in the historical and literary sources that are so important to understanding Martin's work. Martin has explicitly acknowledged his debt to English medieval history, and especially to the fifteenth-century Wars of the Roses, and much of the political and geographical frame of *A Song of Ice and Fire* can be mapped – albeit loosely – onto the geopolitics and dynastic intrigues of this period of internecine warfare.[8] But Martin's work also betrays a profound debt, especially in terms of its elegiac tone, to that most well-known of the literary works that engage with the horror and loss of this troubled period: Malory's *Morte Darthur*.

Malory's retelling of the Arthurian legend is deeply nostalgic in tone, lamenting the loss of a Golden Age of chivalry and masculine behaviour. Expressed most strongly in the Pentecostal Oath, this code of masculine behaviour was one that sought to regulate the role of the knightly classes within society, and to control what was essentially a privileged class of professional killers through an ethos that held the protection of women, innocents and the weak as some of its most cherished ideals. Malory's nostalgia for this lost world – reflecting both the Arthurian ideal and the more peaceable age of his own youth – parallels strongly the similar laments about the state of knightly behaviour that we see repeated so often in *A Song of Ice and Fire*.

The fallen and debased practice of chivalry in the time of the War of the Five Kings is the context for the discussion of Martin's deployment of disability. In the disabled bodies of Jaime and Tyrion Lannister can be read critiques of norms of both masculine appearance and behaviour. In Jaime we have – at first – the ideal image of the knight, whose shining normative exterior masks his debased code of behaviour. In Tyrion – and especially in the Tyrion of the books – we find the near opposite – a twisted form harbouring a heart that, while far from perfect, as often as not comes far closer to the intentions and motivations of one of Sansa's 'true knights' than does his brother, Jaime (Kingslayer, Oathbreaker, incestuous Knight of the Kingsguard).

Jaime was and remains a conundrum. On the one hand, he represents the epitome of masculine form and achievement, excelling as warrior, as lover, as knight; on the other hand, he is an oathbreaker, a slayer of one king, a traitor to a second king – through his incestuous cuckolding – and guilty of the attempted murder of an innocent child, Bran Stark. Inspired in his youth by the shining knights of the Targaryen Kingsguard, he sacrifices his future inheritance as the Lord of Casterly Rock to join the White Cloaks and seek to embody the ideals of chivalry. However, as he later wistfully laments, 'the boy had wanted to be Ser Arthur Dayne, but someplace along the way he had become the Smiling Knight instead' (*SS*, ch. 67). Jaime's story in *A Song of Ice and Fire*, while not, as yet, finished, seemed to be tracing a rather biblical narrative arc of fall and redemption. In the HBO series, his return to Cersei's side and his subsequent death is one of the most jarring discontinuous points for fans of the show; just when he seemed to be following his redemptive arc by joining the combined forces of Westeros at Winterfell, it all falls away as he rejoins his sister. From our reading of his narrative trajectory, the process of redemption that Jaime is currently in the midst of (in the book series) begins with the infliction of the most devastating disability that a knight can suffer: the loss of his sword hand.

The loss of his right hand, on the orders of Vargo Hoat, is both symbolically appropriate for Jaime's chivalric crimes and – ironically – a disability that in fact enables his potential salvation as a chivalric figure. The removal of the right hand was a medieval punishment for the breaking of sworn oaths, removing the oathbreaker's ability to swear any further oaths as he could no longer place his right hand on a bible or other holy relic to do so, thus removing the offender from the social economy of oaths. Thus Jaime's disability is particularly resonant with Catelyn Stark's repeated accusatory appellations of him as an oathbreaker. We note also that it was the hand with which he pushed Bran Stark from the tower, and – of course – it was the primary source of that martial ability that enabled his reputation and prowess in the first place.

But the loss of his hand, and of the martial power that it enabled, is more than just the disabling of his knightly abilities. By stripping away his ability to outwardly perform a chivalric identity through combat, the disability forces Jaime to confront his own interior flaws as a knight. This begins his process of redemption, which is still, as we leave the narrative at the end of *A Dance with Dragons*, incomplete (and, if the show is true to Martin's notes, may be destined to remain so). Through his enabling of the quest of Brienne of Tarth – to seek out and protect the Stark girls – and his equipping her with the Valyrian blade Oathkeeper, Jaime begins on the road to chivalric redemption. We shall have to wait to see whether Martin allows him the grace to complete it. Lambert points out the broader significance of hands in the books, and thus in the series: 'The closest adviser to the king . . . is called the King's Hand and is expected not only to carry out the monarch's will, to transform decision into action, but also to do the king's dirty work, to get his hand dirty in the king's stead.'[9] The loss of Jaime's hand and inheritance is linked not only to each other but also to the problem of the broken body politic; it hardly needs to be pointed out that this is an explicit body metaphor, the king's head directing the action of the king's hands.

In contrast to Jaime, Tyrion seems an unlikely figure through which to discuss Martin's representation of masculinity. Stunted, twisted, bookish, at times besotted and at other times just simply sotted, Tyrion resists, parodies and outright disdains the model of the knight that his brother so exemplarily embodies. Except, of course, he doesn't. Not really. Not in his heart, nor in his actions. Tyrion, even more than a figure like Bran, knows the value of the chivalric ideal and values it all the more so because he cannot outwardly perform it. Tyrion is too cynical and too knowing to think that anyone can really achieve it, especially not a dwarf like himself. But this does not stop him from taking on the chivalric role of the protector of women and the defender of the innocent and the helpless on numerous occasions in the novels. From the protection that he extends to Sansa Stark (from the abuse of his nephew Joffrey), in his role as Hand of the King, to his (at least in part) civic-minded leadership of the defence of King's Landing during King Stannis's siege, and latterly in his protection of the naïve Penny during their voyage to and subsequent captivity in Slaver's Bay, we repeatedly see Tyrion perform what, in a taller man, would be seen as chivalric behaviour.

Tyrion performs such deeds despite himself. In fact, he often resists committing to these acts, and often later regrets doing so, and pays the most appalling personal prices for his literally self- (or at least nose-) sacrificing behaviour. In the disabled body of Tyrion we see Martin's message that Sansa Stark's ideal of the 'true knight' exists not in the perfect body of the deeply flawed Jaime Lannister, or even in the too-perfect form of Loras Tyrell, but rather the ideal lives in the actions of good men. And with this deeds-based definition of chivalry, it is possible to see Tyrion as one of the nearest things to a 'true knight' that we are likely to find in the *Song of Ice and Fire*, even when he is riding a pig.

And yet there is a greater loss associated, indirectly, with the Lannisters, particularly Jaime. By the end of the HBO show, viewers have almost forgotten the real cause of the inciting incident: not the fall of the Targaryens directly, but rather the secret childlessness of the usurper Robert Baratheon, and his lack of a legitimate heir; he has failed to replace the absent Targaryens with a true dynasty of his own. His children are cuckoo's children, secret offspring of the ravenously greedy and rapacious House of Lannister squatting in the House of Baratheon. This secret prompts Jaime's pushing Bran out of the window; following the leads to this secret results in the death of two Hands of the King. This body politic is corrupt at the top, as corrupt bodies politic tend to be.

All of this interrogation of the Westerosi body politic eventually comes into conflict with the narrative's genre, fantasy. The show long tried to avoid this, and many of the problems of Season 8 are rooted in the producers' continuing aversion to the genre.

Leaving disability behind in Season 6 and beyond

As long as I'm standing the war is not over.

– Brynden Tully

Alex Woloch's 2003 book *The One vs the Many* presents a critical approach which can help formulate new ways to consider the relationship between character and plot, described here as the space of the novel: how much of the novel is taken up by particular characters who do not always seem ready to accept their secondariness or minorness. In Balzac's *Le Père Goriot*, the reader is given 'two incomplete protagonists' (Goriot and

Rastignac) locked in an 'undecidable tension', raising the question of which one should be 'the hero': this 'problem of Goriot's and Rastignac's relative centrality comes prior to thematic interpretation; not merely an aspect of critical analysis, it helps condition the grounds for analysis'. In Woloch's terms, and without indulging in too many specifics concerning a novel that is not our focus, *Père Goriot* 'dynamically juxtaposes [Rastignac and Goriot], as character-spaces, within the overall narrative' and subsequently 'claims to present a total picture of Parisian reality' in which these two characters engage in a 'competitive jostling for position within the narrative totality [which] is inseparable from their changing positions within the Parisian totality, a social framework that informs the novel's stylistic, thematic, and structural contours'.[10] Woloch defines his two key terms:

> My interpretive method rests above all in the combination of two new narratological categories which I will formulate and continually return to: the *character-space* (that particular and charged encounter between an individual human personality and a determined space and position within the narrative as a whole) and the *character-system* (the arrangement of multiple and differentiated character-spaces – differentiated configurations and manipulations of the human figure – into a unified narrative structure).[11]

While Woloch notes that texts which feature 'competing co-protagonists are an interesting subset within the broader development of stratified character-fields that call attention to the distribution of attention' in a 'wide range of nineteenth- and twentieth-century novels', his discussion of 'character-space' can be useful for Martin's series with its explicit emphasis on competing characters and narrative arcs.[12] Woloch himself remarks that his study

> is located at an imprecise juncture between form and history: constructing a conceptual model for characterization within narrative poetics and analyzing a specific sequence of literary-historical circumstances. It would be a mistake to delimit the idea of 'character-space' and 'character-system' to the nineteenth-century European novel, even though the significance of narrative minorness, and the social and literary meaning of functionality, develop in specific ways in this period and place. I would instead suggest that the dynamics of distribution – and the tension between structure and reference that emerges in, and formulates, distribution – is inherent to narrativity as formal process.[13]

Woloch begins his study with a brief look at the *Iliad*:

> We might say there are two wars in the *Iliad*. Embedded within the Trojan conflict recounted in the tale we can find a battle on the discursive plane, not between the characters as individual soldiers on the field but between the characters as more or less important figures within the narrative structure. The formal clash between protagonist and minor characters redounds back on, and is motivated by, the clashing world of the story itself.[14]

The *Iliad*, he says, 'is about one life *and* many'.[15] Homer's epic 'includes so many secondary characters because Achilles himself withdraws from the battle in Book I', depriving the epic of its focus, creating a space where even a Thersites ('perhaps the first truly minor character in Western literature') can find his voice, however brutally that voice is subsequently suppressed.[16] The bulk of the *Iliad*'s narrative is concerned with how characters compete to fill the space left by Achilles, a space defined by his lost presence (which is something more than mere absence).

Character-space and character-system are about more than protagonists and minor characters, but about 'how the discrete representation of any specific individual is intertwined with the narrative's continual apportioning of attention to different characters who jostle for limited space within the same fictive universe'.[17] The emphasis on distribution allows Woloch to reveal the 'inherently social dimension' of narrative form, in which

> all character-spaces inevitably point us toward the character-system, since the emplacement of a character within the narrative form is largely comprised *by* his or her relative position vis-à-vis other characters. If the character-space frames the dynamic interaction between a discretely implied individual and the overall narrative form, the character-system comprehends the mutually constituting interactions among all the character-spaces as they are (simultaneously) developed within a specific narrative.[18]

In *Game of Thrones* and its source texts, character-systems compete for space, with the more similar character-spaces (say, would-be monarchs) coming into direct contact, with one eliminating the other. Martin has essentially reified this, making it real by stripping away everything *but* actual conflict. The greatest space thus vacated is not necessarily Robert Baratheon but the Targaryens, who carved out a legitimate political claim which lasted centuries. Robert's Rebellion empties that space but does not fill it: he barely wants to be king, his whole usurpation predicated on pursuing revenge over a mistake.[19] His children are not his children, and he leaves the structure of political life in place but with his own essential emptiness in the centre. He is not a king to be overthrown but an absence to be filled, an invitation to further rebellion and the fracturing of kingdoms.

As the show progressed, the fantasy elements take over: for every dead Wun-Wun the giant, there's a dragon turning into a wight or a new magical act. The show begins to obey generic norms which were built into it in the first place, which come to a natural end with a king on the throne, in this case, one whose primary authority is rooted in a total knowledge of all history and tradition. But even before that, the narrative falls into generic norms as characters and arcs are eliminated or downplayed. As Caroline Spector puts it:

> In *A Song of Ice and Fire*, the threat to civilization is reflected in the Stark motto: 'Winter is Coming.' Winter in Westeros is a multi-year affair that not only blots out the natural progression of seasons, but also brings supernatural menace from beyond the Wall. This phrase hangs over Westeros like a death sentence. It promises

a threat that would, were this a traditional fantasy tale, require the courtly knights to rally, rout the obvious agents of evil, and prevent the destruction of the peaceful shire or duchy that serves as the symbolic heart of the idyllic, morally upright kingdom.[20]

She is only wrong in that this will eventually happen, but not in one epic battle that will mark the climax of the action: indeed, the story is eventually so invested in this trope that it does it twice, once when a band of characters from various arcs come together to nab one of the dead as proof of the threat and again when even more characters join the Battle of the Long Night at Winterfell. These are not all 'courtly knights' but neither were the members of the Fellowship of the Ring, or the characters in countless tabletop RPG games which Martin, by his own admission, was once addicted to. The perception that knights are the ones to gather is an inheritance, again, from Malory rather than the long tradition of fantasy narratives partially descended from his *Morte*.

The show turns away from any real interest in disability at about the same time as fantasy conventions begin to take over, which we locate at Season 6 episodes 'The Broken Man' (6.7) and 'The Battle of the Bastards' (6.9). The Hound's disability, facial scarring which points to internal trauma, had always helped mark him as different, a stigma that marks his character as damaged. He was also a breakout character and thus given an arguably bigger role in the show than he has in the books, which may have necessitated the odd sense that 'The Broken Man' feels like an episode partially out of time.[21] Left for dead in the unfinished books and in the series, he is brought back in this episode in a way that explains his absence: he has effectively retired to help a small, independent community build a sept. Asked how he survived his injuries, Sandor replies, 'Hate'. He does not seem fully absorbed into this community despite having been there some time while he healed, but his renewed presence also seems overdetermined: the community's leader, Brother Ray, interrogates him about his past but portentously suggests that the gods are not through with him. Here, the gods are stand-ins for 'something greater', in Ray's words, which points to an increasing syncretism in the series, a refusal to determine the winners of that other great game, the game of gods which stands behind the song of ice and fire itself. Together with Sandor's hatred – of the brother who cruelly caused his physical and mental trauma – this episode repositions the Hound so that his arc can lead towards the coming together predicted by Spector. He will appear in both 'Beyond the Wall' (7.6) and 'The Long Night' (8.3), one of many strands becoming one, on the way to the only destiny the show can imagine for him: killed by and killing his brother, mathematically eliminating both characters in the show's final purge at King's Landing.

Perhaps the best example of this, also in 'The Broken Man', is the sudden, jarring reappearance of Beric Dondarrion, at this point finally irrevocably dead in the books (replaced by the resurrected Catelyn Stark/Lady Stoneheart, whose arc is absent from the show). The Brotherhood without Banners, across the series, have appeared to deteriorate into thugs, fleecing the people they once sought to protect. As with much else, this is ongoing in the books. In 'The Broken Man', when the unfinished sept is destroyed and its builders slaughtered, the Hound conveniently away from camp, it is the Brotherhood who has done it – but now, represented as a splinter of that group, hunted down by Beric and Thoros of Myr just as the Hound also hunts them. The scene where they meet and divide up the punishments resets the Brotherhood to an earlier version of itself, while also absorbing the Hound's solitary plotline and giving him a new direction – their direction, north to the Wall. Beric, another fan favourite, is brought back at the same time as the Hound in what appears to be a heavy-handed attempt at plot consolidation.

The most obvious example of this new plot consolidation at work is the plot of 'Beyond the Wall', in which several characters come together on an epic quest in the style of the *Seven Samurai* or *The Magnificent Seven*. The better epic analogy is probably the ancient Greek myth of the Calydonian Boar, which also sees several heroes come together in the same cause: a hunt for a destructive creature. There are eight in the group: Jon Snow, Beric, Davos Seaworth, Jorah Mormont, the Hound, Thoros of Myr, Tormund Giantsbane and Gendry; most of these characters were nowhere near each other only a season prior. Unlike in *The Magnificent Seven*, only Thoros of Myr is eliminated here, as the Red Woman is the more important or narratively useful priest of R'hllor, the Lord of Light. The episode consolidates plots by reminding us of elements from the past: the Hound's fear of fire and Gendry's relationship to the Baratheons, both important to the series' final resolution.

Once characters and arcs start being rapidly eliminated or absorbed into other arcs, the structure of the work starts to come clear. 'The Battle of the Bastards', in some sense, should always have been predictable: after the deaths of Robb Stark and Roose Bolton, there are two Snows in the North with rival if tenuous claims to Winterfell. By narrative necessity, let alone the generic norms of fantasy, they *have* to fight. One of them needs to eliminate the other and absorb both his political and narrative place.

The final season tries to return to its anti-fantasy position by ending the White Walker threat at mid-season, rather than at the end. The show is not, after all, called *A Song of Ice and Fire*, but *Game of Thrones*, so on one level it is understandable that the show must end with the Iron Throne. But it is not the natural climax of the narrative, and for all the fury and fire of 'The Bells' (8.5) the last episodes feel more like the Scouring of the Shire than the climax of an eight-season epic.

Our fathers were evil men

Daenerys says: 'Our fathers were evil men. All of us here. They left the world worse than they found it. We're not going to do that. We're going to leave the world better than we found' (6.10). What does Daenerys mean when she says she is going to break the wheel in light of all this? She means she will break the cycle of pain and suffering by uniting the world under her benevolent rule, her conflagration wrapped around a merciful heart. She succeeds but not as she intends; the wheel of primogeniture, which she was first relying upon and then threatened by, has been disrupted – although not entirely by her – and replaced by an extremely limited form of representation. Her partial success can be surprisingly paralleled with that of Frodo Baggins, who succeeds in destroying the Ring even as he fails; he needs Gollum to complete the task just as Daenerys needs Jon Snow, and both come with disruption of the body (complete in

Daenerys's case, partial in Frodo's). This should not obscure the price Essos has paid both to save Westeros from the Night King and then to place Daenerys not on the throne, but at least to let her stand relatively near it for a second.

The spending of Essos is perhaps best encapsulated by the individual fate of Missandei. Beheaded and thrown from the walls of King's Landing at Cersei's order, Missandei's execution triggers Daenerys's quick descent in murderous rage (albeit abetted by other betrayals). Her lover Grey Worm also witnesses the killing, and in the next episode ('The Bells') he will give in to his darkest urges just as his queen does. The abandonment of Daenerys's mission in Slaver's Bay is now echoed in the destruction of the prize everyone has so long sought: as Sean T. Collins argued in a very early response, 'So ends the most daring episode of *Game of Thrones* ever. It's the Red Wedding writ large, a masterpiece that murders all hope of neat closure, and reduces any lingering belief in the redemptive power of violence to ashes in our mouths.'[22] Missandei's death gets lost except as immediate motivation for what many viewers saw as a narratorial betrayal, Daenerys's turn from saviour to maniac. Even here, though, Essos and its inhabitants only exist to further the events in Westeros, a death to launch a million more as all the plots come crashing into one.

'It is not easy', Daenerys says just before she is killed by Jon, 'to see something that has never been seen before' (8.6). She cannot, in fact, really see it herself: her vision is the same as everyone else's in that she longs for totalizing power, hers vaguely different in that her absolutism will somehow translate into a better world for the ruled. Tyrion's minor triumph, then, is to envisage a small never-before-seen something: a system by which the great houses choose each new ruler; a project that is viable, he argues, because of, rather than despite, all the many terrible mistakes they have collectively made. Davos, present at this council but by his own admission unsure if he can vote, had once said to the resurrected Jon that the point was just to go on: 'You go on. You fight for as long as you can. You clean up as much of the shit as you can' (6.3). In other words, no grand gestures, a position with which Tyrion now seems to partially agree. Sam's suggestion that decisions which affect everyone should be made by everyone is met with ridicule by most of the unnamed lords and the foolish Edmure Tully (whose own claim had been rejected moments before), cool smirks from Sansa and Arya and confusion from Brienne and Davos. (We do not see the reactions of characters who have more completely straddled the line between aristocracy and its opposites: Gendry, a bastard now ruling House Baratheon, Tyrion and Grey Worm.) But for the show's producers, famously rumoured to have become tired of it, Davos's earlier statement may betray or echo or reflect their final position: they need to clean up as much of this as they can. A better reading, even if still inadvertently mooted, is that Sam's suggestion – something like democracy – would be too grand a gesture, in Daenerys's words, 'too hard to see'.

And so we get King Bran the Broken, one last nod to disability encoded in his name where he could have been, probably should have been, Bran the Raven. But perhaps that is the point. Leaving aside Tyrion's implausible claim that Bran's is the best of the stories we all just watched for eight seasons, reminding us that he is physically broken is clumsily attached itself to the language of Daenerys, who wanted to break the wheel. In that sense, Bran becomes king because he encapsulates what has been achieved:

wisdom won from hard experience, at the head of a system that has been at least a little disrupted. His knowledge of the past is, of course, perfect; that of the present perhaps less so, as his powers are never fully explored and he only suggests he might be able to find Drogon in the final scene, not that he necessarily will. But even as this could suggest some more fundamental political change, this dreamy king wandering off in his wheelchair to locate the now-absent final fantasy element while his Small Council debates policy, his very powers suggest otherwise: they have put tradition in the form of memory itself on the throne, a return to the status quo that simply looks visually different but is conventionally generic. Bran, despite his strangeness and his disability, is the oldest living son and heir of Ned Stark, and rightful heir to the Kingdom of the North. The power structure remains the same, the means by which decisions are made remains the same and the show ends with Tyrion attempting to tell his oft-interrupted brothel joke one last time.

Is the world of Westeros – let alone Essos – a better place for all the action and tragedy of *Game of Thrones*? Mereen, maybe, if Daenerys's revolutionary regime can survive: Grey Worm makes it clear the Unsullied are not going back there, making the survival of Daenerys's violent experiment unlikely. Westeros? Unclear. While it appears that the Seven Kingdoms have avoided the spectre of a new mad queen, King's Landing is destroyed and the Kingdoms are sundered – albeit only in two, with a new splinter kingdom composed of the North existing in a presumably uneasy relationship to Westeros as whole (wallpapered over, perhaps briefly, by the presence of Starks on both thrones).

In this way, Drogon's destruction of the Iron Throne is not simply an impressive but pointless special effect, nor is it a final faint irony. It is the only way the main action, the one unified story, can end.

Part II

Key institutions

3

The Citadel and the ivory tower

Academia and education in Westeros

Mikayla Hunter

The importance of collective knowledge – preserved and gained through books, stories and shared collective memory – is one of the key themes in George R. R. Martin's *A Song of Ice and Fire* and HBO's *Game of Thrones*. While political acumen and strategy remain at the forefront of the narrative and are essential to the survival of individuals, it becomes increasingly evident that shared knowledge is the key to the survival of humanity. Nearly lost collective knowledge and lack of knowledge – of the White Walkers (or Others, as they are called in the books), dragon glass and Valyrian steel, and dragons, for instance – all put humanity at risk of being defeated by the legions of undead.

In both Martin's work and HBO's TV adaptation of the series, the role of knowledge – both the use and suppression of it – proves instrumental in the war for the Iron Throne as well. Jon's proof of his position as the rightful heir to the Iron Throne through Rhaegar and Lyanna's marriage and Jon Arryn's key to disproving Cersei's children's claims to legitimacy both lie in books and scrolls preserved by maesters.[1] The resurrection of Gregor Clegane, who is then weaponized in the fight for control of the Seven Kingdoms, is the product of a maester's experiments.[2] And the cure for greyscale and effective methods of killing wights are found in texts written and preserved by maesters, and largely unknown to the rest of Westeros's inhabitants.[3]

Indeed, the roles of academics and education in Westerosi society are complicated. Martin is adept at painting the morals and efficacy of his characters and their institutions in shades of grey, and academics are no exception. Lip service is paid to Oldtown as a centre of learning, but Sam's personal experience in the Citadel indicates otherwise. It is an ivory tower that has largely lost its relevance to the ordinary people of Westeros and to the kingdom's government. The title of maester is a highly respectable one in Westerosi society, and yet many of the men themselves – Pycelle, Qyburn, even well-intentioned Cressen – do not inspire much respect in the courts and families they serve. In addition to the maesters' individual characters, the book and TV series grapple with the ethics of experimentation and academic inquiry, notably through the creation and production of wildfire, Qyburn's necromancy and Sam's secret search for cure for greyscale.[4]

Martin has been roundly praised for his historical research in creating his world of ice and fire. In addition to this volume, several books have already been published which point to various historical parallels in both Martin's plots and his characters.[5] However, as with any fictional endeavour, there are some areas in both where historical realism cedes to Martin's or showrunners David Benioff's and D. B. Weiss's artistic sensibilities. The 'reaving, roving, raiding, or raping' culture of the Iron Islands is at odds with the largely agrarian and trader culture of historical Vikings, for instance.[6] With this in mind, this chapter explores academia, education and the Order of Maesters in Westeros. It looks at the structures of the Westerosi education system for both the laity and those pursuing higher education. I investigate the relationship between Citadel and Sept and discuss the secular nature of academia in Westeros, which is in strong contrast with higher education in medieval Europe. It then discusses the strange absence of formal legal training or university-trained jurors within the Seven Kingdoms' court system. An examination of academic ethics follows, including character studies of individual maesters, the majority of whom are portrayed as corrupt, short-sighted or ineffectual. The chapter ends with a consideration of Martin's thematic treatment: warning of the danger to society when academic study is devalued; the importance of educational study in the success of the individual; and the preservation of knowledge for the survival of future generations.

Maesters, the professional academics of Westeros, either reside in the Citadel of Old Town, a city of learning much like Oxford or Cambridge, or they are individually attached to noble houses and royal institutions (specifically, the Crown and the Night's Watch). Those attached to noble houses act as advisers to the head of the house, medics, tutors to noble sons and are in charge of communications. However, it seems that the expense of retaining a maester limits this practice to noble houses: Stark, Tyrell, Greyjoy, Arryn, Mormont, Martell, etc. As Lady Dustin explains, 'Every great lord has his maester, every lesser lord aspires to one' (*DD*, 578). How, then, the nobility of lesser vassal houses like Karstark, Jordayne, Blacktyde and Tarth, or the children of well-off merchants and artisans, are educated is left to the reader's imagination. This must presumably occur through one of two options: tutoring by parents or other adult members of the household (e.g. grandparents), such as was common in most medieval households, or by septas and septons (as with Sansa and Arya's tutelage by Septa Mordane, who fills a governess-like role).[7] Those wishing to pursue higher education and become maesters must go to Oldtown and undergo training at the Citadel. Following Maester Aemon's death at Castle Black, Jon Snow sends Sam Tarly to the Citadel to train as a maester and become Aemon's replacement within the Night's Watch (5.5). However, the Citadel also offers higher education to individuals who do not wish to pursue a career in academia. In 'Breaker of Chains' (4.3), Oberyn Martell is questioned about his possible hand in Joffrey's death, as it is widely known among the nobility that he had studied poisons at the Citadel.

Citadel and Sept

The Citadel functions as the Westerosi equivalent of a university. The first European universities appeared in the eleventh and twelfth centuries, with the foundation of the universities of Bologna (1088) and Modena (1175) and the official recognition of the universities of Paris (1150) and Oxford (1231, though teaching existed as early as 1096).[8] The earliest universities originated in Asia and pre-date European universities by several centuries.[9] Schools and universities in the late Middle Ages were notable for their relative autonomy from the royal courts and, to a degree, from the Roman Catholic Church, though the curriculum centred around Christian beliefs, the institutions were frequently funded by the church and most students attended with the intent of becoming members of the clergy.[10] Similarly, the Order of Maesters exists separately from the Faith of the Seven and the royal court at King's Landing, though Maester Cressen identifies as a lay follower of the Faith and the Grand Maester holds a high position at court. And while the Order of Maesters is a secular order, insofar as their studies do not focus on theological questions, Oldtown used to be a shared centre of both lay and ecclesiastical learning, many years before the events of the book and TV series. The Sept of Oldtown, also known as the Starry Sept, was the original seat of the High Septon before being moved to the Great Sept of Baelor at King's Landing.

Medieval universities taught seven to ten subjects to students pursuing bachelor's or master's degrees: the seven liberal arts – arithmetic, astronomy, geometry, grammar, logic, music theory and rhetoric – and the three Aristotelian philosophies – physics, metaphysics and moral philosophy. Those students wishing to pursue studies beyond the Master of Arts could then specialize in one of three fields: law, medicine or theology.[11] Most medieval formal education was heavily informed by theology. So perhaps the most striking feature of the Order of Maesters and education at the Citadel is its secular nature. Students and maesters at the Citadel study medicine, meteorology and climatology and history; there is no indication that there are any theological studies – those seem reserved for septons and septas. This secularization of academia is in keeping with Martin's overall secularization of medieval society in his creation of Westeros.[12] In medieval Europe, academia and the church may have been nominally independent institutions, yet they were inseparable. Halls and colleges in Oxford, for example, were founded by particular religious orders or as charitable endeavours. In Paris, the major schools (Notre Dame, Ste-Geneviève and Saint-Victor) were culturally and financially intertwined with the university and the diocese, with canons like Pierre (Peter) Abélard, tutor to Héloïse d'Argenteuil (discussed below), in teaching positions: Abélard was master of the cathedral school of Notre Dame de Paris and a canon of Sens.[13] In Westeros, by contrast, religion and academics are regarded as completely separate institutions: the Order of the Seven, now centred in the Great Sept, and the Order of Maesters in the Citadel.

The division between religious and secular thinking breaks down, however, when it comes to portents and prophecies. In Essos, the ability to interpret portents and prophecies (and indeed, to prophesy) is a specific type of wisdom that largely belongs to women affiliated with religious institutions; this wisdom grants status and agency to women in various Essosi cultures. In Westeros, the magical and the metaphysical are not neatly categorized into that which is theological and that which is not. Maester Cressen and Septon Chayle both speculate about the significance of the Red Comet, while Maggy the Frog operates as a wise woman in a freelance capacity (*CK*, 1–2, 64; *FC*, 608–11).

Perhaps the most interesting distinction between the jurisdictions of the secular Order of Maesters and of the clergy of the Sept arises from Martin's organization of the laity's educational system. Formal education for the nobility appears to be as a private tutorial system; there is no equivalent to grammar or other schools or any semblance of classroom-like settings. This system of private tutelage is consequently reserved for the nobility and the future clergy. Martin writes scenes showing the education of the Stark children and discussing other nobles' educations; however, the education of septons and septas must be inferred, as Septa Mordane is not portrayed as a person of noble birth and yet she fulfils an educator's role herself.

A private tutorial system reserved mainly for the wealthy and the clergy is largely reflective of medieval education systems, where children of the noble or wealthy were usually taught at home either by hired tutors or by their parents.[14] However, cathedral and monastic schools, while uncommon until the twelfth century in England, were established as early as the late sixth and early seventh centuries and were intended to educate noble boys in preparation for ecclesiastical careers.[15] And both boys and girls could be educated through '[c]astle schools, court schools, cathedral schools, college church schools, village schools' as well as by parish priests or at home, though girls' education remained, on the whole, 'informal and inferior' to boys' education.[16] No similar schools are mentioned in Westeros. Rather, the home-school private tutorial system seems to be the only option for formal primary and secondary education, unless a (non-noble) child (like Gendry) is apprenticed to a trade. This absence is perhaps in part due to the invisibility of the merchant middle class in King's Landing. The series focuses on the nobility in their civil war, with main and point-of-view (POV) characters mostly coming from the noble class or, like Melisandre and Ser Davos, as characters in close proximity to nobility and deeply invested in their movements. And the audience sees glimpses into the lives of the smallfolk through Arya's adventures, as she befriends Gendry, Lommy and Hot Pie, when she and the Hound encounter the Brotherhood without Banners at a farmer's home, and in her undercover roles for the House of Black and White as Cat of the Canals and the oyster seller.[17] However, we see very little of the yeoman and merchant ranks; these, historically, usually accrued less than the £35–£40 per annum average income of knights, yet they could well afford to pay to have their children educated.[18]

Grammar schools were first introduced in England at the start of the sixteenth century and so perhaps do not fit with the medieval aesthetic of *Game of Thrones* and *A Song of Ice and Fire*; however, boarding schools that were attached to universities are in evidence in the fourteenth century.[19] Boys educated at home until around the age of seven could be given more advanced tutoring until the age of fourteen or so, at which point they could be admitted to university. Be that as it may, Westerosi childhood education is a strictly domestic affair.

In the North of Westeros, this home education is separated by gender. The Stark boys are shown learning the history of Westeros, the symbols and Words of the noble houses, weaponry and strategy. Tyrion and Jorah Mormont were both taught some High Valyrian (the Westerosi equivalent of Latin) and can recite poetry in that language. Sansa and Arya, by contrast, learn needlework and courtesy lessons, and Arya's fencing lessons are disguised as dancing lessons. This in itself is unsurprising in a heavily gendered society like Westeros. However, it is interesting that Martin chooses to separate both the material *and* the types of educators by gender: girls' and boys' education are undertaken by the clergy of the Faith of the Seven and by the Order of Maesters, respectively. The Stark boys, for example, are tutored by Maester Luwin, while Sansa and Arya are tutored by Septa Mordane. Jaime Lannister was similarly tutored by House Lannister's maester, until his father, dissatisfied with the maester's efforts, took over at least part of his education. Tywin recounts:

> I taught my son Jaime to read. The maester came to me one day, told me he wasn't learning. He couldn't make sense of the letters. He reversed them in his head. The maester said he'd heard tell of this affliction and that we simply must accept it. Ha! After that, I sat Jaime down for four hours every day until he learned. He hated me for it, for a time. For a long time. But he learned. (2.6)

Carolyne Larrington has observed that until the High Sparrow's successful conversion of King Tommen and the reinstatement of the Faith Militant, the Faith does not hold much sway over the Westerosi nobility's lives and 'seems to have little impact on people's lives beyond marriages, funerals and of course coronations'.[20] Furthermore, as the Grand Maester is given a permanent post on the monarch's Small Council but the High Septon is not, we can extrapolate that the religious knowledge and wisdom that can be provided by the Order of the Seven holds a lesser status in Westerosi court society than the secular knowledge and learning offered by the Order of Maesters. Girls and women have a significantly lower status than boys and men in Westeros as well, an aspect of worldbuilding that has been alternately criticized and accepted as realistically reflective of a medieval Western society.[21] This lower status of both women and the Sept, and the division of primary home education by both gender and institution, implies that religiously affiliated educators are viewed as lesser than secular- and Citadel-affiliated educators; that by being tutored by Septa Mordane rather than Maester Luwin, the Stark girls are receiving a lesser education than their brothers. Otherwise, readers could reasonably expect septons to be employed by the Great Houses as tutors for their children; and yet they are not. In addition to the Crown's limitations of the Faith's military might (back when King Maegor I disbanded the Faith Militant), the sidelining of the Faith and its uncoupling from elite systems of learning is highly instrumental in limiting its power. Beyond the performance of basic life-cycle rites (marriages, coronations and funerals), religious practice and religious study are largely the province of women and old men: the socially disenfranchised.[22]

By contrast, the Order of Maesters, and indeed the whole of the Citadel, is closed to women. This is in keeping with most historical medieval university conventions for admission, though there were exceptions: Bettisia Gozzadini earned a law degree from the University of Bologna in 1237 and taught at the university in 1239, beginning a tradition of women teaching and studying at the University of Bologna, which continued through and beyond the Middle Ages and Renaissance. Similarly, the universities of Salamanca and Alcalá in Spain began admitting women as both students and instructors in the sixteenth century.[23] Medieval women did not necessarily need to attend university to receive higher education or produce works of academic value, however. Héloïse d'Argenteuil was already a renowned scholar in Greek, Hebrew and astronomy before Pierre Abélard became her tutor. Hildegard von Bingen composed poetry, music and medical texts.[24] Convents offered education to their nuns in subjects such as geometry, rhetoric, ethics, music and Latin as well as midwifery and textile work.[25] Similarly, there are exceptions to the Westerosi norm of girls' education: Ned Stark privately contracts Syrio Forel to teach his daughter to fence (a skill deemed only suitable for men in Westerosi society) and most of the women with claims to queenship (Cersei, Margaery, Daenerys, Sansa) seem to have a healthy grasp of both military and political strategy – though how much of this knowledge was provided by adults in tutoring roles (Petyr Baelish taking Sansa under his wing, for instance, or Olenna Tyrell mentoring Margaery) and how much of it is either innate or hard-won through observation, trial and error varies by individual.

Indeed, throughout the book and TV series, women repeatedly prove themselves to be well-educated in more than mere courtesies, and it is when men underestimate and devalue women's knowledge that they fall into error. Robb Stark does not heed his mother's wisdom about battles being won through alliances as much as battles, and so marries Jeyne Westerling (Talisa in the HBO rendition) and loses his life at Walder Frey's Red Wedding. Jon Snow dismisses his sister Sansa's knowledge of Ramsay Bolton's *modus operandi* and so nearly dies in the Battle of the Bastards. Sam Tarly at first misses the significance of Gilly's discovery that Rhaegar Targaryen secretly annulled his marriage with Elia Martell, wed Lyanna Stark and had a child with her, because though Shireen and Sam took the time to teach Gilly to read, Sam views her capacity to read intelligently for information with a degree of (unconscious) condescension. The folly, and even mortal danger, of limiting access to knowledge and dismissing educated voices (particularly those who are self-taught) is a key theme throughout the series and will be discussed more fully later in this chapter.

Citadel and court

But let us return to the Citadel and the Order of Maesters. In addition to their roles as educators, the maesters are also scholars, researching and experimenting across a variety of subjects. This polymathy is symbolically represented by the chains they wear draped around their necks. Each link represents a mastery of a different subject:

> A maester forges his chain with study.... The different metals are each a different kind of learning, gold for the study of money and accounts, silver for healing, iron for warcraft. And [Maester Luwin] said there were other meanings as well. The collar is supposed to remind a maester of the realm he serves.... A chain needs all sorts of metals, and a land needs all sorts of people. (*GT*, 435)

Meteorology and astronomy are core disciplines at the Citadel. It is the maesters' duty to determine the official beginning of each season, sending out white ravens to the various kingdoms of Westeros to signal the change of the season (*CK*, 2–5). They also study the comet that is seen in the sky concurrently with the hatching of Daenerys's dragons (*CK*, 1–2; *FC*, 10–11, 773–5). They record the history of Westeros, and it is these historical texts that Sam Tarly seems to find most interesting in the Castle Black library.²⁶ Medicine and biology (if that is what we can loosely call Qyburn's area of specialization before he was stripped of his chains) are also under the maesters' purview. And we know chemistry to be an object of study as well, as Oberyn Martell is said to have studied poisons at the Citadel (4.3). However, though it was one of the three areas of study for the master's degree in historical universities, jurisprudence does not appear to be a subject of study at the Citadel: no one with formal legal training is involved in any of the series' legal trials, and defendants must rely on their own wits or representative brawn in trials by jury or combat.²⁷ Martin's selective engagement with the complexities of late medieval society is, in this particular instance, a useful creative decision. Requiring the protagonists to represent themselves in life-or-death trials amplifies the drama and narrative tension considerably. These trials become moments to showcase the intelligence, misplaced confidence or ability to inspire loyalty of the character on trial, rather than displaying the quick thinking and knowledge of a Citadel-trained maester who might have earned his chain link for jurisprudence.

Science and ethics

The final branch of studies which the maesters in *A Song of Ice and Fire* and *Game of Thrones* are shown pursuing is the medical sciences. It is here that the ethics of academia in Westeros come into debate. The two main points of ethical contention are Qyburn's experiments and Sam Tarly's attempt to cure Jorah Mormont's advancing greyscale. While members of the Order of Maesters are granted a certain degree of academic freedom of inquiry, it is clear from the Archmaesters' decision to strip Qyburn of his maester's chain that some degree of ethical accountability is required of maesters, at least when it comes to their experiments. Within the Citadel, Qyburn's experiments are considered beyond the pale – though not, as Cersei makes clear, within the Red Keep. Qyburn's expulsion from the Order of Maesters does not deter Cersei from commissioning him to resurrect Gregor Clegane and raise Qyburn first to the position formerly held by Varys on the Small Council, and ultimately to Queen's Hand (6.10).

It is not, however, Qyburn's necromancy (or, at best, his unnatural preservation of Gregor Clegane's life) which drives the Archmaester to strip him of his chain. Rather, it is that he repeatedly performed vivisections in order to further his medical knowledge. Conducting autopsies and human dissections for the purpose of medical advancement and as a teaching tool is no longer a controversial subject, but for centuries, human dissection was a deeply contentious practice across Europe. In the twenty-first century, autopsies are a standard element of medical education and forensic research, but in the medieval and early modern eras, dissecting the dead was largely viewed as unethical: the ends did not justify the means. Permission to perform autopsies, whether for educational or forensic purposes, was required from the church. A few were performed legally, such as the autopsy of Azzolino Onesti in Bologna in 1302, which was mandated by a criminal judge. Onesti was believed to have been poisoned.²⁸ Others were performed in secret by those wishing to better understand human anatomy, for medical advancement or for artistic understanding. Giovanni Morgagni, Leonardo da Vinci and Michelangelo are known to have illegally performed autopsies to further their understanding of the human body.

Martin has described his approach to writing as follows: 'I take [history], and I file off the serial numbers, and I turn it up to eleven, and I change the colour from red to purple, and I have a great incident for the books.'[29] Dissection may be accepted practice in modern society, but human vivisection remains firmly taboo. To elicit the same ethical discomfort in his contemporary audience that dissections used to elicit in historical audiences, Martin combines elements of Dr Frankenstein's and William Harvey's research in Qyburn's experiments. He turns the historical debate surrounding dissection 'up to eleven' by changing it to a debate within the Order of Maesters around the ethics of medical advancement through vivisection and the ethics of resurrection. William Harvey's seventeenth-century contemporaries, who looked at the advances in anatomy, and particularly the understanding of circulatory system, which Harvey was able to make through his vivisections of animals, stated that they would 'rather err with Galen than proclaim the truth with Harvey'. Like those contemporaries, the audience of *A Song of Ice and Fire* and *Game of Thrones* is invited to be repulsed and revolted by Qyburn's research methods and to approve of the Archmaester's expulsion of Qyburn from the Order.

Qyburn's argument for his research methods is anchored in utilitarian thinking: in his eyes, vivisections of unwilling people are acceptable because of the medical advances these vivisections bring. He believes the preservation of many outweighs the deaths of a few, regardless of circumstances. This fits hand in glove with Cersei's and Varys's political philosophy: that it is necessary and ethical for some to die for 'the good of the realm' – though how Cersei and Varys define 'the good of the realm' differs considerably. On the other hand, the otherwise reprehensible and ethically corrupt Grand Maester Pycelle views Qyburn's vivisections with detestation and thoroughly approves of Qyburn's expulsion from the Order: 'His curiosity was deemed dangerous and unnatural. Rightly so, in my opinion' (4.10). Pycelle's condemnation is a measure of how far beyond the pale Qyburn's abuse of academic research ethics stretches, that even a man as morally corrupt as Pycelle cannot condone his behaviour.

Questions surrounding the ethical bounds of academic freedom are not limited to Qyburn's experiments, however. Sam's pursuit of a cure for greyscale extends this debate surrounding research ethics and provides a counterpoint to Qyburn's research. Greyscale is a disease transmitted through both direct and indirect contact: Jorah contracts greyscale after skin-to-skin contact with an infected person, one of the Stone Men; Shireen contracted the disease by holding a contaminated doll. It slowly spreads first across the skin and then to internal organs, calcifying them. When the disease reaches the brain, it causes insanity that leads to violent behaviour. As with Qyburn, the Archmaester prohibits Sam from medical experimentation, though in this instance, the audience is invited to support Sam's efforts to save Jorah. After all, both Sam and Jorah are portrayed as largely likeable figures; the experiment is successful; Sam saves a life without taking anyone else's; and there are no negative consequences for his disregard for the Archmaester's demands.

Ethical action within the world of ice and fire, whether political or academic, seems to require a balance of means and ends if it is to be treated by Martin, Benioff and Weiss as both justifiable and practical. Sam's approach to academic research and inquiry adheres to this model: he steals textbooks, which violates Citadel rules and yet harms no one; and while his treatment of Jorah is excruciatingly painful for the patient, Sam has his patient's full consent. The alternative if Sam were to comply with the Archmaester's orders is worse: Jorah could die if Sam tries to cure his greyscale and is unsuccessful; he will certainly die if Sam does not experiment at all. In Westeros, the ethical and successful approach for any character, maester, noble, Night's Watch or common folk, is one which inflicts some (yet minimal) damage for maximal preservation of lives and livelihood. Qyburn's experiments could be argued to fall under this ethical standard (minimal damage for maximal preservation) except that the very tangible and immediate deaths he inflicts with his vivisections are for only a possible, but as yet hypothetical, later preservation of more lives. Furthermore, the motive of Qyburn's patron, Cersei, in this revivification exemplifies the Lannister, Baratheon and, as it turns out, Targaryen approach to power: to completely ignore even the utilitarian ethic and to act with the intention of gaining power and taking vengeance on the innocent and guilty alike. Cersei wants the Mountain revived to act as a weapon, to increase her power.

Qyburn's justification for his experiments reflects a theme that plays throughout the series, and particularly in the final season: the line between acting to save people and holding a messiah complex. Daenerys as both Breaker of Chains and conqueror (and earlier when she attempts to use blood magic to heal Khal Drogo) is perhaps the most obvious example of this. The burning of Shireen, revivification of Lady Stoneheart and creation of the Night King are equally horrific results of characters overestimating their abilities and judgement in determining who should live. The right and ability to determine who should die (and who should live again) is fairly clearly the province only of R'hllor, as the only successful resurrections are those of Beric Dondarrion and Jon Snow, when Thoros and Melisandre serve as merely vessels for R'hllor's power and will.

Grey rats and book worms

In comparing Qyburn's and Sam's research methods and results, the audience can clearly see the difference between the dangers of completely regulation- or consequence-free scientific experimentation and those of the suppression of academic inquiry. The Archmaester, however, clearly cannot. The pursuit of knowledge throughout the series remains critical to the preservation of Westerosi people (whether that knowledge be of how to cure a disease, how to defeat a wight or the history of how the Wall was built), and yet the maesters in the highest and most influential positions in the Citadel are repeatedly depicted as either unwilling to uncover new truths at the expense of disturbing a status quo that works well for them or unable to pursue further knowledge and impress its importance upon those in positions of power and influence. As Brian Cowlishaw argues, '[t]he highest-ranking, most learned maesters – the ones most likely and qualified to wield real power – are the most ancient, feeble, doddering, ignored. . . . [O]nly two categories of maesters really exist: those too young to know or do much, and those too old to know or do much.'[30] Even worse, '[m]uch of what the maesters "know" is wrong; much that is essential to know, they deny, ignore, or mistakenly consider a tale for children.'[31] The Citadel is in dire need of educational reform if the maesters are to realize their full potential in influencing the lives of Westerosi citizens.

Throughout the book and TV series, the members of the Order of Maesters are repeatedly depicted as either corrupt or ineffectual (though Maesters Luwin and Aemon are exceptions – and it is no accident that they are both operative in the North). As discussed above, the Archmaester's intellectual conservatism makes him reluctant to allow academic exploration beyond his personal scholarly comfort zone. The restrictive bounds he places on the academic pursuits of both the maesters and the students of the Citadel stifle Westerosi intellectual progress. Larrington correctly contends that '[a]s with the Faith's lack of institutional effectiveness in shaping or enforcing a viable ethical framework for daily life in the southern kingdoms, so the Maesters' detachment from history and the learning they guard so carefully – notably excluding women as well as gifted would-be scholars – demonstrates their intellectual failure'.[32] At the Citadel, the maesters are depicted '[i]nhabiting the worst kind of ivory tower, irredeemably turned in on themselves'.[33]

Grand Maester Pycelle is corrupt and untrustworthy, motivated partly by power but primarily maintaining a life of luxury. His interests appear to consist chiefly of retaining proximity to the Iron Throne (and thus, by extension, retaining his wealth and privilege) and of deflowering virgin prostitutes provided him by Petyr Baelish (5.3). As Grand Maester, his role is ostensibly to serve and advise the monarch. Yet in Robert's Rebellion, it is Pycelle who orders the gates of the Red Keep to be opened to Tywin's invading army (*CK*, 372; *SS*, 507). He proves himself to be in the pocket of House Lannister on multiple occasions. Both Robert Baratheon and Jon Arryn die under his medical care, and Pycelle admits to wilful malpractice: he refuses to provide an antidote to Jon Arryn, aiding in his death in order to prevent the incestuous truth of the royal children's parentage from coming to light, and further admits that he had planned to kill Robert Baratheon under the guise of treating him if the boar had not already given the king a fatal wound (*CK*, 372–3).[34] In *A Clash of Kings* Tyrion, newly made Hand of the King, sets a confidentiality trap for those working closest to him: Pycelle, Varys and Petyr Baelish. Though none is to be trusted, it is Pycelle who breaks Tyrion's confidence most quickly and obviously (*CK*, 371). And even those to whom Pycelle panders, like Cersei, view him with a blend of derision and disgust (*FC*, 269–80). He abuses his position as a learned and powerfully placed man by, in turn, divulging or withholding information to effect harm against others and serve himself. This self-serving behaviour is not merely part and parcel of being a high-ranking member of court: consider, by contrast, Varys, who equally serves on the Small Council, and his repeated and believable assertions that he serves 'the realm, my lord. Someone must' (1.8).

Narrow-mindedness and corruption in top-tier roles such as Archmaester and Grand Maester contribute significantly to enduring problems within the Order, but the dismal opinion of maesters as professional academics held among the nobility is not limited to those in positions of authority. There is a trend throughout Westeros to devalue and downplay maesters' expertise and academic endeavour as a whole. Lady Dustin calls maesters 'grey rats' and tells Theon,

> If I were queen, the first thing I would do would be to kill all those grey rats. They scurry everywhere, living on the leavings of the lords, chittering to one another, whispering in the ears of their masters. . . . Out of gratitude we give them a place beneath our roof and make them privy to all our shames and secrets, a part of every council. And before too long, the ruler has become the ruled. (*DD*, 578–9)

And take, for instance, Maester Cressen, who is maester to Stannis Baratheon and his family. Cressen has served the Baratheon family for years and 'was always summoned for feasts, seated near the salt, close to Lord Stannis' (*CK*, 19). But lately he has no longer been valued for his advice and expertise, and he watches his employer and king increasingly turn to Melisandre's religious zealotry and magic tricks for guidance. He is old, outdated, ineffectual, left out from the feast under the pretence of a concern for his old age. Even his grand final attempt to free Stannis from Melisandre's influence by committing murder-suicide is ineffectual, failing either to harm the Red Woman or to convince Stannis of her unsuitability as an adviser.

Westerosi society, on the whole, does not value traditional, book-focused education. Academic interest is viewed as an ivory-tower hobby, the province of the weak, odd and privileged; and the pursuit, preservation and transmission of knowledge is generally treated as irrelevant, devoid of practical purpose. This is partly due to a lack of accessibility. In the Citadel, the books are visibly chained to the shelves and locked away. Chained libraries were common in medieval England to prevent thieves from absconding with the books, objects of great value. And clearly the Citadel's concern for book theft is well-founded, as Sam steals a great many. But the chained and gated library is also symbolic of the Seven Kingdoms' restricted access to knowledge – as flowing in or flowing out of the ivory tower.

Education then is for the nobility. There are no grammar schools for the small folk and no opportunities for the autodidactic. Gilly wants to learn, but the Citadel and Castle Black libraries are closed to her. Sam (and Shireen) teach Gilly how to read and he provides books for her only by breaking Citadel and Night's Watch rules about allowing women on the premises – or allowing books *off* the premises. Books are largely available only to the wealthy and/or male, and even so, the libraries in the Great Houses tend to be small and neglected. The library at Castle Black is, save for Sam's presence (and Maester Aemon's before his blindness), effectively abandoned.

This brings us to another aspect of the devaluation of academia within Westeros, the relegation of academic interest to the province of those considered by Westerosi society to be weak, odd and privileged. Like Sam's fellow members of the Night's Watch, many of those with access to education and learning materials do not value academic endeavours. Sam is teased and derided for his bookishness by his fellows, and his father disowns him for it. Randyll and Dickon Tarly, Arya and Robb Stark, Jon Snow, Theon and Yara (Asha in the books) Greyjoy, Loras Tyrell, Brienne of Tarth, Robert and Renly Baratheon: most of the nobility – those with access to academic study – place far greater value on physical pursuits, on hunting, reaving, jousting, ranging and fighting. And indeed, there seems to be an inverse relationship within Westerosi society between physical ability and academic interest, as if intellectual study were the bastion for those who cannot advance through physical means – usually fighting. Tyrion and Sam are presented as anomalies in their enjoyment of books and their desire to learn about topics not immediately relevant to their daily lives. It is no coincidence that Tyrion and Sam are also presented as two of the least athletic and physically capable characters. Bran Stark as the Three-Eyed Raven is simultaneously the most knowledgeable and least physically abled character in the series and after his return to the Seven Kingdoms is no longer interested in conforming with the social expectations of the society he belonged to as a boy, which he can never fulfil; he is now a man apart.

However, some of the most dangerous and most successful players in the game of thrones are the ones who value reading and the acquiring and preservation of knowledge. Tywin Lannister is not content with a son who excels in hand-to-hand combat: he forces Jaime to learn to read despite his apparent dyslexia and lectures Jaime on the importance of understanding one's opponents and having a strong grasp of military and political tactics (2.6, 3.3 and 1.7). Varys and Petyr Baelish rise to prominence through their mental acuity and information-gathering networks. Tyrion survives on his wits and knowledge. His research into wildfire and head for strategy (as seen in his repeated wins at cyvasse, a chess-like game) ensures victory at the Battle of Blackwater Bay (*DD*, 324–8; *FC*, 99; (2.9)). His head for legal argument and acquired knowledge of Red Keep architecture are put to use on more than one occasion. His interest in studying people and their motivations repeatedly saves his life and lands him advisory positions as Hand to Joffrey and Daenerys (1.10 and 6.10). He reads widely, telling Jon Snow, 'A mind needs books like a sword needs a whetstone, if it is to keep its edge' (*GT*, 118).

Beyond Westeros, Daenerys proves a successful conqueror because she surrounds herself with and listens to knowledgeable advisers: primarily Missandei, Tyrion, Varys, Jorah Mormont, Ser Barristan Selmy and Grey Worm. As freed slaves, exiles and refugees, her hand-picked advisers are people whom she values for their wisdom and expertise rather than any lands, social status or material wealth. It is only when Daenerys loses, dismisses and ignores her advisers in the final season that she loses her grasp of military and leadership ethics, her various people's support and ultimately her life.

Jon's slow-growing appreciation for the value of education is central to his character development over the course of the series. Though he begins as a teenage boy who finds Tyrion's and Sam's habits of reading for leisure eccentric, he comes around to recognizing the value of what Sam learns through his long hours in the Castle Black library. As a young man at Castle Black, Jon is angry when he is assigned to the Stewards; he only sees opportunities for heroism among the Rangers. Ygritte's refrain, 'You know nothing, Jon Snow', is so strongly attached to his character that it became a popular meme. And yet Jon grows to become a Lord Commander who seeks to learn from the various peoples north of the Wall and who sends his best friend to the Citadel to train as a maester. Despite his desire to keep Sam at his side, Jon learns finally to see the vital importance of education and continuing study in aiding his men's survival at the Wall.

Thus, it is the acquisition, preservation and transmission of knowledge that proves the key to survival, not necessarily of the individual but of humankind. The Others/White Walkers threaten humanity's survival; their advance and initial success arises where knowledge has been lost or hidden. The magic which went into building the wall and the knowledge of what tools to use to destroy it; how to destroy a wight with fire, and an Other/White Walker with dragon glass; where dragon glass can be found; how to hatch, raise and ride dragons; the history of the Children; and the existence of the Three-Eyed Raven. All of these things used to be known among Westerosi people, and the loss of that knowledge threatens the current characters' ability to protect themselves from and defeat the army of the dead – or even to acknowledge the Others/White Walkers as a threat. Knowledge of their existence has, at the point the series begins, faded into Old Nan's tales, dismissed by southerners as 'snarks and grumkins' (*CK*, 368; *FC*, 280; (1.2); (2.2)).

While the book series at the time of publication is not complete, the HBO showrunners make the preservation and transmission of knowledge the central theme of the series' final episode. Sam has apparently become Grand Maester, or at least been given the Grand Maester's chair in the Small Council, and yet he wears no chain, suggesting a reformation among the Order of Maesters. Brienne brings closure to Jaime's narrative by inscribing his deeds in the Kingsguard's *Book of Brothers*. Brandon Stark, the Three-Eyed Raven, becomes king. He possesses the unique ability to access every person's memories, living or dead. The surviving heads of the Great Houses buck tradition and place Bran in the highest position in the realm, convinced that, as the living embodiment of collective knowledge, he will be able to bring an end to the civil war and usher in a new era of peace. The penultimate scene closes on an image of Archmaester Ebrose's book, *A Song of Ice and Fire*, detailing the events of the series. However, Tyrion is left out of its narrative entirely. Though it is played as a joke in the episode, it is an exclusion perhaps foreshadowed by Varys in Season 2: 'The King won't give you any honours, the histories won't mention you, but we will not forget' (2.10). No historical account ever tells the full story, a phenomenon which ensures that academics' work is never complete. As seen in the multiple-viewpoint narrative style of Martin's books, every perspective and piece of additional information adds to a greater understanding of the world at large, even those which seem insignificant at first glance.[35] It is only through the celebration of collective knowledge that civilization thrives.

4

'The Iron Bank will have its due'

Trade and economics in *Game of Thrones*

Caroline R. Batten

George R. R. Martin's *A Song of Ice and Fire* and the associated television show *Game of Thrones* take place in a vividly imagined secondary world based on the social, cultural and governmental structures of fourteenth-century Europe. This world feels detailed and real and obtains its distinctly 'medieval' social flavour, in large part thanks to Martin's provision of information about trade, money, debt and resource production. These fantasy economics are an essential part of Martin's worldbuilding, but their precise workings are often overlooked in studies of his work, and the absence of such detail in other fantasy texts often goes unnoticed. 'Ruling is hard,' Martin noted in an interview with *Rolling Stone*. 'Tolkien doesn't ask the question: what was Aragorn's tax policy? . . . What did he do in times of flood and famine?'[1] An exploration of the economics of the *Ice and Fire* universe serves to illuminate Martin's central ideas about the mechanics of rulership and his interest in the ways sociological restraints influence the decisions of individuals, as well as to highlight fundamental differences in approach between the books and the show. This chapter first seeks to describe the kinds of economies audiences encounter in Westeros and Essos, then to explore the role of trade, finance and debt in the *Ice and Fire* universe by examining two major storylines – that of the Iron Throne's debts and that of Daenerys's experience ruling in Meereen – as well as the role of economics in raiding. Taken together, these analyses demonstrate the ways in which the *Ice and Fire* universe uses the practical realities of finance and trade as a kind of stand-in for a sense of grittiness and realpolitik, a way to explore repeatedly the difference between obtaining and wielding power.

Economies in the world of *Ice and Fire*

Westeros is essentially 'feudal' in its social and economic structures, and some exploration of this frequently used, highly loaded term is useful. The term *feudalism* is not a medieval one but was coined to describe a broad set of social relationships based on obligation, payment, service and land tenure that existed in medieval Europe.[2] The general principle of a feudal society (and thus economy) is that magnates control land and offer land tenure and protection to their vassals in exchange for military support and/or a certain amount of payable land tax. Vassals in turn served as lords to the peasantry who laboured to make the land productive. All goods of value, and the labour required to make them, are created by those at the bottom of the social hierarchy, who are entitled to the smallest percentage of their own production, while the monarch is effectively a lord whose fief encompasses the entire kingdom. The Westerosi economy, like most medieval feudal economies, relies on agrarianism and food production; the 'smallfolk' engage largely in subsistence farming, while lords such as the Tyrells, who hold fiefs in agriculturally rich areas, can acquire enough surplus grain in tax to sell. Craftsmen can also make a living producing both necessities and luxury goods to be consumed by those who can afford to pay.

Feudalism was never a monolithic structure, and the existence of the term can be misleading; numerous complex social and economic relationships existed in the High Middle Ages in Europe. In fourteenth-century England, lords controlled land use and economic production within a manorial system, with some labourers living as serfs bound to manorial lands, others as free persons who engaged in subsistence farming or, more often, entered into contracts with manorial lords for land use.[3] However, the essential idea of feudalism – in which those lower in the class hierarchy pay those higher in the class hierarchy with goods, money or service in exchange for protection and the right to use land – did structure significant aspects of many medieval European royal administrations, and accordingly it governs the workings of Westeros.

The long seasons must have significant economic effects on both Westeros and Essos, though these effects are mostly discussed in terms of the efforts by various rulers to obtain stores of food for the coming winter. Indeed, how everyone gets fed over years of winter – much less how humanity managed to survive a winter that lasted a full generation – is a question that is never satisfactorily answered. The four seasons would create a cyclical pattern of growth and catastrophe: in winter, food supplies are low, and so the population collapses; as spring returns, and production can begin again, labour is in demand, so wages rise, but production would start off slowly and landowners must take losses to employ workers at higher wages. In summer, as food production increases, so does the population, and with plenty of food and plenty of labour, low wages will dovetail with low prices. In autumn, with the advent of harvests and the population at its height, wages are low and demand is high, but so is supply. Then the population crashes again with the advent of winter. This kind of perpetual economic disruption must cause attendant social uprisings. The real-world Peasants' Uprising in England in 1381 was famously produced in part by the backlash to rising wages caused by the population crash of the Black Death in the 1340s; landowners attempted to fix wages at pre-pandemic levels to save their own profits, leading to a workers' rebellion.[4]

At the start of the series, however, Westeros and Essos are at the tail end of a years-long summer, which has clearly allowed for economic flourishing. Westeros is in the midst of a crucial transitional period in its economic structure: the continent is still operating within a 'feudal' system in rural areas controlled by lords of the Seven Kingdoms, but it also contains numerous cities and market towns that can sustain significant populations, with urban economies that rely on the provision of services and skills. Domestic and international trade is essential: wines are imported from Dorne, spices from Qarth. While barter certainly exists, such an extensive network of global trade also relies on coinage. As in medieval Europe, Westerosi coinage is trimetallic. There is a gold standard, as well as silver and copper money.[5] The Master of Coin oversees minting and exchange rates, and all money is issued by the Crown. Gold coins are an example of *commodity money*: the money has value because of its material substance, and a coin is worth exactly the amount of gold that constitutes it. In Braavos, however, the coins are iron; they are *fiat money*, coins that have neither inherent nor use value, but rather have economic value because they are backed by the government or a bank. The development of these significant trade networks – especially in luxury goods, like Cersei's favoured Myrish lace – and the associated regulation and standardization of coinage has facilitated the rise of an upwardly mobile mercantile class, providing ways for people like Petyr Baelish, Illyrio Mopatis and Ser Davos Seaworth to earn enough money essentially to join the ruling class.

Baelish, in particular, represents a particular kind of economic success to other characters in the *Ice and Fire* universe, who speak reverently of his ability to generate gold, associated with his ownership of a string of brothels. It is often noted that sex work has a striking economic prominence in *Game of Thrones*. Some of this is grounded in the show's sensationalism, but the proliferation of brothels does serve as a notable economic benchmark: the leisure class of a city like King's Landing is large enough to sustain numerous and expensive hubs for sex work, which indicates the existence of a significant stratum of the urban wealthy beyond the royal court. Baelish's brothels are a sign of the development of what will eventually become a 'middle class' in Westeros, which will include merchants, clerks, Gold Cloaks and presumably providers of other services: we do not meet any lawyers, accountants or professional scribes in *Game of Thrones*, for example, but an extensive network of global trade and a centralized monarchy collecting taxes from seven distinct vassal kingdoms cannot function without them. In addition to the leisured class, however, large cities also concentrate poverty, creating a class of urban poor (exaggeratedly and grimly visible in Martin's depictions of King's Landing). These people have probably migrated away from subsistence farming in the countryside but find themselves relegated to lives of sickness, hunger and crime in overcrowded, deprived areas like Flea Bottom.

Indeed, the economies of Westeros and Essos both rest, fundamentally, on the maintenance of a profound degree of social and material inequality – but Essos is socio-economically distinct from Westeros in a number of ways. Essos contains numerous city states, which are self-governing and do not relate to a single centralized suzerain. Each city state is oligarchical, run by a council of magisters selected from among the wealthiest citizens; in Volantis, at least, citizens who hold a certain amount of property are able to vote for their triarchs, though in other cities the councils may be essentially self-perpetuating, choosing their own members and presumably therefore breeding complex political and economic rivalries (*DD*, 56). The Free Cities are mercantile, relying heavily on trade; in Slaver's Bay a significant quantity of that trade is in human beings. There is some agrarian underpinning to the economy of Essos as in Westeros, with food grown in the hinterlands of the Free

Cities and the Dothraki engaging in pastoralist practices, but relatively little of it is depicted in the books or show. The use of slave labour creates an economic inequality even more profound than feudalism: some people own property, other people *are* property, and that unpaid labour allows for significantly increased profits for those lucky enough to be free. We encounter relatively few poor, free characters in Essos, for Daenerys's storyline concentrates on the contrast between the wealthy elite and the slaves they own, but such people must exist; there has never been a society that consists exclusively of wealthy masters and completely disenfranchised slaves. We must assume that significant cultural work is invested in preventing class solidarity between poor free persons and enslaved persons in Essos. Presumably, poor free persons are encouraged to identify themselves with the wealthy elite and define themselves as free in opposition to the (reviled) enslaved.[6]

This is the economic world in which *A Song of Ice and Fire* and *Game of Thrones* operate. Martin repeatedly uses the necessity of money, and the profound inequalities of the societies through which our characters move, to force their hands and shape their decisions. Everyone must bow to the power of gold – even the formidable Cersei Lannister, in the most prominent economic storyline shared by both the books and the show, that of the astronomical Crown debt.

The Iron Bank of Braavos and the Crown debt

> Each of the Nine Free Cities had its bank, and some had more than one, fighting over every coin like dogs over a bone, but the Iron Bank was richer and more powerful than all the rest combined. When princes defaulted on their debts to lesser banks, ruined bankers sold their wives and children into slavery and opened their own veins. When princes failed to repay the Iron Bank, new princes sprang up from nowhere and took their thrones. (*AF*, 60)

The Iron Bank of Braavos is first introduced early on in *A Game of Thrones*, when Eddard Stark discovers that the Crown is six million gold dragons in debt, an astonishing amount of money. The Bank remains a shadowy institution in both *A Song of Ice and Fire* and *Game of Thrones*, but its mystique is potent:

> **CERSEI**: There must be someone at the Iron Bank you can speak to, come to an arrangement.
> **TYWIN**: The Iron Bank is the Iron Bank. There is no someone.
> **CERSEI**: Someone does work there. It is comprised of people.
> **TYWIN**: And a temple is comprised of stones. One crumbles and another takes its place. And the temple holds its form for a thousand years or more. That's what the Iron Bank is: a temple. We all live in its shadow and almost none of us know it. You can't run from them, you can't cheat them, you can't sway them with excuses. If you owe them money and you don't want to crumble yourself, you pay it back. (4.3)

We learn only snippets about how the Iron Bank actually functions, however. Professional moneylenders are characterized by their ability to hold partnerships, accept deposits and loan money to others, and we do see glimpses – but often only glimpses – of all these activities in the *Ice and Fire* universe.[7] The financial power of medieval banks, in particular, was derived from capital invested by partners or shareholders, reinvested earnings and money placed on deposit by outsiders.[8] Twice, characters in *Game of Thrones* describe the Iron Bank as demanding interest; the Braavosi institution thus profits directly off its loans (3.3; 7.4). Westerosi merchants owe significant amounts to the Iron Bank in *A Feast for Crows*, which indicates again a reliance on interest payments for profit but also raises the possibility of direct Iron Bank investment of funds in Westerosi industries (*FC*, 535). In *A Dance with Dragons*, the Bank's representative Tycho Nestoris indicates that steady interest payments were made on the Crown debt during King Robert's reign; these ceased after Cersei declared the Crown would not repay the Iron Bank until after the ongoing war is won (*AF*, 55–6). In Martin's histories of Westeros and Essos, he reveals that the Iron Bank originated as a repository for the wealth of twenty-three Braavosi individuals. The bank was formed to utilize the gold, and he notes that other wealthy individuals were eventually allowed to make deposits and contribute gold to the bank for safekeeping (*WIF*, 271–6). This suggests that the Iron Bank functions much like a modern bank, investing money deposited by shareholders ('key-holders' in Braavos) and clients in profitable ventures; indeed, the show once makes reference to the Iron Bank's investments in the slave trade (7.3).

Martin based the Iron Bank of Braavos on the powerful banks of medieval Venice and Florence, which were controlled by the so-called Black Guelph noble families – most prominently the Florentine Bardi, Peruzzi and Acciaiuouli.[9] These banks were established in the mid-thirteenth century and flourished with the support of the Pope; the general improvement in agricultural productivity and growth of silver mining in Europe allowed for a concentration of cash in the hands of the aristocratic elite, a rising demand for luxury goods and an explosion of international trade, all prime conditions for the formation of banking companies.[10] Medieval banking, however, functioned in significantly different ways from our modern systems of deposit, investment and interest. The Bardi, Peruzzi and Acciaiuouli were primarily merchant companies, which commanded such vast resources that they were able to also offer loans to secure advantageous deals and investments; the key to their success was large-scale commodity trading.[11] These merchants made short-term credit available in order to enable international fund transfers.[12] The international merchant bankers were considered distinct from Italian pawnbrokers established in other European cities like Bruges, who extended consumption loans to individuals or families against collateral, and deposit bankers, who accepted deposits to make payments via transfer and created credit by lending, a natural evolution of money changing.[13] This last, the closest in function to a modern bank, was almost always a small-scale local industry, and the offices of most banks would be small booths in marketplaces rather than the grand, imposing edifice of the Iron Bank.[14] Both pawnbrokers and deposit bankers were vulnerable to charges of usury: demanding any interest on a loan was considered a sin by the Catholic Church throughout the medieval period, and so elaborate financial agreements had to be used to avoid difficulties, including inventing a charge for the exchange of silver or gold in a loan contract that would essentially serve as the lender's profit margin.[15] There are no such prohibitions under the Faith of the Seven in Westeros nor the various religions practised in Braavos, and as a result the Iron Bank can operate much more like an early modern or modern financial institution, capable of charging interest explicitly and scaling up the medieval model of a local deposit bank into a world-dominating operation.

The Iron Bank has the resources necessary to make loans to monarchs, despite lacking offices or branches on the Westerosi side of the Narrow Sea. In medieval Italy, only the great merchant banks on the scale of the Bardi and Peruzzi were capable of making such loans, and these tended to receive their repayment through financial privileges rather than interest. Princes pledged royal revenues, including the ability to collect customs, tax fees and house rents, to the banks, allowing them to control large sections of import/export markets deemed important enough to merit direct royal control: grain, salt, iron and, in England specifically, wool.[16]

Only major banks had the financial stability, and resources, to offer loans to monarchs in exchange for trading privileges and revenues. All fourteenth-century European governments required loans to function: taxation was often difficult and expensive to implement, wars were costly and growing more so as the technology of battle increased in sophistication and the standard of living for the nobility was on the rise.[17] The political and mercantile advantages of making loans to the monarch were notable but extending a line of credit to a prince was also a famously dangerous proposition. A loan to a monarch is often long term, immobilizing a bank's funds for a prolonged period of time, and it ties the lender firmly to the political fortunes of the borrower.[18] The high risks of lending to a monarch are perhaps best exemplified by Edward III's relationship with the Bardi and Peruzzi in the 1340s; the banks offered Edward significant loans for his war with France, in exchange for customs management of the wool trade and a large percentage of tax revenue.[19] A series of risky financial decisions on the part of the Bardi and Peruzzi put the banks in a dangerous position, and they were lending to Edward faster than they were receiving reimbursement. Thus they cut off Edward's financial support, forcing him to make peace at Tournai in 1340, and when Edward defaulted on the remainder of his loans it helped to tip the Bardi and Peruzzi into bankruptcy in 1344–5, causing a significant economic crash across Europe. What is interesting, however, as economics scholar Edwin Hunt points out, is that lending to a monarch for profit was out of keeping with the usual Bardi and Peruzzi company policies, precisely because loans to rulers were so risky and relied on such long-term repayment plans.[20] Why does the Iron Bank of Braavos continue to offer loans to unreliable Westerosi monarchs? No mention is made of the Iron Bank receiving trade privileges or similar rewards for their loans, only interest, and – as the events of both English history and *A Song of Ice and Fire* show – monarchs have a poor track record with making steady interest payments. Perhaps the Iron Bank is as vulnerable to poor financial decision-making as any modern institution. Perhaps it is in fact making the bulk of its profits elsewhere, on individual loans, the backing of Westerosi merchants and its noted investments in the slave trade: these might allow the Iron Bank to function in a manner more similar to the northern Italian super-companies on which it is based.

Perhaps more important, however, is the way the Crown's debt to the Iron Bank functions in the *Ice and Fire* narrative. Robert Baratheon's bankrupting of the realm in *A Game of Thrones* and Season 1 is a symbol of his own impotence, and of his fundamental inability to rule Westeros responsibly. We are introduced to the Crown's financial woes in the context of Robert's insistence on throwing a tournament in Ned Stark's name, with excessively large prizes; Ned has no interest in the tournament and the Crown will have to borrow money to provide the prizes, as the king (as noted above) is six million gold dragons in debt. The unnecessary expense, and poor sense of the value of money, indicates a fundamental weakness in Robert. The debt is used as a concrete sign of the moral and practical decay Ned encounters, combats and eventually fails to uproot in King's Landing. Robert's dismissal, in both book and show, of financial management as 'counting coppers' demonstrates to the audience immediately that he has no grasp of the practicalities of kingship (*GT*, loc. 905; 1.3). In Season 1, too, we learn that the Crown owes three million of those gold dragons to Tywin Lannister (1.3); later in this same episode, Robert declares to Barristan Selmy, with great disgust, that he is 'surrounded by Lannisters'. Indeed he is, and more than he knows, as his children are in fact the product of Cersei's incest with her twin brother. Robert's massive debts to Tywin give the Lannisters excessive political influence, an emasculation of Robert that is treated as thematically parallel to Cersei's secret supplanting of the Baratheon line with Lannister heirs.

Robert and Cersei's fundamental misunderstanding of the office of Master of Coin plays a similar role. As Petyr Baelish tells Ned Stark, 'The Master of Coin finds the money; the king, and the Hand, spend it' (1.3), suggesting a fundamental disconnect between Robert's attitude towards money and the labour required to provide it. In theory, the Master of Coin's task should be to maintain the flow of royal income, fulfilling the same role as a medieval European royal bureaucracy: to administer taxation and customs revenue, appoint bureaucrats to engage in fee collection, mint coinage, claim part of the profits from key industries such as the wool trade and secure operating loans from merchant banks. In *A Clash of Kings*, we learn that Baelish

> paid the king's debts in promises, and put the king's gold to work. He bought wagons, shops, ships, houses. He bought grain when it was plentiful and sold bread when it was scarce. He bought wool from the north and linen from the south and lace from Lys, stored it, moved it, dyed it, sold it. (*CK*, 247–8)

Baelish is successful because he understands how to use crown revenues to generate greater profits, but he does not curb Robert's excessive spending, and the Crown's debt has grown alongside its income. (In the show, Tyrion condemns Baelish's borrowing from the Iron Bank without indicating that Baelish is engaged in any profit-generating activities, pinning the blame for the Crown debt on Baelish's bad decision-making, an impression reinforced by Baelish himself, who tells Tyrion, 'They're only numbers, numbers on paper. Once you understand that, it's easy to make them behave' (3.3).) Cersei shows a similar lack of interest in the financial mechanics of rule. In *A Feast for*

Crows, she names the ill and incompetent Lord Gyles Rosby to the position of Master of Coin, saying, 'Rosby will make an adequate master of coin. You've seen that litter of his, with its carvings and silk draperies. His horses are better dressed than most knights. A man that rich should have no problem finding gold' (*FC*, 113). Reducing the function of the Master of Coin to mere provision or possession of money betrays an inability to understand the necessity of careful economic management to the health of the realm, the Crown's finances and the survival of the smallfolk – a miscalculation that will lead to disaster.

It is Cersei's failure to grasp economic principles that lead to her ruin in *A Feast for Crows*. She first makes the decision to withhold payments (presumably interest) on the Crown's debts to the Iron Bank. When Pycelle tells her, 'The Braavosi have a saying... the Iron Bank will have its due, they say', Cersei responds, 'The Iron Bank will have its due when I say they will. Until such time, the Iron Bank will wait respectfully' (*FC*, 245). She dismisses Braavosi representative Noho Dimittis without listening to him, and as a result she is soon fielding pleas from Westerosi merchants, informing her that the Iron Bank is demanding repayment of all its debts and refusing new loans (*FC*, 346–7, 535). Her flippant mental response – 'We need our own bank... the Golden Bank of Lannisport' – demonstrates only that she does not understand how banks work, and where they amass their financial resources that allow them to offer credit. The implication is that Westeros is headed for imminent economic ruin on her watch, which leads, in turn, to her catastrophic offer to the High Sparrow to allow him to re-establish the Faith Militant in exchange for the waiving of the Crown's debt to the Faith of the Seven.

The Sparrows themselves emerge from the economic devastation caused by the War of the Five Kings, pouring into King's Landing from destroyed villages and sacked septs (*FC*, 420). This same economic devastation (including the disruption of trade routes and an influx of newly impoverished refugees) causes food riots in the city even before the arrival of the Sparrows, as prices spike to unaffordable levels for the urban poor, necessitating the Lannisters' alliance with the wealthy Tyrells. Cersei's hatred of the Tyrells is ineffective against the fact of their money and the necessity of securing provisions for King's Landing both in the short term and for the coming winter. Her personal obsession with removing Margaery from power and disproving her virginity, however, distracts her from financial and political realities that she never really understood, despite her belief that it is only her gender that has held her back from rule. She believes the High Sparrow will be her ally in punishing Margaery for fornication with the creation of the Faith Militant, with its accompanying eradication of a portion of the Crown's debt, but instead she finds herself imprisoned. Cersei's obsession with the personal, the individual and the psychological – her viewpoint chapters in *Feast for Crows* dwell obsessively on Margaery – prevents her from ruling with a close eye on the institutions that shape the social and economic realities of her world, and it is precisely that inattention that brings about her fall from grace. In *A Dance with Dragons*, her refusal to pay back the Iron Bank has also led to Tycho Nestoris and his board making an executive decision to back Stannis Baratheon, whose fate in the books is not yet known. Jon Snow thinks to himself that the Iron Bank may well have won Stannis the war, suggesting that this financial decision may have more import in the books than in the show (*AF*, 60).

A Song of Ice and Fire is interested in the way characters' decisions are shaped by the institutions they interact with and the hard social and economic facts they cannot navigate around: these are texts interested in what happens when the unstoppable force of Ned Stark's personal ethics meets the immovable object of fiscal corruption in King's Landing; when Cersei's blithe prioritization of personal vengeance comes up against an emerging religious militia created by unfavourable economic conditions. Main characters can be killed in these books precisely because the narrative is bigger than individuals, and because individual actions based on emotion or desire – Joffrey's beheading of Ned Stark, Robb Stark's impulsive marriage to Jeyne Westerling, Daenerys's appeal to Mirri Maz Duur – have rippling social and political consequences. The television show, however, is (at least latterly) far more interested in psychological narratives.[21] Nowhere is this made clearer than in the handling of the Iron Bank. In the books, the Bank's decision to back Stannis is a business one: they plan to ask him to take on the Iron Throne's debts as well as repay the new loan they extend to him. In the television show, Stannis and Davos go to Braavos essentially as beggars. 'Across the Narrow Sea', Tycho Nestoris tells them, 'your books are filled with words like *usurper* and *madman* and *blood right*. Here, our books are filled with numbers. We prefer the stories they tell. More plain. Less open to interpretation' (4.6). Nestoris asks for numbers of soldiers and ships, amounts of grain and meat produced on Dragonstone; these are the pragmatic factors Martin is interested in, and by placing these statements about a preference for hard numbers in Nestoris's mouth, the show gestures towards these sociological storylines. Yet the episode takes a turn for the individual and the psychological almost immediately: Davos persuades Tycho Nestoris to back Stannis by arguing that Cersei and Tommen are bad investments because they are unreliable as people, as individuals, as rulers, while Stannis is a tested commander (4.6). At this point in the narrative, Stannis looks like a very poor investment indeed for the Iron Bank: he has no funds and his armies are small, Dragonstone produces no foodstuffs and – as with historical loans to medieval monarchs – there is no guarantee that repayment will be prompt or complete. Indeed, with Stannis's death in Season 5, the Iron Bank loses their loan to him in its entirety. (Such an error in modern banking would be career-ending for Tycho.) Yet Davos persuades Tycho to offer Stannis a significant amount of money simply by acting as a character witness.

In its dialogue, the show pushes the myth of the Iron Bank as the implacable temple, the faceless institution that cannot be outrun or put off, but it also removes the Crown debt, previously treated as an insurmountable problem, with a casual wave of the hand. Tycho Nestoris arrives in Westeros to demand full repayment; Cersei convinces him to bet on her, a debt-honouring Lannister, rather than on Daenerys Targaryen, disruptor of Braavosi investments in the slave trade (7.3). Within a fortnight, the Lannisters take Highgarden, which miraculously contains enough gold to pay off millions in debt. If Mace Tyrell could have paid off the entirety of the Crown debt with the gold reserves on his estate all along, he need not have suffered through a dangerous, humiliating and eventually deadly alliance with the Lannisters: but the show does not address this *aurum ex machina*. Tycho Nestoris is so impressed with Cersei's repayment – forgetting, apparently, about years of royal defaulting – that he offers her another loan, with no conditions or collateral, which is never repaid before her death (7.4).

Tycho also claims the Braavosi shareholders have been enjoying the interest payments made on the Crown's debt, but the Crown's dire financial straits, and the fact that they could not repay the 10 per cent of the loan called in by the Bank in Season 5, implied that no interest was in fact being paid. The show ignores the implacable realities of finance for the dramatics of 'fire and blood' and the powers of individual charisma and persuasion. Far harder to ignore, however, are the economic difficulties Daenerys encounters in Meereen, which highlight the profound differences between conquering and ruling.

Slave economies and the Meereenese knot

As noted above, slave labour underpins the economies of the cities of Slaver's Bay: Astapor, Yunkai and Meereen. Presumably these cities also create goods for consumption and export, but slave labour must reduce production costs significantly. Historically speaking, slaves have generally been treated as movable property and therefore can also be used as collateral or in barter. Daenerys's destruction of the slave trade throws an essential element of the entire economy of Essos into disarray. Once established in Meereen, Daenerys's attention is taken up not just with the guerrilla rebellion of the Sons of the Harpy but also with re-establishing a viable economic structure in the city state: 'For centuries, Meereen and her sister cities Yunkai and Astapor had been the linchpins of the slave trade, the place where Dothraki *khals* and the corsairs of the Basilisk Isles sold their captives and the rest of the world came to buy. Without slaves, Meereen had little to offer traders' (*DD*, 237). Daenerys must restore fields that have been burnt, plant new crops and attempt to arrange trade deals with the spice merchants of Qarth, particularly Xaro Xhoan Daxos. Daxos describes Meereen under Daenerys's rule as 'a poor city that was once rich. A hungry city that was once fat' (*DD*, 242). These pressing issues lead Daenerys to make difficult moral compromises, including her marriage to Hizdahr zo Loraq and her allowance of the reopening of the fighting pits. There are no easy solutions to the problems of ruling in Meereen, and the narrative in both books and show eventually avoids the complex realities of the new Targaryen regime in Slaver's Bay by simply removing Daenerys, on dragon-back, from the immediate situation. In the show, Meereen is more or less narratively abandoned when Daenerys decides to go to Westeros with her newly enlarged army; she leaves Daario Naharis as regent and the city is never mentioned again. It remains to be seen how Daenerys will negotiate her ongoing relationship with Meereen in the books; Martin has referred to the difficulties of this plot line and its various moving parts as 'the Meereenese knot'.[22] The problems of practical rule within the narrative even create meta-narrative difficulties for their author.

Daenerys's liberation of Astapor, her use of the Unsullied against their former masters and her burning of Kraznys mo Nakloz are savvy political and economic decisions when taken in isolation, because they allow her to obtain possession of an army she cannot otherwise pay for, without surrendering one of her priceless dragons (*SS*, 304–15; 3.4). Obtaining the Unsullied in this manner also solves a thornier social and psychological problem: Jorah notes that Daenerys could benefit hugely from an army that does not rape or pillage, while Barristan Selmy argues that she needs an army that follows her out of love (3.3). Freeing the Unsullied and asking them to follow her out of gratitude and loyalty achieves both aims. The problem with the Targaryen motto of 'fire and blood', however, is that it encompasses only conquest, not rule. It is easy to see the moral repugnance of a slave-based economy, but both the books and the show insist on considering the pragmatic realities of the situation. Daenerys is offered a part in the slave economy of Essos: before his death, Kraznys suggests to her that she blood the Unsullied by sacking other cities and bringing captives to Astapor, whom he will buy from her for a good price; 'thus all shall prosper' (3.4). Daenerys burns down this self-perpetuating economy, and the result is the strategic destruction of Meereenese agriculture, the crucifixion of 163 slave children and the immediate reversion of Astapor and Yunkai to slave-based economies once Daenerys has moved on to Meereen. The show renders explicit a point that is made clear only by degrees in the books: Daenerys does not understand the social and economic structures that previously governed Meereen, and so she struggles to maintain her power there and is forced to make moral compromises she resents. Later she is approached by a former slave called Fennesz, who asks to be allowed to sell himself back to his master. He explains to her that she doesn't understand the purpose and respect he was able to command as a slave to a powerful man, and that the halls she has set up to feed and house former slaves are unregulated and squalid, places where the young prey on the old (4.10). Daenerys is caught between two moral imperatives: the need to let individuals make their own choices, navigating the intractable economic realities set before them, and the need to prevent wealthy elites from taking advantage of former slaves. A better social safety net – better food and housing for the newly freed, real protection for the poor and elderly from the predations of others – would eliminate this particular conundrum, but Daenerys lacks the resources to achieve this ethically preferable outcome.

Once again, trade, resource production and the navigation of economic structures are used to create a sense of realpolitik in the Meereen storyline. The realities of being a ruler are explored in economic terms because these have the merit of being concrete: people need to be fed, housed and paid; no amount of dragon fire can provide those resources; and the consequences of not providing those resources are clear and destructive. Daenerys's difficulties in Meereen are also as much cultural as economic. She is repeatedly described as failing to understand the Meereenese. Much of Martin's worldbuilding in Essos is notably Orientalist: he offers us a familiar vision of the 'mysterious East' populated by spice traders, nude dancers and bed slaves, which inherently flirts with bigotry. Daenerys's economic struggles in Meereen, however, demonstrate that she is not, and cannot be, a 'white saviour' of the city, capable of untangling its social complexities in a way that the Meereenese are somehow unable to see or achieve themselves. The show's infamous ending shot of Season 3, an aerial view of the pale, blonde Daenerys surrounded by a sea of anonymous brown people reaching up to her in supplication, reverts to the white saviour narrative, and in removing many of the economic details of Daenerys's reign in Meereen – for example, her attempts to resow the fields, her politico-economic discussions with Xaro Xhoan Daxos – it fails to undermine or subvert this problematic image. Paying attention to the pragmatic realities of Daenerys's rule in Meereen does not erase the problems with the portrayal of Essos in the world of *Ice and Fire*, nor the lack of concrete detail in its politics and history, especially in comparison with Westeros. It does, however, offer the suggestion that Essos is not merely a monarchical 'training ground' for Daenerys, much as she might treat it that way, and that the practical concerns of ruling require moral sacrifices that cannot be glossed over with the title 'Breaker of Chains'.

Predatory economies

There are also several ancillary economies operating in Westeros and Essos, and one of the most notable models is what might be termed *predatory economies*, societies whose financial models are built on or mandate raiding and pillaging. These economies are inherently parasitic, seizing resources they had no hand in producing, and some of them are more effective than others.

The most notable predatory economy in Westeros is that of the Ironborn, whose motto is 'We Do Not Sow'. The Iron Islands are famously low on natural resources, and the smallfolk struggle to scrape a living. As Theon Greyjoy thinks to himself upon his return home:

> Death is never far here, and life is mean and meagre. Men spend their nights drinking ale and arguing over whose lot is worse, the fisherfolk who fight the sea or the farmers who try and scratch a crop from the poor thin soil. If truth be told, the miners have it worse than either. . . . Iron, lead, tin, those are our treasures. Small wonder the ironmen of old turned to raiding. (*CK*, 123)

The aristocratic Ironborn, who are not particularly financially distinct from the smallfolk they rule over, pride themselves on not engaging in agrarian production, but achieving all their wealth through 'reaving': that is, pillage. Engaging in monetary trade is considered emasculating, as Theon is reminded when he returns home and is confronted by his father Balon: 'That bauble round your neck', Balon says. 'Did you pay the iron price for it, or the gold? . . . Did you pull it from the neck of a corpse you made, or did you buy it, to match your fine clothes? . . . I'll not have my son dressed as a whore' (2.2). Balon rejects the entire economic model of commodity trade as antithetical to the culture of the Iron Islands, antithetical to the masculinity of the Ironborn, in large part because the Ironborn have little ability to engage with it.

Balon's own economic model – paying only the 'iron price' – is, however, fundamentally unsustainable. As Carolyne Larrington has noted, Martin's Ironborn draw heavily from popular images of the Vikings, who are imagined as bloodthirsty raiders constantly seeking out new villages from which to pillage silver.[23] Medieval Scandinavians, however, never subsisted entirely off raiding. The Icelandic sagas make clear that young men would go off on raiding expeditions to acquire silver, earn glory and serve kings abroad, but those men would then return to Iceland to take up land, farm and raise livestock, father children and engage in local politics.[24] Trade was essential to medieval Scandinavian economies, both in terms of imports and exports and in terms of goods acquired abroad by Scandinavians who returned to Iceland or Norway with their new luxury items.[25] It is very difficult to obtain goods and services entirely by force; the Ironborn cannot possibly go raiding every time they need to eat. Predatory or raiding-based economies are inherently precarious because they depend entirely on economic structures in which the raiders do not participate and which they struggle to influence. If you can only take goods from a corpse, moreover, eventually all the people who make the goods you need will be corpses. Raiding and pillaging exhaust small towns and villages extremely quickly. If the Ironborn survived solely off raiding, they would soon simply run out of food and valuables to take. The population of the Iron Islands must be very small indeed to be sustained only by poor agriculture, dangerous fishing and plundering from others. At the same time, though, if the island's industries are really so impoverished, Yara's promise to Daenerys in Season 6 of 'no more reaving, roving, raiding, or raping' raises a significant question: if not raiding, then what (6.10)? Will the Ironborn starve? The economy of the Iron Islands is unsustainable with or without the income from plunder.

A more successful predatory economy is that of the Dothraki, and in large part their success comes from the fact that they can self-sustain in between raids for long periods on the Great Grass Sea. The Dothraki, like the Ironborn, are generally wary of money and commodity trading as concepts, and similarly consider buying and selling to be emasculating, operating instead within a loose gift economy. Yet the Dothraki have a more sustainable economy than the Ironborn because they are not Greyjoy hardliners. They still trade slaves seized in raids for necessary goods and rationalize this practice as an exchange of gifts rather than barter. The Dothraki also breed their own horses, upon whom they rely for transport, milk, meat and hides, utilizing the superb natural resource of the Great Grass Sea to keep their livestock fed essentially without monetary cost. Perhaps more importantly, a *khalasar* will often choose to demand tribute from a city with threat of violence rather than hold themselves to the need to kill for money and goods (SS, 271; 1.3). Raiding often enough to keep the threat alive, but exacting tribute often enough that cities are not razed to the ground and can continue producing the goods the Dothraki require, is simply better economic policy than an insistence on paying the 'iron price' every time one wishes to acquire a luxury product. However, the Dothraki are far less successful militarily and economically than their real-world counterparts: Martin based the horse lords loosely on the nomadic tribal confederations of the Mongolian steppe, but in the thirteenth and fourteenth centuries those tribes were united into the Mongol Empire, the largest contiguous land empire in history. Part of their success is attributable to their encouragement of trade to make up for the fact that they produced relatively few goods. They created mutually beneficial arrangements with merchant partners (*ortoqs*), developed an effective administrative bureaucracy for managing trade and tax and carefully maintained the safety and usability of the trade routes collectively known as the Silk Road.[26] Martin's exoticizing of the Dothraki diminishes their social, cultural and economic power, much as his use of popular misconceptions about the Vikings limits the reach of the Ironborn.

Where economically driven narratives in King's Landing and Meereen are employed to ground ideologically and emotionally motivated characters in the practical realities of rulership, with Cersei and Daenerys both coming up against non-negotiable political, cultural and financial obstacles, the economies of the Iron Islands and the Great Grass Sea would be profoundly precarious in 'real life'. Dothraki and Ironborn refusals of commodity trading are used instead to highlight the conflict, perpetual in the *Ice and Fire* universe, between the maintenance of social and economic institutions and the destruction of those same institutions in acts of extreme violence. Viserys demands payment for arranging the *khal*'s political marriage to his sister; rather than negotiate, Drogo pours melted gold over his skull. The Ironborn choose Euron Greyjoy as their king because he promises them seizure of the North as plunder; there is no mention of the Ironborn taking over, say, the Northern trade in furs. Daenerys operates in a fashion befitting a *khaleesi* in Astapor; rather than pay for an army she needs but cannot afford, she takes it instead. The Ironborn and Dothraki insistence on seizing rather than negotiating is an explicitly masculinist fantasy of dominance (despite Daenerys being one of the most prominent practitioners of scorched-earth violence in the narrative) that meets with mixed success. Sometimes 'fire and blood' win the day, as in Astapor, Vaes Dothrak or Highgarden. Sometimes money is the highest law, as in King's Landing, Meereen and Braavos. The narrative derives its sense of the medieval real, its grittiness and shock value alternatively from violence and from focusing on economic imperative. 'We who serve the Iron Bank face death full as often as you who serve the Iron Throne,' Tycho Nestoris tells Jon Snow (*AF*, 60). In the *Ice and Fire* universe, the day is always won by blood or gold.

Conclusions: Sociological and psychological narrative

Fans expressed great frustration over the death of Petyr Baelish in Season 7 of *Game of Thrones*. Baelish is treated as the consummate manipulator, the man who prepares for every eventuality, and whose financial abilities have allowed him to climb the ranks of the aristocracy while keeping his gaze firmly fixed on his own advancement rather than loyalty to any patron:

> **BAELISH:** Do you know what the realm is? It's the thousand blades of Aegon's enemies. It's the story we agree to tell each other over and over until we forget that it's a lie.
> **VARYS:** But what do we have left once we abandon the lie? Chaos. A gaping pit waiting to swallow us all.
> **BAELISH:** Chaos isn't a pit. Chaos is a ladder. Many who try to climb it fail, never get to try again. The fall breaks them. And some are given a chance to climb, and they refuse; they cling to the realm, or the gods, or love. Illusions. Only the ladder is real. The climb is all there is. (3.6)

Baelish's death in the show, however, comes not at the hands of one of the institutions he has manipulated, not as a slip off the ladder, but because of an ill-conceived attempt to set the Stark sisters against one another, for reasons the show never fully explains. Baelish's error is emotional and psychological, despite the fact that Baelish is a character whose successes and missteps have all previously operated at the level of the sociological. Martin's Baelish is a 'master juggler' who has increased the Crown's revenues tenfold while also allowing its debt to accumulate, and who is working to create a profoundly powerful alliance between the North and the Vale (rather than selling Sansa to Ramsay Bolton, as he does in the show). This shift is typical of the change in tone that marks the show's later seasons, as Zeynep Tufekci writes:

> At its best, [*Game of Thrones*] was a beast as rare as a friendly dragon in King's Landing: it was sociological and institutional storytelling in a medium dominated by the psychological and the individual. This structural storytelling era of the show lasted through the seasons when it was based on the novels by George R. R. Martin, who seemed to specialize in having characters evolve in response to the broader institutional settings, incentives and norms that surround them. . . . Benioff and Weiss steer the narrative *lane* away from the sociological and shifted to the psychological. That's the main, and often only, way Hollywood and most television writers tell stories.[27]

A Song of Ice and Fire derives its trademark sense of danger and darkness precisely from Martin's interest in the sociological, which allows him to kill off major characters without losing narrative momentum. The economic imperatives of food riots, slave rebellions and interest rates offer storytelling opportunities to remind the audience of institutional pressures and highlight the difficulties attendant upon being a ruler who needs to have a tax policy and whose responsibility it is to feed a significant population during a winter that might last years. The show's interest instead in, say, Daenerys's spontaneous madness or Petyr Baelish's sudden desire to set the Starks at one another's throats feels in comparison like an oversimplification of a story that is as much about the fate of a world as about the individuals who navigate it. When the show abandoned sociological storylines – when it erased the Crown debt to Braavos in a single stroke, for example – it lost much of its potency as a commentary on the difficulties of ethical governance.

The economics of Westeros and Essos give necessary depth to the *Ice and Fire* universe. Trade, debt and resource management bring individuals into contact and conflict with institutions; they set parameters on choices and provide consequences for actions. The drama between characters is sharpened, the stakes heightened, by the acknowledgement that their interpersonal relationships operate in the shadow of sociocultural systems that must be navigated or broken, often with devastating consequences. No matter Cersei's courtly machinations, Daenerys's ideological commitments or Balon Greyjoy's paternal disappointment, debts must be paid, trade routes must be maintained, smallfolk must be fed – and winter is coming.

Part III

Faith and salvation

5

The dog, the cynic and the saint

The case of Sandor Clegane

Thomas Honegger

The dog and the hound – animal symbolism in Westeros

First impressions count, and appearances may be deceptive – or at least they do not tell the entire story.[1] This is certainly true of Sandor Clegane, Joffrey Baratheon's horribly disfigured bodyguard or, to use Martin's medievalizing term, his 'sworn shield'.[2] Book and TV show differ in the way they introduce him. The very first view we get of Clegane in the printed text of *A Game of Thrones* is through the eyes of Eddard Stark, Lord of Winterfell. He gives us very brief sketches of some of the members of King Robert's retinue and informs us that 'there [was] Sandor Clegane with his terrible burned face' (*GT*, 39). Although it is not explicitly stated, Eddard's comment suggests that Clegane is riding bareheaded. In the HBO series, however, he enters Winterfell in full armour and his face is covered by his helm in form of a snarling hound. The dog/hound theme is thus introduced very graphically and is only later continued and developed in the conversational references to Clegane as 'dog' and 'hound'.

Helmets and headgear in form of animal heads or heads of fabulous creatures were known throughout history, and Martin is once more dipping his ladle into the Cauldron of History to serve us a tasty and richly suggestive morsel. We may not be able to identify an exact historical primary world counterpart to Clegane's helmet, yet it has the ring of authenticity and, viewed alongside historical helmets of similar design (see, for example, the picture of the lion's head helmet below), it blends in so perfectly that hardly anyone would spot it as the creation of a twentieth-century mind.[3]

Although the book does not mention the helmet at first, it introduces the dog/hound theme later in the narrative, namely on the day after Bran's fateful fall from the tower. Our point-of-view (POV) character this time is Tyrion, and the first reference to Clegane as 'the Hound' occurs when Tyrion sees the tall warrior in the courtyard getting ready for the morning training session: 'Tyrion glanced down and saw the Hound standing with young Joffrey' (*GT*, 87). In the ensuing conversation Joffrey jokingly alludes to Clegane's epithet in his proposal to '[s]end a dog to kill a dog!' (*GT*, 87). The full transformation of the man into man-hound takes place shortly afterwards

Figure 1 Sandor Clegane enters Winterfell. © Anke Eissmann, by permission of the artist

Figure 2 Sallet in the shape of a lion's head (Italy, *c*.1475–80). © The Metropolitan Museum of Art, New York (Creative Commons CC0 1.0)

when Clegane closes his visor and his 'soot-dark armor seemed to blot out the sun. He had lowered the visor on his helm. It was fashioned in the likeness of a snarling black hound, fearsome to behold' (*GT*, 88). Fearsome, but not to Tyrion, who follows Joffrey's habit of addressing Clegane with 'dog': 'If he [Joffrey] forgets, be a good dog and remind him' (*GT*, 88), thus making explicit Clegane's subordinate position by means of power semantics. Some of Martin's readers may not know the exact difference between

Figure 3 Sandor Clegane's helmet. © Anke Eissmann, by permission of the artist

'hound' and 'dog' but it will soon become clear that the two terms are not used as full synonyms. 'Hound' occurs mostly when people think or talk about Sandor Clegane, whereas 'dog' is, as a rule, used when he is addressed directly by one of his superiors, most often Joffrey. The following passage nicely illustrates the complementary uses of these two terms: 'He [Joffrey] looked at Sandor Clegane. "And you, dog, away with you, you're scaring my betrothed." The Hound, ever faithful, bowed and slid away quietly through the press' (GT, 146).[4]

The key expression in this passage is, of course, 'ever faithful'. Faithfulness is the most dominant characteristic ascribed to dogs in the Middle Ages and beyond, a primary association that is responsible for the presence of numerous dogs on medieval tomb effigies.[5]

Yet people in the Middle Ages would also have been aware of the less savoury characteristics of dogs. On the spiritual level, the Old Testament especially provided the basis for an *interpretatio in malam partem* (negative interpretation).[6] The modern world has inherited this ambiguity so that the dog is, on the one hand, the despised and ignoble animal of insults and curses ('You stupid dog!') and, on the other, man's valued and trusted companion.

The dog's ferociousness constitutes the third and last aspect determining the medieval view of this animal. The use of dogs in warfare goes back (at least) to antiquity, best known in the context of the Roman army employing big mastiffs.[7] The dog's capacity to attack enemies and to defend its master has been valued highly throughout the millennia and forms part of the medieval characterization of dogs. Bestiaries, such as the *Rochester Bestiary* (*c.*1230), often have illustrations depicting dogs that attack their master's enemies (see below), thus making them the ideal bodyguards.

Martin then combines all these three elements in the figure of the Hound. He is presented as unwaveringly loyal to his master Prince Joffrey and seems to obey his commands without question.[8] Furthermore, he is feared as a ferocious fighter. Lastly, he himself stresses his non-nobility by distancing himself from his brother and the

Figure 4 The loyal greyhound at his (dead) master's feet. The late-fourteenth-century Beauchamp Tomb in Worcester Cathedral. © Hugh Llewelyn (Creative Commons Attribution 2.0 Generic)

Figure 5 King Garamantes, being rescued by his dogs; from the *Rochester Bestiary*, England (Rochester?), *c*.1230, Royal MS 12 F. xiii, f. 30v. © British Library, London (Creative Commons CC0 1.0)

other anointed knights. This last point will be discussed in greater detail in the next section of this chapter. First, however, I focus on Martin's use of the 'faithful dog' topos in his books in general, and in relation to Sandor Clegane in particular.

The world of Westeros is a feudally organized, largely pre-industrial world that shows numerous parallels to late antiquity and the European Middle Ages, where dogs were present both as pets and fighting dogs, along with utilization for herding cattle and hunting.[9] The first three categories are not prominently represented in Martin's epic, whereas the hunting dogs gain some importance in their role as Ramsay (Snow) Bolton's companions.[10] Roose Bolton's bastard son not only (mis)uses them to chase and hunt down his victims but also to savage and kill his stepmother Walda and her newborn baby (6.2). Dogs are, like ordinary soldiers, tools in the hands of their masters, loyally obeying their orders, and are presented as morally neutral in themselves. However, there are limits even to a dog's loyalty, as Ramsay Bolton finds out to his chagrin. His penultimate words, 'They're loyal beasts,' says Ramsay to Sansa in 'The Battle of the Bastards' (6.9), a statement contradicted by the fact that his starved dogs hesitate only briefly before eating him alive. This gives the lie to the idea that dogs will risk their own survival for their master's life and is part of the larger theme of the 'rising of the oppressed against their unjust masters' or, more appropriately, the subtheme of 'servants/subjects turning against their masters' which runs through Martin's epic.[11]

A similar development is seen in Sandor Clegane, who begins the slow but irreversible process of discovering, listening to and following his own conscience. His first step is to desert his sadistic master Joffrey since, as Sandor puts it, '[e]ven a dog gets tired of being kicked' (*SS*, 658), demonstrating that he increasingly resents the immorality of his master's behaviour. The confrontation with fire before the walls of King's Landing during the Battle of the Blackwater serves to bring into the open that hidden resentment and triggers a development that is foreshadowed in Clegane's contemptuous attitude towards knights and knighthood. Sandor Clegane, the Hound 'ever faithful', becomes 'unfaithful' to Joffrey, like the hound Huan in Tolkien's tale 'Of Beren and Lúthien', and, as I will argue in the last section of this chapter, deserts him to find a new and better master.[12] He thus stands in contrast to his brother Ser Gregor Clegane, 'Lord Tywin's mad dog' (*GT*, 467), who shows neither remorse nor repentance and develops into Ser Robert Strong, a Frankenstein's monster-type bodyguard for Cersei Lannister.[13]

Sandor Clegane's characterization through animal symbolism seems to originate in his physical and mental characteristics. The reference to and explanation of the Clegane family sigil, three dogs on yellow ground, strikes me as a suitable afterthought inspired by the rapidly expanding heraldic universe connected with the families and houses of Westeros.[14] The first time we come across the Clegane family sigil is towards the end of *A Game of Thrones* when Tyrion 'saw the standard . . ., three black dogs on a yellow field. Ser Gregor sat beneath it' (*GT*, 685).

So Martin creates a matching banner for the Hound and 'Tywin's mad dog' that fits the heraldic universe of Westeros, taking up and varying the animal symbolism already introduced in the first chapter in form of the direwolf (*GT*, 17–21) that graces the banners of House Stark (*GT*, 20), and the stag of the House Baratheon, ominously alluded to by the length of shattered antler (*GT*, 18) buried in the direwolf's

Figure 6 Sigil (or coat of arms) of the Clegane family. © Lord Evermore (Creative Commons Attribution 2.0 Generic)

throat.[15] The meaning of a stag killing a direwolf as a portent for the conflicts to come is immediately grasped by the adult protagonists, yet neither by the POV character Bran (cf. *GT*, 18) nor, consequently, by (first-time) readers. They are likely to make the connection only after the introduction of the crowned stag as the sign of the House Baratheon at King Robert's arrival at Winterfell: 'Over their heads a dozen golden banners whipped back and forth in the northern wind, emblazoned with the crowned stag of Baratheon' (*GT*, 39).

The HBO show differs in two points. First, Eddard and his men come across the carcass of the stag before finding the direwolf. Second, attentive viewers may have already spotted the (dire)wolf (House Stark), the lion (House Lannister), the dragon (House Targaryen) and the crowned stag (House Baratheon) making an appearance in the opening credits of each episode. This is obviously a symbolic depiction of the major conflict between the Houses of Lannister, Stark and Baratheon on the one side and the Targaryens on the other – which had led to the fall of the Targaryen dynasty and the seizing of the Iron Throne by Robert Baratheon. The showrunners thus creatively apply Martin's animal symbolism in the new TV medium.

Martin not only furnishes the Clegane family with a fitting animal for their banner in the second volume of *A Song of Ice and Fire*; he also provides an aetiological tale explaining the origin of the three hounds on the yellow field. As the Hound accompanies Sansa back to Maegor's Holdfast, she asks him:

'Why do you let people call you a dog? You won't let anyone call you a knight.'
'I like dogs better than knights. My father's father was kennelmaster at the Rock. One autumn year, Lord Tytos came between a lioness and her prey. The

Figure 7 Direwolf, lion and crowned stag attacking the dragon. Animal symbolism in the opening credit sequence of the HBO *Game of Thrones* series. © Anke Eissmann, by permission of the artist

> lioness didn't give a shit that she was Lannister's own sigil. Bitch tore into my lord's horse and would have done for my lord too, but my grandfather came up with the hounds. Three of his dogs died running her off. My grandfather lost a leg, so Lannister paid him for it with lands and a towerhouse, and took his son to squire. The three dogs on our banner are the three that died, in the yellow of autumn grass. A hound will die for you, but never lie to you. And he'll look you straight in the face.' (*CK*, 288)

The tale takes up and elaborates the topos of the dog/hound's faithfulness and willingness to risk its life in order to defend its master. Sandor seems to identify (at least partially) with the animal on his family's banner, implicitly comparing its lack of guile with his own bluff honesty and contrasting these two qualities with the implied treacherousness of the lioness that turns against her 'own kin', so to speak.[16] Sandor is not a cleric trained in allegorizing tales and events, yet he can instinctively read the underlying symbolism of the animals involved in the incident.[17] Indeed, the 'treacherousness of lions' is a motif that Martin introduced at the beginning of the narrative when Jon tells the reader about Jaime: 'They called him the Lion of Lannister to his face and whispered "Kingslayer" behind his back' (*GT*, 51). The motif of the 'treacherous lion' finds its ironic climax in the 'little lion' Tyrion Lannister killing his father, Tywin Lannister (*SS*, 1073). No wonder that the behaviour of the most noble animal, the lion, turns Sandor Clegane into a cynic – in every sense of the word.

The cynic – the hound on chivalry

The *Merriam-Webster Dictionary* defines *cynic* as 'a faultfinding captious critic, especially one who believes that human conduct is motivated wholly by self-interest', and the etymology of the word provides the connection to the 'dog' theme.[18] As the *Online Etymology Dictionary* points out, *cynic* (n.) derives

> from Greek *kynikos* 'a follower of Antisthenes, literally 'dog-like', from *kyon* (genitive *kynos*) 'dog'. . . . Supposedly from the sneering sarcasm of the philosophers, but more likely from *Kynosarge* 'Gray Dog', name of the gymnasium outside ancient Athens (for the use of those who were not pure Athenians) where the founder, Antisthenes (a pupil of Socrates), taught. Diogenes was the most famous. Popular association even in ancient times was 'dog-like' (Lucian has *kyniskos* 'a little cynic', literally 'puppy'). Meaning 'sneering sarcastic person' is from 1590s.[19]

And indeed, Sandor Clegane's canine fidelity to his master is counterbalanced by his cynical disdain for the chivalric establishment at large – with good reason, as the reader begins to realize.[20] One of the first instances when his contempt for the knightly class becomes obvious occurs at the Tournament of the Hand. The readers have not only seen close up the brutal (and possibly intentional) killing of the young and inexperienced Ser Hugh of the Vale by Ser Gregor (*GT*, 295) but have also witnessed Ser Loras Tyrell's trick with the mare in heat to score against the Hound's older brother in the lists, and Ser Gregor's subsequent uncontrolled outbreak of murderous violence (*GT*, 314–16).[21] The young knight is saved only by the timely intervention of Sandor Clegane, who is shortly afterwards proclaimed winner of the tournament by Ser Loras with the words: 'I owe you my life. The day is yours, ser', to which Sandor replies: 'I am no *ser*' (*GT*, 316).

At this point in the narrative, readers have all the more reason to sympathize with Sandor Clegane since they have become privy to the true story behind Sandor's horrible disfigurement: Gregor, older and much stronger than his brother, had pressed Sandor's face into the burning coals of a brazier to punish him for playing with one of Gregor's toys, a wooden knight, without having asked permission. His father's reaction and his brother's military career must have caused Sandor's lasting disenchantment with the chivalric ideal and his antagonism to his violent brother becomes the defining element of his personality so that he proudly proclaims: 'I am no knight. I spit on them and their vows. My brother is a knight' (*GT*, 301).[22]

Vows and oaths play an important role in the feudal, largely authoritarian and pre-legalistic society of Westeros. Thus, the ceremony of knighting involves swearing an oath 'to be a good knight and true, to obey the seven gods, defend the weak and innocent, serve my lord faithfully, and defend the realm with all my might' (Ser Duncan to the master of the lists (*KSK*, 28)). The reality may look very different, as Clegane points out to Sansa, who argues that

> 'True knights protect the weak.' He [Clegane] snorted. 'There are no true knights, no more than there are gods. If you can't protect yourself, die and get out of the way of those who can. Sharp steel and strong arms rule this world, don't ever believe any different.' Sansa backed away from him. 'You're awful.' 'I'm honest. It's the world that's awful.' (*CK*, 757)

Yet behind Sandor's bluff warrior persona, his realist and disillusioned view of the world hides a disenchanted and traumatized idealist. Widespread chivalric hypocrisy and the betrayal of knightly ideals irritate him so much that he defines himself primarily through honesty and, consequently, the only vows he seems to have sworn, and kept, up to his second traumatic experience at the Battle of the Blackwater, are those to protect and obey Joffrey. He thus tries to avoid the problem of (potentially conflicting) chivalric duties by casting himself in the role of the pre-chivalric warrior.[23] Clegane refuses to play at being 'the lion on the battlefield and lamb in the hall', and as a dog/hound he intends never to fall prey to chivalric hypocrisy. His position as Joffrey's sworn shield, or 'dog', relieves him of listening to and obeying the voice of his conscience and thus make it possible to avoid moral conflict.

The Hound is only one protagonist in Martin's extended discourse on knighthood and chivalric ethics.[24] *A Song of Ice and Fire* presents a system in decline that is rotten to the core.[25] The one true and honourable knight left, Ser Barristan Selmy, is soon dismissed from the Kingsguard (*GT*, 624) and goes into exile, and the two publicly admired representatives of chivalry, Ser Loras Tyrell and Ser Jaime Lannister, turn out to be not quite what one expects true knights to be. It is from the margins and the marginalized figures that we can expect moral renewal and the reformation of the chivalric ideal. Figures such as Brienne of Tarth, whose beneficial influence on Jaime is vital for his further development, the exiled Ser Jorah Mormont, the 'Onion Knight' Ser Davos Seaworth and to some extent also Sandor Clegane stand at the centre of the negotiation of ethically responsible behaviour.[26] In the next and final part of this chapter I focus on the slow, and, at the time of writing, still unfinished conversion of Sandor Clegane.[27]

The saint – Sanctus Sandorus Cynocephalus

To a significant extent, the career of Sandor Clegane basically follows the trajectory of the 'villain turned (near) saint' type, known as 'The man promised to the devil becomes a priest' (Aarne-Thompson-Uther type 811, henceforth ATU 811). Prominent examples of this type among medieval texts are the romances *Sir Gowther*, *Robert le Diable*, *Tydorel* and also *The Legend of Gregorius* or *The Life of St Alexius*. They all feature (very) bad and sinful men who undergo a process of conversion and not only atone for their earlier sins but in some cases even become saints. *Sir Gowther*, for example, features a protagonist who is fathered on his innocent and noble mother by an incubus and who develops into a 'warlocke greytt' (l. 22).[28] Gowther already shows his demonic nature as an unnaturally fast-growing baby who causes the death of several wet nurses so that he has to be fed solid food. Once grown up, he terrorizes the countryside, raping, pillaging and killing, especially members of the clergy. Accused of being a devil's son, Gowther asks his mother about his true parentage and, upon learning the truth, decides to repent and seek penance and absolution for his sins directly from the Pope in Rome. The Pope hears his confession and orders him to spend a time of penance being mute and eating only food that has been touched by the mouth of a dog. Gowther leaves Rome and ends up as the mute fool Hob at the court of the Holy Roman Emperor, where he fed with the dogs, since this is the only way that the mute man will accept nourishment. Yet when the sultan, who demands the emperor's (also) mute but beautiful daughter in marriage, attacks the emperor, Gowther miraculously receives armour and weapons and on three successive days defeats the pagan army. The final redemption comes when the emperor's daughter, who has fallen from a tower, is brought back to life by God and proclaims the end of Gowther's penance. Gowther is shriven by the Pope, marries the emperor's daughter and leads a saintly life. The significant element here is, of course, the 'canine phase' where Gowther becomes dehumanized and turns into a 'dog' before he is able to complete the atonement for his former sins.[29]

I have chosen *Sir Gowther* as an illustrative example of ATU 811 since it contains an interesting dog element. However, among the tales belonging to ATU 811 an even better and arguably closer analogue to Sandor Clegane's development exists: the legend of Saint Christopher. Martin, as a (lapsed) Catholic, is very likely to be familiar with the basic tale, which can be found in Jacobus de Voragine's *Legenda Aurea* (translated into English and printed by Caxton in 1483 as the *Golden Legend*). The story in brief runs as follows: Reprobus, a mighty warrior of 'a right great stature, and . . . a terrible and fearful cheer and countenance' (48) wants to serve the mightiest and most powerful ruler in the world.[30] He enlists in the service of a powerful king, yet when finding out that his lord is afraid of the Devil, he leaves him and enters into the service of Satan. However, when he learns that his new master fears 'a man called Christ which was

Figure 8 A dog-headed *cynocephalus*, one of the Plinian races, from the *Schedelsche Weltchronik* (also known as the *Nuremberg Chronicle*) from 1493. © Nanae (Creative Commons Attribution 2.0 Generic)

The Dog, the Cynic and the Saint

Figure 9 Fourteenth-century manuscript illustration to Marco Polo's *Il Milione* showing the dog-headed inhabitants of the Andaman Islands. © Bibliothèque nationale de France, Paris (Creative Commons CC0 1.0)

Figure 10 Saint Christopher Kynokephalos (Doghead). Seventeenth century, Kermira, Cappadocia. Byzantine and Christian Museum, Athens. © Byzantine and Christian Museum, Athens (Creative Commons CC0 1.0)

Figure 11 Saint Christopher carrying Christ (woodcut, Buxheim, Germany, print by unknown artist, c.1423). © The John Rylands University Library, University of Manchester, England (Creative Commons CC0 1.0)

hanged on the cross' (49), Reprobus decides to search for this mighty lord and offer his services to him. This proves difficult and, in the end, he follows the advice of a hermit to serve Christ by serving his fellow men – which Reprobus does by carrying them across a river. One night a little child asks for this service and Reprobus discovers that he has carried Christ – and takes on the name Christophorus ('Carrier of Christ'). He turns to converting pagans in the area and is consequently arrested and martyred. However, since he immediately works a posthumous miracle, the heathen king and his kingdom convert to Christianity.

This is all well and good, but where is the 'canine link' to the Hound? It is to be found, in my opinion, in the ancient tradition of depicting Reprobus/Saint Christopher as a member of the *cynocephali*. The *cynocephali* constitute one of the Plinian or monstrous races believed to live either somewhere far away in the East or on the edges of the Known World.

In his *Il Milione* (last quarter of the thirteenth century), for example, Marco Polo mentions dog-headed barbarians on the Andaman Islands. The iconographic tradition originating from the illustrated manuscripts of Pliny's *Naturalis Historia* and the depictions of dog-headed men by later authors adapting his works are likely to have inspired the depiction of Saint Christopher as a *cynocephalus*.

Figure 12 Saint Christopher with a dog's head carrying Christ (Romania, Biserica 'Naşterea Domnului' din Sărata, no date given). © Ivan Polikarov (Creative Commons Attribution 2.0 Generic)

Conclusion

So could Sandor Clegane, the Hound, be heading for sanctification, to become the 'Carrier of the Saviour' in the Known World? As things stand, the Hound does not turn into a dog-headed saint – at least not in the HBO show which concluded in summer 2019 with Season 8. Sandor Clegane finds himself unmistakably on the side of the 'good guys', and there are moments where he comes close to 'sanctification', which is, in the end, never realized.[31]

The development of Sandor Clegane is a good example of how Martin manages to exploit the potential in characters by connecting them not only to general narrative 'motifs' (such as ATU 811) but also to more specific literary or cultural motifs and analogues.[32] Furthermore, this storyline illustrates Martin's predilection for at least a partial subversion of patterns and the frustration of expectations. Thus the Hound does not progress towards a purely spiritual and transcendent salvation but finds himself drawn back into the all-too real and violent world of politics, powerplay and warfare. The TV showrunners (likely taking their cue from Martin) revive the motif of sibling rivalry as the dominant theme so that Sandor finds his end in the fall that also kills his monstrous brother.[33] This is not exactly a martyrdom in the manner of Saint Christopher, but it fits the overall theme of the cleansing destruction that paves the way for a new era with Bran the Broken as king of Westeros, Samwell Tarly as Grand Maester, Podrick Payne as member of the Kingsguard and Brienne of Tarth as Commander of the Kingsguard.

6

The figure of George R. R. Martin's Septon Meribald and the Franciscan legacy

Maria Błaszkiewicz

This chapter proposes to place the character of Septon Meribald from Martin's *A Song of Ice and Fire* in the wider context of the Franciscan tradition, concentrating on the figure of St Francis of Assisi. The validity of the comparison lies in the exceptional position of the septon in Martin's secondary world. Martin's presentation lays stress on both his spirituality and appearance and a variety of character traits which seem to point to the figure of this particular saint and to the ethos of his order. As *A Song of Ice and Fire* has been in existence for some time alongside the TV show, a further implication of the subject is the problem of the evolution of the septon as a motif in HBO's *Game of Thrones*.

The sources available for the study of the figure of St Francis of Assisi consist of his own literary legacy plus very rich medieval material and an unusually diverse and profound modern response. In both cases scholarly and serious works exist alongside more popular and emotional approaches. The same can be said about the writings of Francis, some of which, especially his *Canticle of the Creatures*, have been popularized in the Anglophone world as Henry Draper's hymn *All Creatures of Our God and King*: not so much a translation as a paraphrase, often found wanting.

The pivotal early medieval source is the *Life of St Francis* of 1229, commissioned by Pope Gregory IX at the time of the saint's canonization to promote his cult. This was written by Thomas of Celano, a scholarly hagiographical corpus which 'reflects his knowledge of the Latin classics and the tradition of ecclesiastical hagiography'.[1] What is most important for both the present study and, more importantly, for the Franciscan legacy is that Thomas sees Francis as a new type of saint, who, while 'living like a monk in his prayer and asceticism', was nevertheless free from the confinement of the cloister and who 'took the Gospel out into the world. He achieved what the traditional forms of religious life could not, that is, effective witness and preaching of the Gospel in the midst of the people.'[2] A number of texts composed soon afterwards, such as the *Life of St. Francis* by Julian of Speyer (1232–4), show clear dependence on Celano's *Life*. Less than ten years later, however, Thomas was commissioned to revise his work, as he had not included in his earlier version significant facts about the last period of Francis's life. It is important to note that as not much time had passed since the saint's death (3 October 1226), those early Lives were based on actual accounts of people who knew him and who witnessed a number of important events connected with him and his cult. This new version of Thomas of Celano's *Life* is not the only important work of the period. The *Legend of the Three Companions* and the *Florilegium* offer a collection of short, often miraculous accounts which accompany and supplement the major work. The situation is further complicated when, after the composition of the *Major Legend of St. Francis* by the Franciscans' minister-general, Bonaventure, in 1263, the general chapter's decree ordered all previous hagiographical texts about Francis to be destroyed. Nevertheless, such texts would continue to appear over the next century and a half.

Here we come to a significant source for modern knowledge of St Francis, the so-called *Little Flowers of St. Francis of Assisi*. The official biographies were quickly augmented by the emergence of more popular texts, some of which were later translated into the vernacular. One in particular, the vernacular version of the Latin text of *The Deeds of Blessed Francis and His Brothers* by Ugolino Boniscambi of Montegiorgio, universally known as the *Fioretti* or the *Little Flowers of St Francis of Assisi*, has ruled supreme in its imagination and devotion over the ages. Interestingly, the *Fioretti* were translated into English as late as the nineteenth century. On the one hand, this coincided with the partial reintroduction of Catholic thought into the intellectual atmosphere of England through such figures as John Henry Newman and, on the other, it resulted in the special treatment of Francis in America, where the Protestant reading of the figure was stressed. A fascinating study by Patricia Appelbaum, significantly called *St. Francis of America*, shows a variety of such approaches, from attempts to highlight a Protestant dimension in the saint's life and teaching, through his affinities to the theology of liberation to a secularized version of Francis as a champion of nature.[3] In an influential study from 1923, G. K. Chesterton attacked the tendency to secularize Francis. In a colourful analogy, he exclaims, 'to tell the story of a saint without God ... is like being told to write the life of Nansen and forbidden to mention the North Pole.'[4] Appelbaum refers to the paradox of a Protestant reading of the figure of the saint.[5] It is also significant that the modern image of Francis should highlight his ecological stance without exploring its roots. The unity of creation, famously praised in Francis's *Canticle of All Creatures*, is the unity of the Creature and the Creator. While Draper's Victorian paraphrase of the song consists of several apostrophes to 'All creatures of our God and King' to praise the Lord, the original *Canticle* both addressed God and praised him through the same catalogue of creatures; yet after a startling reference to Sister Death came a stern exhortation against mortal sin. The early hagiographies stress the fact that the *Canticle* is the fruit of the whole life of Francis, while the last stanzas were composed on his deathbed. The change of perspective in Draper's paraphrase replaces the intensity of the original with a bland if joyful tone.

Similarly, modern, popular reception of Francis finds his sermon to the birds, depicted in Giotto's frescoes, most attractive without endeavouring to learn – for example, from the *Fioretti* – what he was actually preaching. The most famous story from the *Fioretti*, as noted earlier, is undoubtedly the Wolf of Gubbio. Numerous images present the scene where the Wolf makes a pact with the saint, endearingly raising its paw, or where a smiling Francis is simply embracing a smiling canine. The story, however, is just one of more than a hundred episodes which present the saint's attitude towards the animals in the context of his deep, often shockingly radical spirituality. Giotto's frescoes show Francis among the birds but also pierced by the penetrating light of the cross in the scene of the reception of the stigmata.[6] The Francis of the *Fioretti*, however simplified, is the same Francis whom we read about in scholarly biographies and theological studies. The modern Francis is not.

My attempt to place *A Song of Ice and Fire* within the Franciscan context thus raises two important questions: one is about the nature of Martin's medievalism, the other, more specific and stemming from the first, is the nature of the Franciscan legacy Martin uses.

In her monograph discussing Martin's medievalism, Shiloh Carroll comments upon the comparison often made between Martin and Tolkien and the claim that, contrary to the idealistic and escapist Tolkien, Martin comes closer to a realistic depiction of the Middle Ages.[7] Truly remarkable as Martin's effort is in many respects, the whole comparison is questionable because it judges Tolkien for something he never intended to do. Tolkien's medievalism and artistic achievement have nothing to do with the realistic depiction of the epoch, if understood as a faithful depiction of historical and material details. If we are to trace medieval connections in his work, certainly a very fruitful exercise, we should look at medieval art, especially literature, medieval philosophy or medieval thought more generally. Tolkien's medievalism draws a connection between his literary works and the cultural and theological context of the Middle Ages, a field he was deeply knowledgeable about. The case of Martin is more complicated. First of all, he himself acknowledges a different approach and points to his historical interests as being the most important. The history, including the material history, of the period can definitely be discussed as a source of Martin's inspiration.

Interestingly, a parallel study of the influence of medieval literature and the medievalist cast of mind in both authors has unveiled an extremely rich layer of medieval allusions and intimations on most of the levels of *A Song of Ice and Fire*, from narrative strategies and structures to generic conventions. Martin's attitude to the historical sources resembles romance epic Italian poets of the late fifteenth and sixteenth centuries who, given Michael Murrin's insistence on that genre's 'trend to historical verisimilitude', seem more important for the genre of fantasy than is usually assumed.[8] Murrin stresses that 'Boiardo differs from other writers of romance in the late fifteenth century for he invented a purely fictional world'.[9] The author 'told a story without precedent in the old chronicles', since in writing about Charlemagne he

> imitated history, its formal devices rather than its content. He discusses his romance as if it were history, exploiting the ambiguities of the term *storia* or *istoria*, which can mean simply 'a narrative' or 'a history'. . . . Formal imitation lent a certain verisimilitude to this, the most fantastic of the late fifteenth-century romances.[10]

However, this does not mean that Martin managed, or even tried, perhaps, to recreate the medieval world fully in his cycle. Certain fundamental aspects are tangibly absent, some have conveniently been added and others ignored. There is, potentially, nothing wrong in this, if one bears in mind that, however indebted it is to certain aspects of the primary world, Martin's work is not a set of historical novels (see Carolyne Larrington's chapter in this volume) but belongs to a genre whose major constituent is the creation of a secondary world.[11] On the other hand, as Tolkien once so aptly demonstrated, the whole point of the successful construction of secondary worlds, and consequently good fantasy works, is the establishment of an inner consistency which makes the secondary creation impervious to readerly doubt.[12] One may therefore wonder whether omitting an essential ingredient from the primary source of inspiration does not jeopardize this consistency.

The most tangible absence in Martin's secondary world is the striking lack of spirituality in the Seven Kingdoms. To all appearances, while clearly interested in and ready to use the historical background for his world, Martin clearly did not bother overmuch with the religious dimension. The resulting contrast with the meticulous and consistent presentation of a number of feudal intricacies jars unpleasantly. Martin's problem in *A Song of Ice and Fire* is not so much the fact that he does not create a credible ecclesiastical structure in his fictional world but rather that he chooses to refer to such a structure in a most sketchy and perfunctory manner, as if exposing the thinness of the canvas and cardboard backdrop imitating the real thing. Contrary to the comprehensive and credible construction of the Citadel, which takes over the educational role of the medieval church (see Mikayla Hunter's chapter in this volume), the Faith of the Seven seems unconvincing and ephemeral, especially in contrast to the series' other cults which, though often merely sketched, possess inner consistency and strength sufficient to persuade and captivate the reader. The best example seems to be the cult of the Drowned God and, to an extent, also the cult of R'hllor. There is also no credible suggestion that the religious climate of the past, before Targaryen times, was significantly different, which would explain the present as a decadent stage; this could potentially have amended the situation by creating a picture of a cult that has run its course.[13]

Against this uninspiring background one figure stands out with unexpected force. Not only is he strikingly well if briefly presented but also, even more importantly, he seems uniquely rooted in the spiritual context of the primary world, even though this context is neither comprehensive nor uniform in its evocation. While Martin clearly does not try to incorporate the monastic and ecclesiastical tradition of the Middle Ages into his secondary world, what he definitely makes use of and projects upon his created world is the popular, American reception of St Francis; thus he may occasionally startle the reader by a sudden and incisive reference to the original medieval legacy.

The character of Septon Meribald appears solely in *A Feast of Crows* in an episode that is equally exceptional and isolated within *A Song of Ice and Fire*. During her hopeless quest for Sansa, Brienne and her companions join a septon for a period on his yearly circuit of the poorer part of the Riverlands, since he might apparently be useful as a guide. After several days spent in a slow journey and general conversation, the septon assists them to the Quiet Isle where their roads separate. *A Song of Ice and Fire*, as it stands now, does not seem to have any further use for him.

Brienne's quest has led her back to Maidenpool, after a circular and fruitless pursuit of the fool who is rumoured to be hiding in a remote and isolated bay, whom she has wrongly identified as the supposed companion of Sansa, Ser Dontos. Contrary to a typical quest structure, however, this return does not create closure; she has accomplished nothing, is neither welcome nor wanted in Maidenpool and the next stage of her journey is equally hazy and aimless. Her companions are even more ill-assorted than before: Ser Hyle Hunt is driven by motives opposite to her own, and may be of use but may also prove a serious obstacle, whereas the person temporarily assuming the role of guide, Septon Meribald, does not seem to be in a position to offer any valuable counsel.

There is nothing of the typical sage in Meribald. Not only is he low-born, poor and illiterate, but he also belongs to one of the lowest and humblest strata in the Westerosi clergy, a 'septon without a sept'. Even though no other such character is presented in the story, Meribald is introduced in a way which consciously downplays him, stressing that he is just one of a large and insignificant class: 'Meribald was a septon without a sept, only one step up from a begging brother in the hierarchy of the Faith. There were hundreds like him, a ragged band whose humble task it was to trudge from one flyspeck of a village to the next, conducting holy services, performing marriages, and forgiving sins' (*FC*, 293). This social gap between the septon and his high-born companions is widened by his early confession that he is doing lifelong penance for his youthful abuse of the cloth and (at least attempted) seduction of young women; this, slightly humorously, makes Brienne uneasy. If their short journey together in any way enlightens or transforms Brienne or Podrick, it has happened in an exceptionally subtle way.

Contrary to the aimless and spasmodically directionless movement of Brienne, Septon Meribald's journey not only has a very firm direction and purpose but also, as he has been following the same regular route for more than forty years ('from Maidenpool to Maidenpool, my circuit takes me half a year and ofttimes more' (*FC*, 276)), its regularity and steadiness acquire a ritualistic aspect of imposing order through its measurable circularity. His regular visits to the lonely villages and humble settlements of the Riverlands, places where poor and illiterate people regulate their lives by the cycles of nature, serve as the most rudimentary liturgical calendar. The introduction of the septon and his purposeful route provides a counter-motif in *A Feast of Crows*, where randomness of movement and of purpose becomes a universal predicament.

This particular part of the narrative is set in a surprisingly sparse landscape. Unlike Westeros's other lush, ravaged or hostile settings, the Riverlands are almost sketchy, basic horizontal lines of shallow dunes, marches and vast barrenness. On the other hand, they have a certain quality of peacefulness. The stark nakedness of the land is the result of neither war nor the perennial struggle between man and nature, and thus it creates a paradoxically peaceful, almost restful atmosphere of quiet humility. These flatlands are regularly traversed by a barefoot, poor man, his donkey and his dog on their unambitious yet essential circuit. The result is strangely soothing and reassuring:

> Near midday they stopped at a tiny village, the first they had encountered, where eight of the stilt-houses loomed above a small stream. The men were out fishing in their coracles, but the women and young boys clambered down dangling rope ladders and gathered around Septon Meribald to pray. After the service he

absolved their sins and left them with some turnips, a sack of beans, and two of his precious oranges. (*FC*, 296)

Meribald took them off to hear their sins, 'What will you do with them?' 'Feed them. Ask them to confess their sins, so that I might forgive them. Invite them to come with us to the Quiet Isle.' (*FC*, 295-6)

A striking feature of this quotation is the insistence on Meribald's power of absolution, a concept and a rite never mentioned anywhere else in *A Song of Ice and Fire*. Confession, an extremely important practice of Catholicism and a significant element in medieval culture, does not form any part of the routine or mentality of Westeros. While marriages have a definite religious character in both the official faiths of the Seven Kingdoms, no further sacramental life in a cult clearly modelled, at least to a certain extent, on Christianity is ever mentioned or suggested, apart from this episode; here it returns almost obsessively several times, solely in the context of Meribald's vocation.[14]

One possible explanation, if one assumes Martin's conscious use of the motif, is an intertextual reading of Meribald in dialogue with Chaucer's Friar in 'The Friar's Tale'. If we accept the critical suggestion that Martin's ideas about the corruption of the clergy derive not just from historical but also literary sources, then – on the one hand – there is a further yawning gap in the construction of his secondary world, yet – on the other – the figure of Meribald acquires additional meaning.[15] For Chaucer and his contemporaries those aspects of decadence were projected against a vast background of ecclesiastical tradition and the ingrained religious dimensions of every layer of life; no equivalent can be found anywhere in the modern Western world. Even if some medieval people did not consciously participate in this spiritual dimension, yet they were nevertheless steeped in it. Satirizing a corrupt monk drew on the fact that behind this individual stood a vast edifice of monastic tradition which indicated the decadence of his behaviour as described. Although the mendicant orders could not rival the richness or length of the monastic tradition, Chaucer's Friar is also set against both the ideals of the orders' founders and the contemporary stereotypical criticism based on the difference between common fraternal practice and those ideals.[16] Martin's fantasy cycle does not have this kind of background and his world is markedly devoid of any monastic life. A begging brother is not the member of a mendicant order, or any order, but is simply a very poor and insignificant member of the Faith, who lives by begging; why he is called a brother is never explained. Admittedly, the Quiet Isle community may resemble a friary and its members are also called brothers, but this seems rather to be a conscious way of evoking certain connotations from the primary world necessary to create the scene's desired effect than a gesture towards any significant ecclesiastic institution. Similarly, being only a step away from a begging brother, like Chaucer's Friar, Meribald is presented hearing the confessions of sins, but, unlike Chaucer's Friar, he neither exploits this opportunity nor tries to find rich or important penitents. Rather he seeks those who have no one else to help them. Yet the septon confesses that, in the past, just like the Friar, he had been prone to seducing women capitalizing on the attraction of his habit. Meribald the contrite, poor and devout confessor becomes thus an anti-Friar, or rather shows his remote literary brother a way of redemption.

The contrast between a septon without a sept and a septon with an affiliation, as it were, may not strike the reader, due to the series' general lack of emphasis on ecclesiastic ways of living. Nevertheless, Meribald's total lack of a permanent abode and his dedicated ministration to the poor in themselves may well point to the Franciscan ethos and the specific character of Francis, noticed as early as Celano's *Life*.

The action, repeated several times in the episode, of giving out food seems evocative of something deeper than just charity: 'three women emerged from the reeds to give Meribald a woven basket full of clams. He gave each of them an orange in return, though clams were as common as mud in this world, and oranges were rare and costly' (*FC*, 295). However heavy the donkey's load may be, it cannot possibly sustain the needs of the septon on a circuit of six months, nor can it change the situation of the people he visits. The kind of food he gives out, even the simple vegetables, may be rare in the area, but the luxury of his oranges seems excessive to the point of incongruity. Nevertheless, this very luxury invests the gesture with a meaning that transcends mere sustenance. There is no equivalent of the Eucharist in the Faith of the Seven, nor even a vague approximation of the story of the Redemption, nor for that matter, Incarnation. Apart from vague references to confession, the concept of sacramental life is totally absent from the Faith. That marriage has a religious dimension and even more vague references to the naming ceremony do not fill this gap. Nevertheless, there is something sufficiently powerful and mysterious in the act of Meribald's giving out precious food to justify the suspicion that there is a sacramental dimension to his gesture.

Even though neither Brienne nor her companions seem particularly impressed by this, the septon displays a characteristic almost entirely lacking in the Seven Kingdoms – a spirituality which has nothing to do with fanaticism. Asked whether his life of constant solitary walking in the Riverlands does not feel lonely, the septon simply replies: 'The Seven are always with me' (*FC*, 276). There is neither pathos nor exultation in this statement of fact, so entirely unique in the whole of Martin's work. For Meribald, the constant presence of God(s) does not require explanation, nor, for that matter, particular emphasis: the scene makes it quite clear that he regards this with the same level of certainty as the presence of his two animal companions, whom he talks about in the same sentence: 'and I have my faithful servant, and Dog' (*FC*, 276).[17] However laconic it is, or perhaps precisely because it is so laconic and matter of fact, this is practically a declaration of being in a state of permanent mystical experience. In this context, a later conversation in which Meribald explains more specifically his particular devotion to the Smith, in his aspect of a Cobbler, transcends this rather commonplace story: it becomes a subtle theological interpretation. Even more striking is the encounter with the three women; this cannot fail to impress Meribald's companions even if they tried to shrug it off as a joke:

> One of the women was very old, one was heavy with child, and one was a girl as fresh and pretty as a flower in spring. When Meribald took them off to hear their sins, Ser Hyle chuckled, and said, 'It would seem the gods walk with us . . . at

least the Maiden, the Mother, and the Crone.' Podrick looked so astonished that Brienne had to tell him no, they were only three marsh women. (*FC*, 295)

The women may be simply what they seem, but then the reactions of Meribald's companions show they could not fail to grasp the possible implications of the scene. Is Meribald simply ministering to three women? Or are they Three of the Seven who come to him both as they are, and yet as humble small folk, in order to commune with him? Is the gift of the orange returned a thousandfold? Can this scene be read in the context of one of the pivotal episodes in the life of St Francis: the meeting with the leper, who turns out to be Christ? This event is mentioned both in Francis's own writings and in his hagiographies; it lays stress on his inner struggle to acknowledge brotherhood with a man perceived by his contemporaries as an outcast not only from society but almost from the human race. Francis's act of kissing the leper, an unthinkable deed, is followed not only by the wretched man's miraculous vanishing, uniformly interpreted as a revelation of Christ in him, but it also initiates a new, permanent stage in the life of the saint, symbolized by his efforts to rebuild the ruined church of San Damiano and his lifelong call for penance. In the novel, the three women come to a septon who had already embarked on the road of penance years before and who does not need to be reminded that he walks in the presence of God(s). If this is a divine revelation, it is not Meribald who needs it, but rather his companions, whom he does not endeavour to convert through his words, but who are offered the possibility of religious experience through his mere presence. Meribald, like Francis before him, as Celano put it, 'made a tongue of his whole body in the service' of the Seven.[18]

Currently, St Francis's most recognizable feature is his love of animals and the natural world. Christians may also be aware of the fact that he has become the patron saint of ecology. A range of more or less religious ceremonies that try to incorporate the animal world into the liturgy are commonly associated with his name.[19] Septon Meribald's Franciscan associations may, probably, first be noticed in the scene when he speaks about his dog while also mentioning the Seven in a casually intimate way:

> 'Does your dog have a name?' asked Podrick Payne. 'He must,' said Meribald, 'but he is not my dog. Not him.' The dog barked and wagged his tail. He was a huge, shaggy creature, ten stone of dog at least, but friendly. 'Who does he belong to?' asked Podrick. 'Why, to himself, and to the Seven. As to his name, he has not told me what it is. I call him Dog.' 'Oh.' Podrick did not know what to make of a dog named Dog, plainly. The boy chewed on that a while, then said, 'I used to have a dog when I was little. I called him Hero.' 'Was he?' 'Was he what?' 'A hero.' 'No. He was a good dog, though. He died.' (*FC*, 295)

The most universally loved episode from the *Fioretti*, as noted earlier, is the story of the Wolf of Gubbio. The tale's popularity in modern secular culture makes it absolutely certain that the appearance of a canine in the Meribald episode should evoke this charming Franciscan legend. 'Dog' is praised for his ability to fight most wolves and thus is a great help in the septon's journeys; however, he is no match for Nymeria gone wild. This introduces into the episode, with its Franciscan flavour, the question of domestication and wildness, raising a more general issue about the attitudes towards wildlife and the animals in general in Westeros. Interestingly, the Seven Kingdoms' uniformly utilitarian and hierarchical attitude towards animals is set against this only instance when a human recognizes a creature's autonomy.[20]

There is a significant difference between the way Meribald treats Dog and the way he treats other animals. He is far from sentimental or even, if judged by modern sensibilities, understanding and compassionate, about his donkey. There is no difference between his lack of empathy for the overburdened creature he calls 'his faithful servant' and the later quite utilitarian approach to the usefulness of the Hound's warhorse on the Quiet Isle. Both are simply beasts of burden. Ser Hyle's sudden burst of sympathy for the stallion facing gelding evokes a stern rebuke and uncompromising differentiation. As well as a half-seriously expressed male solidarity, Ser Hyle's compassion also reflects his class-oriented feudal attitude. Interestingly, Meribald's calm acceptance of the feudal view of his class and the burdens borne by the small folk seems absolute, even though he does not appear affected by the fact that his temporary companions are his social superiors.

There is, however, one significant exception to this serene view of the social order. Neither Dog nor the wolves can be read in the context of the Wolf of Gubbio, yet a startlingly apt parallel can be observed in another key aspect of the episode: the theme of the Broken Men. The actual point of the *Fioretti* story is that Francis is able to tame the wolf. In exchange for a constant supply of food, the wolf will protect the inhabitants of Gubbio from dangers posed by the wild. This transformation of a wild beast into a tame ally is implied in the Meribald episode and later apparently realized in the suggested resolution of the Hound's narrative arc on the Quiet Isle. Meribald declares his willingness to seek the so-called Broken Men, who have reportedly appeared in the area, not in order to help to hunt them down but to help them in a very thorough if simple way: '"What will you do with them?" "Feed them. Ask them to confess their sins, so that I might forgive them. Invite them to come with us to the Quiet Isle."' (*FC*, 296). The introduction of the theme of the Broken Men in the episode leads to a long passage where Meribald describes very passionately the process of breaking the peasant men brutally brought into contact with war. To some extent, these dispossessed and stranded ex-foot soldiers are reduced in his story to a pack of strays. Their regression is presented as a gradual breaking down of the feudal structure, depicted here as the guarantee of relative security and a sense of belonging. The consequent alienation of the peasant foot soldier leads to his despair and his dehumanizing rejection of the society he turns against in order to survive. While he is never sentimental about real wolves (and is unaware of Nymeria's identity as a kind of stray), Meribald, it transpires, has been a Broken Man himself; thus he expresses his unusual wish to reclaim and tame the human strays. We do not know if it remains only a wish, or becomes part of his regular duties, but the last time Meribald appears in the story is the moment when he visits the Quiet Isle, a place on his route that is a haven for all the dregs of war, literal and otherwise. It is also a place where, it appears, his intentions are implemented, as implied by the figures of the Elder Brother and the Brother Gravedigger.

The Quiet Isle closure of the Meribald episode is also significant; while it introduces very positive, therapeutic ecclesiastical imagery into a world so far totally bereft of this aspect of life, it also provides an elegant and surprisingly discreetly devised closure to the Hound plotline, one that is obscure for Brienne but crystal clear for the reader. The rumours about the Hound give Brienne some kind of purpose and direction after the futile lead she was following, just before meeting Meribald. In this way, two important plot lines cross and the stories of Brienne and the Hound intertwine. The irony, perceptible only to the reader at this point, is that in her pursuit of the Hound Brienne is no longer following Sandor Clegane nor, for that matter, a Stark girl. Thus, Brienne and Sandor Clegane, who never meet in *A Song of Ice and Fire*, although their plot lines and character formation run surprisingly and ironically parallel, find rest and consolation in the same place. It is impossible to say at the present stage of *A Song of Ice and Fire* whether Sandor Clegane has come to his final sanctuary and whether he has indeed irrevocably shed his identity; Brienne is given no such chance as her quest forces her to continue. Nevertheless, the journey with Meribald and her respite on the Quiet Isle give her an opportunity for inner cleansing and inner self-recognition, a unique luxury for Martin's characters.

The HBO show *Game of Thrones* transforms this suggestive network of interrelationships almost beyond recognition. However, a parallel ecclesiastical figure does emerge who may be seen as a counterpart to the Meribald and the Elder Brother pairing. We encounter Brother Ray (played by the charismatic Ian McShane) in a single episode, but this character is no less memorable than Meribald. Ray is probably closer to the figure of the Elder Brother, as he is the leader of a community. Nevertheless, his relatively vague but, at the same time, extremely marked, spirituality places him in the same order as Meribald. The meeting has nothing to do with Brienne and appears in 'The Broken Man' (6.7); at this point in the adaptation, while the plot retains fragmentary strands of *A Song of Ice and Fire*, as a whole it has already crossed the point of no return after which it can only use the remaining material from the novels to create a new entity. Season 6 is still relatively consistent and perhaps because of this opportunity to recycle and reorganize the existing material, it marks a transition between the increasingly weaker, shallower improvisation of the last two seasons and the earlier more anchored story. Brienne's quest has been so changed that there is no place in it for a spiritual respite. Moreover, she becomes an important factor in the Hound's plot line, as the previous season ends with their climactic if rather unmotivated duel. Instead of the Hound's journey with Arya ironically ending before they have the chance to reach any destination, he is wounded by Brienne and left to die while the Maid of Tarth, rebuffed by Arya, apparently returns to Riverrun.

The Hound thus reappears in the next season in 'The Broken Man' as member of a rather curious community. The opening scene shows surprisingly idyllic surroundings, where a smiling, tranquil group of people are clearly enjoying a quiet and prosperous communal existence. Everybody looks content and well fed, if simply dressed. There is a special emphasis on the abundance of food prepared by the women while the men are engaged in erecting a wooden structure, seemingly a tower or a rudimentary sept. The scene strongly resembles the iconic image from Peter Weir's 1985 film *Witness* where the whole Amish community gathers to raise a barn. The reference is clearly intended and suggests the similar nature of the group. This idyllic, almost prelapsarian tone underlined by slightly incongruously sentimental music is stressed by the close-up on one of the men hammering a wooden peg into the structure. Later, when Brother Ray assures the bandits that they do not have any iron, this assertion underlines their unearthly peacefulness rather than poverty. By the standards of war-ravaged Westeros they may be simple but are definitely not poor. Nothing is said about their history, and frankly, their very existence seems implausible. In contrast to the very pessimistic view of man as almost always ready to use all his potential for violence and deceit in the universal struggle, a view characteristic of both the world of the novels and the adaptation, the people in this valley seem totally to lack the survival instinct. They are docile, meek and consequently undercharacterized. Apart from the Three Women, Meribald's parishioners, who are mentioned, but do not appear in the story, are nevertheless tangibly present, not idealized, and yet not dehumanized. Organically connected to their harsh and humble environment they seem eternally there and eternally in need of the ministration of a septon. They create an effect of basic stability, just like Meribald's circular and repetitive journeying. Brother Ray's congregation is ephemeral and improbable, a world impossible to maintain, a passing dream waiting to be destroyed by implacably brutal reality. The appearance of the hostile members of the Brotherhood, their confrontation with Brother Ray and the episode's violent conclusion resembles countless such scenes from almost every western movie; this further contributes to the feeling of unreality.

We do not have access to the whole story of Meribald's life, nor can we assess his progress towards sainthood at the moment when we see him. Is the encounter with the Three Women the culmination of some process, the beginning of a new stage or just a manifestation of a constant state of communion with the divine? The story of his traumatic youth, told largely in an impersonal and generalized way, has no conclusion. Meribald does not tell his companions what happened after he became a Broken Man, even though it is evident that something momentous must have transformed him into a septon. His confession about his early transgressions and his need of penance suggests that there was more than one pivotal moment in his past, but we can only surmise what they might have been. A parallel effect is achieved in the case of Brother Ray in the scene when he evidently begins his sermon with the exemplum from his biography. However, he only manages to describe his youthful depravity and taste for killing with gusto before the appearance of the group of horsemen and a conversation filled with veiled threats further reveals his present inner strength, integrity and benevolence. In both cases a pivotal, hagiographically significant scene, or scenes, of conversion is missing. In the case of Meribald this makes him more mysterious and striking. His role is not clear and there is still a possibility that Martin has planned or will plan some further role for him in the unfolding story. As for Brother Ray, the episode concludes with his death. Sandor Clegane finds him hanged from the unfinished tower surrounded by the bodies of his congregation. Yet his undepicted death transforms him into a martyr figure; his short conversation with Sandor Clegane bears unexpected fruit later, perhaps because of the dramatic ending of the idyll.

Whatever happened in the life of Septon Ray, the equivalent of the Broken Men from *A Song of Ice and Fire* here is the Hound, who finds healing in Ray's boldly agnostic doctrine. The ironless structure erected with wooden tools, 'guiltless of fire' is a symbol of the special status of the community to which the Hound is admitted. He is the only one who wields metal tools. His strength and ability to use the axe is unduly stressed. It is also ridiculous that he seems to be the only one able to provide firewood, hacking at a heap of stupidly wet branches in a place so remote that he cannot hear any hypothetical cries for help. From a realistic point of view the scene does not really work. From a symbolic perspective, however, it is replete with meaning. The prelapsarian colouring makes the act of cutting green branches seem sinister; the community, whose existence is so improbable, is improbably wiped out. The Hound takes the axe and goes to seek revenge. Has he learned anything from the episode?

The grave-digging scene is completely dissociated from this episode; it recurs in the next season (7.1), when the Hound comes back to the cottage he once robbed to find the inhabitants dead. His decision to bury them does have a penitential dimension, but only in a limited and personal sense. As Brother Gravedigger on the Quiet Isle (in the books) the Hound embarks on a path of penance that has an impersonal and protracted nature. He will not simply try to atone for one of his own sins, rather, as digger of graves for all who have died in the senseless wars and are washed down by the river, he tries to atone for the evils of his kind. In fact, just like Meribald, he would have fitted very well into a story from the *Fioretti*, while the show's Brother Ray and his Sandor Clegane belong in a western.

To conclude, however divergent Martin's secondary world is from its primary source in respect of its presentation of the spiritual dimension, Martin successfully incorporates into it a characteristic and easily recognizable reference to a popular medieval image of the saint, thus creating a desirable medieval ambience. Clearly the departure from this paradigm in *Game of Thrones*, in the direction of a more familiar American pattern, suggests that the medieval in the HBO series is merely a prop. Maybe there is a St Francis of Westeros, but there is no St Francis of HBO.

Part IV

Chivalry

Theory and practice

7

The warrior(s) in crisis

The knights of Westeros and the process of civilization

Anja Müller

On the very first pages of the 'Prologue' to George R. R. Martin's *A Game of Thrones*, the reader is introduced to the first knight of many to come in the *Song of Ice and Fire* series:

> Ser Waymar Royce was the youngest son of an ancient house with too many heirs. He was a handsome youth of eighteen, grey-eyed and graceful and slender as a knife. Mounted on his huge black destrier, the knight towered above Will and Gared [two fellow members of the Night's Watch] on their smaller garrons. He wore black leather boots, black woollen pants, black moleskin gloves, and a fine supple coat of gleaming black ringmail over layers of black wool and boiled leather. Ser Waymar had been a Sworn Brother of the Night's Watch for less than half a year, but no one could say he had not prepared for his vocation. At least insofar as his wardrobe was concerned. His cloak was his crowning glory, sable, thick, and black and soft as sin. (*GT*, 2–3)[1]

Given this attention to his apparel, which is derogatorily commented on by both the narrator and Royce's brothers of the Night's Watch,[2] Martin's Ser Waymar obviously represents a variety of knighthood that is implicitly criticized and admonished in the following precept from Geoffroi de Charny's *A Knight's Own Book of Chivalry* (c.1350):

> And if you want to be armed elegantly and stylishly and desire that your arms be remembered, recognized, and adorned above others, seek constantly and diligently opportunities to perform deeds of arms. [. . .] You should make your armor more elegant with such work; and whosoever achieves most is the most transformed and adorned.[3]

Like so many other knights to be encountered in *A Song of Ice and Fire*, Ser Waymar seems to care more for his outward appearance than for the fulfilment of core chivalric ideals such as prowess, honour, piety, loyalty and largesse – and he duly pays for this ill-advised priority with his life.

In this chapter, I am going to scrutinize the problematic image of knighthood in Martin's *A Song of Ice and Fire* series. Reading Martin's novels alongside Norbert Elias's remarks on the 'process of civilization', I shall suggest that the notion of crisis that obviously informs chivalry and knighthood in Westeros responds to a structural development within the society of this fictitious world, which can be seen as analogous to the changes described by Elias as a transition from medieval warrior societies to court culture. The argument of my chapter largely concerns this structural analogy between Martin's novels and Elias's conjectures. Avoiding intentional fallacies, it is immaterial for the argument whether Martin has read Elias or any of the other sources cited in this chapter. The chapter neither explores how far Martin's fictitious, neomedievalist world reflects historical concepts or phenomena, nor does it assume that the sources it cites on the concept of knighthood (such as Geoffroi de Charny and Ramon Llull) mirror actual historical realities.[4] Together with Richard W. Kaeuper, I understand these texts as part of a discourse about 'an accepted or desired set of ideas and practices' that contained a 'core cluster of common values and practices' with shifting accentuations.[5] Reading Martin alongside Elias suggests a heuristic tool to explore the position and function of knighthood for the worldbuilding of *A Song and Ice and Fire* and to understand and appreciate certain character developments.

I shall begin by briefly tracing evidence of transitional processes in the historical and societal structure of Westeros before focussing on various concrete manifestations of the apparent crisis in Westerosi knighthood. Particular attention will finally be given to the two characters who may serve as epitomes of this crisis, while simultaneously suggesting that there are options for renegotiating or even re-establishing knighthood: Brienne of Tarth and Ser Jaime Lannister.

My argument will be based on a close reading of Martin's novels rather than on the HBO TV show, because I maintain that chivalry and knighthood have a deeper significance for both worldbuilding and characterization in the novels than in the TV show (especially from Season 4 onwards). The character of Jaime Lannister in particular has been adapted in such a way, in Benioff and Weiss's version, that the profound engagement with chivalry that informs Jaime's character arc from *A Storm of Swords* on has been largely sacrificed in favour of an almost exclusive focus on the Lannister family struggles. Of course, Jaime's further development in the novels is yet unknown. Nevertheless, I perceive in Jaime's renegotiation with chivalry (which makes him reject and abandon sexual intimacy with his sister immediately after returning to King's Landing having one final incestuous encounter in the Great Sept of Baelor) a stark contrast to Benioff and Weiss's grossly inconsistent version. Therefore, I shall concentrate on the novels in what follows, and will only refer to the HBO series, where necessary and conducive to the argument, in occasional remarks or footnotes.

With regard to the transition from the Middle Ages to the Early Modern period, medievalist scholars have frequently and in various ways commented on sociological transformations. A common denominator in this respect is the perception of a transition from a warrior to a court society, entailing transformations from heroic warrior codes to courtly codes of chivalry. Maurice Keen describes this development in rather general terms; to him, 'Chivalry essentially was the secular code of honour of a martially oriented aristocracy', with an origin in the social code of honour of the warrior groups of the early middle ages. [. . .] The rise of the secular courts [then . . .] provided the context for it to grow up from a warrior's code into a sophisticated secular ethic, with its own mythology, its own erudition, and its own rituals which gave tangible expression to its ideology of honour. As such, it [. . .] also left [. . .] a very deep imprint on the times that followed.[6]

Aldo Scaglione perceives chivalric/heroic knighthood, courtly knighthood and chivalric *courtois* knighthood in coexistence rather than succession.[7] A literary equivalent to such historical observations can be found in Beverly Kennedy's distinction between three types of knighthood in Malory's Arthurian romance. According to her classification, the heroic knight 'is most at home on the field of battle and although nominally a Christian, he is also a fatalist like the warriors of the first feudal epics'.[8] The 'worshipful knight' (corresponding to Scaglione's courtly knighthood) 'is most at home in the court of the King and, although culturally a Christian, he is also a rational pragmatist like the courtiers and princes of the early Renaissance'.[9] The 'true knight', finally, 'is most at home in the mysterious forests of "adventure" performing the sacral mode of doing justice by means of trial by battle. He is a radical Christian, a mystic and a providentialist who believes that knighthood is a "high order" established by God to do "true justice" in the world.'[10] From such considerations emerges a typology distinguishing between heroic knights, courtly knights and true knights.[11]

These typologies correspond to the larger sociogenetic perspective put forward by Norbert Elias, where he argues for a transformation from a territorial warrior culture to a centralized civilized society characterized by a functional differentiation into individual units that each held separate responsibilities (e.g. politics, the military and education). According to Elias, this transformation of societal structures was accompanied by a transformation of behavioural codes, affecting the codes of chivalry too.[12] Alfred Schopf, therefore, perceives (courtly) knighthood as a measure taken, as it were, to civilize feudal nobility.[13] For Kaeuper, this conclusion ignores the 'complex and sometimes self-contradictory' self-understanding of knighthood.[14] His own assessment of different phases of chivalry perceives shifts in the chivalrous codes rather as an internal process, while emphasizing the continuity of a core set of chivalric values. When trying to read *A Song of Ice and Fire* alongside Elias, the exact historical nature of the transformation claimed by Elias is immaterial, for the transformation merely serves as a heuristic tool. Employing this tool, the first step we need to establish is whether these sociogenetic transformations are also discernible in Westeros.[15]

According to Martin's *The World of Ice and Fire*, one can trace a development in the history of Westeros from an early age of settlement (Dawn Age), followed by a long phase of territorial government in the Age of Heroes: 'Petty kings and powerful lords proliferated, but in time some few proved to be stronger than the rest, forging the seeds of the kingdoms that are the ancestors of the Seven Kingdoms we know today.'[16] This stage not only corresponds quite neatly to that of the warrior culture described by Elias and other scholars. It also displays the tendency to a gradual decrease in the number of players, as power focused on 'some early domains – generally centered on a high seat, such as Casterly Rock or Winterfell – that in time incorporated more and more land

and power into their grasp'.[17] With the Targaryen conquest, a process of centralization as described by Elias set in, including a tendency towards territorial concentration. Aegon I took residence in Dragonstone and then entered the ongoing territorial strife between the warring Seven Kingdoms. The warfare ended advantageously for him, due to the internal quarrels of the other competitors and, of course, his own weapons of mass destruction (also known as dragons). The moves towards centralization under Aegon I include the establishment of King's Landing as capital and new centre of trade, the forging of the Iron Throne as the symbol of a united violent power monopoly, the promotion of the arts (under Aegon's sister Rhaenys) and the foundation of the chivalric order of the Kingsguard.

Nevertheless, the societal and governmental structures under Aegon I still mark a transitional stage, for, despite these steps towards centralization, Aegon's constant progresses through his realm, with a train of knights, septons and maesters, are comparable to the practices of medieval travelling warrior kings. Moreover, legislation in Westeros was still regionally diversified. Central rule was only consolidated under the fourth Targaryen king, Jaehaerys I, who managed to unify the country under one law, and – more importantly – under one faith (that of the Seven), after his predecessors Aenys I and Maegor I had almost precipitated a religious civil war, the former due to his weakness, the latter due to his tyrannical rule. Jaehaerys I reconciled crown and faith, unified the code of law, improved hygienic conditions in King's Landing, achieved infrastructural cohesion through road building and thus prepared the realm for economic prosperity and internal security.[18] His successor Viserys I was able to enjoy the most prosperous era under Targaryen rule, but the seeds of later conflicts among his successors were sown during his reign, culminating in the so-called Dance of Dragons.[19] That event almost saw a relapse into territorial struggle, and the following Targaryen rulers all had to deal with the problem of a single monarch, as outlined by Elias: he is weaker than the society he rules, and his position rests on a congruity of his interests with his subjects' (especially the nobility's) and on ambivalent alliances.[20] Once the last dragons had disappeared, it becomes clear that, in Westeros, too, central monarchic power no longer derives only from economic or military strength but predominantly from the skilful handling of power structures in society and from different discourses of legitimation. This applies to the Targaryen rulers up to Aerys II, as well as to their successors from Robert Baratheon to Joffrey and Tommen. Thus, the prehistory of *A Song of Ice and Fire* contains the basic characteristics of a development that implies the different concepts and positions that will eventually unfold in the conflict about the Iron Throne. Where then – to come back to my topic – do knighthood and chivalry stand in this world and its social and power structures?

The conflict that develops about who is the legitimate heir to the Iron Throne also affects knighthood in Westeros, which seems to be in deep crisis. This does not mean that Martin's representation of knights and knighthood is essentially a harsh, bloodthirsty, 'real' counterpart to idealized representations of chivalry in medieval literature. As Charles Hackney has argued, the novels confront ideal and 'practice' in Westeros in a similar way to European medieval literature.[21] Corinna Dörrich, in turn, discerns a broad range of highly differentiated manifestations and concepts of knighthood in Martin's novels.[22] Already in the Middle Ages, such authors as Chrétien de Troyes or Thomas Malory had assessed the ambivalence of chivalry in view of the violent potential inherent in knighthood and the resulting discrepancy between ideal and reality.[23] In medieval texts, however, deviations from the ideal normally serve to affirm the value system which is implied by the ideal and, thus, have a normative character.[24]

In fact, the chivalrous ideal of medieval romance is also a mere ideal or myth in the world of Westeros. True knights populate the world of songs and are either relegated to the Age of Heroes or to the tales about individual knights who had made a name for themselves under Targaryen rule, such as Duncan the Tall. In Bran's or Sansa's early point-of-view (POV) chapters, different versions of heroic knighthood can be distinguished. Bran's chapters focus on prowess, Sansa's on courtly knighthood with an emphasis on service to the lady. Both idealizations are promoted by and reside in fictions – the 'songs', which, like medieval romance, consolidate these ideals in the cultural memory of Westeros. However, the narrative soon makes clear that these idealizations differ vastly from the harsh reality. It is also significant that, among living knights, the few specimens who are presented as following the ideal of the loyal knight all belong to an older generation: Ser Rodrik Cassell and, especially, Ser Barristan Selmy, who seems like a living anachronism, the sole survivor of the Kingsguard, which once used to be a body of heroic and legendary knights.

The Kingsguard was established under Aegon I, modelled on the ancient celibate order of the Night's Watch. At the wish of Queen Visenya, the chief requirement of a Kingsguard knight was not prowess but rather unfaltering and exclusive loyalty to the king.[25] Thus, the Kingsguard represents a type of knighthood that is already removed from the heroic warrior ideal (where prowess was prominent), to a courtly ideal, emphasizing the vassal's pledge to his lord. The oath of celibacy inevitably excludes courtly love from that ideal, too, and indeed, it seems as if that particular element was largely absent from the chivalric codes operating in Westeros. It only surfaces in tournaments, in the form of a public display of venerating women; this appears to be rather aimed at the audience than reflecting an actual chivalrous devotion to the lady as such.[26] With the rule of Mad Aerys II, however, this knightly ideal of loyalty becomes questionable the more one learns about the atrocities committed by order of the king – with the silent acquiescence of his Kingsguard; these knights thus broke the pledge to protect the weak and innocent for the sake of their loyalty to their lord.[27] The problem of unwavering loyalty is again raised under Joffrey's erratic rule, when he commands Kingsguard knights to mistreat Sansa. Under King Tommen, the Kettleblack brothers, who were personally appointed by Queen Regent Cersei, may be loyal to her but are morally utterly corrupt, to the point that they have sexual relations with her.

In *A Storm of Swords*, as well as in *A Feast for Crows*, the crisis of the Kingsguard is inextricably connected with the crisis of legitimation of the monarch. If loyalty to the lord is deemed the most important virtue of knighthood, this priority presupposes that lord's legal and moral legitimation. A challenge to his legitimation inevitably entails a challenge to the ethics of absolute loyalty. So far, the readers and characters of the world of *A Song of Ice and Fire* have been confronted throughout with rulers whose respective legitimacy is at least questionable and whose rule can hardly be considered just, let alone ideal.[28] One can therefore contend that the larger crisis of sovereign legitimacy contributes considerably to the crisis of knighthood in Martin's novels, as the former notion of crisis obviously destabilizes the gravitational centre of the sovereign lord, around which the chivalrous virtues revolve. Following the code of chivalrous virtues becomes a matter of individual ethical choice. Knighthood in Westeros is thus represented as a concept in transition. What is more, there is no original, ideal knighthood in Martin's world, not even on the fictional level. The most plausible 'original ideal' of Westerosi chivalry, the Kingsguard, is explicitly characterized in the *World of Ice and Fire* as a construct motivated by power politics; and this functional definition of knighthood is correlated with a functional differentiation within society in Westeros. The narrative structure of Martin's novels is shaped by the concomitant crises of legitimation and dilemmas of loyalty, for, from a narratological POV, the crisis of knighthood drives the plot onwards and produces new reconfigurations of character constellations.

Besides the consistent challenge to the legitimacy of the liege lord in Martin's novels, we can simultaneously discern a further significant development in Westerosi chivalry: its opening up beyond the ranks of nobility and promoting a meritocratic concept of knighthood. This is not without medieval precedents. Ramon Llull, for example, on the one hand insisted on the noble birth of knights and on the other hand paved the way for a performance-oriented definition of knighthood, emphasizing equally the inner attitude and disposition a knight should possess.[29] Ser Davos Seaworth is probably the most prominent example in *A Song of Ice and Fire* of a man who may be reckoned to embody upward social mobility. With his plebeian origins and largely devoid of prowess, the former smuggler, dubbed the so-called 'Onion Knight', can nevertheless be regarded as a model courteous knight because of his unerring loyalty to his respective lords.[30] Uniting the observance of chivalric duties with the emphasis on his humble origins, Ser Davos represents what might be called a habitual form of knighthood – that is, knighthood as a habitus: one which identifies a knight foremost by a consistent performance of certain practices that have come to be regarded as a 'second nature' to a knight.[31] Since any habitus is produced by the historical conditions from which it has emerged, it is essentially conservative. Most importantly, the notion of habitus draws attention to the social practices someone exhibits as the major criteria by which to identify the social group to which that person belongs. In our case, knighthood as habitus is determined by the maintenance of traditional chivalric virtues and the exclusive pledge to one single lord, one with unquestionable legitimacy; since Ser Davos clearly fits into this pattern, he is recognizable as a knight.

The group that also represents both potential for social mobility and a certain conservativism is called the hedge knights. Although hedge knights do not possess landed property, they still define themselves not only by their title but also by their (non-)possession of land, as the epithet 'hedge knight' self-ironically declares the hedge as the knight's home. Binding themselves to a lord as vassals with mutual obligations, the contracts of hedge knights include a complex conglomeration of obligations and oaths, beyond mere financial considerations. While the hedge knights in *A Song of Ice and Fire* are largely treated as minor side characters and/or notorious fortune hunters (such as Hyle Hunt), whose adherence to codes is largely a matter of form, Martin's prequel series *The Hedge Knight* about Ser Duncan the Tall actually presents a proletarian knight, who rises from Flea Bottom to the Kingsguard as an (almost anachronistic) epitome of true knighthood.[32] Whereas the high-born knights around Ser Duncan only intermittently honour their vows to protect and serve those in need, Ser Duncan acts as a relic of heroic and even courtly knighthood – a figure that calls for a meritocratic, democratic reconsideration of the hedge knight's status and habitus.[33] Whereas the foundation of Ser Davos's loyalty is the supposedly indisputable legitimacy of his lord, hedge knights' loyalties are functional and pragmatic: they offer their fidelity and service in exchange for accommodation, sustenance and material support. If Ser Duncan leaves one of his lords whose claim he has found to be illegitimate, this indicates – in comparison to the more conservative social climber Ser Davos – a higher degree of functional definition in the bond between a liege lord and a vassal knight, while also indicating a higher degree of agency on the side of the vassal.

As a habitus, knighthood in Westeros has become disconnected from hereditary social status and is on the point of being reduced to a matter of abilities and codes. It thus returns to those medieval origins, according to which knighthood could not be inherited.[34] As such, the medieval codes of knighthood offer an effective means of social elevation in a stratified society – provided the structures of that society permit mobility of social rank in the first place. In the Westeros of *A Song of Ice and Fire* this is clearly not (yet) the case. Instead, the various knights reflect the condition of crisis in the Seven Kingdoms. In relation to the various typologies of medieval knighthood mentioned above, Martin's readers encounter numerous bad examples of knighthood. Some of them earn this evaluation because they deviate from the ideal of prowess – such as Ser Waymar Royce, who pays more attention to his wardrobe. This display of rich apparel, so frowned upon by Geoffroi de Charny, in fact seems to be a consistent feature of Westerosi knights, as revealed by the splendour at the Hand's tourney. Martin's narrative of this event revels in detailed descriptions of fancy (if not always functional) armour and dress. In fact, the chapters on the Hand's tourney reveal that among chivalry's four most prominent virtues – which, according to Keen are: prowess, loyalty, largesse and courtliness – the pre-eminent feature of a Westerosi knight is his prowess, that is, his courageous fighting skills. Even in splendid armour, Ser Loras Tyrell can thus win the favour of the crowds. Sheer prowess alone, however, can also be problematic, as is reflected in the case of Ser Gregor Clegane, The Mountain that Rides, whose brutal strength and propensity to extreme violence severely undermine his status as a knight.

The emphasis on prowess would align Westerosi knighthood with what Beverly Kennedy termed the 'heroic knight' ideal, as foregrounded, for example, in the writings of Geoffroi de Charny. In view of Elias's theories on the process of civilization, this type largely corresponds with a warrior society. However, as noted, by the period in which *A Song of Ice and Fire* is set, the world of Westeros has already undergone a structural transformation towards centralization and social diversification. During this progress towards civilization, chivalrous codes in Westeros have become more intricate. At least at the tourney and in the 'songs' one can find, for instance, traces of the idea of courtly love, although the concept as such does not seem to be a prominent part of the performative practice of knighthood in Westeros. I would argue rather that *A Song of Ice and Fire* reserves the practice of courtly love to characterize relationships between very particular individuals; for instance, this is the case with Prince Rhaegar and Robert Baratheon, fighting over Lyanna Stark; Ser Jorah trying and failing to please his former lady and Daenerys Targaryen; Ser Loras's love for Renly Baratheon; Brienne's infatuation with Renly and, later, Ser Jaime; and, last but not least, the incestuous love, which nevertheless falls within the pattern of courtly love, of Ser Jaime Lannister and Queen (Regent) Cersei. Therefore, I suggest that courtly love and service are rather part of a narrative strategy for characterization than a true feature of Westerosi culture. Nor does largesse seem to play any significant role as a chivalrous virtue.

Loyalty is a different matter, frequently evoked as a major knightly virtue and decisive for their honour. Loyalty to the sovereign lord and the oaths determining that loyalty are, according to Kennedy's typology, the defining virtues of the 'worshipful', or 'courtly' concept of knighthood. This courtly knighthood is a feature of the stage of emerging civilization, binding the knight to his sovereign by oaths – and thus also demanding from him a certain regulated behaviour. In Westeros, this type of knighthood is epitomized in the Kingsguard, whose White Book, by recording the deeds of its members, offers the possibility to practice the self-control mechanisms characteristic of this 'more civilized' stage of chivalry. The vows of the Kingsguard betray awareness of a diversified social structure, demanding that the knight take cognizance of the various duties imposed on him in an intricate social net of complex relationships and obligations. Unlike the Night's Watch vow, the Kingsguard oath is not rendered verbatim in Martin's novels, but Ser Jaime's reply to Catelyn Stark's reproaches that he is an oathbreaker implicitly expresses much of the extent of these obligations: 'Defend the king. Obey the king. Keep his secrets. Do his bidding. Your life for his. But obey your father. Love your sister. Protect the innocent. Defend the weak. Respect the gods. Obey the laws' (*CK*, 796).[35]

Ser Jaime's important comment on the conflicting nature of vows very neatly summarizes the dilemma created by the virtue of loyalty. Within the context of medieval chivalric codes, this virtue presupposes the unquestionable legitimacy of the sovereign lord, whose position has been ordained by divine powers and whose rule is just beyond doubt. The world of *A Song of Ice and Fire*, however, has so far confronted its readers and characters with sundry sovereigns, whose legitimacy was and is far from indisputable and whose reigns have been marked by gross deviations from justice, let alone ideal, sovereign government. Strictly speaking, this observation is not confined to Mad King Aerys II; it applies to all the rulers after the Targaryen conquest, which was, after all, a violent seizure of power. The crisis of government that manifests itself in Martin's novels also presents a challenge to chivalric virtues and thus is a considerable factor contributing to the crisis in knighthood, because the gravitational centre upon which chivalrous virtues hinge – the lord – is apparently destabilized. As a consequence, following the behavioural codes of knighthood becomes a matter of individual choice and ethics far more than is the case in medieval romance, where the framework of right and wrong was both clear and regulated.

Above I elucidated some of the consequences of this crisis, summarized as a general notion of decline in the state of chivalric practice. Yet Martin's series also contains characters who, while epitomizing the crisis of knighthood in Westeros, also offer possibilities of renegotiating or re-establishing knighthood. In the remaining part of this chapter, I want to focus on two of these characters. The first is Brienne of Tarth. Brienne sternly upholds chivalrous virtues, but despite her undisputable merits the so-called Maid of Tarth (whose byname's echoes of Joan of Arc are certainly no coincidence) is – at least in the novels published so far – excluded from Westerosi knighthood because of her sex.[36] In Season 8, episode 2 of the TV show, Tormund Giantsbane dismisses such an exclusive, gender-biased definition of knighthood, asserting that he would 'knight [Brienne] ten times over' – whereupon Ser Jaime Lannister seizes the opportunity and uses his prerogative as a knight to elevate another to knighthood, dubbing Brienne in what is probably one of the most touching scenes of the final season.[37] Throughout the novel, Brienne attempts to uphold chivalrous ideals by simply putting them into practice. Without being granted the official status of a knight, Brienne thus enacts knighthood as a habitus, detaching the behavioural code from its social status. This uncompromising attitude earns her ridicule, and she often resembles a Westerosi version of Don Quixote, acting as if she lived in the 'songs' of the bards rather than in the novels' real world.[38] Yet despite that ridicule, Brienne of Tarth also earns a deep respect from those characters who, even if they do not share her idealism, appreciate her attempts to preserve a habitus that has almost become obsolete in its original social environment, by transferring it into a new context, namely that of female knighthood. And it seems in the novels as if respecting Brienne's chivalric habitus serves as a moral litmus test for the characters she encounters. Those who reject or even try to destroy her have so far been identified as depraved or monstrous. Brienne's acceptance as a knight by other characters generally depends on whether they have an essentialist or a performative understanding of knighthood. An essentialist understanding of knighthood assigns constant, typical features and meanings to the concept, and if this understanding rests on rigid patriarchal premises, it excludes women from becoming anointed knights.[39] In contrast, a performative understanding of knighthood that defines knighthood as relational and functional, in other words, as the successful practical embodiment of a habitus, allows flexibility in its definition. In Martin's novels, the essentialist understanding appears to bear negative connotations, whereas the performative understanding is seen more positively.

In academic criticism, Brienne has been commented on as a feminist revision of the heroic warrior type, who may serve as a corrective to the failed development of an earlier ideal of masculinity.[40] I am a little wary of following such arguments, not least because Brienne's femininity needs further reconsideration. I would argue that her femininity is at least ambiguous, because this character so clearly works with gender reversals and androgynous patterns that also affect other characters, while her innocent insistence on chivalric ideals is simultaneously very much connected to her femininity and virginity.[41] What one can safely say, however, is that when it comes to situating this character within the civilizational transformation process in Elias's sense, Brienne successfully manages to combine the ideal of heroic knighthood and its potential for violence with a discernible ability for self-control and sublimation of affect. This ability resonates with courtly knighthood and is essential for the stage of a diversified, civilized society. While the figure of Ser Davos signifies an opening up of knighthood with regard to rank, the figure of Brienne envisages such an opening up with regard to gender. However, Brienne clearly represents a less conservative version of knighthood than Ser Davos. Pledging herself by oath to various lords and ladies, Brienne has become entangled in a far more complex web of social, legal and moral obligations than has Ser Davos with his singular devotion to Stannis (and, in the TV show, later to Jon Snow). The ensuing conflict of loyalties culminates when Brienne is forced by Lady Stoneheart to choose between the lives of her companions Podrick and Hyle Hunt, as well as her own and delivering Jaime Lannister.[42] The current cliffhanger in this story arc in *A Dance with Dragons* prevents us from drawing conclusions about Brienne's eventual choice at the present moment. What one can contend, though, is that Brienne's situation with these conflicting loyalties corresponds with the complex differentiations of sociological functions, which Elias claims for the civilized, whereas Ser Davos, with his exclusive adherence to one lord only, tends to repudiate and avoid such complexities.[43]

An ultimate evaluation of Brienne's character, of course, cannot be arrived at until the series' sixth volume, *The Winds of Winter*, reveals (hopefully) the resolution of the current cliffhanger in Brienne's story arc. This resolution will certainly have an impact on our overall reading of knighthood in Martin's novels. Since the TV show omits the Lady Stoneheart plot altogether and thus never confronts Brienne with a comparable choice, I refrain from drawing any conclusions from the show about this character's further development. If, however, the claims are correct that the final outcome of the characters in the TV show corresponds to what George Martin has in store for them, then Brienne's promotion to Lord Commander of King Bran's Kingsguard in the series' final episode could either hint at a possible reward for her meticulous adherence to chivalrous virtues or at her eventual compliance with the prevailing chivalric system of Westeros, after having discovered that she could not live up to her ideals. At least her completion of Jaime's entry in the White Book of the Kingsguard, which preserves her version of Jaime Lannister for future generations, suggests that Brienne has found a way for herself to retain her belief in chivalrous virtues (as represented by Jaime's recorded deeds) despite experiences of personal disappointment.[44] The resolution of the current cliffhanger in the Brienne and Jaime storyline will also add deeper insight into the character who is arguably the most notorious and controversial knight, Ser Jaime Lannister. For the sake of brevity, I will not go into details about the ambiguity of Ser Jaime's chivalry but will restrict myself to a reading of the character in view of the societal transformation processes outlined by Elias.

From the beginning of the series, Jaime is known as one of the best swordsmen in Westeros. He defines himself through his sword hand and, as the reader learns in Jaime's POV chapters, even after his maiming he has little interest in or understanding of anything that is not related to the warrior skills of fighting and riding. *A Feast for Crows* thus depicts Jaime as 'more comfortable' (*FC*, 703) and at ease in the warrior environment of the camp than at court in King's Landing.[45] Even when it comes to religious faith, he can only relate to the Warrior. Scrutinizing Jaime's acts and inclinations, we can therefore conclude that Jaime's self-identification corresponds to a great extent to what Elias describes as the behavioural codes of a warrior. These are characterized, for instance, by exerting violence and by awareness of being exposed to violence and pain, hence the constant experience of physical threats. This, in turn, results in a radical attitude of living in the here and now, the experience of living between extremes and, as a consequence, an unrestrained indulgence in affect and desires. This kind of behavioural mode also informs what the novels have so far revealed about Ser Jaime: his impulsiveness, combined with his readiness to face the consequences of his recklessness, testifies to such an attitude towards life.[46] Psychological explanations for Ser Jaime's behaviour could be offered, such as the early death of his mother or the traumatizing events he had to witness in the Mad King's Kingsguard. Yet in the logic of a warrior society, to which Ser Jaime apparently belongs and to which he considers himself as belonging, this is not necessary. His incestuous love for Cersei, his shoving Bran Stark out of the window and attacking Eddard Stark in the streets of King's Landing equally fit into that warrior behavioural pattern. And within this pattern, those acts are, in fact, morally legitimate and justifiable.

Ser Jaime's problem is, however, that the society he lives in has already undergone a structural transformation which renders the behavioural codes of a warrior society obsolete. For a knight, at least in this society, is no longer the same as a warrior. I argue that many of the external and inner conflicts with which Ser Jaime is confronted can be explained by the clash of a warrior society's behavioural codes with those of a centralized, diversified society. The former codes may be an anachronism, but this anachronism forms a residue within the ideals of knighthood in the social sphere to which Ser Jaime belongs. We have seen that the codes of knighthood are in a state of crisis in Westeros, manifested in the clash between the residual codes of the past and the unsatisfactory practice of these codes in the present, due to the shift in social structures. If true knighthood surfaces (as in the case of Brienne), it does so in form of a habitus now disconnected from its original social environment.

In the character of Ser Jaime Lannister, Martin concentrates and illustrates the various ethical dilemmas resulting from this clash or impasse. Jaime's so-called 'soiling' of the white cloak of the Kingsguard was occasioned by the collapse of the simplistic warrior culture logic in face of the complex obligations in a diversified society, which are – as the novels make clear – not easy to comply with. When Ser Jaime frames his summary of the Kingsguard vows to Lady Stark with the words 'So many vows ... they make you swear and swear. It's too much. No matter what you do, you're forsaking one vow or the other' (*CoK*, 796), he is by no means being evasive but simply stating the truth of a central moral dilemma emerging alongside the process of civilization. The passage shows that Ser Jaime is apparently at a loss when it comes to coping with the complexities of the new social structures he inhabits. Slaying Aerys was a decision that essentially followed from warrior logic. It was an extreme choice in an extreme situation, executed in full awareness of, and with readiness to accept and bear, the consequences. Yet, as we learn, it asserted Jaime's insistence on that fundamental code of knighthood: to protect and to serve – not the king but the weak and innocent, and thus, he took his liege lord to task for not fulfilling his part of the oath.

Despite his notorious reputation (in both Westeros and among readers), I would argue that Ser Jaime is, in fact, the character who – together with Brienne of Tarth – comes closest to displaying all the virtues of knighthood, albeit qualified by adaptation to his particular situation. He is a skilled fighter (and pursues sword practice even after his maiming), he is fiercely loyal (especially to his family and those close to him), he is protective (e.g. towards Tyrion, Cersei, Tommen, Brienne or the servant

Pia), he can be generous (see his behaviour towards his squire Peck and towards Pia) and is one of the few characters actively involved in a courtly love relationship (both with his sister and, one might argue, with Brienne). Jaime's traumatic experiences in Aerys II's Kingsguard cause him to adopt the habitus of a cynical knight, who, by retaining his title and his position in the Kingsguard, comes to embody the paradox of chivalry without virtues or other moral points of reference. His encounter with Brienne makes it obvious that he used to share the ideals to which she still adheres, and although he can no longer subscribe to this idealism, he attempts to reinstate a new form of the cultural practice of knighthood that can reconcile these ideals with the reality in which he finds himself. Like Brienne, he thus also cultivates, as it were, knighthood as a habitus, but in his case, this habitus is not disconnected from its former social sphere but rather from the essentialist claim chivalric values have held. For Ser Jaime's practice of chivalric ideals seems to be based on the assumption that the meaning of individual virtues cannot be entirely fixed but will have to be adapted to their respective contexts – as implied in the remark to Lady Catelyn, mentioned above.

This renegotiation of chivalric ideals is, of course, also enforced by Jaime's loss of his sword hand, which abruptly excludes him from his warrior existence. Deprived of the capability of further fulfilling the virtue of prowess, Ser Jaime can only continue as a knight if he adapts himself to the codes of courtly knighthood: that is, if he undergoes the transition from warrior culture to court culture. To quote Elias: 'Here, the individual is largely protected from the sudden assault, the shocking attack of physical violence on his life; but he is also forced to suppress his own passions, the urges to physically attack others.'[47] The turn in Jaime's story arc can clearly be read along these lines: as a gradual adaptation process to the behavioural codes of court culture. Accordingly, Ser Jaime begins to curb his desire towards Cersei, serves his king loyally and, in an ironic, even queer twist, plays the lady's part in the courtly love constellation with Brienne, by sending her on a quest.[48] With regard to the cliffhanger in *A Dance with Dragons*, there is much speculation whether Jaime's story arc is one of redemption and how this arc will eventually terminate. Without attending to the moral implications of such a reading (which I find highly problematic), I suggest what one can safely say is that Jaime's story arc is definitely a process of civilization.

This process also finds its expression in the novel's narrative mode, which mirrors the continuous self-reflection that Elias describes. Civilized individuals take this turn when they have to negotiate various demands and pressures in a ceaseless process of self-control. In Martin's novels, Ser Jaime's transformation is accompanied by a shift in narrative representation. As long as Jaime is still in the warrior stage, the reader is only provided with an external presentation of this character. Once Jaime is given a POV of his own, from *A Storm of Swords* onwards, his chapters reveal the self-reflexive stance he must assume while undergoing his process of civilization. In these chapters, the reader can take note of the new battlefield on which Ser Jaime finds himself: a 'battlefield [that] is projected inside as it were: Part of the tensions and passions one used to fight out in single combat, now have to be fought within oneself'.[49] It is on this internal battlefield that *A Song of Ice and Fire* allows Ser Jaime to renegotiate his position as a knight and to retrieve and develop a code and a habitus of knighthood which, in my opinion, offer glimpses of a possible recuperated practice of knighthood in the world of Westeros.

I argue that the strongest deviation from the novels in Jaime's representation in the TV show does not consist in Jaime's eventual break-up with Brienne and return to Cersei ('The Last of the Starks', 8.4) – whether this is a deviation at all can only be judged after Martin has completed his novels. I maintain that the series fails to acknowledge sufficiently Jaime's attempt at re-establishing himself and the Kingsguard according to chivalrous ideals. In the novels, this attempt includes Jaime's sexual impotence when facing Cersei in his quarters, whereas Benioff and Weiss make him have intercourse with his sister right on the White Table. Indeed, the TV show largely jettisoned this renegotiation of knighthood in Jaime's character arc; apart from occasional, inconsistently pursued hints at his status as a knight, Jaime Lannister is almost exclusively defined through his incestuous relation to Cersei, which extends throughout the entire series. Although occasional recollections of or meetings with Brienne may (re)kindle traces of chivalrous behaviour in Jaime, and despite the fan service to so-called Jaime-Brienne shippers (who support this pairing against any other options) in the first four episodes of Season 8, Benioff and Weiss decided to discard this essential part of Jaime's character: a decision which produces an annoying inconsistency in the representation of Ser Jaime Lannister. Readers will therefore have to wait for Martin to finally publish *The Winds of Winter*; until then, it remains tantalizingly open how the residues of chivalry or processes of civilization I have discussed will eventually work themselves out in the world of *A Song of Ice and Fire*.

8

Tournaments and judicial duels in George R. R. Martin's *The World of Ice and Fire* and *A Song of Ice and Fire*

Przemysław Grabowski-Górniak

The Middle Ages have always served as a source of inspiration for fantasy literature. As a result, a standardized assortment of kings, knights and castles, supplemented by magical weaponry and fantastic creatures taken directly from chivalric romances, has served as an easily recognizable blueprint for the genre's ever-growing collection of secondary worlds. However, while quasi-medieval environments are rather common for high fantasy, few authors have utilized the cultural richness of the real Middle Ages, and fewer still have displayed any discernible understanding of the period and its customs. One aspect of the medieval world that is often disregarded is the richness of its martial culture. A good example of this usual lack of nuance is the regular absence of depictions, or even indications of the existence of any tournaments or other martial games. As engagement in various war games was an inseparable part of knights' lives, and the development of the tournament movement was visibly intertwined with the evolution of chivalry, one could not overstate the importance of such events for any narrative aiming to recreate the medieval knightly culture in a believable manner. George R. R. Martin's *A Song of Ice and Fire*, arguably the most widely admired fantasy series of recent years, deviates from the simplistic portrayal of the chivalric tradition and features many examples of tournaments and judicial duels of paramount importance to the plot, also ascribing to them the kind of narrative importance arguably last seen in Sir Walter Scott's fiction. After all it might be claimed that the state of Westeros at the beginning of the series was the ultimate result of a series of events started by the famous tourney at Harrenhal.

The following study examines and compares the tournaments and judicial duels featured in selected volumes of *A Song of Ice and Fire*, as well as in *The World of Ice & Fire*, and a short story set in the same universe, entitled 'The Hedge Knight', with their historical counterparts. The martial games selected from George R. R. Martin's series are the tourney at Ashford Meadow, the tourney at Harrenhal and the Hand's tourney as the three adequately represent distinct aspects of medieval tournaments and contain descriptions helpful in highlighting the changes such events underwent historically. The Trial of Seven described in 'The Hedge Knight' and the duel between Prince Oberyn and Ser Gregor Clegane shall be used in turn as a reference point for a discussion on judicial duels. Since Martin's Westeros as it is depicted in 'The Hedge Knight' seems to be representative of the first half of the late medieval period and the plot of the book series is set almost a century after that of the short story, knightly tournaments, or tourneys, are a well-established and commonly recognized form of martial games in this secondary world.[1] It is, however, essential to understand the historic source and subsequent evolution of such martial games in order to illustrate how the tourneys of Westeros correspond to the European knightly tournaments. For that reason, the analysis of each of Martin's tourneys and judicial duels shall be conducted through the prism of our current knowledge and understanding of the medieval tournaments.

Within the internal chronology of Martin's secondary world, the earliest tournament of those chosen for this analysis is the tourney at Ashford Meadow, which constitutes the main focus of 'The Hedge Knight', the action of which takes place almost one hundred years before the events of *A Song of Ice and Fire*. The story follows the exploits of Dunk, a squire to a hedge knight, who, following his master's death, decides to pose as a knight and seeks his fortune in a tourney held at Ashford Meadow.[2] The protagonist is to some extent similar to William Marshal, as both are warriors of low standing who perceive tournaments as a viable method of improving their financial situation.[3] In itself, however, the tourney at Ashford Meadow represents a fairly late stage of medieval martial games and as such suggests a long pre-existing tradition of organized armed competition. Historically, knightly tournaments did not emerge from a void; in fact, tournaments and judicial duels were a constant presence throughout the post-classical era, in some incarnations predating the existence of mounted knights. Some derive early medieval martial games from the *hippika gymnasia* or *militari ludi* of Roman cavalry units.[4] A later instance of such war games can be found in Carolingian times, as in 842 when the conclusion of an alliance between Charlemagne's grandsons, Louis the German and Charles the Bald, was celebrated with a display of horsemanship in which groups of cavalrymen simulated charging at one another, pretending to flee, and skilfully shifting their formations.[5] However, the Roman and the Frankish war games can hardly be called tournaments, since in those coordinated cavalry manoeuvres there was no place for actual armed combat. The first written records of actual medieval tournaments come from the twelfth century, even though some of those refer to incidents claimed to have occurred in the previous century.[6] However, one needs to be aware that while the term 'tournament' is used in relation to twelfth-century martial games, one would be sorely mistaken to expect them to have taken the form of that described in Martin's 'The Hedge Knight' or Sir Walter Scott's *Ivanhoe*.[7]

In our history, tournaments resembling the tourney at Ashford Meadow were predated by the mêlée, 'a battle in all but intent, fought *en masse* over open large expanses of open terrain, generally between two towns'.[8] Interestingly enough, Martin presents what seems to be a direct reference of such martial games in his depiction of the North in *The World of Ice & Fire*: 'Northmen fight ahorse with war lances but seldom tilt for sport, preferring mêlées that are only this side of battles' (*WIF*, 136). Historically, aside from certain areas established as places of rest and recuperation, the entirety of the countryside served as a battlefield. This aspect is also true in Westeros's mêlée, as 'there are accounts of [such] contests that have lasted half a day and left fields trampled and villages half-torn down' (*WIF*, 136). However, early tournaments also lacked the orderly structure of their later incarnation as there were no clear rules of conduct and the sheer size of the tournament ground made any supervision by local marshals or judges impossible. As a result, serious injuries or even deaths of the participants were not unheard of.[9] Again, Martin reflects that state in his description of the Westeros games, informing the reader that 'serious injuries are common in such a mêlée, and deaths are not unheard of', further underlining the point by mentioning 'the great mêlée at Last Hearth' in which 'eighteen men died, and half again that were sorely maimed'.[10] Thus, given the fact that Martin's North seems to be consistently presented as somewhat culturally and technologically outdated when compared to the South of Westeros, one may speculate that the men of the North participate in an older type of martial games, no longer cultivated in more advanced areas but nonetheless representative of the common source of the joust-centric tourneys prominently featured in the series. On that basis it is sensible to presume that while George R. R. Martin was fashioning the tournaments of Westeros on the basis of their medieval counterparts, he also adhered to the historical pattern of the latter's development.

The reason why Martin chose to focus on later style of knightly tournaments may be dictated by the fact that there was never a single champion in the twelfth-century tournaments. Arguably therefore the more organized formula lends itself better to telling a story of individual growth and success. That being said, it cannot possibly be claimed that there was no success to be had in the mêlée. While there was no champion title to be won, the actual measure of success lay in the number of knights one captured and the amount of armour, horses and ransom received from them. As the wealth one could gain through such acquisitions was considerable, many participants resorted to trickery and ambushed smaller groups of combatants for an easy victory. For this reason, those of higher social standing often employed armed retinues to fend off unwanted attackers. The social importance of the tournaments is best exemplified in the biography of William Marshal, one of England's most famous knights, who rose to prominence and wealth mainly through his great skill in tournament fights. In 1168 William had entered the household of Henry II's son Henry 'the Young King' to train the prince and he accompanied him to a number of French tournaments. Here one might draw an interesting comparison between William Marshal and Ser Duncan the Tall. Dunk, as the latter is referred to in the short stories, also makes his fortune through his tournament exploits and is even employed to look after a young member of the royal family of the Targaryens and to train him in knightly craft. However, even though William Marshal is hailed by many as one of the best knights that ever lived, his behaviour during tournaments would probably seem quite unbecoming to anyone used to the Victorian perception of chivalry, and thus quite at odds with the more idealistic attitude of Ser Duncan. Reportedly, William could often be found grappling with his opponents, tearing off their helmets and attempting to take hold of their horses' bridles as these were more certain means of subduing one's opponents than engaging them in swordplay.[11] Additionally, Marshal's biographer mentions the knight being on one occasion admonished by the prince 'for leaving him alone on the battlefield to pursue his own glory'.[12] It should be noted than Marshal's behaviour did not deviate from the norm; his contemporary, Count Philip of Flanders, was known for purposely entering the mêlée late as this allowed his team to easily capture those tired and scattered by the ongoing battle, a tactic from which the Young King's retinue suffered a number of times.[13]

Still, even if there are some superficial similarities to be drawn between Sir William Marshal and Ser Duncan, their tournament experiences are hardly comparable. In the short story the narrator states that during that time there was 'a dozen different forms a tourney might follow', listing 'mock battles between teams of knights', mêlées and formulas 'where individual combats were the rule' (*HK*, 40). While mêlée and individual combat should be rather understandable at this point, one might wonder what the author means by 'mock battles'. It is possible that he is referring to the *bohort* (or *buhurt*), a less formal fighting contest between mounted knights. As bohorts were often fought with wooden staffs, whalebone weapons or blunted swords, they were generally regarded as a valuable martial exercise. The bohorts' non-lethal nature and easily controllable organization made them an ideal practice for squires. Bohorts were also a popular form of entertainment for the highest echelons of the chivalric nobility. According to one account, while he was in Sicily King Richard I took canes from a passing peasant and used them as weapons in an improvised bohort between his household knights and some French crusaders.[14] Be that as it may, it is jousting that constitutes the actual focus of the story's tournament.

Although jousts, in which two mounted knights charged at one another with couched lances in order to unhorse their opponent, originally did occur before the mêlée, they were not considered an important part of the tournament until the thirteenth century. One possible reason for jousts' rise in prominence might be the increasing popularity of chivalric romances in which scenes of mounted duels abound. Additionally, a shift from massive mêlée battles to focused and localized struggles between individual contestants allowed for a more effective display of fighting prowess. The usual joust consisted of three runs, in the course of which both knights were expected to break their lances on the opponent's breast or helmet, preferably unhorsing him in the process. Removing one's helmet was a widely understood signal of a desire to end the joust.[15] If one of the knights was unhorsed but wished to continue the fight, the other was expected to dismount and face his opponent with a sword, an axe or a mace in hand.[16] From the thirteenth century onwards, jousting lances had safe, coronated tips, although those craving a real challenge sometimes agreed to use sharp weapons both when mounted and on foot.

Upon arrival at Ashford Meadow, Dunk sees the tourney grounds filled with pavilions and merchant stalls. That and the fact that all the martial games take place in the lists clearly indicates that the tourney at Ashford Meadow is most likely based on tournaments of the late medieval period. It is unfortunately impossible to point to any exact century as the definite point of reference for 'The Hedge Knight' as the story contains descriptions of an assortment of objects and activities, some of which could be connected with the thirteenth century, while others would better fit in the fourteenth century. For example, if the type of armour that Dunk orders from an armourer is to be any indication, the first half of the thirteenth century seems more likely. In his first conversation with the armourer, Dunk lists a suit of mail, a gorget, grieves and a greathelm as the parts he requires for his tournament armour (*HK*, 14).

Additionally, the reader is told that Dunk's master used a halfhelm with a nasal, a type of head protection popular only up to the first half of the twelfth century. Of course, the mention of the halfhelm does not necessarily contradict the suggested date as it is possible that Dunk's master is deliberately shown to be an old knight who had kept the same armour for most of his life, either due to his outmoded habits or simple lack of funds. Nonetheless, the greathelm evolved in the 1220s and remained a popular tournament helmet even in the latter part of the fourteenth century.[17] Although the lack of a reinforced surcoat, or a coat of plates, may be a little baffling, just as is mentioning greaves rather than shynbalds, Dunk's selection of equipment is largely consistent with a broader imagined background of the thirteenth century. At the same time, Dunk discusses the usefulness of helmet visors and is seen carrying a longsword, and using steel gauntlets, which would suggest the fourteenth century (*HK*, 41, 39, 96). Thus, while 'The Hedge Knight' clearly represents an amalgamation of images and designs from both the thirteenth and fourteenth centuries, the tourney it describes should be considered in relation to the broader historical background of those two centuries.

Historically, the thirteenth and fourteenth centuries were the time when the tournament became more formalized and found wider social acceptance. Initially little more than mock battles, tournaments gradually became important cultural events, often organized to celebrate momentous occasions, including royal weddings and coronations. Organized with pomp and ceremony and at a considerable cost, the tournaments of the fourteenth century often alluded to chivalric romances and introduced costumes and theatrics for the entertainment of the audience. A good example of such events is the tournament held at Windsor on 19 January 1344 to which not only knights but also 'all the ladies from the south of England and wives of the citizens of London were invited'.[18] The proceedings opened with a great banquet for the ladies, who entertained themselves in the castle hall while all the knights, aside from two French guests of honour, ate in their tents, followed by a dance. For the following three days, King Edward III and nineteen of his household knights fought against all challengers. After the tournament had ended the king and queen appeared in the castle chapel in luscious velvet robes tailored specially for the tournament and invited all participants to join them in a great feast after the mass.

Obviously, smaller, less spectacular tournaments were still being organized. In his chronicle Jean Froissart describes one such tournament held at Saint-Inglevert in 1390. According to Froissart, three French knights waited for challengers in their three crimson pavilions, each of which had two shields, one of peace and one of war, hanging at the entrance.[19] The three knights would then joust with any challenger who struck one of their shields. In this particular detail, Martin's description of the tournament's challenge procedure matches Froissart's. Other than there being only one shield displayed before knights' pavilions in Martin's short story, the arrangement is largely the same as at Saint-Inglevert. The only real difference is in the actual course of the tournament as Martin's knights joust all at the same time. Although group fighting was not uncommon in the medieval martial games, as evidenced by mêlées or bohorts, the joust was typically a competition between two knights. As already mentioned, the central goal of the joust was to allow individual knights to fully display their martial prowess, a feat nearly impossible with numerous fighters in the lists. Interestingly, in the descriptions of the tourney at Harrenhal, taking place seventy-nine years after that of Ashford Meadow, and the Hand's tourney, all jousts are shown to be conducted with only two knights at a time (*GT*, 285–8). Clearly, while the difference could be dismissed as the author's mistake, it is sensible to expect those cultural and social elements in Martin's writing that were taken directly from history to function similarly in the same context. As the knights of Westeros are consequently shown to be almost exactly the same as their medieval counterparts, and the Ashford Meadow tourney strongly resembles similar historical events, we should consider the possible significance of such a considerable alteration. Arguably, the most logical explanation is tied to religion. As Westeros did not have popes who would have condemned mêlées, a strong distinction between group fights and jousts would not be needed. It is entirely possible that the joust of the Ashford Meadow tourney is in fact a diminished form of the Westerosi brand of the mêlée. Alternatively, this unusual situation may be explained by the special nature of the event as it is stated that the tournament was organized by Lord Ashford to celebrate his daughter's thirteenth name day, and thus the atypical formula might be a part of the celebration (*HK*, 40). In that respect, the number of contestants should not be seen as diverging from historical precedent but rather a stage in the development of a tournament movement in a quasi-medieval society without the clergy's bias against mêlées, or a representation of a larger cultural variety of tournament formulas.

While the precise historical antecedents for the tourney at Ashford Meadow against the background of the historical tournaments are, to put it mildly, problematic, the above-mentioned tourney at Harrenhal and the Hand's tourney can be easily identified as the Westerosi equivalents of the fifteenth-century tournaments. The abundance of plate armour and the use of richly embellished battle gear evidently made for the lists rather than the battlefield reflects the growing extravagance of fifteenth- or even sixteenth-century tournaments. While the course of the individual jousts follows the medieval rules virtually to the letter, and therefore they are of no merit to further discussion, the social aspects of both events are definitely worth exploring. The central incident of the tourney at Harrenhal was undoubtedly Rhaegar Targaryen's choice of Lyanna Stark to be named 'the Queen of Love and Beauty' (*GT*, 608). As could be seen in the instance of the Windsor tournament of 1344, the presence of ladies at the medieval tournaments was not only normal but also desirable in the late Middle Ages. As tournaments were increasingly influenced by courtly culture and literature, ladies, in whose name knights could compete, became an inseparable element of such events. Numerous sources mention ladies awarding kerchiefs, ribbons and garters to knights, to be worn in the lists as a sign of love and devotion. Sometimes the winner of the tournament could request a kiss, or a 'gift of loving thanks', from a chosen lady, and if he had fought on a lady's behalf she would be named 'the Queen of the Tournament'.[20] The literature of the time, including numerous Arthurian romances and Chaucer's 'The Knight's Tale', provided its audience with many tales focused on the role of courtly love in martial contests. However, a relatively safe joust was not the only means of honouring one's lady, especially if one needed to protect her good name and avenge any slights she might have suffered.

Judicial trials were a unique category of martial contest. It was believed that if two disputing parties entered a duel, God would assist the one that was in the right. In the high and late Middle Ages judicial duels were a widely agreed-upon way of resolving all sorts of legal disputes. What is interesting is the fact that trial by combat was not restricted to knights only. Different rules and equipment were used in judicial duels between members of particular social classes. In the latter part of the medieval period, judicial duels were so important that numerous manuals detailing fighting techniques for every possible configuration, including a duel between a woman and a man, were created. Hans Talhoffer, author of one of the best-known medieval fighting manuals, and an umpire in several judicial duels, listed murder, treason, heresy, urging disloyalty to one's lord, betrayal, falsehood and taking advantage of a maiden or lady as the seven causes for a trial by combat.[21] Additionally, as it was possible to employ the services of a champion there were a number of people who fought in judicial duels professionally.[22]

In the texts chosen for this analysis there are two instances of trial by combat, the first arising from a dispute between Dunk and Prince Aerion Targaryen, the second meant to establish whether Tyrion Lannister is guilty of murder. It is noticeable that both trials differ considerably from the medieval equivalents, albeit each in distinctive ways. The Trial of Seven, as the judicial combat in 'The Hedge Knight' is called, follows medieval standards in that it is an armed struggle, the end of which can be either the death of one of the disputants or the surrender and confession of guilt by either of them. The first, most obvious dissimilarity lies clearly in the number of fighters. As the name indicates, the judicial duel has only two participants, while the Trial of Seven requires two groups, each consisting of seven knights. Religious symbolism aside, such a judicial combat structure must seem curious as it no longer tests the mettle of the individuals directly involved in the dispute. In fact, a large number of fighters would allow for a situation in which a group of warriors could attack the opposing disputant all at once, which has little to do with an honourable fight. Even more baffling to a modern spectator is the information that if someone were unable to find six supporters, he would be immediately found guilty. One might expect that, even if in Westeros group fights were somehow considered a viable method of resolving disputes between two individuals, a culture designed to be so similar to that of medieval Europe should acknowledge the possible value of a less numerous party's victory over a larger one, and should thus allow a subset of seven to fight their opponents if they so wish. If Westerosi knights are hailed for single-handedly overcoming several enemies in battle and in a tournament joust, such restrictions for what is, essentially, a ceremonial display of martial prowess seem inconsistent. Also strange is the ruse devised by Prince Baelor who instructs Dunk's supporters to carry tournament lances into the trial, as they exceed the length of the war lances used by their opponents. In the Middle Ages, all weapons used in judicial duels were inspected before the fighting started in order to make sure both sides had an equal chance.[23] While it serves as a great plot device, Baelor's trickery would be impossible in a historical judicial duel. As the martial games of 'The Hedge Knight', as well as the clearly formalized Trial of Seven, demonstrate how both tournament and judicial combat are well organized and established in the storyworld, one can hardly overlook how out of keeping with the rest of the picture such a complete lack of supervision over the arms used for a sacred trial is.

The questionable quality of the judicial duel described in *A Storm of Swords* is also connected with the combatants' battle gear. The background of the duel is that both fighters are serving as champions of the disputing parties; Prince Oberyn additionally aims to force the confession of guilt from his opponent. This aligns itself perfectly with the laws and standards of the Late Middle Ages. As both champions are knights, fighting each other in armour and on foot is accurate. What makes this duel different from those that were held in the Middle Ages is the disparity in the armour and weapons used by each of the champions. As evidenced by written records and graphic depictions in medieval fighting manuals, at all times the disputants were supposed to use exactly the same weapons: these consisted usually of a choice of daggers, short and long swords and spears.[24] The greatsword, the weapon Ser Gregor Clegane wields, was used only in battle and, due to its size and purpose, was never used with a shield. Of course, although one could argue that using a greatsword one-handed is meant to signify Clegane's immense physical strength, the fact remains that this type of weapon is designed for a two-handed grip; its effectiveness would be severely limited, if it were used in combination with a shield.[25] Additionally, as Clegane is said to wear 'heavy plate [armour] over chainmail', he would have no use for a shield (SS, 395). All the plates from Talhoffer's and Fiore dei Liberi's medieval fencing manuals show that armoured knights engaged in judicial duels carry no shields as the protection provided by the plate armour made them obsolete. This fact notwithstanding, even if he were to use the greatsword two-handed, as it was intended to be used, Clegane is at a visible disadvantage as the readers are told that Prince Oberyn's spear 'was two feet longer than Ser Gregor's sword, more than enough to keep him at an awkward distance' (SS, 398). Whereas Prince Oberyn may benefit from a longer weapon, he is at a severe disadvantage when it comes to armour. It is even stated by the narrator himself that '[Oberyn's] mail and scale together would not give him a quarter the protection of Gregor's heavy plate' (SS, 396). It is safe to say that no similar situation would ever have been allowed in a medieval trial by combat, as both combatants had to be provided with the same type of weapons and armour.[26] Given the accuracy with which George R. R. Martin recreates the intricacies of knightly culture and tournaments in his works, it seems that in the case of both judicial combats discussed the requirements of plot and tension-building supersede consistency and accuracy. In fact, a single combat between two so contrastingly armed fighters, one of whom is evidently presented as lightly armed and nimble while the other is obviously better protected, but slower and at a range disadvantage, evokes associations with the duels of Roman gladiators, which purposefully paired asymmetrically equipped warriors for dramatic effect.

The martial games of the Middle Ages are arguably the perfect exemplification of the complexity and cultural contradictions of the period. Through combining the ruthlessness of war with the conventions of courtly love, adorning mortal danger with a veneer of colourful pageantry, medieval tournaments were a fascinating mixture of seemingly conflicting values. What was originally little more than military training eventually developed into a cultural phenomenon of romanticized and often theatrical displays of highly formalized violence that outlived the period that gave birth to them. Serving as far more than a simple means of entertainment for local lords, medieval tournaments constituted important social and political events and were frequently responsible for the rise or ruin of a given knight. To a large extent, the same could be said of the tourneys in George R. R. Martin's *A Song of Ice and Fire*. In fact, an argument could be made that the state of affairs presented in *A Game of Thrones*, the series' first volume, is the fallout of one such event. As both *A Song of Ice and Fire* and other literary works tied to this cycle feature tournaments and other forms of formalized combat, such as judicial duels, to an extent rarely seen in the fantasy genre, it is safe to say that their significance in Martin's fictional world is on a par with the social status they enjoyed in the Middle Ages. In conclusion, it needs to be stated that even though some of Martin's depictions of martial games and judicial duels may contradict the rules and patterns of their historical antecedents, the real value of those representations lies in their apt recreation of the immensely important role such events played in the medieval world. Hopefully, the popularity of George R. R. Martin's literary cycle will help the general audience acknowledge the often overlooked multifaceted qualities of medieval knightly culture.

Part V

Memory

On medieval dream tradition in George R. R. Martin's *A Song of Ice and Fire*

Bartłomiej Błaszkiewicz

As ever more scholarly and critical effort is spent on the elucidation of the fine points of literary composition that contribute to the artistic grandeur of *A Song of Ice and Fire*, the full scope and depth of George R. R. Martin's indebtedness to the wealth of medieval cultural tradition is emerging as a reward for meticulous study. Martin's work reflects the use of medievalism as a consciously pursued literary mode of secondary world creation, determined by a creative interconnection between the uniquely idiomatic cultural context which once shaped the literary tradition that modern heroic fantasy draws upon for its generic identity and the background of modern cultural sensibilities which reflect the genre's contemporary context. The true meaning of the high fantasy text is thus negotiated somewhere between the reverence of an antiquarian fascination with human history and the urge to make the sense of the mythical past an element in the expression of the modern existential condition.[1]

Among the elements of literary composition that reflect the modern appropriation of, and dialogue with, the medieval cultural heritage, the motif of dreams and dreaming is unique, intersecting as it does many vital aspects of the medieval philosophical and spiritual outlook. Moreover, the medieval perception of the topic of dreams not only evolves dynamically throughout the period but also produces no uniform consensus of approach at any given moment in its one thousand years of intellectual history.

The foundations of the medieval attitude to the question of dreams were laid right at the dawn of the epoch in formative philosophical works which witnessed the forging of a new mentality: one which reformulated the cultural legacy of disintegrating Roman civilization. The most important of these was Macrobius's commentary on Cicero's *Somnium Scipionis*, which provided a hugely influential typology of dreams, arranged in a continuum from the prophetic dream stemming from direct contact with the divine (*oraculum*), or containing a divinely inspired vision of the future (*visio*), through an enigmatic reflection of the waking reality (*somnium*), to a confused projection of wakeful apprehensiveness (*insomnium*), and a hallucinatory trance-like experience at the intersection of the mental projection of inner distress and virtual contact with the netherworld of the spirits (*visum*). A divergent classification, built around a corresponding gradation reflecting a progressive interpenetration of the spiritual into the sleepers' psyche, was provided by Calcidius in his commentary on Plato's *Timaeus*; this comprises a descending hierarchy of *revelatio, spectaculum, admonitio, visum* and *somnium*.[2]

Both classifications reflect the medieval outlook on the position of human cognition, against a continuum composed of: the natural phenomena accessible through the five senses, the marvellous, which reaches deep into the core propensities of the four elements and may be accessed through recourse to spiritual insight, and finally the direct operation of the miraculous, where the human intellect is directly enlightened at the behest of a divine power. This ascending hierarchy of vision is elaborated in St Augustine's commentary on Genesis. Here he describes a scheme involving three kinds of vision: corporeal vision, stemming from the five external senses; spiritual vision, the domain of the imagination, or phantasy – one of the four internal senses; and, finally, intellectual vision, an action of the faculty of the intellect.[3]

As all the above formulations reflect the Neoplatonic character of the intellectual environment of the early Middle Ages, they naturally conflict with the different approach adopted in the High Medieval period, under the overwhelming influence of Aristotelian thought. Aristotle himself had been adamant in his rejection of any supernatural context and origin in the activity of dreaming. Aristotle located all activity of dreaming in the domain of the internal sense of imagination, which, during sleep, operates without the overriding control of the superior faculties of the Intellect and the Will: 'the dream is a sort of presentation which presents itself when the sense-perceptions are in a state of freedom.'[4] Consequently, it is because of the Intellect's lack of involvement in dreaming that Aristotle rules out the possibility of dreams being either divinely inspired or containing prophetic messages. As additional proof Aristotle argues that

> the power of foreseeing the future and of having vivid dreams is found in persons of inferior type, which implies that God does not send their dreams; but merely that all those whose physical temperament is, as it were, garrulous and excitable, see sights of all descriptions. . . . For it would have regularly occurred both in the daytime and to the wise had it been God who sent it.[5]

This line of argumentation inevitably clashes with the Christian tradition concerning prophetic dreams, as in Luke 10.21: 'In that hour Jesus rejoiced in spirit, and said, I thank thee, O Father, Lord of heaven and earth, that thou hast hid these things from the wise and prudent, and hast revealed them unto babes: even so, Father; for so it seemed good in thy sight.' Given the abundance of prophetic visions in the Old Testament books of Exodus, Ezekiel and Daniel, as well as their importance for determining the Christian perception of the interaction between the divine agent and human cognition and understanding, it was inevitable that the Aristotelian tradition, which exerted a defining influence on the dominant philosophical trends during the High Medieval period, should be adapted to function within the Christian world view.[6] The most incisive treatment of the theme of dreams is found in the work of St Thomas Aquinas. While discussing the topic of prediction of the future by divination in the second part of *Summa Theologiae* St Thomas begins by adopting a typically Aristotelian perspective which rules out any automatic connection between dreams and future occurrences, except for the case when dreams may stem from the sleeper's apprehensiveness about future occurrences and thus contribute to decisions concerning a course of action in the future.[7] Aquinas outlines a fourfold scheme accounting for all the possible causes of dreams.[8] The crucial element here is the central position of *phantasia*, or *imaginatio*, one of the four internal senses (along with *sensus communis*, *aestimativa* and *memorativa*, which collectively constitute the middle section of the human cognitive apparatus). He defines *imaginatio* elsewhere in the *Summa* as a 'storehouse of forms received through the (external) senses'.[9] Its role is to form *phantasmata*, or phantasms, interpreted by the highest faculty: Intellect. This relies on the phantasms to interpret reality because 'in the present state of life in which the soul is united to a passible body, it is impossible for our intellect to understand anything actually, except by turning to the phantasms'.[10] Consequently, all kinds of dream experiences have to pass through the faculty of *imaginatio*.

Thus, in the second part of *Summa Theologiae*, Aquinas proposes a classification comprising two inward and two outward causes of dream experiences.[11] The first of the inward causes results from *imaginatio* reflecting the Intellect's waking preoccupation with daytime events and considerations. This kind of dream cause corresponds most closely to Aristotle's explanation, and it constitutes the case of *phantasia* being influenced 'from above' in the ascending hierarchy determining the spiritual/corporeal continuum that makes up the human being. Conversely, *phantasia* can become disturbed during sleep by an imbalance in the four humours in the sleeper's body. *Imaginatio* is now influenced 'from below'. In either case the dreams experienced by the sleeper result from the normal functioning of the human body and soul in conjunction.

Correspondingly, the outward causes of dreams may be corporeal or spiritual. For corporeal causes, the sleeper's body is influenced by the surrounding elements, most typically air, or by 'an impression of a heavenly body', here conceived of as a natural phenomenon happening routinely due to the capacity of more refined substances to influence cruder ones: a known characteristic of Created Nature.[12]

The last, spiritual cause of dreams relates to the direct intervention of either God or the *substantiis separatis* (separated substances – i.e. angels and demons). In this case, although the ultimate cause of the dream vision is a divine, or demonic, intervention, the actual experience is still transmitted through the faculty of *imaginatio* because, as Aquinas explains elsewhere in the *Summa*, 'incorporeal things, of which there are no phantasms, are known to us by comparison with sensible bodies of which there are phantasms' because 'the human intellect . . . cannot grasp the universal truth itself unveiled; because its nature requires it to understand by turning to the phantasms'.[13] It is because of its reliance on phantasms that the human intellect is open to demonic deception. The potentially unreliable *imaginatio* is required initially to process the visions occurring in dreams, calling upon what Aquinas calls 'imaginative vision' (corresponding to St Augustine's spiritual vision), without the benefit of the reassuring lucidity of intellectual insight.[14] Sometimes then the divine visitation engages directly with the superior discerning powers of the Intellect:

> An angel causing an imaginative vision, sometimes enlightens the intellect at the same time, so that it knows what these images signify; and then there is not

deception. But sometimes by the angelic operation the similitudes of things only appear in the imagination; but neither then is deception caused by the angel, but by the defect in the intellect to whom such things appear.[15]

This philosophical theory of the operation of dreams in the human psyche provided a lasting foundation for the understanding of dream-related phenomena in high medieval and early modern European culture; the inherently conflicting nature of medieval intellectual tradition continued to reverberate through the literary canon.

A corresponding dichotomy underlies the treatment of dreams in George R. R. Martin's *A Song of Ice and Fire*. The medievalized setting for the fantastic secondary world brings with it some of the deeply ingrained mental attitudes and culturally conditioned patterns of behaviour typical of the medieval period.

We begin in the castle of Winterfell, the seat of the most powerful of the ancient Houses of the north of Westeros, House Stark. The fortunes of war result in the eight-year-old Bran, recently crippled by a freak accident which has left him paralysed below the waist becoming the head of the House. Bran is afflicted by recurrent dreams of falling and the enigmatic figure of the Three-Eyed Crow. The boy confides in Maester Luwin, a lifelong trusted servant of the House. Typically for his profession, the maester adopts an attitude of rational scepticism, reminiscent of what Aristotle had to say about dreams. When confronted by the coincidence of the two surviving Stark brothers dreaming of encountering their absent father in the crypt beneath the castle, Maester Luwin attributes the phenomenon to a rationally explainable result of the mental strain the boys experience because of their parents' prolonged absence:

> I agree that it is odd that both you boys dreamed the same dream, yet when you stop to consider it, it's only natural. You miss your lord father, and you know that he is a captive. Fear can fever a man's mind and give him queer thoughts. Rickon is too young to comprehend –
>
> [. . .]
>
> but you, Bran, you're old enough to know that dreams are only dreams. (*GT*, 673)

Maester Luwin's explanation of the causes of what seems to be a most uncanny coincidence relegates the whole experience to the category that Aquinas classifies as the type of dream whereby the phantasms produced by the *imaginatio* echo the restlessness of the waking Intellect; this roughly corresponds to what Macrobius calls the *insomnium*. Ironically, Maester Luwin himself points out that the age gap between the brothers, and the consequent difference in the Intellect's capacities to take stock of the situation, would normally result in the dream experience being different in each case.

This context is underscored when the unfortunate maester is attacked by Bran's direwolf when he takes an empirical line: descending to the crypts with the two boys in an attempt to demonstrate that their father is not, in fact, physically there. The emphatic symbolism of the scene when Maester Luwin is unexpectedly confronted with 'darkness [which] sprang at him, snarling' from the depths of the crypts (*GT*, 671) reinforces the air of implicit irony surrounding the maester's dogged rationalism.

When the Reed siblings come to renew the pledge of allegiance of one of the Starks' principal vassal houses in time of war, the maester is confronted with the idea of 'green dreams'. This type of dream contains prophetic visions of the future and Luwin obstinately refuses to accept that such phenomena may have any value. Yet, as he elaborates further on the cause for his deep-seated scepticism, it is clear that his argument depends on a rationalist empiricism reminiscent of Enlightenment attitudes towards the supernatural rather than on the Aristotelian premise that only the superior powers of the Intellect may be deemed reliable in recognizing the supernatural character of dream visions.

Thus, Maester Luwin represents the sceptical end of a wide spectrum of opinion concerning dreams. The bipolar character of this continuum mirrors, to a significant degree, the medieval intellectual environment. Yet, the learned maester's stubbornly rationalist position, made to represent the opinion prevalent in his profession, is founded upon a wider phenomenological gap than was the case with medieval philosophical arguments. The Thomist perspective essentially appropriated Aristotelian scepticism towards dreams in order to normalize and classify the various causes of dreams; the mundane psychosomatic experience could thus be distinguished from divinely sanctioned contact with the supernatural. In contrast, Maester Luwin's wholesale denial of any form of the supernatural effectively limits, or flattens out, the potential scope of the Intellect's operation; he assumes that the capacity to dream significant dreams might be possible only as an inherent power of the Intellect to grasp a certain reality by the exercise of its inner powers. Dreams can never be produced by an external influence, or entity, capable of penetrating into the sleeper's psyche: 'but remember as well all those tens of thousands of dreams that you and Rickon have dreamed that did not come true' (*CK*, 276). Thus, Maester Luwin's opinion of dreams results from his prior rejection of the existence of the web of organic links encompassing the whole of Creation which Aristotle, Macrobius and Aquinas would have taken for granted.

The maester's stubborn and disparaging attitude towards dreams results, to a significant extent, from the abject failure of his own youthful attempts at dabbling in the magical arts. Behind this failure lies the deep conviction that magic is 'only a different sort of knowledge' (*CK*, 274), a branch of learning studied as an intellectual pursuit which ultimately earns the accomplished scholar another metal link in the maester's chain:

> Perhaps magic was once a mighty force in the world, but no longer. What little remains is no more than the wisp of smoke that lingers in the air after a great fire has burned out, and even that is fading. Valyria was the last ember, and Valyria is gone. The dragons are no more, the giants are dead, the children of the forest forgotten with all their lore.
>
> No, my prince. Jojen Reed may have had a dream or two that he believes came true, but he does not have the greensight. No living man has that power. (*CK*, 276)

Thus, in Maester's Luwin's rationalist view, magic is understood as an ability to impose a certain pattern of alteration into the set of the physical laws that determine the functioning of the natural world. It is not the ability to penetrate more deeply into the elemental texture of natural phenomena that cognition – based on the external senses – would allow (as would have been the medieval conceptualization). Hence, for Luwin, magic could only exist as a stable element occupying a niche within the system of physical laws, rather than as an intermediate level in the Intellect's contact with the realm of the spiritual where the Intellect is the junior partner, dependent on the active influence and guidance of the spiritual agent.[16] Consequently, he emphatically rejects the possibility of an external cause for dream visions.

Looking at the wider context a clear symbolic aura surrounds Maester Luwin. His bitter dismissal of the supernatural is voiced in the northernmost bulwark of human civilization, close to the Haunted Forest, the greatest and most intricate symbiotic organism of his world. The Forest possesses a form of collective consciousness that extends well beyond the sensorially accessible layer of Nature. In this context, Maester Luwin is clearly conceived as one of two polar opposites, both vying for influence over Bran, destined to become the chief receptacle and catalyst for the Westeros-Wide-Web of collective consciousness. Implicitly juxtaposed with the instinctive, unpremeditated insights of Old Nan, Maester Luwin represents the narrowly rationalist mental circuit of the civilization that has developed in Westeros under the conditions prevalent in the last two centuries: a viewpoint that will be obliterated by the dramatic developments unveiled in the course of the narrative.

It is essentially for this reason that Maester Luwin's persistent rationalism becomes, in context, crushed by the weight of heroic fantasy's generic conventions; these stem from the narrative textual tradition that inherits the medieval embrace of the marvellous and the spiritual. In fact, beyond Winterfell, the belief in external causation of dream visions has wide currency among the population. Archmaester Marwyn moots the idea to Samwise Tarly during his sojourn in Oldtown, speaking of 'the sorcerers of the Freehold' who 'could enter a man's dreams and give him visions' (*FC*, 537–8). The idea is enshrined in the prayer formulae of the Faith of the Seven: 'The Maiden dances through the sky, she lives in every lover's sigh / Her smiles teach the birds to fly, and give dreams to little children' (*SS*, 439). These two examples not only testify to the ubiquitous character of the belief that dream visions are efficacious across Martin's secondary world but also show that the phenomenon transcends barriers of culture and religion. The two above-mentioned references to externally influenced dream visions could be referred back to Macrobius's *visum* and *oraculum*, respectively. The whole medieval spectrum of possible dream interactions with the supernatural, we might expect, be encountered in the course of *A Song of Ice and Fire*. However, neither of the two above types of dream is directly presented in the narrative; yet these references still create the expectations determining the scope of narrative possibilities within this secondary world.

To repeat: Martin's narrative never attempts to convey a simple reflection of the medieval hierarchization of the dreaming experience, nor does it ever aim at reinstating a medieval conceptualization of the dream-phenomenon. Instead it seeks to revitalize the idea of the inherent meaningfulness of dreams by resorting to a modern conception of dreams: one derived from the early twentieth-century psychoanalytical approach. This treats dreams as reflecting the innermost psychological impulses of the individual consciousness. This focus on what Aquinas terms 'the inwards causes of dreams' is Martin's starting point in the hierarchy of signification produced by the dreaming experience as one element in his narrative's psychological reality.

Many instances of the *somnium* kind of dream are experienced by various characters of *A Song of Ice and Fire* in the course of their troubled careers. Thus Jon Snow is visited by hectic reminiscences of the daily fighting routine while defending Castle Black against the wildlings: 'His dreams were strange and formless, full of strange voices, shouts and cries, and the sound of a warhorn, blowing low and loud, a single deep booming note that lingered in the air' (*SS*, 647). Two key words convey the vague nature of this form of dream experience for most of the characters: 'strange' and 'formless'. So too in the restless dreams of Catelyn Stark during her effective house arrest at Riverrun: 'That night Catelyn slept fitfully, haunted by formless dreams of her children, the lost and the dead' (*SS*, 28). Tyrion's anxious dreams, which haunt him during his journey up the Rhoyne in the company of Ser Jorah, are similarly indistinct: 'His dreams were full of grey, stony hands reaching for him from out of the fog, and a stair that led up to his father' (*DD*, 734). This kind of dream experience is a projection of present waking anxiety: unfocused, twisted images reflecting a current preoccupation, and occurs frequently in the novels. A common motif in this sort of dream is the dreamer's sense of losing his or her identity: '"I dreamed about the queen," he said. "I was on my knees before her, swearing my allegiance, but she mistook me for my brother, Jaime, and fed me to her dragons"' (*DD*, 138). This, however, is not the only mode in which a prolonged trauma experienced in waking hours manifests in dreams. Other dream visions frequently take the form of idyllic projections of the character's innermost wishes and provide solace amidst current hardships. Sam Tarly dreams of his home during his desperate march to reach the Wall after the Watch's raid debacle. Here, as the lord of the family estate (and presumably as husband of Gilly), Sam takes his father's place at the head of the table during a feast in honour of his Night Watch companions (*SS*, 440–1). Similarly, Daenerys dreams of herself and Daario Naharis as 'man and wife, simple folk who lived a simple life in a tall stone house with a red door' during her troubled time as the ruler of Meereen (*DD*, 252).

Arya and Sansa both regularly experience dreams that bring them back to Winterfell. Arya continues to be haunted by the visions of home happiness on her way north with Yoren and the Night's Watch recruits (*CK*, 22–4), while Sansa has this type of dream in the days after her forced marriage to Tyrion, and also later, during her sojourn at the Eyrie (*SS*, 543): 'She had been back in Winterfell, running through the godswood with her Lady. Her father had been there, and her brothers, all of them warm and safe. If only dreaming could make it so' (*SS*, 543). Brienne of Tarth experiences a homecoming dream vision during her final night as a prisoner of the Brotherhood without Banners before she is led out for execution: 'This time she dreamed that she was home again, at Evenfall. Through the tall arched windows of her lord father's hall she could see the sun just going down. I was safe here. I was safe' (*FC*, 499). All these dreams represent deeply personal projections of yearning for an unattainable state of psychological equilibrium; comfort is provided by the reassuring presence of loved ones. Yet, despite their decidedly intimate nature, the visions that visit the characters in their most turbulent and psychologically demanding moments all centre around domestic idylls in the family environment. This establishes a sort of common denominator between characters who are otherwise quite dissimilar, even those who feel intense enmity towards one another. This common ground reinforces a sense of basic humanity in responses and impulses; on the intellectual level this objectivizes the foundation of the inner psychological experience. Within the text, the uniformity of emotional responses helps to develop characters whose basic function in the narrative would normally require only a one-dimensional, stock quality. Compare two passages describing this particular kind of dream, affecting Catelyn Stark and Cersei Lannister: 'As she slept amidst the rolling grasslands, Catelyn dreamt that Bran was whole again, that Arya and Sansa held hands, that Rickon was still a babe at her breast. Robb, crownless, played with a wooden sword, and when all were safe asleep, she found Ned in her bed, smiling' (*CK*, 209) and: 'Cersei dreamed a long sweet dream where Jaime was her husband and their son was still alive' (*DD*, 1175).

Dreams which project the innermost concerns, constituting personalized incarnations of some of the human psyche's most profound instinctual impulses, are vital in deepening the psychological portrayal of some key characters in the narrative, broadening the presentation of their emotional scope. This technique clearly reflects a modern outlook, extending significantly beyond the medieval understanding of this type of dream. This approach – enhancing the psychological depth of characters by relating them to basic human instincts – is quite distant from medieval conceptions of personality: there a character's significance corresponds to the intensity of their articulation of a shared emotion.

A unique example of this is the sequence of two dreams experienced by Tyrion Lannister during his troubled convalescence after the siege of King's Landing. The first of the dreams is the familiar escapist vision where the adversities of waking life are overcome by a vision of harmony and tranquillity:

> This time he dreamed he was at a feast, a victory feast in some great hall. He had a high seat on the dais, and men were lifting their goblets and hailing him as hero. Marillion was there, the singer who'd journeyed with them through the Mountains of the Moon. He played his woodharp and sang of the imp's daring deeds. Even his father was smiling with approval. When the song was over, Jaime rose from his place, commanded Tyrion to kneel, and touched him first on one shoulder and then on the other with his golden sword, and he rose up a knight. Shae was waiting to embrace him. She took him by the hand, laughing and teasing, calling him her giant of Lannister. (*CK*, 575–6)

The idyllic character of this dream appears so far removed from reality that, more than in any other case, its effect is likely to be a subtle psychological torture rather than any compensatory psychological boost. For this reason, it clearly indicates how far a lifetime of social exclusion has had a traumatic effect on Tyrion's tender psychic constitution. Tyrion's vision is unique; it is the only one of the escapist dreams experienced by the characters of *A Song of Ice and Fire* that is not constituted by the domestic bliss of quiet family life. The true significance of this fact emerges in Tyrion's second dream during his period of imposed oblivion in the depths of the Red Keep: 'He dreamed of a better place, a snug little cottage by the sunset sea. The walls were lopsided and cracked and the floor had been made of packed earth, but he had always been warm there, even when they let the fire go out. She used to tease me about that, he remembered' (CK, 576–7). This lengthy passage describes an escapist dream which is not an idyllic visualization of all the wished-for things that the current waking reality fails to deliver. Instead, it is evoked from the deeper recesses of memory, constituting a lucid recollection of past bliss. The activity of dreaming allows Tyrion to recover a deeply suppressed memory, dreamed as it is remembered. Viewed in this context, Tyrion's mental projection, recalling his short-lived married happiness with his first wife, provides the solace of recollecting personal fulfilment in the most concrete form. There is no nostalgic idealization that might blur the scene's detailed character. In this sense, of all inwardly produced dreams, Tyrion's is most lacking in what Milton would have called the 'addition strange' which, in *A Song of Ice and Fire*, is a ubiquitous feature of dreams originating in recollection of the past.

The uniqueness of Tyrion's dream emerges most clearly when juxtaposed with other comparable dream experiences. For most of them the recollection of the past that resurfaces in dreams is connected to some pivotal, traumatic moment, the consequences of which continue to haunt the person's present life in waking reality. Daenerys returns obsessively to the moment of Khal Drogo's gruesome execution of her brother:

> Viserys stood before her, screaming. 'The dragon does not beg, slut. You do not command the dragon. I am the dragon, and I will be crowned.' The molten gold trickled down his face like wax, burning deep channels in his flesh. 'I am the dragon and I will be crowned!' he shrieked, and his fingers snapped like snakes, biting at her nipples, pinching, twisting, even as his eyes burst and ran like jelly down seared and blackened cheeks. (GT, 687)

> She dreamt of her dead brother.
> Viserys looked just as he had the last time she'd seen him. His mouth was twisted in anguish, his hair was burnt, and his face was black and smoking where the molten gold had run down across his brow and cheeks and into his eyes. (DD, 1532)

Although with the passage of time between the two dreams the horrific quality of the remembered vision of Viserys's dramatic death recedes into gruesome realism, the image continues to catalyse Daenerys's sense of guilt and bereavement. The phantasm itself remains essentially unchanged, continuing to mark the same past trauma. Yet, as the paralysing fear that Daenerys experiences in the first dream gives way to aching wistfulness, it is clear how the subsequent incarnation of the traumatic memory indicates her progress towards mental maturity.

Throughout *A Song of Ice and Fire*, there are numerous instances of dreams stemming from traumatic memories of the past. Sansa is visited by a dream where she is attacked by a crowd of 'faces twisted into monstrous inhuman masks' after she is mobbed and nearly raped in the Riot of King's Landing (CK, 469). Later she is repeatedly visited by various nightmarish reminiscences from the period of her incarceration in the capital: 'Once she dreamed it was still her marrying Joff, not Margaery, and on their wedding night he turned into the headsman Ilyn Payne' (*SS*, 157). Similarly, Stannis Baratheon is troubled by dreams recalling Renly's murder (*CK*, 381), Varys returns to the moment of his mutilation (*CK*, 402), Theon is visited by spectral images of the people he killed while ruler of Winterfell (*CK*, 496–7), Jaime Lannister relives in a dream the killing of King Aerys (*SS*, 110–11), while Brienne's dreams return, once again, to the death of Renly, and her confrontation with the bear in the Harrenhal bear pit (*FC*, 110, 496). Tyrion's dreams centre on the time he spent in the Sky-Cells at the Eyrie (*SS*, 179) and the moment of his killing of Tywin (*DD*, 878). Davos's dreams remind him of the dramatic death of his sons in the battle for King's Landing (*SS*, 51). Finally, Cersei repeatedly returns to the memory of her girlhood visit to the fortune teller who so accurately predicts her future (*FC*, 188; 424–6).

The vast majority of dreams that evoke past experiences are projections of guilt, either for one's own wrongdoing or for failure to fulfil a social or moral obligation. They may also provide a painful reminder of past powerlessness in the face of adversity. Dreams about the past are invariably presented as destructive experiences: the sense of ethical failure results in a weakening of the characters' ability to cope with the challenges posed by the present. The dreams themselves are treated as resulting from psychic trauma; they are never instruments of mental healing or divine intercession. Nor do the dreams ever effectively predict the future, for they merely project present apprehension onto expectations, devoid of any extraordinary form of insight.

Arguably, the most informative example of dreams in this context emerges when we juxtapose the two respective dreams of Eddard Stark and Jaime Lannister that recall the dramatic events surrounding Robert Baratheon's rebellion against the last Targaryen king. These feature the very same knights, comprising the last Kingsguard of Aerys II:

> They were seven, facing three. In the dream as it had been in life. Yet these were no ordinary three. They waited before the round tower, the red mountains of Dorne at their backs, their white cloaks blowing in the wind. And these were no shadows; their faces burned clear, even now. Ser Arthur Dayne, the Sword of the Morning, had a sad smile on his lips. The hilt of the great sword Dawn poked up over his right shoulder. Ser Oswell Whent was on one knee, sharpening his blade with a whetstone. Across his white enameled helm, the black bat of his House spread its wings. Between them stood fierce old Ser Gerold Hightower, the White Bull, Lord Commander of the Kingsguard. (*GT*, 392)

> He saw them too. They were armored all in snow, it seemed to him, and ribbons of mist swirled back from their shoulders. The visors of their helms were closed, but Jaime Lannister did not need to look upon their faces to know them.

> Five had been his brothers. Oswell Whent and Jon Darry. Lewyn Martell, a prince of Dorne. The White Bull, Gerold Hightower. Ser Arthur Dayne, Sword of the Morning. And beside them, crowned in mist and grief with his long hair streaming

behind him, rode Rhaegar Targaryen, Prince of Dragonstone and rightful heir to the Iron Throne. (*SS*, 419–20)

Both noblemen are afflicted by their respective dreams in very similar circumstances and in corresponding physical conditions: Lord Eddard dreams of the confrontation at Prince Rhaegar's Tower of Joy during his imprisonment in the dungeons beneath the Red Keep, when he is in considerable physical pain and has a high fever. Jaime Lannister dreams of his fellow members of the Kingsguard during his stay in Harrenhal following his capture and mutilation by the Brave Companions; his physical state is similar to Eddard's and his prospects of survival seem equally bleak. While these circumstances naturally account for the nightmarish character of their dreams, significantly, the figures of the Kingsguardsmen allow the articulation of the self-accusations troubling the two characters in their hour of weakness and pain. For Lord Eddard the contempt and scorn expressed by the knights reinforces the sense of guilt he felt in the wake of his failure to free Lyanna from presumed captivity at the Tower of Joy. For Ser Jaime the same figures project the full ethical context of his killing of Aerys. These visitations by the ghosts of the past do not offer a point of contact with a transcendental reality but rather show how the subconscious reasserts itself over higher intellectual registers in times of stress and physical frailty. In Martin's secondary world we do not directly witness instances of any extra-natural intrusion into the individual psyche of the kind that would result in the *visum* type of dream, yet the more modern incarnation of the category of *insomnium* may be identified here as a powerful destructive force against which particular characters must continuously strive in order to keep their mental balance.

In Jaime's feverish dream in Harrenhal, the master swordsman still enjoys full command of a healthy right hand: 'I felt it, I felt the strength in my fingers, and the rough leather of the sword's grip' (*SS*, 420). Similarly, we learn later that: 'In his dreams Jaime always had two hands; one was made of gold, but it worked just like the other'(*FC*, 389). This detail becomes a crucial marker for a very special example of a dream experience. Uniquely for Martin's narrative, this might be classified as *oraculum* in Macrobius's classification, or *admonitio* if we choose to follow Calcidius. The dream in question occurs to Jaime when staying as guest of honour at Riverrun, now commanded by Lord Emmon Frey:

That night he dreamt that he was back in the Great Sept of Baelor, still standing vigil over his father's corpse. The sept was still and dark, until a woman emerged from the shadows and walked slowly to the bier. 'Sister?' he said.
But it was not Cersei. She was all in grey, a silent sister. A hood and veil concealed her features, but he could see the candles burning in the green pools of her eyes. (*FC*, 528)

As we can see, the dream unveils itself on a fundamentally different cognitive plane from those in which Lord Eddard and Jaime succumb to troubled recollections of the events of Robert's Rebellion. There the identity of the dream-persons, the context evoked by their presence and their relation with external reality are determined by the dream visions functioning as internally produced projections of subconscious psychological impulses. Here, in contrast, Jaime is visited by a person he initially has trouble identifying. His mysterious interlocutor has a better understanding of the nature of the reality within which the meeting takes place:

> 'Who are you?' He had to hear her say it.
>
> 'The question is, who are you?'
>
> 'This is a dream.'
>
> 'Is it?' She smiled sadly. 'Count your hands, child.'
>
> One. One hand, clasped tight around the sword hilt. Only one. 'In my dreams I always have two hands.' He raised his right arm and stared uncomprehending at the ugliness of his stump. (*FC*, 528)

As in the numerous examples of dreaming discussed above, Jaime's dream has its origins in the past, but, unlike the other dreams, this one does not stem from a personal memory or a recollected image. Considering that Jaime's mother, Lady Joanna Lannister, died in childbirth when he was seven years old, his initial lack of recognition seems justified. Any memory that Jaime had of his mother would reflect the childlike cognitive powers through which they were originally impressed in his memory. If this figure is not recognized, it must be because Jaime's adult perception is confronted with a vision which seems to exist independently from the phantasms that *imaginatio* would form based on impressions evoked from *memoria*. In other words, adhering to the principles of the medieval cognitive model, what Jaime experiences possesses a quality of existential clarity which elevates it above the level of the internal senses. Consequently, Jaime sees his mutilated hand not as a projection of what his *imaginatio* would select for him on the basis of the memorative power as the preferred image but rather as how his Intellect knows his hand is at present.

This places the dream in the category of externally inspired intellectual visions (i.e. Aquinas's category 4), akin to the revelatory or instructive dreams typical of dream allegory.[17] This seems to be the main thrust of what Lady Joanna bequeaths to her eldest son for his further meditation:

> 'We all dream of things we cannot have. Tywin dreamed that his son would be a great knight, that his daughter would be a queen. He dreamed they would be so strong and brave and beautiful that no one would ever laugh at them.'
>
> 'I am a knight,' he told her, 'and Cersei is a queen.'
>
> A tear rolled down her cheek. The woman raised her hood again and turned her back on him. Jaime called after her, but already she was moving away, her skirt whispering lullabies as it brushed across the floor. Don't leave me, he wanted to call, but of course she'd left them long ago. (*FC*, 528)

We might, of course, still choose to treat Joanna Lannister's message for her son as merely reflecting Jaime's dawning realization of the ultimate futility of his family's ambitions and aspirations. Yet if we choose this model, the figure of Lord Tywin's wife would still preside over a mental process in which her son achieves a novel kind of insight into his present situation. This brings his Intellect to a new level of clarity, causing Jaime to see through the appearances of formal titles and honours and leads him to consider the more profound existential reality behind them. For the Lannister family, this becomes the reality of disintegration and failure. The important thing is that the mental perspective to which Jaime is exposed in his dream extends far beyond his personal experience; it manifestly reflects Lady Joanna's wealth of wisdom, the sum of what she experienced during her lifetime and the evident profound awareness and understanding of her family's present situation.

All this has the effect of placing Lady Joanna on some more objective and real plane of existence than the realm of *imaginatio*'s *phantasmatas*, setting Jaime's dream apart from most of the dreams experienced by the characters of *A Song of Ice and Fire*. Thus it falls within the medieval tradition of the enlightening dream vision, one which extends beyond the sphere of the natural, making more direct use of the Intellect in absorbing and digesting the experience. The uniqueness of Jaime's dream visitation is all the more noticeable if we consider that, in Martin's narrative, there is no instance of any dream vision resulting from direct contact with any of the archetypes who reflect the divine aspects in the Faith of the Seven. Secondly, the only dreams clearly and objectively based on an external intrusion into the characters' psyche rely on the projections of phantasms (or at least, originate in this form), rather than being a clearly conveyed message destined for the operation of the Intellect.

Martin's secondary world does take from the medieval tradition the category of externally induced dream visions that convey to the dreamer a reliable prediction of future events or a message of advice or admonition. The absence of any objectively verifiable spiritual presence in this fictional world causes this category to function differently than would have been the case in a medieval narrative. Thus, in *A Song of Ice and Fire*, we adhere to the assumption, unanimously recognized in the medieval outlook, that it requires an infinitely superior form of consciousness to exert an external influence on the human psyche. The only entity endowed with such a form of consciousness is the collective natural organism which is made up of the web of weirwood trees which extends over the whole of Westeros, one which is also capable of sensorially accessing the past. This imposing natural formation has its command centre in the Haunted Forest north of the Wall, where the human catalyst for the collective consciousness is the resident Greenseer: in the books, Ser Brynden Rivers. A human mind is thus positioned at the pinnacle of this awesome natural organism, one which is able to interpret the staggeringly extensive data available from this massive apparatus of universal prescience; thus the whole organism continues to devote its symbiotic interest to the fortunes of human civilization.

This natural entity is responsible for three kinds of dreams experienced by various of Martin's characters: the greendreams, such as those which routinely affect Jojen Reed; the warg dreams experienced by the younger Starks; and Bran Stark's three-eyed crow visions. Although both Jojen and Osha refer occasionally to 'the gods' as the source of these types of dreams, this seems to be a mere figure of speech, expressing the incredible nature of the interaction between the natural monster-mind and the individual human psyche.

Jojen Reed's greendreams consist in the dreamer's being given occasional access to visions of future occurrences. They are frequently enigmatic, allegorical visions; this renders them useless for intellectual analysis, and they are effective solely as conveyors of intuitive premonitions: "'The green dreams take strange shapes sometimes,' Jojen admitted. 'The truth of them is not always easy to understand'" (*CK*, 324). The greendreams correspond neatly to the medieval rationale behind the formation of dream visions; Jojen's experiences may be interpreted as the *imaginatio*'s inexpert transformation of externally induced sensory impulses into phantasms.

Thus, the information about the Ironborn's future invasion of the north and the sack of Winterfell is conveyed to Jojen through an unsettling vision veiled in allegorical imagery:

> I dreamed that the sea was lapping all around Winterfell. I saw black waves crashing against the gates and towers, and then the salt water came flowing over the walls and filled the castle. Drowned men were floating in the yard. When I first dreamed the dream, back at Greywater, I didn't know their faces, but now I do. That Alebelly is one, the guard who called our names at the feast. Your septon's another. Your smith as well. (*CK*, 324)

Typically for this sort of prophecy, the full realization of its significance is achieved when one recognizes its predictions coming true in the present reality: 'One of the ironmen handed Reek a sword, and he laid it at Theon's feet and swore obedience to House Greyjoy and King Balon. Bran could not look. The green dream was coming true' (*CK*, 417). To apply the medieval terminology here, Jojen's greendreams can be categorized as a specific variant of *visio*. While this type of dream would have been quite recognizable to the medieval mind, the nature of the causative agent behind its operation reflects Martin's modern outlook on the role and propensities of the supernatural.

Similarly, the skin-changing dreams experienced by Bran, Arya, Sansa and Jon seem to originate in their symbiotic relationship with the Westeros-Wide-Web of weirwood wisdom. The warg dreams experienced by the siblings who inadvertently entered into a symbiotic relationship with the direwolf pups are, again, a projection of the intense bond developed between humans and animals at the sensory level. Consequently, these dreams allow the human mind to experience the more intense forms of sensory perception natural for the animal's interaction with the environment:

> The smells filled his head, alive and intoxicating; the green muddy stink of the hot pools, the perfume of rich rotting earth beneath his paws, the squirrels in the oaks. The scent of squirrel made him remember the taste of hot blood and the way the bones would crack between his teeth. Slaver filled his mouth. He had eaten no more than half a day past, but there was no joy in dead meat, even deer. He could hear the squirrels chittering and rustling above him, safe among their leaves, but they knew better than to come down to where his brother and he were prowling. (*CK*, 51–2)

From the standpoint of medieval psychology, this type of dream experience does not penetrate above the level of the internal senses and does not directly involve the Intellect. Although the notion of skin-changing was current in medieval culture, it was not particularly connected to the idea of dreaming, nor is it so associated in the modern fantasy genre. Martin's association of the two concepts lies in the idea that Nature is a single big collective organism, consisting in a web of symbiotic relations between its constituent elements. Thus, the development of a link between humans and direwolves is Nature's way of extending assistance to selected members of the human species by extending to them the protective benefits of a symbiotic relationship.[18]

The relationship itself is based on sharing those levels of consciousness that function in relation to the five external and four internal wits (or what we would now properly call sensory perception and the instinctive interpretation of its data) which both species share. The fact that most of the time the interconnection between the humans and the direwolves manifests itself in dreams would not have been surprising to any medieval scholar; it would have been considered a natural consequence of the fact that neither the Intellect nor the Will plays any part in the processing of the phantasms through which a skin-changing dream experience could be conveyed. No relation with the animal consciousness may be established at this level as beasts do not possess an intellectual soul, but merely the *anima sensitiva*.[19]

Despite the fact that many characters are not granted 'greensight', through skin-changing dreams they are enabled to interact with the complex natural world that Martin envisages. They come into direct contact with the sphere of collective perception, as with Jon Snow when he encounters the apprentice Greenseer who once was his (presumed) half-brother, Bran Stark:

A weirwood.

It seemed to sprout from solid rock, its pale roots twisting up from a myriad of fissures and hairline cracks. The tree was slender compared to other weirwoods he had seen, no more than a sapling, yet it was growing as he watched, its limbs thickening as they reached for the sky. Wary, he circled the smooth white trunk until he came to the face. Red eyes looked at him. Fierce eyes they were, yet glad to see him. The weirwood had his brother's face. Had his brother always had three eyes?

Not always, came the silent shout. Not before the crow. (*CK*, 474)

Indeed, across all of Martin's secondary world, there is no more elaborate case of externally induced dreams than that of Bran's Three-Eyed Crow visions. These are all relatively cryptic messages veiled by allegorical images based on phantasms; they evolve with each successive dream and contain no directly intellectual form of illumination. Yet they do represent an echo of the medieval conception of dream visions as appropriate mental vehicles for exhortation to perform a specific action or to undertake a life-transforming mission. These come from a superior external agent and would roughly correspond to Calcidius's concept of *admonitio*.

The first of the numerous visions in which Eddard's younger son meets the Three-Eyed Crow is especially significant. The outside influence intruding into his dream seems to become decisive in his finding the mental and physical strength that allows him to regain consciousness and wake from the coma caused by his fall, enabling his final recovery:

> The ground was so far below him he could barely make it out through the grey mists that whirled around him, but he could feel how fast he was falling, and he knew what was waiting for him down there. Even in dreams, you could not fall forever. He would wake up in the instant before he hit the ground, he knew. You always woke up in the instant before you hit the ground. (*GT*, 156)

Bran's phantasm-based imagistic dream vision may be traced back to medieval antecedents. Animal figures frequently appeared in medieval dreams as representations of people; Chaucer's Criseyde sees Troilus as an eagle in a dream, while Troilus encounters his adversary Diomede as a boar. Consequently, it is not surprising that Bran is visited by Lord Brynden in the shape of a raven. This dream-vision feature is a logical extension of the capacity to access the collective consciousness of the weirwood trees, here allegorized as enjoying a bird's-eye view as if flying high over numerous locations.

The idea of falling has always been common in dream visions as conveying foreboding, or else of losing mental control or succumbing to negative outside pressure. Here the traditional meaning is reinforced by modern modes of decoding the signification of dreams. Thus, the motif may equally be construed as originating in an intertextual reference to Eve's disturbing dream in *Paradise Lost*: a projection of the psychosomatic process involved in the boy's struggle to muster the strength to recover consciousness. The ultimate meaning of Bran's dream experience would be compromised if we failed to incorporate a modern psychological context in its interpretation. The dream vision's medieval heritage is most prominent here because the narrative provides a cross-referential context confirming the objective existence of the superior external agent who influences Bran's visions. This, consequently, lends credibility to the visions and makes them an important element of the secondary world's objective reality. Viewed in this context, Bran's dreams not only provide the overriding motivation for his actions and determine his consequent behaviour but also define his role: special status has been bestowed on him, communicated through an external agent who penetrates his psyche in a dream. In this way, Martin's narrative redefines the externally induced dream vision by reinterpreting it in a modern psychological context, at the same time he preserves its textual role as an objective element in the consensual reality of the fictional world.

The creators of the HBO television series effectively exploited this tendency to see Bran's visions as a way to access the wider reality beyond the immediate experience of the characters. As the show moved beyond the original template of Martin's novels, Bran Stark's visitations of the past in the company of the Three-Eyed Raven allowed the introduction of pivotal past moments to the audience. Thus, it is through Bran's participation in the store of memories preserved by the collective consciousness of the weirwood as interconnected organism that the past emerges as context for the present action in the TV show. The audience is able to witness glimpses of the prehistory of Westeros, when the Children of the Forest flourished. Subsequently, Bran's visions converge ever more closely on scenes and situations relating increasingly directly to the main plot line's dramatic fulcrum. Bran's visions enable the audience to glimpse the everyday life of Brandon, Eddard and Lyanna Stark during their early adolescence spent under their father Rickard's principled guidance at Winterfell, before the dramatic developments of Robert's Rebellion. As Bran's visions begin to converge around the present, we see how the uncanny penetration of the present into the past caused Hodor's trauma – one which leaves him permanently stigmatized with a supposed mental disability.

Finally, Bran's visions focus on the one key event of the time of Robert's Rebellion: the confrontation between his father Eddard and the remnant of the King's Guard left to protect Lyanna in her presumed captivity at the Tower of Joy. In the novels, the reader experiences this specific moment in Westeros's history through the personal, troubled visions of Eddard Stark and, partly, through Jaime Lannister, at a much earlier juncture in the narrative. The TV audience is exposed to the events much later in the story, when it is becoming increasingly clear that, contrary to the received version of events preserved in Westerosi collective memory, knowledge of the actual facts may be the decisive factor in determining the whole narrative's final outcome. Consequently, the air of detached objectivity surrounding Bran's visions is enhanced, becoming the means through which Jon Snow's true identity is convincingly revealed. The TV plot introduces a novel element: the revelation of the unchivalric character of Eddard Stark's victory in single combat against Ser Arthur Dayne.

The revelations concerning Jon Snow's true parentage are thus offset by revelations about Lord Eddard's less-than-noble behaviour and his subsequent propagation of the untrue version of the story. This provides a counterpoint for Eddard's selflessness in protecting his nephew; it may imply that one motive behind his decision to protect the boy is his concern for his House's public image, along with a genuine care for the fruit of his sister's reckless affair with the prince.

Incorporating this new element into the story structure at this moment enhances the role of Bran's visions as the ultimate mental mechanism through which contact with timeless objective reality is achieved. Bran's increasing abilities allow him to access these coldly objective visions of the past: this test verifies the ultimate reality of the cinematic secondary world. Thus, the TV dream visions further enhance the medieval idea that dream visions may have an oracular character; some form of contact is achieved with an actual, tangible level of reality, one which remains inaccessible to the operation of the senses in regular, waking life.

The many manifestations of the dream experience that various characters are confronted within Martin's secondary world reflect the scope and variety implied in the medieval categorizations. The modes of understanding human cognitive processes most symptomatic of the High Medieval philosophical outlook are still useful in explaining some of the mechanisms behind the formation and psychological significance of the many dreams affecting the characters of *A Song of Ice and Fire*.

The hierarchical model of the human perceptive and intellectual functions current during the Middle Ages decisively determined the contemporaneous categorizations of the various types of dreams. The medieval range of opinion about the inherent validity and reliability of dream visions is reflected in Martin's narrative. Dream vision is highly significant in indicating the dramatic shifting and rearrangement of ontological boundaries as Martin's secondary world moves towards a more intense contact with the supernatural, a move typical of heroic fantasy. Thus the nature and content of the dream visions are as central to the psychological portrait of particular characters and to the definition of their narrative roles as they would once have been in medieval heroic narrative.

That the experience of dreaming has immanent significance is, in Martin's work, transformed by modern conceptions of dreaming as reflecting psychological processes – the influence of the contemporary psychoanalytical approach. Consequently dreams are highly internalized and their propensity to reflect the burden of past mental trauma dominates the text-worlds more emphatically than would have been the case in medieval literary texts. Key here is the lack of any tangible presence of the spiritual absolute in Martin's secondary world. The prophetic, visionary quality of externally induced dreams is significantly redefined, distancing them from the medieval legacy. Absent an objective providential presence in Martin's fictional universe, the oracular dream vision is anchored to an empirical conception of the organic character of Nature as macrocosm. The revelatory dream vision does not elevate the dreamer into hierophantic contact with the divine but rather permits him to penetrate deeper into the recesses of the collective subconscious stored in, and supported by, the symbiotic superintelligence of Nature.

Despite the inherently modern conceptualization of the mechanism responsible for revelatory dream visions, their textual function is evidently to reinforce the traditional concept of the seer, prophet or *magus*, a special character invested with supernatural abilities. Their narrative presence enhances the reader's ethical and ontological perspectives. This narrative mechanism lies at the heart of George R. R. Martin's eloquent dialogue with the medieval tradition.

10

The medievalist emotional economy in George R. R. Martin's *A Song of Ice and Fire*

Anna Czarnowus

In the *Introduction* to the *Cambridge Companion to Fantasy Literature* Edward James and Farah Mendlesohn develop a metaphor that is highly relevant to the discussion of medievalism in fantasy texts and also in the context of analysing the medieval and medievalist emotions in them:

> Fantasy is not so much a mansion as a row of terraced houses, such as the one that entranced us in C. S. Lewis's *The Magician's Nephew* with its connecting attics, each with a door that leads to another world. There are shared walls, and a certain level of consensus around the basic bricks, but the internal décor can differ wildly, and the lives lived in these terraced houses are discrete yet overheard.[1]

George R. R. Martin's *A Song of Ice and Fire* is built from similar bricks to those that construct other medievalist fantasy novels and all of them share the walls of medievalism as a fictional reproduction of, and fantasy about, the Middle Ages.[2] Yet, its internal décor remains original. What I shall focus on is an important part of this décor, namely how what I read about in the novel cycle relates to medieval emotions and, particularly, medieval theories of them. Furthermore, I shall examine how emotions in the novel cycle (and the TV show, where it is relevant to this discussion) are 'medievalized' to make us, the readers (and the viewers), feel that the fantasy characters belong to a distant past. All these are forms of medievalism, which means here trying to imagine how emotions were expressed and how they were present in the Middle Ages but also recreating them for use in Martin's fantasy narrative.

If there are differences between emotions in the fantasy cycle and in what can be observed in medieval culture, then the emotional economy of the cycle is not entirely medievalist. This image of emotions relies largely on our modern sensibility and manners of emotive expression. Here I shall analyse how emotions are presented in Martin's fantasy cycle and how they are distributed: to what extent they are present and in which directions they go. The circulation of emotions will also be discussed.[3] This study also attempts to further fill the earlier gap in criticism on medieval emotions other than love, a gap observed by Barbara H. Rosenwein in her introduction to the essay collection *Anger's Past: The Social Uses of an Emotion in the Middle Ages*.[4] Much research has been done on medieval emotions from its publication in 1998 onwards.[5] This chapter will not focus exclusively on love, which would otherwise be the easiest strategy to adopt in the case of Martin's cycle, where romance is an inseparable part both of aristocratic lives and those of the low folk. In an article published in 2018 Carolyne Larrington focuses on pride and shame as attached to the idea of personal honour, anger and romantic love as emotions that are 'imagined as typically medieval'.[6] Here I will also argue that emotions 'medievalize' the text but will look at these three representative 'medievalizing' emotions in the cycle from the perspective of the medieval theories of emotions with which they appear to engage. I will look at not only how love is represented in the text but also how honour (and its concomitant emotions of shame and sympathy) acts in *A Song of Ice and Fire* and *Game of Thrones* and what role anger plays in this narrative.

Here the terms emotion/affect/passion/appetite/sentiment will be used interchangeably, even though there are distinct differences between them that go back to the philosophical and proto-psychological background examined within the field of the history of emotions.[7] This does not mean that this background will not be touched upon, since understanding the medieval expression of emotions is not possible without referring to St Augustine and St Thomas Aquinas.[8] Ute Frevert's constructivist approach, visible in her idea of emotions 'lost and found', will be invoked most frequently, since she treats emotions as constantly in a state of flux; the specific cultural norms in a given society depend on their expression. Over time emotions can be lost irretrievably, as exemplified by honour, but some of them can be 'found' again, in the sense that they can be examined from the perspective of the history of emotions, even if the emotions themselves do not exist any longer.[9]

Medieval emotions

When talking about medieval emotions it is safer to investigate the ones expressed rather than the ones that might be felt.[10] Ute Frevert insists that the distinction is necessary, since in medieval literature investigating what is felt is difficult if not impossible, unless the narrator or the characters themselves explicitly state what the character's inner emotions are.[11] From the perspective of emotion history, for a long time there was a fallacy that in the Middle Ages people felt completely different emotions than we do in modernity. In fact, emotions are probably neither entirely universal nor entirely socially constructed: historical emotions may appear to have been completely different from ours, but this may be a matter of how feeling is expressed.[12] The fallacy that the medieval period was both more emotional and differently emotional from modernity has often been exemplified with the famous passage from Huizinga's *Waning of the Middle Ages*, where he stated that, 500 years before he wrote these words in 1919, that is, in the late Middle Ages, 'the contrast between suffering and joy, between adversity and happiness, appeared more striking'.[13] What is often overlooked by critics is that he refers here to the outer forms of human life: ultimately he means the expression of emotions rather than the emotions themselves. In contrast with what often has been claimed, he does not argue that the emotions themselves were different from ours nor that they were the same as ours. This is an important fallacy which demonstrates that the 'search' for medieval emotions, also those 'lost and found', started early in the history of medieval studies and that readers wanted to hear from Huizinga what he did not say.[14] From our point of view it is safer to claim, after Huizinga, that late medieval mob expressed their emotions vehemently. It was probably socially acceptable to do so and even encouraged, since loud expression of emotions created an atmosphere of togetherness and the sharing of feelings, for example, in religious devotion or expressing attachment to a ruler.[15] The model in Martin's cycle is medievalist in this respect, since any popular gathering in King's Landing tends to be accompanied by shouting and other expressions of emotional reactions. Such are the reactions when Ned Stark is exposed to the crowd as a traitor: 'A thousand voices were screaming, but Arya never heard them. Prince Joffrey [. . .] no, *King* Joffrey [. . .] stepped out from behind the shields of his Kingsguard' (*GT*, 702). The crowd reacting to the king's words and actions is an indispensable part of the execution, as was in fact the case at various historical executions in the Middle Ages. The expression of feelings of hostility and the sharing of them is thoroughly medievalist here, since it attempts to recreate how most readers imagine medieval expression of emotions must have been – and how it actually was.

The basic medievalist nature of the universe of Martin's cycle cannot be questioned. There are knights and ladies, values such as honour, cruelty and violence (discussed by Kristina Hildebrand in this volume), and blood feud, to mention only the most obvious elements of this imagined world. In his monograph devoted to fantasy literature, Tomasz Z. Majkowski lists the key medievalist elements of Martin's text: architecture, feudalism, tournaments, minstrels, supernatural creatures and genealogy.[16] For Majkowski, however, the list would not be complete without discussing the emotional background of the actions described, since Martin 'introduces the three most important emotions that cement the community of romance knights: the sense of brotherhood, which is expressed in the institution of a chivalric order, the requirement of fidelity symbolized by the oath of allegiance, and romantic love that cannot be fulfilled directly, hence it is expressed through chivalric actions'.[17] Majkowski's presentation of the emotion perspective is valuable, even though the brotherhood he lists is not an emotion, since the sense of brotherhood and fidelity characterizes behaviour rather than constitutes anything that one may feel. On the other hand, emotion is demonstrable through behaviour and in the case of medieval, rather than medievalist, literature it is more tangible than speculating about what people may be assumed to have felt. For as, Michael Champion and Andrew Lynch observe, all that can be examined are only 'human emotional remains "left behind" from the pre-modern world'.[18] Medievalist fantasy literature, I argue, appears to record some of those emotional remains, even if the sense of brotherhood is actually grounded in some other emotions. As for the position of love as an emotion, that is indubitable. Yet once again the presentation of love in the novel cycle is so diverse that it could be the subject of this whole chapter; this study aspires to be more inclusive.

Medievalist emotions and philosophy

In the eighteenth and nineteenth centuries interest in emotions flourished, but even then they were perceived from different angles due to different philosophical systems that shaped the contemporary worldviews. In an article from 2014 Ute Frevert writes:

> What made the eighteenth and nineteenth centuries so special was the parallel existence of different systems of thought, each of which defined its own concepts and differentiated them from others. There was the long-established Aristotelian tradition, which had been systematized by Thomas Aquinas, and which was influential well into the modern period. Its core concept was pathos/pathé, or *Leidenschaft* in German. The soul (anima) was the site of these passions, moved by them and able to pick up sensation of pleasure or displeasure. This sensation, this movement, was transferred from the soul to the body and set it in motion.[19]

The Aristotelian vision of the body as animated by passions that provoke movement put passions at the centre of human existence. It also claimed that the movement of the soul comes first; then the body is animated by the soul. Aquinas had taken over this perspective and made it relevant for the Middle Ages. The other model, which coexisted with the ancient and medieval ones in the eighteenth century, was that of Hobbes and Spinoza. They, as Frevert writes, 'ascribed a positive and vital function to affect and passion'.[20] Nevertheless, like Descartes and Leibniz before them, Hobbes and Spinoza distinguished between what the medieval models included as 'passions', that is, 'life-preserving drives and bodily instincts', and 'conscious morally relevant *sentiments*'.[21]

These two perspectives – emotions which agitate the soul and then the body and Hobbes's and Spinoza's theorization of bodily instincts and conscious sentiments – coexist in *A Song of Ice and Fire*. On the one hand, the relationship between Cersei Lannister and her brother Jaime may be seen as a feeling that agitates their souls, reflected in how their bodies are moved. After all, the erotic love between them is unquestionable and it even leads to the initial fall and the final reconstruction of House Stark (in the TV show) through Bran's accession to the throne. On the other hand, love is equally an unconquerable bodily instinct here, as in Hobbes and Spinoza. Love moved the Lannisters' bodies, and upon the discovery of their secret by Bran, the fear of disclosing the secret made Jaime push Bran off the tower with Cersei's approval. Yet, this crippling ultimately led to Bran's survival, to his achieving the status of 'the keeper of all our memories' and to his kingship (8.6).

The love between Jaime and Cersei resembles what Aquinas termed 'passions of the soul'. Heribertus Dwi Kristano defines them as those that 'happen to corporeal animate beings because such passions involve both a somatic dimension as their material component and a psychical dimension as their formal component'.[22] In the case of love between the two siblings, the somatic dimension is when their blood heats up whenever they see each other and the psychical dimension is their desire to be together regardless of the consequences.[23] Thus, the somatic part of their mutual attachment is as important as the psychical one. Their incestuous love affair is medievalized in this manner. I cannot argue that Martin recreates Aquinas's theory of passions consciously, but by conflating the bodily drive with what is otherwise mental he creates an image that is more in accordance with this particular medieval theory of emotions than it would be otherwise.

All the above, however, contradicts a later element within the theory of emotions: the seventeenth- and eighteenth-century idea of emotions as morally ennobling sentiments. Jaime cannot detach himself from Cersei completely, even though this corporeal and psychical drive is destructive from the perspective of morality. This passion is stronger than any conventional sense of morality, one that bans incest and it is stronger than loyalty towards the king. Love as passion, as defined by Aquinas, makes Jaime a highly conflicted character, since his love affair with the queen makes him break the oath of loyalty to the king. It may be even seen as an act of treason; hence the incestuous love is degrading rather than ennobling. It is much less justifiable than the slaying of the Mad King Aerys that Jaime felt compelled to do. This made him not only an oathbreaker but also the saviour of Aerys's people, whom the king would otherwise have exterminated. Being disloyal is a vice as the love affair of Jaime and Cersei proves, but it may also save the lives of others.

Aquinas's model of emotions as passions is not, however, the only medieval element that is traceable in Martin. Another is Augustine's concept of will as an important determinant in emotions. To quote Monique Scheer, 'Augustine more or less followed Neoplatonic ideas and divided the human soul into understanding, memory, and will, viewing the passions as being in the service of the will.'[24] In the novel cycle, Robb breaks the promise to marry Walder Frey's daughter and he marries Jeyne Westerling instead. This is how Larrington explains it: 'In the books Robb is trapped into marrying a minor nobleman's daughter, Jeyne Westerling, for whom he has little feeling: his idealistic adherence to the honour-code drives him to atone for her defloration through marriage. The showrunners, in contrast, reference Robb's marriage as a true and modern love; yet it is his undoing.'[25] The novel cycle makes frequent reference to the medieval idea of honour, also practised in personal relations, and shows how complex this practice of honour can be if it leads to Robb's death during the Red Wedding. Shannon Wells-Lassagne calls Robb's union with Jeyne Westerling a relationship made 'not for love, but for honor, after having taken her innocence in his grief at the supposed death of his brothers'.[26] As for the TV show version, it does not have to be regarded as a narrative in which Robb's marriage is 'modernized'. It can just as well be attuned to Augustine's concept of emotions as subjected to the will. Robb may have married Talisa in order to show that his will as a ruler had a primary importance. Then, following Augustine's argument, Robb's emotions followed what he wished for. If so, Robb's marriage to Talisa may not have resulted from what Mariah Larsson called the 'follies of love' in the cycle but rather from subjecting his emotions to the will.[27]

The model of emotions is Augustinian here: the will follows passions and not reason. The passions are likely to lead one astray and this may cause wilfulness, since reason does not control the process. In the TV series will and the passions that coexist with it bring about numerous deaths and the further depletion of House Stark, even if this house is relatively triumphant in the end. This is how William J. Bouwsma summarizes the Augustinian perspective:

The will, in this view, is seen to take its direction not from reason but from the affections, which are in turn not merely disorderly impulses of the treacherous body but expressions of energy and quality of the heart, that mysterious organ that is the center of the personality, the source of its unity and its ultimate worth. The affections, therefore, are neither good nor evil but the essential resources of the personality; and since they make possible man's beatitude and glory as well as his depravity, they are, in Augustinian humanism, treated with particular respect.[28]

What apparently inhabited the heart of Robb Stark was strong amorous passion and this passion led to misery and death. Whether Martin is aware of it or not, his perspective could be Augustinian: Robb's passion was not condemned but commented on as an inseparable part of his personality. It was also presented as the 'follies of youth', when one follows the heart and not the reason. Love as a drive that follows the will, rather than a purely spontaneous emotion, may be a concept that was 'lost' after the Middle Ages; it is 'found' again in Martin's fantasy epic in order to increase the medievalizing effect.

During the seventeenth and eighteenth centuries, philosophers adopted the perspective that emotion is an ennobling phenomenon, since it then becomes 'a "mental condition" in which the subjectivity of a human being [is] expressed'.[29] This is yet another perspective adopted in Martin's cycle and its TV adaptation. Love does not have to be taboo, like Jaime's, or reckless and leading to disaster, like Robb's. The love between Ned and Catelyn Stark is primarily shown as noble, since it grew with time as the couple got to know each other and had children. It does not end with Ned's death, since Catelyn remains devoted to him in her grief as well. This would correspond to a modern-day vision of love as an emotion that is expressed through loyalty and fidelity, if not for the fact that it was an arranged marriage. The love turned out to be romantically ennobling, even though the idea of Ned and Catelyn's arranged marriage is in itself medieval. The concept of arranged marriage sends readers back to historical upper-class marriages in the Middle Ages. Rikke Schubart and Anne Gjelsvik comment on this: 'When Martin created his female characters, he took inspiration from the European medieval age, during which royal marriages were political, and women used as pawns.'[30] Marital love as a means of emotionally connecting with one's spouse transforms Catelyn. She no longer sees herself as a pawn in an arranged marriage but as an independent woman who chooses to love her husband despite his supposed love affair and despite the introduction of Jon as an extramarital child into her household.[31] This is an idea that could be thought of as integral to the modern-day concept of love, were it not that medieval authors used to define marital love as growing with time, like the love between Catelyn and Ned.[32] Their marriage is then both 'medieval' in its evolution from an arranged union to a mature, loving relationship and romantic, since their identities are fully expressed through this relationship. This love is not only felt but also 'distributed' through their actions and it circulates in the narrative. Both Catelyn and Ned make each other feel loved, since they do a lot for the other person.

What medievalizes the world of *Game of Thrones* even further is honour. In the chivalric world of Martin's cycle honour features prominently as an apparently 'lost emotion'. The chivalric code imposes honourable behaviour on all knights and while they may have problems with the observance of this code, they always relate to these standards even when they do not observe the rules for some reason. The label of 'Kingslayer' becomes attached to Jaime for good, as if his breach of his feudal oath excluded him from the circle of real knights. Honour, however, is not one of the six basic emotions, which have been specified as fear, anger, disgust, sadness, joy, shame and guilt, despite the ahistoricity of this perspective.[33] In *Emotions in History* Frevert calls honour 'an emotional disposition' rather than an emotion itself.[34] Pierre Bourdieu has described honour as 'a powerful *habitus*, . . . a system of "emotional dispositions" that is turn produces and structures social practices'.[35] Honour then becomes what Monique Scheer discussed as a 'habituated practice of the body'.[36] The idea of honour as an emotional disposition is highly relevant in light of the distinction between emotions, moods and dispositions, where 'an emotion is generally seen as having a specific occasion and intentional object'.[37] Honour is an emotion in this sense only in relation to particular occasions, but, as a disposition, it does not have a specific occasion, nor does it function with respect to an intentional object. It is rather a certain readiness to act in a specific manner. The study of honour thus involves values, which are as important as perceptions, gestures and relations in any study of emotions from the past.[38] In *A Song of Ice and Fire* Martin explores the validity of honour in the world he creates. Other characters act as foils to Jaime, all too human in his fallibility. Even if he acts contrary to honour as an emotional disposition, he realizes this very well and feels it more or less acutely, depending on the circumstances. An incestuous love affair with Cersei is not honourable and it is an act of treason towards Robert Baratheon, but Jaime does not feel as bad about it as he did about slaying King Aerys, which happened at a point when this murder became absolutely necessary for the survival of his subjects.

This can be related to the medievalizing role of shame in the cycle. The manner in which this concept is developed does not necessarily belong to medieval Christian philosophy, but it may be related to it. In *A Song of Ice and Fire* Jaime is a character who develops morally once he becomes more or less haunted by guilt and shame, those which Antonio Damasio calls 'social emotions'.[39] Brienne, the Maid of Tarth, accompanies Jaime and acts as a foil both to his past actions, including the crippling of Bran, and his present sense that all honour is lost to him, since he is disabled.[40] What activates the emotions of guilt and shame is his transfer from the realm of the rich, beautiful and powerful to the world of the disabled, who need to rely on the good will of others in various ways. His nobility is overlooked when Vargo Hoat and his men, who are allies of the Boltons, cut off his hand in order to strengthen the position of the Boltons as a House in competition with the Lannisters. The crippling appears metaphorically to sever Jaime's relationship with his previous arrogance and his feeling that he remained outside and above morality and social conventions. Jaime feels humiliated when he loses his hand, but this humiliation is necessary for his growth in psychological terms. He begins to see honour as an emotional disposition he no longer has at his disposal, but paradoxically the guilt and shame, the key medieval emotions related to honour, make him act more honourably. Humiliation does not have to be the opposite of honour in this situation, since Jaime's feelings allow him eventually to regain this emotional disposition: this transforms him into someone governed by the code of honour once again, at least in the novel cycle. Cersei, in contrast, operates contrary to this code when she commits adultery, and hence acts against her husband's honour. She undergoes no transformation that could be compared to Jaime's, perhaps because she undergoes no shock in the novel cycle, while in the TV show the shock related to her children drives her to paranoia.

Jaime's shame can be seen as both a medievalizing and a medieval emotion. In terms of medieval philosophy, shame is a passion, but it is a praiseworthy one. According to Aquinas it is a fear of a disgrace in the view of others; this makes people act more nobly than they otherwise would.[41] Thus it is not praiseworthy in itself, but rather indirectly, as is true of many other passions.[42] As is characteristic in Aquinas's thinking, reason is indispensable for the passion of shame to develop. Aquinas discusses the shame-related terms *verecundia*, *erubescentia*, *confusio*, *pudor* and *turpido* as important for the moral growth of a human. *Verecundia* is a sense of shame, *erubescentia* a reason for blushing, *confusio* is both good and bad shame, *pudor* is sexual shame and *turpido* is disgrace.[43] Even though they were difficult to endure, they all led to virtue.

In the case of Jaime Lannister his emotional condition does not develop in the way discussed by Aquinas. Jaime does not feel shame because of a fear of being disgraced. After his humiliation, namely his being forced to occupy the position of a crippled man, he starts to feel ashamed about everything he has done and not simply about those acts from the past that might be revealed to others. This is an idea that is found in Aquinas: shame has ennobled Jaime and made him a more complete human being. Martin challenges the categories 'normal' and 'disabled' in this manner, as Pascal J. Massie and Lauryn S. Mayer point out.[44] When he was 'normal' in the bodily sense, Jaime was able to perform the most monstrous deeds, such as the crippling of Bran. Once he became crippled himself, he gradually stopped thinking and acting like a monster.

Other social emotions, such as sympathy, also largely contribute to the development of the plot.[45] When someone is humiliated as Sansa is when her father is executed and she is forced to stay in King's Landing as his killer's fiancée, they expect to elicit another emotion from others: sympathy (or empathy). As a result, Sansa naively thought that Littlefinger sympathized with her while he only wanted to take advantage of her vulnerability. In the world of *A Song of Ice and Fire* hardly any characters feel sympathy for one another, an idea which may belong to a stereotypical vision of the Middle Ages as a time of cruelty and brutality.[46] Even Catelyn Stark, otherwise a tender wife and mother, has a certain air of hardness around her, since expressing sympathy in this masculine world would be a dangerous weakness. Furthermore, her tender motherhood does not embrace Jon Snow, to whom she is a 'hateful stepmother', as Schubart and Gjelsvik write.[47] Ned exposes his weakness only once, when he is deluded into thinking that Littlefinger is a sympathetic friend of the family and when Ned confesses to him that he has doubts about Robert fathering Joffrey. He pays for this weakness with his life. These are the hallucinatory thoughts he has when imprisoned for treachery and waiting for his execution:

> *I failed you, Robert*, Ned thought. He could not say the words. *I lied to you, hid the truth. I let them kill you.*

> The king heard him. 'You stiff-necked fool', he muttered, 'too proud to listen. Can you eat pride, Stark? Will honour shield your children?' Cracks ran down his face, fissures opening in the flesh, and he reached up and ripped the mask away. It was not Robert at all; it was Littlefinger, grinning, mocking him. When he opened his mouth to speak, his lies turned to pale grey moths and took wing. (*GT*, 607)

He feels powerless and exposed to violence from his enemies. Yet, this vulnerability makes Ned even more human. This is similar to Jaime's vulnerability, even though Jaime started to show signs of being less ruthless only once he becomes a disabled person. There is no ruthlessness of this sort in Ned at the beginning of the story, at least if one thinks that he is a 'medieval' human in the novel cycle and the show, but his weakness makes him more of an ordinary person than the aristocratic lord he initially was.

Powerlessness and empowerment

Powerlessness and emotions as empowering are two important themes in Martin's cycle that also 'medievalize' it, since they are recurring themes in medieval literature as well. This may be evidenced by the example of anger. In Martin's novel the ancient humoral theory, a discourse very much present in the Middle Ages and Renaissance, seems to influence the manner in which some characters are presented. What is expected of women is the coldness that allegedly characterizes them, which is similar to the Galenic model in medieval and early modern culture. To quote Paster:

> Men's bodies were thought to be hotter and drier, women's bodies colder and more spongy. This was not a difference that applied universally: most theorists believed that some men, especially old or melancholy ones, were colder than some women. But generally, as part of the order of things, females started off their lives colder in temper than males of the same age and, with rare exceptions, stayed that way.[48]

There are hardly any old men like this in Martin's cycle, but the woman who is exceptional in her lack of coldness, motivated by the strong emotions she often feels, such as anger, fear and competition with others as an emotional disposition, is Cersei. She experiences these difficult emotions in the male-dominated world, but it is debatable whether this makes her strong or weak. She is generally devoid of honour as an emotional disposition, and honour is empowering for men since it situates one firmly within the higher social class which one occupies. Cersei places her ambitions in her children instead. Interestingly, however, when she is in a state of rage, it makes her powerful, regardless of the social position of women in the world of this fantasy epic.[49] The expression of anger is what medievalizes it: this is what makes the characters' reactions, as exemplified by Cersei, similar to the reactions of the medieval mob famously described by Huizinga. They cried and roared in public, and crying out of anger and roaring with rage is indeed what Cersei performs. Such displays of strong emotions, for example, anger, make her more visible in the patriarchal world she lives in. She 'spends' her anger on, and 'distributes' it among, those who surround her. The expression of anger by a powerful woman is not an emotion now entirely 'lost' for us, yet Martin 'finds' it by making it central to Cersei's characterization. Cersei's anger is an emotion that could have been visible in the reactions of medieval queens.[50] Importantly, she saw herself primarily as a queen, since this was a promise she made to herself in her youth and she fulfilled it.[51] Her anger in the story is not only a case of female *furor*, described by writers as early as antiquity. Cersei is not only enraged in the manner in which Dido was enraged in Virgil's *Aeneid* when she was abandoned by Aeneas.[52] Her anger resembles the medieval *ira regis*, the anger a ruler consciously directed against his subjects.[53] She wishes to punish others with her displays of this emotion. This medievalizes the fantasy cycle, even though Cersei is not presented in accordance with the Galenic doctrine of female bodies as 'cold' and hence less emotional than male ones.

When looking at the medievalism of *Game of Thrones*, understood here as both the novel cycle and its TV adaptation, I discover a range of medieval and medievalist emotions that are expressed, hence 'spent' or 'distributed' in the social sense. My emphasis here has also been on emotions 'lost and found', here specifically: love, honour and anger. Augustine's and Aquinas's theories had to be invoked in order to see how Martin has 'medievalized' emotions in the cycle. The emotions in question refer us back from the fantasy cycle to the historical Middle Ages. The result is that feeling in these texts and their adaptation can be both disconcertingly alien and yet appealing to our modern sensibilities.

Part VI

The 'HBO effect'
Violence and misogyny

11

From romance to rape

The portrayal of masculine sexuality in *Game of Thrones*

Kristina Hildebrand

Violence as realism

As we all know, *A Song of Ice and Fire* and *Game of Thrones* have been immensely successful, both as a series of novels and as a TV show. Part of that popularity seems to be the idea that it presents a realistic image of the Middle Ages, especially in the portrayal of violence in general and sexual violence in particular. That *Game of Thrones* is perceived as realistic due to its level of violence is hardly a novel idea. For example, in a 2013 article in *The Guardian*, Tom Holland discusses how *Game of Thrones* appears more realistic than actual historical novels and drama such as Hilary Mantel's series about Thomas Cromwell. It is striking that the level of violence, while never explicitly cited in the article as part of the realism, is still constantly present as an aspect of it: the headline claims that *Game of Thrones* is 'More Brutally Realistic Than Most Historical Novels', and Holland adds that 'the appeal of Westeros is less that it is fantastical than that it seems so richly, so vividly, so brutally real', and

> no fiction set in the 14th century, for instance, has ever rivalled the portrayal in *Game of Thrones* of what, for a hapless peasantry, the ambitions of rival kings were liable to mean in practice: the depredations of *écorcheurs*; rape and torture; the long, slow agonies of famine.[1]

In discussing realism, Holland explicitly links it to the violence depicted: that violence is a large part of what makes *Game of Thrones* realistic seems too self-evident to need stating explicitly. It appears, then, that readers and viewers come to the text already equating realism with brutality and violence.

There is more division among fans on the subject of historical accuracy, with arguments about whether the show depicts the medieval world correctly and what is fantasy rather than fact. There are obviously valid discussions of how the text draws on medieval history and medieval historical figures, but here I am referring to the debate beyond scholarly circles about the accuracy of the depiction. This might seem a pointless discussion: while drawing on history, perhaps especially the War of the Roses, for inspiration, *Game of Thrones* does not attempt faithfully to portray historical events: it is unclear what 'historical accuracy' would mean for a fantasy world (see Larrington's chapter, this volume). Yet this argument, carried on in various corners of the internet, also points to the idea that *Game of Thrones* is a realistic depiction of history – if we compare it to *The Lord of the Rings*, there is lively discussion on how true to Tolkien's books the films are, but, as Kavita Mudan Finn also points out, it would be rare indeed to come across a debate on the historical accuracy of Middle-earth.[2] Unlike *The Lord of the Rings*, *Game of Thrones* lays claim to realistic representations of life in a quasi-historical past, and thus 'realism', for any given meaning of that term, is key to the believability of the text.

Drawing on Helen Young's work, Shiloh Carroll points out that the realism is created inside the text: 'readers are caught in a "feedback loop" in which Martin's work helps to create a neomedieval idea of the Middle Ages, which then becomes their idea of what the Middle Ages "really" looked like, which is then used to defend Martin's work as "realistic" because it matches their idea of the real Middle Ages.'[3] This feedback loop also applies to the portrayal of sexuality, where male sexual violence is portrayed as 'natural' and projected back onto an imagined past. Since this past, as we have seen, is still presented as realistic regardless of its imagined state, the audience is further convinced that sexual violence was, indeed, natural and ubiquitous in the Middle Ages.

Sex and violence

Martin's novels and the TV series both feature many instances of sexual violence. As is also the case outside fiction, the persistent presence of the threat of sexual violence serves to keep all women afraid, even those women who, as Shiloh Carroll points out, 'have a layer of protection from sexual assault on account of their status and relationship to men who can protect them'.[4] Even these women, and those able to physically defend themselves, like Brienne, are, under certain circumstances, also at risk of rape.[5] The protection lasts only as long as such status and relationships last and offers no security from sexual assault within those relationships. This ubiquitous threat of sexual violence, considered by Martin to be an integral part of his realistic worldbuilding, serves, as we shall see, to present male sexuality as naturally and unavoidably predatory.

Nevertheless, while authenticity and historical accuracy are promoted as a significant feature for both novels and show, their depiction of sexuality is still constructed both as dwelling in an imagined past and as contemporary. Mariah Larsson points out that 'the various paradigms featured in the fictional universe of Ice and Fire are constructed from ideas about how sexual relations were organised in a long gone, pre-modern world', offering a window into an imagined past.[6] Yet contemporary views on sexuality also inform the portrayal: 'ideas of gender equality, mutual pleasure, consent, and romantic love color the reception of the sex scenes in *Game of Thrones*, but also any notions about sexual positions, virginity, female and male sexuality, submission and domination.'⁷ I would claim that not only is reception coloured by these ideas, but that the portrayals themselves cannot escape being coloured by them as well. The creators of the show themselves possess the same horizon of expectations as the viewers. The dichotomy of 'pre-modern sexuality' and 'contemporary sexuality' is, as Larsson makes clear, an illusion: our understanding of the pseudo-medieval world is a contemporary one. I would add that this pseudo-medieval world becomes a repository for many contemporary ideas about sexuality, perhaps especially those that are not openly admitted to. We should note the possibility of the pseudo-medieval setting providing viewers of the series in particular – who are more forcefully reminded of the setting due to it being constantly visually present – with an alibi for watching and enjoying sexual violence. The setting represents a time from which the viewer can safely distance themselves, in a way that is not possible with depictions of sexual violence in contemporary settings. I will return to this when discussing the titillation factor of the show.

Sexualized violence in *Game of Thrones*: The wedding night of Daenerys and Khal Drogo

As we have seen, 'realism' in *Game of Thrones* is associated with violence and brutality. Unsurprisingly, the TV show became famous partly due to its levels of sexual or sexualized violence, generally aimed at women, and its many rape scenes. While there are several studies on overarching themes of sexuality and violence in *Game of Thrones*, both the novels and the TV show, I will focus here on one plot event: Daenerys and Khal Drogo's wedding night and the beginning of their marriage. This is a specific focal point for the issues of sexuality and violence, especially taking into account that the scene differs significantly in the text and in the TV episode. The scene constitutes an interesting example of the attraction of perceived realism, but also of contemporary views of sexuality and masculinity. In the novel Daenerys is seduced by her new husband, and she has the clear possibility of turning him down. The TV show, on the other hand, shows this scene as a rape. This has been discussed before, notably by Valerie Estelle Frankel, by Mariah Larsson and (briefly) by Rikke Schubart, and I will be engaging with their analysis here.⁸ I would, however, like to focus not only on the differences between the novel and the TV show but also on the results of these differences. The TV episode introduces changes which serve, first, to present violent male sexuality as 'natural' and rooted in biology and, secondly, as more sexual and even titillating. This, in its turn, both caters to and creates a male dominance over the narrative. The TV episode removes focalization from Daenerys and instead allows the viewer to identify with Khal Drogo; Daenerys is presented to the male gaze with her body consistently exposed; the marriage is not made more equal with time but instead involves a power imbalance tilted in the woman's favour, referring to male fear of manipulation and loss of autonomy through sex; and the rape scene, through the withdrawal of Daenerys as the focalizer, allows the reader to experience it as sexually arousing.

The novel

The first time we encounter Daenerys in the novels, she is an ambiguous character: the focalizer or point-of-view (POV) character of her story, yet initially completely passive. She remains the focalizer through the chapters I am dealing with here; we never see her through the eyes of another character and have access only to her own interpretation of how others look at her. We experience the plot through her eyes but are also constantly reminded of her passivity; to some extent, her position as focalizer strengthens the impression of passivity, as for many of her earliest appearances, she watches and listens but does not act. As readers, we have no choice but to share in her inaction.

By placing her as the focalizer and denying that position to the other characters around her, such as Viserys and Khal Drogo, the text gives her the same privileged position as the other focalizing characters, even though we do not, at first, see her act except at the direction of others. This creates an interesting identification with a character who only gradually acquires any agency.

Daenerys's age is emphasized by her childish dependence on her brother and her lack of experience. We see her marvelling at a beautiful gown, only for her brother Viserys to enforce his will on her through sexualized violence: 'His fingers brushed lightly over her budding breasts and tightened on a nipple. "You will not fail me tonight. If you do, it will go hard for you. You don't want to wake the dragon, do you?" His fingers twisted her, the pinch cruelly hard through the rough fabric of her tunic. "*Do you?*" he repeated' (*GT*, 29). Daenerys is thus presented to us as feminine, submissive and defenceless in front of her brutal brother. As we are told that 'she had always assumed that she would marry Viserys when she came of age. For centuries the Targaryen had married brother to sister' (*GT*, 32), her brother's sexualized violence is given a context of potential marital rape. This mention of Targaryen marriage practices, especially combined with Daenerys's age of thirteen, is likely to unnerve the reader. Although she is still just as young, the marriage to Khal Drogo here acquires the positive aspect of saving Daenerys from marrying her brother.

Throughout the preparations and the wedding, Daenerys is a passive prop rather than participant. The next scene depicts her being washed and dressed by servants and making no choices about attire or ornaments. Throughout the wedding feast she is also a passive observer, fearing the wedding night and unable to speak to anyone (*GT*, 101–6). Her interaction with others has so far been only as a silent recipient of attention, advice and aggression. The first hint of independent activity comes when she receives a horse as bride gift from her husband (*GT*, 106). This is the first indication of Khal Drogo's treatment of her as an actor with agency: by giving her a means of transportation not dependent on anyone else he indicates his desire for her to have at least some degree of independence. She rides the horse, feeling that 'for the first time in hours, she forgot to be afraid. Or perhaps it was for the first time ever' (*GT*, 106). She responds to the power and speed of the horse by saying, 'Tell Khal Drogo that he has given me the wind', which makes him smile at her (*GT*, 106). This should not be overlooked: Khal Drogo's gift gives her freedom from fear and a certain amount of autonomy, and they both recognize this.

The wedding night emphasizes this respect for Daenerys's wishes and is sharply contrasted with her brother's disregard for them. Once they are alone, she starts crying. 'Khal Drogo stared at her tears, his face strangely empty of expression. "No", he said. He lifted his hand and rubbed away the tears roughly with a callused thumb' (*GT*, 107). While the gesture is described as 'rough', it is an expression of caring that Daenerys has not, so far as we have seen, encountered from her brother. When touching Daenerys's hair, Drogo is referred to as 'murmuring softly' and expressing 'warmth' and 'tenderness' (*GT*, 107). This behaviour is repeated throughout the wedding night scene: even when ignoring her refusal, such as when he tells her 'No' and move her hands when she attempts to cover her bare breasts, even that is described as being done 'gently but firmly' (*GT*, 108). While this is, of course, a rejection of her right of refusal, it strikes the reader as a contrast to her brother's brutality.

Khal Drogo also chooses to symbolically place them as equals: 'taking her lightly under the arms, he lifted her and seated her on a rounded rock beside the stream. Then he sat on the ground facing her, legs crossed beneath him, their faces finally at a height' (*GT*, 107). Rather than emphasizing their different roles as a helpless child and an ultra-masculine man, the scene indicates a more equal relationship. In fact, many of Khal Drogo's actions during the wedding night are essentially coded feminine. Let us start with his hair. In the novels it is described thus: 'Drogo's braid was black as midnight and heavy with scented oil, hung with tiny bells that rang softly as he moved. It swung well past his belt, below even his buttocks, the end of it brushing against the back of his thighs' (*GT*, 37). While the braid is a marker of masculinity in Dothraki culture, being cut off after a lost fight, its style – scented and adorned – is not explicitly masculine. In the TV show it is long, kept in a ponytail and adorned only with the occasional ribbon holding it together at various points – a considerably more traditionally masculine style.

Considering the importance of hair in Dothraki culture, it is unsurprising that the first physical contact initiated by Daenerys on the wedding night is to first help remove the bells from Khal Drogo's hair and then to unbraid it. In sharp contrast to the earlier scene where she is washed, clothed and adorned while standing passive, this makes her an active participant in the process (*GT*, 107). Once the braid is undone, Drogo displays his hair: 'He shook his head, and his hair spread out behind him like a river of darkness, oiled and gleaming' (*GT*, 107–8). While recognizing the erotic aspect of hair, this is also a curiously domestic and feminine scene: the help with unbraiding and the shaking out of the hair are both scenes primarily associated with women.

The wedding night is a seduction, carried out with regard not just for Daenerys's comfort but with respect for her capacity to consent. The sexual encounter involves long foreplay, carried out slowly and with concern for Daenerys's inexperience: 'He cupped her face in his huge hands and she looked into his eyes. "No?" he said, and she knew it was a question. She took his hand and moved it down to the wetness between her thighs. "Yes," she whispered as she put his finger inside her' (*GT*, 108). The wedding night is thus marked by Khal Drogo starting out with the domestic and calming ritual of undoing braided hair, presenting himself as sexually attractive and proceeding with slow foreplay and a request for consent.

It is clear from the novel that Daenerys's sexual relationship with Khal Drogo, after the first night, often lacks her consent, and he shows no consideration for the pain and soreness riding brings her: 'her lord husband could not see the tears that wet her face, and she could use her pillow to muffle her cries of pain' (*GT*, 228). However, this eventually changes: as she gets more used to riding, she begins 'to notice the beauties of the land around her' (*GT*, 229) and 'she began to find pleasure even in her nights, and if she still cried out when Drogo took her, it was not always in pain' (*GT*, 30). Daenerys eventually talks to one of her slave women about how to please a man and learns how to take the initiative in sex. She waits for Drogo, undresses on his arrival and leads him outside, according to the Dothraki belief 'that all things of importance in a man's life must be done beneath the open sky' (*GT*, 236). This encounter marks a change in their relationship: 'When he tried to turn her over, she put a hand on his chest. "No," she said. "This night I would look on your face." . . . She rode him as fiercely as she had ever ridden her silver, and when the moment of his pleasure came, Khal Drogo called out her name' (*GT*, 236). While Daenerys's confidence has been boosted by her connection to the dragon eggs, and her defiance of her brother, her willingness to initiate sex with Khal Drogo draws on that initial encounter, which showed that he could feel compassion and tenderness for her. In the course of the relationship, from the moment she is given the horse and treated with gentleness for what appears to be the first time in her life, Daenerys comes to trust in her own strength and will and transfers her loyalty from her brother to her husband.

This plot development makes a great deal of sense. Daenerys's willingness to support her husband against her brother and her firm loyalty to her husband can all be explained by the first night when her consent was sought. As Frankel points out, 'Daenerys has never had a choice about anything, thanks to her vicious brother.'[9] Unlike Khal Drogo, her brother has never considered her consent in their interaction – which is uncomfortably sexualized – and faced with the possibility of a consensual relationship, Daenerys shifts her loyalties.

The TV show

Unlike the novel, the TV show does not offer us focalization through Daenerys: as a media form, film does not lend itself as easily to individual focalization but is more likely to present a third-person view. Nevertheless, we might note that other characters are given scenes seen through their eyes, for example, Catelyn Stark experiencing the dire wolf foiling the attack on Bran in 'The Kingsroad' (1.2). We only see things through Daenerys's eyes for a brief moment, as she comforts herself by looking at the dragon eggs; at all other times, the camera maintains a third-person view or, occasionally, the view of another character. We are, in fact, offered much more of Khal Drogo's perspective than of Daenerys's. When he first meets Viserys and Daenerys, the camera lingers on them as they are introduced, indicating Drogo's gaze.

The first effect of the loss of focalization is the possibility of identifying with other characters. With Daenerys as focalizer, in the novel we are always aware of what she is thinking and feeling. In the TV show, the viewer ends up a voyeur, observing the rape of Daenerys while not being made to know what she feels, except through her outwards signs, such as crying. This distancing built into the medium allows the viewer to escape from Daenerys's perspective, should they so desire. Readers of the novel are given no opening for identification with Khal Drogo, as we do not know anything of his emotions or thoughts but can – with Daenerys – only observe them from the outside. Not just in presenting Daenerys from the outside but as viewed consistently through a desiring male gaze, the TV show not only enables but also seems to invite identification with Khal Drogo.

In the show, Daenerys is consistently presented to us from an outside perspective which also repeatedly exposes her body. This display of her body emphasizes how much we are watching her from the outside: we are never allowed to forget that our position versus Daenerys is voyeuristic rather than empathic. In the very first scene, her dress exposes her back down to the buttocks, and we then see her brother undressing her. Interestingly, in the TV show her brother's physical violence, discussed above, is absent; while verbally violent, we do not see him commit the sexualized violence of the novels. The wedding dress she is then seen wearing does not hide her body so much as veil it, and she is thus on display not only to her prospective husband but also to us as viewers.

Daenerys's helplessness and vulnerability are emphasized through the constant exposure of her body; this strongly signals sexual vulnerability/availability throughout the show. Similarly, the Dothraki women, whom we see having sex (of doubtful consent) at the wedding feast, are largely bare-breasted rather than wearing leather vests like the men's, as in the novel (*GT*, 101). Khal Drogo's body is also displayed as sexually attractive, with the emphasis on his upper body, in keeping with 'modern sensibilities, which eroticize the chest and abdomen and upper arms of the young male body'.[10] However, this display of naked muscle, while it does sexualize Drogo, does not present him as vulnerable or sexually available: male sexuality is portrayed as grounded in strength and control.

The sex and killings at the wedding are seen to make Khal Drogo smile, creating an expectation that he will not be inclined towards gentleness or compassion. The gift of the horse appears also in the show, but here Daenerys does not ride it on her own, and her comment is on its beauty, not its speed. The implicit promise of greater independence and consideration is absent.

As opposed to the novel, the TV show clearly shows the wedding night as a rape. Larsson claims that since the TV version of Daenerys is not as young as she is in the novel, 'the TV series needed to emphasise the rape aspect of the wedding night more, in order to provide the same sense of victimhood as the novel does by making her so young'.[11] However, while the TV series does make her fifteen rather than thirteen, I would argue that it still presents her as a victim just as strongly, or even more so, as in the novel. Daenerys in the TV show is still very young, her partly dressed or undressed body is repeatedly displayed and the actor's body is presented as physically fragile – especially, as Larsson points out, in contrast to that of the tall and broadly built Jason Momoa.[12] This fragility is further emphasized by the TV series leaving out the physical activity that we see Daenerys undertake in the novel, such as riding her wedding-gift horse. In the light of this, the rape not only outweighs the character's increased age but in fact adds to the sense of Daenerys's victimhood.

The TV show episode subverts the text by retaining the 'no' used to Daenerys as she covers her breasts, but leaving out any tenderness, not to mention the entire seduction and her final consent. Instead, we are shown Khal Drogo simply bending Daenerys forward and proceeding as she cries. Later sexual encounters between them are also brutal: she is always seen suffering and crying, and comforting herself by looking at the dragon eggs, as mentioned earlier; this is one of the few examples of our seeing the scene from her perspective. It should be noted that the dragon eggs are also a promise of future power – although Daenerys does not know that yet, it is likely that a large part of the audience does – and, as Finn puts it, '[d]ragons are a gender equalizer'.[13] Daenerys's glance at the eggs, with the knowledge the audience has, is a hint of the change from powerless pawn to powerful queen that Daenerys will undergo.

Debra Ferreday points out that 'although there is a tender consensual scene between Daenerys and her husband, this occurs only after he has repeatedly, graphically raped her and she has learned seduction techniques in order to take back control'.[14] Daenerys learning about sex from one of her slave women is indeed present in the TV show. However, here it is no longer a conversation, as in the novel, but a pseudo-lesbian scene focused entirely on the fantasy of two women having sex in order to (learn how to) please a man. Frankel points out that it is a 'performance for the camera, with straddling and grinding'.[15] The instructions given to Daenerys focus entirely on the attaining of power through sexual attraction and skills, not on any desire for mutual pleasure. The resulting sex scene shows Khal Drogo as violent when she tells him 'no', until she convinces him that she wants only a change in position, not to abstain from sex, and this reinforces our image of marital rape from the wedding night. Larsson argues that the change in position, by drawing on our own cultural understanding of sexual positions, indicates a change in the relationship: 'when Daenerys and Khal Drogo begin to have sex face-to-face, with Daenerys on top or in the missionary position, their relationship becomes more respectful and equal.'[16] However, I would read this a little differently: the relationship here involves a transfer of power which is not entirely unproblematic. In this scene Daenerys does not, for once, undress: this reminds the viewer of how disempowering her lack of clothing has been. This is especially clear in that this is also the first time Khal Drogo's naked body is displayed to the viewer. Once Daenerys gains a small amount of control in the marital bed, she is no longer naked, and her husband is. As mentioned above, the conversation with her slave woman that preceded it has focused entirely on sex as manipulation and power. The crying out of Daenerys's name is also absent from this scene, implying that Drogo's recognition of her as an individual has not been achieved. This can be seen not so much as a movement towards greater equality as a loss of power on the man's part, due to the manipulative sexual power of the woman – a much less positive portrayal than in the novel. Indeed, the suggestion that Drogo is manipulated, even brought to ruin, by his sexual desire for his wife, is one that is underlined by his subsequent story arc in Season 1.

Schubart points out that Daenerys's 'impossible task is not to endure, but to master Drogo'.[17] While she is referring both to the novel and the TV show, they are not, in my view, equivalent in this aspect. Instead, the mastering indicates the central problem of Daenerys and Khal Drogo's marriage in the TV show: there can be no mutuality or consent in a relationship where one must have power at the expense of the other. In the claim that the slave woman will teach her how to make Khal Drogo fall in love with her, the TV show can indeed be read as 'less transgressive and more conventionally romantic' than the novel.[18] Nevertheless, we should note that, while in the novel a more equal relationship is desired and achieved, in the TV series the desired outcome of Daenerys's sexual initiative is not mutual understanding but rather a power shift. This is a conventional view of heterosexual relationships, but I would not call it conventionally romantic in the eyes of a female audience: it speaks much more to a basic male fear of being controlled through their sexual and emotional attraction to a manipulative woman.

The effects of the changes

Interestingly, showing the wedding night as a rape was more important than keeping the plot development believable. Larsson points to this change and claims that it fundamentally influences even Daenerys's reasons for standing up to her brother: in the novels, Daenerys's defiance of her brother allows her to become more confident in her position as wife and khaleesi, whereas in the TV series her improved relationship with Khal Drogo allows her to defy her brother.[19] However, I would argue that the novel is even more complicated than that: the gift of the horse, with its connotations of freedom both of movement and from fear, and the respect for her consent on the wedding night, is what allows Daenerys to envision a relationship where she is not constantly abused and controlled by a man. Why, then, is Daenerys's consent removed in the TV show, and what are the effects of this removal?

I would argue that these changes, creating a male dominance over the narrative, are dependent on – and support – two underlying assumptions: firstly, that sexual violence is perceived as more authentic than consensual sex in this pseudo-medieval setting, and secondly, that the show seeks to titillate the (male) audience by presenting a form of sexual contact that is seen as, essentially, sexier.

With the loss of focalization and thus the option for the viewer to identify with other characters than Daenerys, the gender of the audience comes into play. *Game of Thrones* does not have a strongly predominantly male audience: Valerie Estelle Frankel points out that 42 per cent of the viewers are women, an assessment also made in other sources.[20] Indeed, in Season 7 at least, the conversations about *Game of Thrones* on social media involved more women than men, 52 per cent and 48 per cent, respectively.[21] Nevertheless, the show is often perceived as being more interesting to a male audience – see, for example, the *New York Times* review of the first season for comments of that ilk.[22] At least in the early seasons, the actual presence of a large female audience does not seem to impact the expectation that the audience should be primarily male.[23] It is a well-known fact that the male gaze is much more present than the female in contemporary TV, and we should not be surprised that this is the case in *Game of Thrones* as well. The presentation of sexual violence as 'realistic' and the desire to titillate the viewers with violent sex is thus unavoidably tied to the showrunners' and HBO's expectation of the audience to comply with the male gaze, identify with the male characters and accept a narrative dominated by a male perspective.

We have already seen that *Game of Thrones* is presented as 'realistic' largely due to its depictions of violence, whether that violence is sexual or non-sexual. This carries over, predictably, into seeing violence against women as realistic, more so than a lack of violence. *Game of Thrones* includes multiple scenes of violence, whether sexual or otherwise, against women, and, as Larsson points out, 'some scenes in the TV series further develop, exaggerate and even add sexual violence to the story'.[24] This is despite the fact that 'since we engage with moving images differently, in particular with regard to depictions of sex and violence, than we do with written fiction – in a sensorial and embodied way – the perception of sex and violence in the TV comes across as stronger than in the novels'.[25] The impact is thus increased twofold: by the addition of more sexual violence and by the change of medium.

As George R. R. Martin has had the opportunity to influence the TV show, his opinion on the portrayal of sexual violence must be considered to apply to both the novels and the show. Martin explains the presence of violence against women in an interview, stating,

> Now there are people who will say to that, 'Well, he's not writing history, he's writing fantasy – he put in dragons, he should have made an egalitarian society.' Just because you put in dragons doesn't mean you can put in anything you want. . . . I wanted my books to be strongly grounded in history and to show what medieval society was like, and I was also reacting to a lot of fantasy fiction.[26]

Here, as we can see, the subordination of women (and other minorities) is presented as an unalterable fact of medieval life. Leaving aside the Eurocentricity of the view of the Middle Ages, it still begs the question of why dragons do not detract from the realism of the portrayal. Martin proceeds to present a depiction of a world without sexual violence as fundamentally dishonest:

> And then there's the whole issue of sexual violence, which I've been criticized for as well. I'm writing about war, which [is] what almost all epic fantasy is about. But if you're going to write about war, and you just want to include all the cool battles and heroes killing a lot of orcs and things like that and you *don't* portray [sexual violence], then there's something fundamentally dishonest about that. Rape, unfortunately, is still a part of war today.[27]

It is an interesting approach to claim that imagining a world where rape is not part of warfare is not only unrealistic but in fact dishonest. This suggests that to Martin, rape is an unavoidable part of the practice of violence, and its presence might be hidden but not removed in a fantasy world, if it is to be realistic. And realism is, as we have seen, both a significant feature of both novels and show and marked by the presence of violence.

As mentioned above, the show portrays sexuality in a long-gone world but relies on the audience's ideas about sexuality in creating that portrayal. It can also be read as harbouring ideas about sexuality that are not often displayed in public, or displayed only implicitly. One such idea is that male sexuality is naturally predatory and violent, often camouflaged under the portrayal of men as pursuers and women as pursued.

The portrayal of male sexuality in popular culture and public discourse favours a depiction of men as pursuers and women as pursued. In much heteronormative discourse, this implicitly shades into a metaphorical framing as a pursuit of prey by a predator. Bock and Burkley point out that this is 'a common metaphor used to describe heterosexual relationships', and it would also appear that when asked to identify with an animal, men are more likely than women to pick a predator.[28] The portrayal and self-identification of men as predators would appear to increase their inclination towards sexual violence: Bock and Burkley state that their study's results 'provide initial evidence for [their] prediction that men-as-predators and women-as-prey dating metaphors encourage men to adopt attitudes that help to perpetuate sexual violence'.[29] This hegemonic view is internalized unless actively resisted, and through it we perceive men as pursuers or as predatory due to biology, not culture. It is thus 'authentic' and 'realistic' for men to be violent.

The portrayal of male sexual violence against women thus both draws on and promotes a framing of predator/prey that is then projected back in time. This creates a feedback loop similar to and concurrent with that of the 'realistic' Middle Ages discussed previously: if male sexual aggression is biological, it must be depicted as present in all times and spaces, especially if those are to be seen as realistic, and this depiction strengthens the idea that male sexual aggression is ubiquitous. Showing men as sexually aggressive and inclined to violence against women, and encouraging men to internalize that identity, would thus be likely to increase violence, creating a self-fulfilling prophecy of violent masculinity as 'natural' and biological. *Game of Thrones*, with its heavy investment in 'realistic' portrayal, is then almost unavoidably going to show male sexuality as violent and aggressive, encouraging the idea that this is the natural state of affairs. If this is the accepted view, Khal Drogo, who is portrayed – especially in the TV show – as 'barbaric' and therefore less sophisticated and cultured than other men, must become a sexual predator in order to retain his masculinity. Indeed, in the change to the scene portraying loving and mutual sexual contact with Daenerys initiating sex, we see her empowered and a hint that Khal Drogo is correspondingly disempowered; sex on the woman's initiative carries a danger of manipulation and loss of power.

This 'realistic' sexuality is also used for titillation. Although, as mentioned above, Larsson suggests that 'the perception of sex and violence in the TV comes across as stronger than in the novels', in this instance the audience is simultaneously offered the possibility of distancing themselves through a third-person perspective and voyeuristic position.[30] Despite containing a large number of women, the audience is expected to comply with the male gaze and is offered more opportunities to identify with male characters such as Khal Drogo than the novel provides. If the identification is not expected to be with a terrified young woman being raped, it will land either on the hypermasculine rapist or in a third-person distancing, which allows the viewers, if they so wish, to approach that scene as simultaneously shocked and excited. The scene can be enjoyed and found arousing while a proper rejection of rape is maintained.

It should also be noted that violent sex is often presented as masculine and/or pornographic, whereas gentle sex is seen as feminine and/or romantic. With the viewers able to identify with Khal Drogo rather than Daenerys, and the male gaze present in the scene, the sexual encounter is masculinized by being presented as violent and non-romantic. Larsson argues that 'representations of sexual violence can, indeed, be sex; that is, they can invoke sexual feelings in the viewer'.[31] Since we are offered the option of distancing ourselves from the scene, the option of finding it exciting is more easily accepted. Frankel also points to the strong sexualization of the scenes of marital rape as 'titillating with full nudity and no lasting trauma seen'.[32] By changing the wedding night from a seduction to a rape, the creators of the TV show have chosen to present the sex as more pornographic, catering to the male gaze and allowing identification with the male character without questioning his hypermasculinity.

The end of the series

The series ends with Daenerys's death at the hands of her lover: this scene, of course, has no equivalent in the novels yet. Here, too, we see Daenerys with outside focalization, as she gazes on the Iron Throne. For a brief moment, we look over her shoulder, as she notes the arrival of Jon Snow. Her face is serene and contented, sharply contrasted against Jon's agitation as he tells her of the killing happening outside. In a clear subversion of expected gendered behaviour, she is calm whereas Jon is distressed almost to the point of tears. However, his emotion is expected and approved, considering the level of atrocity he has witnessed, whereas her calm presents her as inhuman and unfeminine. He appeals to her to make her opponents understand and to forgive, calling on her to act in a way coded feminine. Daenerys's comments about a new world not 'built by men loyal to the world we had' rings more cruelly when voiced by a woman, as it breaks the expectations of consideration and care from a female character. The choice made by Jon, to distract her by kissing her so that he can stab her, seems immensely predictable. The killing is deeply sexualized, carried out in the middle of an intimate kiss and with a penetrating weapon. We watch it from the same outside focalization as we saw Daenerys's wedding night, and the camera focuses briefly on Daenerys's dying face, then switches to Jon, seen alternatingly up close and from a distance. He is audibly and visibly distressed, the scene clearly presenting this as his tragedy and loss. As with the wedding night, Daenerys's interaction with men results only in pain and misery for her, yet her pain is never at centre stage except as titillation or as an example of 'authentic' brutality.

Game of Thrones changes the novel's portrayal of Daenerys's and Khal Drogo's marriage to make it less respectful and more violent. In doing so, the TV show caters to the male gaze and an imagined male audience, allowing the narrative to be dominated by male desire and male fears.

12

The Rise and Fall of Cersei Lannister

Neomedievalist misogyny in George R. R. Martin's *A Song of Ice and Fire*

Sylwia Borowska-Szerszun

Muscular medievalism, defined by Amy S. Kaufman as a construct of the Middle Ages that 'imagines the past as a man's world in which masculinity was powerful, impenetrable, and uniquely privileged', can serve, as Kaufman argues, as 'collective justification for the worst traits of both patriarchy and humanity'.[1] Such an approach seems to inform George R. R. Martin's *A Song of Ice and Fire* (1996–) and its HBO TV adaptation, *Game of Thrones* (2011–19). Enjoying tremendous popularity worldwide, both the novel cycle and the TV show draw the attention of both readers and critics to some misogynistic preconceptions about the roles of women in society, inviting them to ponder whether such anti-woman stereotypes are supported or challenged by the narrative(s).

The patriarchal society of Martin's fiction is vividly depicted as a quasi-medieval world of brutal individualism, torture, mutilation and sexual abuse. The political and religious ideology of most of Westeros, especially its southern regions, allows women to assume the archetypal roles of the Maiden (representing innocence and chastity), the Mother (epitomizing motherhood and nurturing) and the Crone (standing for wisdom), and the echoes of these archetypes inform, yet do not determine, the construction of all female characters in the cycle. In Martin's take on these deep-rooted patterns, positive and negative attributes associated with them are blended, transformed or reversed to create multidimensional female characters and comment on the clichéd depiction of femininity in much popular fantasy fiction. Hence, in his prose, innocence can turn into naivety; motherly love might verge on madness; wisdom may be mistaken for cunning. While some women of *A Song of Ice and Fire* reject the values stereotypically attributed to womanhood, cross-dress or venture into the realm of men (e.g. Arya Stark, Asha Greyjoy, Brienne of Tarth), and some try to play by the rules to gain their share of power through matrimony and childbearing (e.g. Margaery Tyrell, Catelyn Stark), others defy clearly delineated boundaries of gender, combining both masculine and feminine features (e.g. Cersei Lannister, Daenerys Targaryen). Even though women are dynamically involved in the action and frequently play vital roles in the 'game of thrones', few of them, if any, actually escape violence, abuse, rape (or threats thereof) and sexual objectification.[2] This ambiguous depiction of women, especially when transposed to the TV screen, has drawn a mixed fan response and considerable critical interest.[3] The following analysis of the figure of Cersei Lannister, the 'evil queen' of the cycle, aims to contribute to this ongoing discussion by revealing not only the extent of anti-woman stereotypes evident in her portrayal and their connections to medieval tradition but also the mechanisms through which they are revisited and reshaped in a contemporary literary fantasy. For the sake of clarity, the discussion will refer chiefly to the narrative of *A Song of Ice and Fire*, highlighting only the most relevant aspects developed in the TV show.

When asked about the level of sexual brutality and violence in his narratives, Martin usually justifies it by emphasizing his authorial intent of representing the 'real' Middle Ages. In the interview by John Hodgman he claims, for instance, that J. R. R. Tolkien and his followers 'were getting it [the Middle Ages] all wrong' and produced 'a sort of Disneyland Middle Ages, where they had castles and princesses and all that', and yet despite this medieval decorum, 'the sensibilities were those of 20th century Americans'.[4] It remains questionable whether *A Song of Ice and Fire* truly escapes contemporary sensibilities, yet Martin makes it clear that he is primarily preoccupied with creating an aura of 'historical' realism and authenticity, with which he explains any instance of gruesome violence in his fiction. If we follow this line of argumentation, any question such as 'is there misogyny in *A Song of Ice and Fire*?' might simply be answered, 'Yes, but it is not of our times – it's only medieval.' While the attribute 'medieval' is meant by Martin to refer to the historical period, or at least to distant past that has no influence on the present, it is not devoid of negative connotations and remains strongly coloured by the pun resulting from the homophonic association of *-eval* with *evil*.[5] This seems to reflect a wider problem with the term as it is frequently used today. Apart from providing a neutral reference to the Middle Ages, the adjective 'medieval' has acquired many evaluative meanings that stand in opposition to 'classical', 'renaissance' or 'modern'. Thus, in the contemporary imagination, the 'medieval' primarily embraces the archaic, primeval, cruel, violent, barbarian, uncultivated and irrational within its scope.[6] Obviously, the term may also entail the more positive connotations involved in the nostalgic reconstructions of the Middle Ages that look back to the period for something that has been lost. In fantasy literature this can be exemplified by the works of such authors as William Morris, C. S. Lewis, J. R. R. Tolkien and many of his followers.[7] Yet to Martin, who re-evaluates the past in a largely negative way, such visions appear unrealistic, immature and naive. Although he appreciates Tolkien's 'originality' and 'deep abiding love of myth and history', Martin strongly criticizes his followers for 'produc[ing] these endless series of dark lords and their evil minions who are all very ugly and wear black clothes'. Perceiving such visions of the Middle Ages as oversimplified and lacking the aura of realism, the author of *A Song of Ice and Fire* dismissively relegates them to the realm of Disneyland.[8]

Martin's narrative borrows heavily from European history and medieval tradition, yet his revision of the Middle Ages is far from monolithic in terms of inspirations. Anna Czarnowus observes that the setting of *A Song of Ice and Fire*, reminiscent of both

Old English and Anglo-Norman worlds, appears to be 'situated at a cross-section of the two historical periods or rather of the two literary images of these periods'.[9] Exploring how the narrative resonates with medieval history and culture, Carolyne Larrington compares Martin's worldbuilding technique to using the blocks 'chiselled out of the historical and imaginary medieval past', which entails the incorporation of a range of elements associated with the medieval North, the West, the Mediterranean and the exotic East.[10] In a recent collection of essays, Martin's historical inspirations have been given considerable critical attention in an attempt 'to help readers understand and appreciate the vast tapestry of George R. R. Martin's fiction by hanging it alongside the great vista of history'.[11] On the whole, the imagined Middle Ages of Martin's novels seem to be simultaneously recognizable and unrecognizable to the historian and the literary critic, as the author bends chronological timelines of historical events, transcends geographical boundaries and spices everything up with a touch of magic; this, in fact, remains marginal to the narrative (quite literally relegated to the exotic Essos and beyond the Wall). Thus, despite Martin's interest in history, what he aims to present as the 'real' Middle Ages is, in fact, a clear instance of neomedievalism, which can be conceptualized as 'a self-conscious, ahistorical, non-nostalgic imagining or reuse of the historical Middle Ages that selectively appropriates iconic images, often from other medievalisms, to construct a presentist space that disrupts traditional depictions of the medieval'.[12] This seems to have significant consequences for the discussion of misogynistic preconceptions in the depiction of Cersei Lannister. To say that anti-woman stereotypes are medieval is to imply that they belong to the past, that they are merely part and parcel of the Middle Ages – something ugly but safely sealed off in a distant, imprecise, bygone era. However, a closer examination of Martin's novels and the TV show reveals that although these stereotypes are rooted in the past, they do remain strikingly contemporary. Proposing to conceptualize them as neomedievalist rather than medieval, I suggest that examining the instances of misogyny in *A Song of Ice and Fire* and *Game of Thrones* 'can bring one closer to understanding the ways in which the Middle Ages operates as its own cultural fantasy'.[13] This fantasy clearly looks back to the past but also – purposefully or not – reflects the present, and as such deserves our attention.

Although a history of misogyny spans the centuries, originating long before the Middle Ages and continuing well beyond them, the scope of this article permits me to highlight only certain aspects that might shed light on Martin's depiction of Cersei.[14] While the picture of medieval misogyny is complicated by a more positive, 'profeminine' vision of femininity, anti-woman rhetoric is present in serious works of philosophers, theologians and medical experts, canon law, conduct manuals, literature and theatre.[15] As Howard R. Bloch observes, '[t]he ritual denunciation of women constitutes something on the order of a cultural constant, reaching back to the Old Testament as well as to Ancient Greece and extending through the fifteenth century.'[16] Not surprisingly, all throughout the Middle Ages, women were predominantly depicted as belligerent, ill-tempered, selfish, demanding, complaining, irrational, unreasonable, uncontrollable, unbalanced and lustful. Interestingly, all these epithets can justifiably be attributed to Cersei Lannister, the incarnation of medieval and neomedievalist misogynists' nightmares.

The medieval construction of female inferiority is firmly grounded in the interpretation of the biblical story of creation, in which Eve is created from Adam's rib, as a derivation of man and a 'help meet' for him (Gen. 2.18-22). This account is usually favoured over Gen. 1.27, which shows men and women as equally participating in God's divinity. In this version of the story, God created Adam and Eve on the sixth day in his own image, blessed them both and commanded them to multiply and subdue the earth. Thus, the roles of man and woman are implied to be complementary rather than hierarchically opposed to each other. However, the dominant narrative developed in Gen. 2.18-22 construes woman as the one created not in the image of God but in that of man, which makes her more distanced from God than man is, and thus more inclined to corruption and sin. In his analysis of the scene of creation as the cornerstone of misogynistic prejudices, Bloch argues that for medieval thinkers 'man enjoys existence (substance), being, unity, form and soul', whereas 'woman is associated with accident, becoming (temporality), difference, body and matter'.[17] This substantial contrast is also accentuated in scientific works of the period, including Aristotle's physiology and Galenic medicine, to produce a coherent and powerful picture of female inadequacy.[18]

Detached from God and situated within the earthly sphere of carnality, woman becomes closely associated with all the sins of the body, especially lust. In fact, the idea that women are more lecherous than men was disseminated through religious manuals, sermons, exempla, fabliaux, farcical and satirical tradition, art, literature and theatre. For instance, medieval works of art frequently depict the sin of lust as a woman, and the morality plays also tend to gender this vice as feminine (e.g. *Interlude of Youth*).[19] In fabliaux and farces, women whose excessive sexual appetites cannot be satisfied by their henpecked husbands often resort to adultery (e.g. Alisoun in Geoffrey Chaucer's 'Miller's Tale', Tyb in John Heywood's *Johan Johan*). A thirteenth-century Latin satirical poem, *Against Marrying* (*De coniuge non ducenda*), preserved in fifty-five manuscripts, blatantly asserts that 'A woman will receive all males: / No prick against her lust prevails'.[20] While such examples could easily be multiplied, they demonstrate that similar attitudes towards female sexuality were expressed in various genres throughout the period. As Ruth Mazo Karras notes:

> The particular attribution of lust to women was in part an effort to displace onto them the responsibility for the sins of men who could not control their own temptations. The placing of blame also indicated a real fear of women – that they would disrupt the established order of things by leading men astray, by causing bastards to inherit, by destroying clerical celibacy, by polluting the nunnery.[21]

Thus, female sexuality, construed as excessive, unrestrained and uncontrollable, is not only a cause of man's fall, which endangers individual salvation, but also a major threat to the functioning of a healthy society.

The echoes of chief medieval misogynists ring in the words of the High Sparrow, a religious leader of Westeros and a skilful political player with his own agenda, who claims that 'all women are wantons at heart, given to using their wiles and their beauty to work their wills on men' (*DD*, 792). Although these particular words are meant to diminish Cersei Lannister's influence as Queen Regent over young King Tommen (her son) quite late in Martin's narrative, similar ideas have shaped her portrayal from the very beginning of the novels. Cersei Lannister is indeed the arch-seductress of *A Song of Ice and Fire*, whose ambition coupled with sexual transgression leads to the murder of the rightful king, usurpation of the line of succession and bloody civil war. Of all the women in the series, she is the most bound to the corporeal, effectively using her body and sexuality in the quest for power, which is evident in the lesson given by her to Sansa during the siege: 'Tears are not a woman's *only* weapon. You've got another one between your legs, and you'd best learn to use it. You'll find men use their swords freely enough. Both kinds of swords' (*CK*, 845). It seems, however, that a common cheating wife would not be 'medieval' enough for Martin's revision of the Middle Ages, which is after all aimed at contemporary readers, who in all likelihood would not find adultery as repulsive and hazardous to social order as their medieval counterparts. Thus, to reinforce the negative image of Cersei, her infidelity is structured as an incestuous relationship with her twin brother. In Westeros, as in contemporary Western society, brother–sister incest is seen as 'a monstrous sin', the offspring of which are labelled 'abominations', and the rule applies to anyone except for the Targaryens, who 'like their dragons ... answered to neither gods nor men' (*CK*, 498). Here, Martin seems to diverge from medieval narratives, in which sibling incest, both incidental and deliberate, seems to have been considered as less atrocious than a parent–child relationship and was usually treated as a subplot rather than the major theme.[22] Observing that its consequences were usually tragic, Carolyne Larrington draws attention to the social circumstances surrounding incest, observing that '[f]rom a medieval moral perspective, both parental neglect and overindulgence provide opportunity for children to go morally astray'.[23] Although in *A Song of Ice and Fire*, the close relationship between Cersei and Jaime is in fact the consequence of their mother dying and being neglected by the father in childhood, the trope of incest is presented as a heinous act, emphasizing the siblings' – especially Cersei's – moral decadence.

Paradoxically, Cersei's biggest political achievement is plotting against her husband, Robert Baratheon, who is not a paragon of royal virtue himself. It is here that she spectacularly succeeds in getting him killed and securing the throne for her and Jaime's underage sons through the use of rhetoric and behind-the-scenes manoeuvres, which make it possible to read her as the female Machiavellian of the court.[24] It is also here that Cersei refuses to perform the proper role of the queen 'to act as a vessel, a passive body that will bear children from the king's line', introducing into the line of successions the offspring of the relationship with her twin, which can be interpreted as 'a form of self-replication or *auto-impregnation*'.[25] At this point her actions have a strong potential for subverting the patriarchal order through the introduction of a matriarchal line of succession. The very idea is strongly discredited, however, as her rule proves to be disastrous. Acting in the capacity of Queen Regent and ruling on behalf of her son Tommen, Cersei commits mistake after mistake, surrounds herself with fools and becomes increasingly paranoid, which, as Shiloh R. Carroll demonstrates, only 'conforms to unfortunate stereotypes that reinforce misogynistic ideas about women's ability to rule'.[26] Unable to distinguish between the well-being of her people and her own insatiable appetites, she proves unfit as a ruler, becoming an epitome of the medieval tyrant, whose fall must inevitably follow. While her downfall is motivated by the lack of leadership skills, the loss of political power is structured as the loss of control over her body and sexuality. In the beginning of the narrative Cersei is a strikingly attractive woman, taking pride in her emerald-green eyes, golden hair, fair complexion and graceful figure, as well as firmly believing in the power of her body to manipulate men into acting according to her wishes. However, as the story progresses, the firepower of her chief weapon diminishes considerably. As fit for a woman defined by carnality and succumbing to the sins of the body, in *A Feast for Crows* she is shown as overindulging in food and drink, which results in weight gain and loss of looks, becoming a visual representation of her moral bankruptcy.

More importantly, losing political influence is also structured as a sexual degradation and fits a regular pattern – the men with whom Cersei is involved become less and less powerful and more and more deplorable. Her incest with Jaime can be interpreted not only as private revenge against her abusive husband but also as a sort of rebellion against the rules imposed on women, manifesting itself in taking control of her own sexuality. Particularly in its initial stages, the relationship is also presented as one that provides her with psychological comfort and a sense of identity: 'Jaime and I are more than brother and sister. We are one person in two bodies. We shared a womb together. He came into this world holding my foot, our old maester said. When he is in me, I feel . . . whole' (*GT*, 485). In Jaime's absence, however, Cersei gets involved in a love affair with her cousin, Lancel Lannister, 'a poor copy' of her brother, who has been instrumental in the murder of Robert but turns out to be a man of neither political substance nor stamina, and who betrays her in the end (*CK*, 447). Finally, she resorts to Osney Kettleblack, to whom she offers sex in exchange for providing evidence against Margaery Tyrell, a rival queen married to her underage son. The whole scheme proves ineffective, and Cersei's failure is highlighted by a shift in the power structure of her relationship with Kettleblack: 'He thrust his fingers inside the bodice of her gown and yanked, and the silk parted with a ripping sound so loud that Cersei was afraid that half of the Red Keep must have heard it. "Take off the rest before I tear that too," he said. "You can keep the crown on. I like you in the crown"' (*FC*, 837).

While Cersei in this scene appears powerless and unable to protest, Kettleblack is the master of the situation. With her clothes unceremoniously torn and the crown becoming nothing more than a sexual fetish, she is bluntly commanded to fulfil his erotic fantasy. From being a powerful woman who exercised control over her body and enjoyed her sexuality, Cersei is reduced to a passive object of male desire and treated no better than a common woman. This becomes even more evident in the scene featuring the 'Walk of Shame'. Here, her naked body is exposed to public view and reveals further signs of deterioration: excess fat, stretch marks and sagging breasts. With shaved head and reduced to her ageing nakedness, the queen loses more than her personal dignity and becomes 'soiled goods' – the term which frames her shame in economic terms (*DD*, 1040). This ritual punishment has nothing to do with personal penance; its sole aim is to make a spectacle of the queen's body, devaluing her in the eyes of her subjects so as to prevent her from regaining control and power in the future. This is in fact the last appearance of Cersei in the novels, leaving the readers with the impression that the 'game of thrones' is over for the power-hungry queen. Yet, her narrative continues on screen, demonstrating that the punishment failed to break her spirit and made her even more cold-hearted and merciless in the long run.

The sixth season of *Game of Thrones* makes it clear that Cersei refuses to surrender and chooses agency (associated with masculinity) over victimization (linked with femininity). While her authority and power are seriously diminished, Cersei tries to regain her influence over her son and become a significant political player again. When she is approached by a group of armed members of the Faith Militant in the Red Keep and ordered to go and speak with the High Sparrow, she refuses. When she is threatened that her disobedience will lead to violence, she responds, 'I choose violence' and calmly watches Ser Gregor Clegane literally tear off one of the men's head.[27] Cersei's choice of violence in this scene foreshadows the season's finale, in which she gets rid of all her enemies at one go – by blowing up the Great Sept of Baelor, where they are gathered to witness her trial. Dressed in fine clothes and adorned with exquisite jewellery, Cersei is shown as watching from afar the explosion that killed not only those who opposed her but also the innocent citizens of the city. When Cersei learns Tommen committed suicide, her moment of triumph is slightly marred; yet she proceeds to be crowned the Queen of the Seven Kingdoms and finally sits down on the Iron Throne. Becoming queen in her own right at last, she appears unmoved by the hatred of the nobles gathered for her coronation, who swear their loyalty to her only out of fear.

In one of the interviews, Lena Headey, the actress playing the role of Cersei Lannister, said, 'I don't play her as a villain. I just play a woman who is a survivor and will do exactly what a man [would] do.'[28] Although Cersei is indeed a survivor, she is not perceived as such by the audience due to her selfishness and cruelty. Her choice of violence indicates that she is capable of aggression – a stereotypically masculine trait. Yet, as Anne Campbell explains, aggression is perceived differently in men and women:

> Both sexes see an intimate connection between aggression and control, but for women aggression is the failure of self-control, while for men it is the imposing of control over others. Women's aggression emerges from their inability to check the disruptive and frightening force of their own anger. For men, it is a legitimate means of assuming authority over the disruptive and frightening forces in the world around them.[29]

Thus, when she emulates masculine behaviour to achieve her goals, her actions are perceived negatively by the audience and contribute to the accumulation of negative stereotypes about the figure of Cersei, who increasingly resembles a monstrous and evil witch who would refrain from nothing to achieve what she wants. In Seasons 7 and 8 she is unchangingly portrayed as a woman who is so focused on keeping her power at any cost that she ignores the broader picture and the threat from the army of the Night King in the North. Being overconfident in her strategic and military skills, she alienates herself even from Jaime and eventually fails to protect herself and her kingdom from the attack of Daenerys Targaryen, which once again calls into question her ability to make wise decisions.[30]

In both *A Song of Ice and Fire* and *Game of Thrones* Cersei's transgressive sexuality and adultery go hand in hand with her instability, irrationality and paranoia. For a medieval audience such a connection was obvious, as it was reinforced by medical tracts that linked female physiology and sexuality with emotional and mental imbalances on the grounds that the very possession of a womb affected a woman's senses. Although Galen, a significant medieval medical authority, dismissed the idea expressed by Aretaeus of Cappadocia that the womb was almost an independent creature, or at least 'a living thing inside another living thing', which could move up and down a woman's body in search of satisfaction, such a belief was quite widespread.[31] Whether considered a living creature or not, in early texts devoted to gynaecology the womb was often presented as capable of wandering within the female body. Excessive movement, caused by lack of sexual intercourse or menstrual fluid retention, could lead to the damage of other organs and death. A dissatisfied womb was believed to be capable of negatively affecting a woman's speech, senses and mental faculties, forcing its owner to look for sexual pleasure. Furthermore, as Laurinda S. Dixon writes, '[u]nder Christianity the popular image of the victim of *furor uterinus* changed from a woman beset by organic physical illness to one plagued by demons and at the mercy of supernatural forces.'[32] It is difficult to prove whether George R. R. Martin is actually familiar with the medical theory of the Middle Ages outlined above or not. Yet, it would probably be hard to convince the twenty-first-century readers that Cersei's transgressive sexual behaviour and irrationality are caused by her wandering womb or being possessed by demons. Consequently, another, clearly non-medieval, layer is added to her portrayal.

Firstly, there is an attempt to build some psychological credibility of the character by equipping Cersei with contemporary motivations. Thus, her rage and distrust of men are set against the context of her relationship with Robert, from which she emerges as physically and sexually abused. Rather than becoming a withdrawn victim of domestic violence, which would perhaps bring her more sympathy from the audience, Cersei wears her bruises as 'a badge of honour' and takes revenge on her assailant (*GT*, 429). Her objection to being treated as a political pawn, a currency in the marriage market or, in her own words, 'a brood mare' will also be understandable to contemporary readers (*SS*, 266). It seems only natural that as a woman equipped with ambition, she should strive to make room for herself within a system that does not favour women. However, even if her actions can be partly justified, her own inclination towards violence and cruelty become so prominent that the readers are led to believe she is in fact capable of any abominable act (e.g. the murder of Jon Arryn is easily attributed to her until it turns out much later in the cycle that it was plotted by Jon's wife Lysa and Petyr Baelish). One of the reasons for this is that until the fourth novel in the cycle, Cersei is not a point-of-view (POV) character, so events are not depicted from her perspective. Interestingly, when she finally becomes one, the technique is used differently from its application in the case of other characters. Rather than presenting the complexity of her circumstances, the chapters focalized through Cersei invariably emphasize the negative aspects of her personality: shallowness, pride, lust, political short-sightedness, errors of judgement, instrumental treatment of power and growing paranoia.

Secondly, the depiction of Cersei lacks any positive qualities traditionally associated with femininity. Setting herself apart from the despised representatives of her own sex, she perceives herself as a better version of the men she knows. Interestingly, Cersei's famous words to Robert – 'What a jape the gods have made of us two. . . . By all rights, you ought to be in skirts and me in mail' (*GT*, 429) – not only imply his cowardice but also sound like a paraphrase of the words of the Host's wife in Chaucer's 'Monk's Tale Prologue': 'False coward, wrek thy wyf! / By corpus bones, I wol have thy knyf, / And thou shalt have my distaf and go spynne / Fro day to nyght!' (ll. 1905–8).³³ Chaucer's choice of 'knyf' and 'distaff' to represent masculine and feminine spheres of activity in this passage is not incidental. Although the items do not necessarily need to change owners, they can be found in the depictions of carnivalesque reversal of gender roles on the margins of medieval manuscripts, as well as in literature and theatre. The image of a wife beating her husband with a distaff features, for instance, in *The Luttrell Psalter* – one of the most famous English manuscripts of the fourteenth century. Here, a tool traditionally related to the feminine activity of spinning is also a 'symbol of her appropriation of phallic power' and aggressive female sexuality while the masculine attribute of a knife is not 'a protective sign of male strength but embarrassingly exhibits the priapic lust that subjugates him to the female'.³⁴ Female hunger for power over her husband is also famously voiced by Chaucer's Wife of Bath in her tale: 'Wommen desiren to have sovereynetee / As wel over hir housbond as hir love, / And for to been in maistrie hym above' (ll. 1038–40).³⁵ Finally, shrewish and domineering wives are characteristic in fabliaux and drama, where, as transgressors against social order, they earn their share of ruthless ridicule and satire. Probably the best-known example of such a wife on the English medieval stage is Mrs Noah, who appears in the York, Chester and Towneley Cycles and stands in vivid contrast to the meek wife of the biblical Noah narrative. In each play, the rebellious woman initially disobeys her husband's orders and refuses to enter the Ark; and in all of them she is finally physically coerced into obeying. The Towneley Play Mrs Noah is the character who opposes her husband most violently and even wishes him dead, yet she also submits in the end.³⁶

The woman who wants to take over male power is a stock image in the medieval imagination, yet the issue of the reversal of gender roles is depicted quite literally in *A Song of Ice and Fire*. Let us consider a few examples of how Cersei perceives herself:

When we were little, Jaime and I were so much alike that even our lord father could not tell us apart. Sometimes as a lark we would dress in each other's clothes and spend a whole day each as the other. Yet even so, when Jaime was given his first sword, there was none for me. . . . Jaime learned to fight with sword and lance and mace, while I was taught to smile and sing and please. He was heir to Casterly Rock, while I was to be sold to some stranger like a horse, to be ridden whenever my new owner liked, beaten whenever he liked, and cast aside in time for a younger filly. Jaime's lot was to be glory and power, while mine was birth and moonblood. (*CK*, 848–9)

When Tywin Lannister spoke, men obeyed. When Cersei spoke, they felt free to counsel her, to contradict her, even *refuse* her. *It is all because I am a woman. Because I cannot fight them with a sword.* (*FC*, 507)

While the masculine sphere of activity is seen as a battleground that brings 'glory and power', femininity is defined by 'being sold to a stranger like a horse' and childbearing. Not surprisingly then, Cersei is embittered by the constrictions imposed on women and jealous of the male freedom to act and fight. What catches our attention though is the mention of cross-dressing in childhood, which in a way prefigures her later transgressive behaviour, and the fact that both passages make the sword a necessary attribute of masculinity. Taking into account that the word 'sword' is frequently used by Martin to mean 'penis' (see, for instance, the lesson given to Sansa during the siege mentioned earlier), Cersei's envy of her brother's weapon can be read as a literal reference to the Freudian concept of penis envy, which seems to be another addition to a long-established tradition of female inadequacy and imperfection.

While the theory has obviously received its share of criticism from feminist critics for continuing the tradition of representing women as broken or deficient men, it has also taken hold of the popular imagination. In short, Freud theorized penis envy as a natural stage of psychosexual development in girls, observing that 'the discovery that she is castrated is a turning point in a girl's growth' and that girls 'fall a victim to "envy for the penis," which will leave ineradicable traces on their development and the formation of their character'.[37] Siegfried Zepf and Dietmar Seel explain it in relation to the Oedipal stage in the following way:

> In the context of the rivalry with the mother, penis envy refers to the maternal power over the father's penis that the daughter wants to have in herself, while, in the context of the rivalry with the father, penis envy arises from the jealousy of the father's penis that the daughter believes is necessary to have on herself in order to satisfy her mother.[38]

If this stage of development is properly resolved, a girl transposes her initial desire for the father onto men generally, assumes a passive role in the relationships and sublimates her desire for a penis into a yearning for a baby. If not, she might suffer from sexual inhibition or remain a neurotic victim of penis envy as an adult. In this case Hilary M. Lips writes, '[s]he may try to be masculine, become resentful and jealous of men, and reject the feminine fulfillment of pregnancy – all the while completely unaware that it is her unconscious wish for a penis that is making her so cranky.'[39] The description can easily be linked with Cersei, who at one point of the narrative states: 'A pity Lord Tywin Lannister never had a son. I could have been the heir he wanted, but I lacked the cock' (SS, 1005). Here, it becomes evident that she perceives herself as her father's son who lacks nothing but a penis, claims she should have been born a man and attributes all her problems and failures to being 'castrated' and thus unable to compete with men in the public sphere.

Cersei's feelings of envy towards men could probably gain her some sympathy from readers. After all, as Mari Ruti writes, 'in a society that rewards the possessor of the penis with obvious political, economic, and cultural benefits, women would have to be a little obtuse not to envy it; they would have to be a little obtuse not to want the social advantages that automatically accrue to the possessor of the penis.'[40] Yet, in the course of the narrative Cersei fails to substantially change the social pattern that promotes female passivity and subordination. When in power, she strives to emulate traditionally masculine attributes so much that she eventually becomes a caricature of Robert Baratheon. Throughout *A Feast for Crows*, her original delight in good food turns into gluttony coupled with increasing consumption of wine. Significantly, her consequent weight gain becomes a visual indication not only of her moral depravity but also of her growing resemblance to Robert. The culmination of the process becomes apparent in the scene of Cersei's sex with another woman, Taena. Here, Cersei disregards her partner's complaints of pain and actually imagines herself to be acting as Robert, the reminiscences of marital rape informing the whole scene:

> She wondered what it would feel like to suckle on those breasts, to lay the Myrish woman on her back and push her legs apart and use her as a man would use her, the way Robert would use *her* when the drink was in him, and she was unable to bring him off with hand or mouth.
> Those had been the worst nights, lying helpless underneath him as he took his pleasure, stinking of wine and grunting like a boar. . . . She was always sore afterward, raw between the legs, her breasts painful from the mauling he would give them. (*FC*, 685)

These painful memories seize Cersei's imagination, driving her to perform the role her husband did in their marital bed. Like him, she puts the blame for her brutality on the wine and domineers over her partner, claiming her rights to sex as the queen and imagining, quite disturbingly, that 'her fingers were a boar's tusks, ripping the Myrish woman apart from groin to throat' (*FC*, 693). It is emphasized that Cersei derives neither pleasure nor satisfaction from the homosexual intercourse; the only attraction lies in acting like a man and taking absolute control of the situation in which another woman is at her mercy. Furthermore, the image of the boar ambiguously lingers over the whole scene. Referring to Robert first, it is later connected with Cersei, signalling that her metaphorical transformation is complete. Yet, the boar is also the animal that caused Robert's death early in the cycle and as such gloomily foreshadows Cersei's forthcoming political fiasco. The scene, blending a detailed description of sex with interior monologue, reinforces the negative stereotypes used in the construction of the most prominent female villain of the cycle, insinuating that in her penis envy-driven attempts to emulate male behaviour, Cersei Lannister has become a glutton, a drunk, a rapist and a fool unable to foresee her downfall coming.

The depiction of Cersei is indicative of Martin's overall neomedieval approach to creating his secondary world as a gritty rather than nostalgic version of the Middle Ages. As Kavita Mudan Finn succinctly puts it, 'the problem with Cersei Lannister is not that she conforms to negative medieval stereotypes; it is that Martin – and the HBO producers – insist on incorporating *all* of those stereotypes at once.'[41] While the construction of this character depends to a great extent on misogynistic discourse inherited from the Middle Ages, it is also 'translated' into more contemporary terms by adding layers of meaning comprehensible to a contemporary audience. Yet, the underlying principles have remained strikingly similar. Despite the fact that Cersei Lannister has done no more than male villains have, her rise to power through sexual manipulation and violence is seen as an unforgivable transgression, requiring a ritual punishment, which involves exposing her naked body to humiliate her. Although she is at one point ironically described as 'as gentle as King Maegor, as selfless as Aegon the Unworthy, as wise as Mad Aerys' (*DD*, 308), and thus epitomizes all the male tyrants known to Westeros, they have been recorded in the chronicles as fearsome despots, while she will perhaps be best remembered as a common woman, forced to parade naked through the jeering crowd. Finally, even though she proved a tough political player capable of overcoming her enemies and becoming the queen, her death in the final season highlights her helplessness rather than bravery. While the viewers probably expect to see her fighting to the end, Cersei appears weak, fearful and paralysed when she witnesses Daenerys and her dragon destroying the city. The impression that lingers beyond the show's finale is that Westeros had a glass ceiling of its own, which Cersei, despite all her frantic attempts, failed to break. While she indeed lacks the qualities of an effective leader, her incompetence is gendered as specifically feminine, rather than merely human, by highlighting her carnality, monstrous sexuality and transgressive behaviour. This resonates well with the medieval construction of misogyny but simultaneously repeats more contemporary negative stereotypes of female rule, which implies perhaps that the 'medieval', encompassing the meaning of 'a bygone era' and 'irrationally barbarous', is not as removed from the present as we would optimistically like it to be.

Postscript

Carolyne Larrington

The global pandemic that raged from the beginning of 2020 onwards had a marked impact on the fictional universe of *A Song of Ice and Fire* and *Game of Thrones*. Where in 2019 concrete plans for a number of prequel TV shows, the opening of the *Game of Thrones* theme park at Linen Mills Studios in Banbridge, Northern Ireland, and even the long-anticipated completion of the sixth novel in Martin's series, *The Winds of Winter* were on the horizon, all these developments were derailed by studio shutdowns, financing problems and Martin's involvement in a good number of other projects unrelated to the *Game of Thrones* universe. Yet, as the 'Known World' industry cranks slowly back into action, ten years after the first broadcast of the TV show and the publication of *A Dance with Dragons*, interest in Martin's creation remains strong.

What kept readers reading, audiences watching, people connecting with the transmedia franchise all across the world in this time of unprecedented crisis? In part, it was the global fascination with power and how effectively it can be used: for fantasy epic reaches outside itself to ask big contemporary political questions. Who constitutes 'us' and who are 'them'? Who should be allowed to pass through the Wall to the relative safety of the Seven Kingdoms, given the existential threat the White Walkers pose to all humanity? How long can the introduction of Western, liberal values – like the abolition of slavery in Slaver's Bay – be sustained if the threat of overwhelming (dragon-based) firepower is removed? Also critically, the plot lines are deeply invested in narratives of the family: each of the younger generation had to find their own paths in life, escaping the often toxic legacies of their House and parents: from the Mad King to the über-patriarch Tywin, to the soul-destroying aggression of Balon Greyjoy. Third, the series was invested in exploring different kinds of identity: characters with disabilities, like Tyrion and Bran, or born into poverty, like Davos and Bronn – even some women, like Brienne and Sansa and Yara the lesbian, all came out as winners. Even if the TV show eventually lost its nerve in asking its far-reaching questions about Western imperialism and other challenges to the established Western social order as it galloped towards the finish, a key storyline, developed beyond the book material, gave a touching romance to Grey Worm and Missandei, two fine actors of colour.

Lessons have been learned though over the last ten years; critical reception of Martin and Benioff and Weiss's vision of Westeros and Essos has highlighted questions about their depictions of gender and sexuality, violence, including sexual violence, and race across printed and visual media. The showrunners proved nimble enough to respond to the criticism; gratuitous nudity, 'sexposition' – long speeches to explain key backstory and plot points, enlivened by romping prostitutes in the foreground – and graphic dramatizations of sexual violence were all curtailed as the showrunners began to respond to the criticisms of women commentators and a female fanbase.

The one prequel in production in the summer of 2021 and slated for broadcast in 2022 is *House of the Dragon*, relating the events of the Targaryen dynastic civil war known as the *Dance of the Dragons*. This is set a hundred years before the history that unfolds in *A Song of Ice and Fire*. Importantly, a British Black actor, Steve Toussaint, takes the key part of Corlys Velaryon, also known as the 'Sea Snake', a famous sea lord from Valyria. Velaryon's son Laenor is also prominent in the story, and John Macmillan, another Black British actor, has been cast in the role. Laenor is also gay, according to the books; increased visibility for and acceptance of a gay character builds on the positive depictions of Renly and Loras in the books and perhaps can counteract the problematic imagining of Yara's lesbian sexuality in the show.

George Martin has a five-year deal with HBO to work on other adaptations of fantasy material, including his own writing. There is even the possibility that a Broadway show about the tourney at Harrenhal may be staged in 2023. *The Winds of Winter* is now forecast to be many hundreds of pages long, and the publication of teaser chapters has stalled. Meanwhile, Martin's publication of the first volume of *Fire and Blood*, a history of House Targaryen and its impact on the Seven Kingdoms, in 2018, pre-empted the completion of *The Winds of Winter*. Will the intricately imagined, medievalized fantasy universe that Martin has built over the decades become as lucrative, productive and mesmerizing as the comparable Marvel Comics Universe? Content-hungry entertainment media seem set to fund fantasy franchises well into the future – though they are also ruthless in pulling the plug on shows that don't pull in the audiences.

In the end, *A Song of Ice and Fire* and *Game of Thrones* has enlarged our vision of what fantasy epic could achieve, as it asked its vital and resonant questions about gender, power, violence and possibilities of change. As this book has shown, George R. R. Martin has built a remarkable world, transmuting and reimagining historical material and engaging in a neomedievalism that alludes to, challenges and renegotiates familiar medieval fantasy tropes. With its multiple male and female heroes and, famously, the many 'cripples, bastards and broken things', whose storylines reflect different responses to violence and disempowerment, books and show allowed people across the globe to debate how treachery, violence (often against women) and ethical behaviour played out for its characters, how individual self-realization and rather limited versions of political liberation could be achieved and, more satisfyingly, how collective resolution and solidarity in the face of an existential threat to all humanity could overcome nihilism and despair.

Notes

Introduction

1 Helen Young, *Race and Popular Fantasy Literature: Habits of Whiteness* (New York and London: Routledge, 2016), 11.
2 Ibid., 63.
3 Ibid., 12.
4 David Matthews, *Medievalism: A Critical History* (Cambridge: D. S. Brewer, 2015).
5 See Shiloh Carroll, '"Tone Deaf?" *Game of Thrones*, Showrunners and Criticism', in *HBO's Original Voices: Race, Gender, Sexuality and Power*, ed. Victoria McCollum and Giuliana Monteverde (Abingdon and New York: Routledge, 2018), 169–82 See also Carroll's 'Introduction: Martin and Medievalist Fantasy', in *Medievalism in A Song of Ice and Fire and Game of Thrones* (Cambridge: D. S. Brewer, 2018), 1–22, in particular 13–21 and 'Adaptation and Reception', in the same volume, 131–80, in particular 144–8.
6 Leslie J. Workman, 'Editorial', *Studies in Medievalism*, 7 (1995): 2. Compare also Shippey's definition on the *Studies in Medievalism* home page; quoted in Matthews, *Medievalism*, 11.
7 Tison Pugh and Angela Jane Weisl, *Medievalisms: Making the Past in the Present* (New York and London: Routledge, 2013), 1.
8 Ibid.
9 Carol L. Robinson and Pamela Clements, 'Living with Neomedievalism', *Studies in Medievalism*, 18 (2009): 55–75 (62). See also Marshall's definition, 'a self-conscious, ahistorical, non-nostalgic imagining or reuse of the historical Middle Ages that selectively appropriates iconic images … to construct a presentist space that disrupts traditional depictions of the medieval'. David W. Marshall, 'Neomedievalism, Identification, and the Haze of Medievalism', *Studies in Medievalism*, 20 (2011): 21–34 (22).
10 Matthews, *Medievalism*, 39.
11 See Carolyne Larrington, '"(No More) Reaving, Roving, Raiding or Raping": The Iron-Born in George R. R. Martin's *A Song of Ice and Fire* and HBO's *Game of Thrones*', in *The Vikings Reimagined: Reception, Recovery, Engagement*, ed. Tom Birkett and Roderick Dale, Northern Medieval World (Kalamazoo: Medieval Institute Press, 2020), 162–78.
12 Matthews, *Medievalism*, 1.
13 Thomas A. Prendergast and Stephanie Trigg, *Affective Medievalism: Love, Abjection, and Discontent* (Manchester: Manchester University Press, 2018), 119.
14 Matthews, *Medievalism*, xii.
15 Ibid.
16 Ibid., ix.
17 See Sarah Salih, 'Cinematic Authenticity Effects and Medieval Art: A Paradox', in *Medieval Film*, ed. Anke Bernau and Bettina Bildhauer (Manchester: Manchester University Press, 2009), 20–39.

18 Mikal Gilmore, (2014), https://www.rollingstone.com/culture/culture-news/george-r-r-martin-the-rolling-stone-interview-242487/.
19 See Carolyne Larrington, *Winter is Coming: The Medieval World of Game of Thrones* (London: I.B. Tauris, 2015), 49–53; Larrington, *All Men Must Die, Power and Passion in Game of Thrones* (London: Bloomsbury Academic, 2021), 165–9.
20 Shiloh Carroll, *Medievalism in A Song of Ice and Fire and Games of Thrones* (Cambridge: D. S. Brewer, 2018), 8.
21 Anne Gjelsvik and Rikke Schubart (eds.), *Women of Ice and Fire: Gender, Game of Thrones, and Multiple Media Engagements* (London: Bloomsbury, 2016); Zita Eva Rohr and Lisa Benz (eds.), *Queenship and the Women of Westeros: Female Agency and Advice in Game of Thrones and A Song of Ice and Fire* (Basingstoke and New York: Palgrave Macmillan, 2019).
22 Valerie Estelle Frankel, *Women in Game of Thrones: Power, Conformity and Resistance* (Jefferson: McFarland, 2014); Ken Mondschein, *Game of Thrones and the Medieval Art of War* (Jefferson: McFarland, 2017); Carol Parrish Jamison, *Chivalry in Westeros: The Knightly Code of A Song of Ice and Fire* (Jefferson: McFarland, 2018).
23 Jes Battis and Susan Johnston (eds.), *Mastering the Game of Thrones: Essays on George R. R. Martin's A Song of Ice and Fire* (Jefferson: McFarland, 2015); A. Keith Kelly (ed.), *Power and Subversion in Game of Thrones: Critical Essays on the HBO Series* (Jefferson: McFarland, 2022).
24 Bartłomiej Błaszkiewicz (ed.), *George R. R. Martin's A Song of Ice and Fire and the Medieval Literary Tradition* (Warszawa: Wydawnictwo Uniwersytetu Warszawskiego, 2014).
25 Amy S. Kaufman, 'Muscular Medievalism', *The Year's Work in Medievalism*, 31 (2016): 56–66.

Chapter 1

1 Alex Gendler, ed.ted.com/lessons/the-wars-that-inspired-game-of-thrones-alex-gendler
2 See Martin's Foreword(s) to the 2013–15 republished editions, and 'My Hero: Maurice Druon', https://www.theguardian.com/books/2013/apr/05/maurice-druon-george-rr-martin. Compare Martin's blog, http://www.georgerrmartin.com/maurice-druons-the-iron-king/
3 'My Hero: Maurice Druon'.
4 Mikal Gilmore, http://www.rollingstone.com/tv/news/george-r-r-martin-the-rolling-stone-interview-20140423
5 The French reprints carry on the cover band Martin's guarantee: 'Si vous aimez *Game of Thrones*, vous adorerez *Les Rois Maudits*' (If you love *Game of Thrones*, you will adore *Les Rois Maudits*).
6 They shared great-grandparents in Robert I of Artois and Matilda of Brabant and are consequently second cousins.
7 See, for example, Douglas Kelly, *The Art of Medieval French Romance* (Madison: University of Wisconsin Press, 1992).
8 *The Lily and the Lion*, 137.
9 Martin elects to grant such POV status only to Westerosi characters, with the exception of Areo Hotah, captain of Doran Martell's guard in Dorne, and (in a single chapter,

Dance with Dragons, ch. 31), Melisandre. See Carolyne Larrington, *All Men Must Die: Power and Passion in Game of Thrones* (London: Bloomsbury, 2021), 193–4.
10 See *SS*, ch. 5, after the Battle of Blackwater Bay; *FC*, ch. 24, when Davos is reported as executed by Lord Wyman Manderley.
11 *The Poisoned Crown*, 240.
12 See *The Strangled Queen*, Prologue: 'He had curbed the powerful, maintained peace in so far as it was possible, reformed the law, constructed fortresses that the land might be cultivated in their shelter, united provinces, convoked assemblies of the middle class so that it might speak its mind, and watched unremittingly over the independence of France.'
13 http://asoiaf.westeros.org/index.php?/topic/87914-the-accursed-kings-characters-in-asoiaf-ak-spoilers/
14 *The Iron King*, 227–31.
15 *The Strangled Queen*, 144–62; *The Royal Succession*, [online edition] loc. 745–836.
16 *The She-Wolf*, Prologue: 'Driven by blind and vaguely mystical impulses, primitive dreams of sanctity and adventure, by their condition of poverty and by a sudden frenzy for destruction, country boys and girls, sheep-, cow- and swineherds, young artisans, young spinners and weavers, nearly all of them between fifteen and twenty, abruptly left their families and villages and formed barefoot errant bands, provided with neither food nor money. Some wild idea of a crusade was the pretext for the exodus.'
17 See Carolyne Larrington, *Winter is Coming: The Medieval World of Game of Thrones* (London: I.B. Tauris, 2015), 184.
18 *FC*, ch. 28.
19 *SS*, ch. 36; HBO *Game of Thrones*, 'Second Sons' (3.8). See also Larrington, *Winter is Coming*, 15–16.
20 *The Iron King*, 17.
21 Ibid.
22 Ibid., 18.
23 *SS*, ch. 61.
24 *The Iron King*, 243–50.
25 *The Poisoned Crown*, 233–4.
26 See below; *The Royal Succession*, loc. 2731–94.
27 *The Lily and the Lion*, 132–3.
28 Ibid., 137.
29 Ibid.
30 See Larrington, *Winter is Coming*, 177–80, 72–3.
31 *The Iron King*, 101–6.
32 Larrington, *Winter is Coming*, 180.
33 Commemorated in Lombard Street in the City of London's banking district.
34 *The She-Wolf*, 239–40. Cf. *The King without a Kingdom*, 208, 'You take his place on the throne, you take on his obligations also'.
35 *The Lily and the Lion*, 247. The visit took place in April 1331.
36 *DD*, ch. 44.
37 HBO *Game of Thrones*, 'The Laws of Gods and Men' (4.6).
38 A fuller account of the credit squeeze Cersei faces as a result of her default is given in this article: Carolyne Larrington, https://www.1843magazine.com/culture/the-daily/game-of-loans
39 See Larrington, *All Men Must Die*, 101–2, and Daniel W. Drezner's account of the Iron Bank Board's likely view of the new régime in Westeros, 'Minutes from the Iron Bank's

Board of Directors' Meeting: A One-Act Play', https://www.washingtonpost.com/outlook/2019/05/20/minutes-iron-banks-board-directors-meeting-one-act-play/?noredirect=on&utm_term=.0242aa94400a.
40 Jon Stark's parentage was finally elucidated in the show. In *A Dance with Dragons*, Aegon Targaryen, apparently the son of Rhaegar and Elia Martell, emerges as a new Targaryen heir, gaining the strong support of Varys. *A Dance with Dragons*, Epilogue.
41 Larrington, *All Men Must Die*, 70–1, 114–15.
42 Ibid., 99–100.
43 *The Royal Succession*, loc. 2731–94.
44 Ibid., loc. 2827–910.
45 *The Lily and the Lion*, 341–76.
46 *The She-Wolf*, 155.
47 Ibid., 397.
48 Ibid.
49 *The Royal Succession*, loc. 2942–57: 'this law which was to triumph in history after it had ruined the kingdom by a hundred years of war' (2057).
50 *FC*, chs. 13, 21, 40.
51 Larrington, *All Men Must Die*, 127–8, 202–5.
52 *The Lily and the Lion*, 285–6.
53 Ibid., 328–9: 'So great was the light from the burning French ships that the coming of night was scarcely noticed' (329).
54 *The King without a Kingdom*, 259.
55 Gilmore, http://www.rollingstone.com/tv/news/george-r-r-martin-the-rolling-stone-interview-20140423.
56 Ibid.

Chapter 2

1 Shiloh Carroll, *Medievalism in A Song of Ice and Fire and Games of Thrones* (Cambridge: D. S. Brewer, 2018), 21.
2 Adam Debosscher, '#ForTheThrone: A Study of the Emphasis on the Medievalism in the Paratext of G. R. R. Martin's *A Song of Ice and Fire* in HBO's *Game of Thrones*', *The Year's Work in Medievalism*, 33 (2018): 82–6.
3 Ibid., 78.
4 Ibid., 91.
5 William P. MacNeil, 'Machiavellian Fantasy and the Game of Laws', *Critical Quarterly*, 57, no. 1 (2015): 34.
6 Charles Lambert, 'A Tender Spot in My Heart: Disability in *A Song of Ice and Fire*', *Critical Quarterly*, 57, no. 1 (2015): 24.
7 Carroll, *Medievalism*, 23–53.
8 See Larrington's chapter in this collection.
9 Lambert, 'A Tender Spot in My Heart', 24.
10 Alex Woloch, *The One vs the Many: Minor Characters and the Space of the Protagonist in the Novel* (Princeton and Oxford: Princeton University Press, 2003), 244–5.
11 Ibid., 14.
12 Ibid., 245.

13 Ibid., 30.
14 Ibid., 3.
15 Ibid., 2.
16 Ibid., 4.
17 Ibid., 13.
18 Ibid., 18.
19 Valerie Estelle Frankel, *Women in Game of Thrones: Power, Conformity and Resistance* (Jefferson: McFarland, 2014), 71; Lynsey Mitchell, 'Re-affirming and Rejecting the Rescue Narrative as an Impetus for War: To War for a Woman in a *Song of Ice and Fire*', *Law and Humanities*, 12, no. 2 (2018): 229–50.
20 Caroline Spector, 'Power and Feminism in Westeros', in *Beyond the Wall: Exploring George R. R. Martin's A Song of Ice and Fire*, ed. James Lowder (Dallas: Smart Pop Books, 2012), 171.
21 See Maria Błaszkiewicz's chapter in this volume.
22 Sean T. Collins, 'Game of Thrones' Recap: For Whom the Bell Tolls', *Rolling Stone*, 19 May 2019. Online.

Chapter 3

1 For the scroll containing the account of Rhaegar and Lyanna's marriage, see 'Eastwatch', (7.5). For the book that convinces both Jon Arryn and Ned Stark of the illegitimacy of Cersei's children, *The Lineages and Histories of the Great Houses of the Seven Kingdoms* by Grand Maester Malleon, see episodes 1.4, 1.5 and 1.6.
2 Though Qyburn was stripped of his maester's chain prior to his revival of Gregor Clegane, the experiments he performed and knowledge he accrued to perform this revival happened while he was still a maester: See episodes 5.2, 5.3, 5.8 and 5.10.
3 Shireen Baratheon survives greyscale but the disease disfigures her; her siblings do not survive. In the books, Maester Cressen's role in curing the disease is unclear, though he feels guilt over the outcome. In 5.4, Stannis Baratheon, Shireen's father, tells her that he hired 'every maester on this side of the world. Every healer, every apothecary' to stop the disease. Which healer's method worked and which healers' methods did not is unknown. See also *CK*, 2–3. Sam discovers the cure by combing through the Citadel's library in 7.2 and 7.3. Sam learns how wights are created and the best way to stop them in 'A very old book in Maester Aemon's library' in 1.7.
4 Wildfire is not the result of maesters' experiments but rather it is a proprietary secret of the Alchemists' Guild, whose fully trained members are styled as 'Wisdoms': *CK*, 279–83; episode 2.5.
5 Ayelet Haimson Lushkov, *You Win or You Die* (London: I.B. Tauris, 2017); Carolyne Larrington, *Winter is Coming* (London: I.B. Tauris, 2016); *Game of Thrones versus History: Written in Blood*, ed. Brian A. Pavlac (Hoboken: Wiley Blackwell, 2017); *Queenship and the Women of Westeros*, ed. Zita Eva Rohr and Lisa Benz (Cham: Palgrave Macmillan, 2020).
6 Larrington, *Winter is Coming*, 68–74, esp. 68–70; Carolyne Larrington, '"(No More) Reaving, Roving, Raiding, or Raping": The Ironborn in George R. R. Martin's A Song of Ice and Fire and HBO's *Game of Thrones*', in *The Vikings Reimagined*, ed. Tom Birkett and Roderick Dale (Boston: Medieval Institute Publications, 2019), 164. Similarly, Martin's depictions of the limited means of power for Essosi women

(namely via religious institutions) do not reflect the diversity of roles available to women throughout medieval Asia and northern Africa; see Mikayla Hunter, '"All Men Must Die, but We Are Not Men": Eastern Faith and Feminine Power in *A Song of Ice and Fire* and HBO's *Game of Thrones*', in *Queenship and the Women of Westeros*, ed. Zita Eva Rohr and Lisa Benz (Cham, Switzerland: Palgrave Macmillan, 2020), 148–52.
7 Nicholas Orme, *Education and Society in Medieval and Renaissance England* (London: Hambledon Press, 1989), 1.
8 Hastings Rashdall, *The Universities of Europe in the Middle Ages*, 2 vols (Oxford: Clarendon Press, 1945), I, 119; Charles Homer Haskins, *The Rise of Universities* (London: Cornell University Press, 1957), 1–12; 'Introduction and History', *University of Oxford*, 20 October 2014, https://www.ox.ac.uk/about/organisation/history (accessed 10 August 2020).
9 The University of Al Qarawiyyin was founded by Fatima bint Muhammad Al-Fihriya Al-Qurashiya in 895 CE in Fez, which is now in Morocco; the university-cum-monastery of Nalanda in India was founded circa the fourth or fifth century. Jeffrey T. Kenney and Ebrahim Moosa, *Islam in the Modern World* (New York: Routledge, 2015), 128; M. B. Rajani, 'The Expanse of Archaeological Remains at Nalanda: A Study Using Remote Sensing and GIS', *Archives of Asian Art*, 66, no. 1 (2016): 1.
10 Orme, *Education and Society*, 23–31; Julia Barrow, 'Churches, Education, and Literacy in Towns 600–1300', in *The Cambridge Urban History of Britain*, ed. D. M. Palliser (Cambridge: Cambridge University Press, 2000), 145–9.
11 Orme, *Education and Society*, 5, 52; Hilde de Ridder-Symoens, *A History of the University in Europe*, 4 vols. (Cambridge: Cambridge University Press, 1992), I, 47–55.
12 Larrington, *Winter is Coming*, 132–7; Daniel J. Clasby, 'Coexistence and Conflict in the Religions of *Game of Thrones*', in *Game of Thrones versus History: Written in Blood*, ed. Brian A. Pavlac (Hoboken: Wiley Blackwell, 2017), 201.
13 Pierre Abélard, *Historia Calamitatum*, trans. Henry Adams Bellows, Fordham University Medieval Sourcebooks (New York: Macmillan, 1972), https://sourcebooks.fordham.edu/basis/abelard-histcal.asp.
14 Orme, *Education and Society*, 1–2.
15 Ibid., 2, 5–7, 166.
16 Shirley Kersey, 'Medieval Education of Girls and Women', in *Educational Horizons*, 58, no. 4 (1980): 188; Orme, *Education and Society*, 2–5.
17 Arya's friendship with Gendry, Lommy, and Hot Pie begins in *CK*, 27–33 (in the show, in episode 3.2), and grows through *A Storm of Swords*. For the incident at the farmer's home, see episode 7.1; for the Cat of the Canals and the oyster seller see Martin, *FC*, 569–85, and episode 5.9.
18 By the mid-fourteenth century, a typical knight's income was approximately two shillings a day or £36.5 per annum. May McKisack, *The Fourteenth Century 1307–1399* (Oxford: Oxford University Press, 1959), 238. By the end of the sixteenth century, anyone with an annual income of £40 or more was considered suitable for knighthood, as set out in British Library Additional MS 5832, fol. 206r-v.
19 See, for example, Peter Ingulf, *Ingulf's Chronicle of the Abbey of Croyland*, ed. and trans. Henry T. Riley (London: Henry G. Bohn, 1854), 125.
20 Larrington, *Winter is Coming*, 133–6, esp. 133.
21 See, for example, Shiloh Carroll, *Medievalism in A Song of Ice and Fire and Game of Thrones* (Cambridge: D. S. Brewer, 2018), 54–7, 61–4, 69–71, 82–4; Rikke Schubart and Anne Gjelsvik, 'Introduction', in *Women of Ice and Fire*, ed. Anne Gjelsvik and Rikke Schubart (London: Bloomsbury, 2016), 7–9; Valerie Estelle Frankel, *Women in*

'Game of Thrones': Power, Conformity, and Resistance (Jefferson: McFarland, 2014), 161–76.
22   Larrington argues for this in part by pointing to the characters in the Sept at the eve of the Battle of Blackwater: girls, women and old men who pray because they cannot fight. In Essos, conversely, religious institutions frequently provide women with agency and power. Larrington, *Winter is Coming*, 134; Hunter, '"All Men Must Die, but We Are Not Men"', 151–7.
23   Costina Denisa Bărbuceanu, 'Athena Rising? Mentoring in Higher Education', in *Revue des Sciences Politiques*, 62 (2019): 48; Kersey, 'Medieval Education of Girls and Women', 190–2.
24   Juanita Feros Ruys, 'Heloise', in *The Oxford Encyclopedia of Women in World History, Volume I*, ed. Bonnie G. Smith (Oxford: Oxford University Press, 2008), 445; Susannah Mary Chewning, 'Hildegard of Bingen', in *The Oxford Encyclopedia of Women in World History, Volume I*, ed. Bonnie G. Smith (Oxford: Oxford University Press, 2008), 452–3.
25   Kersey, 'Medieval Education of Girls and Women', 188.
26   Grand Maester Malleon's *The Lineages and Histories of the Great Houses of the Seven Kingdoms* has been mentioned above; Archmaester Ebrose's *A Song of Ice and Fire*, mentioned at the end of the TV series, details the recent history of Westeros. For Sam's interest in historical texts in the Castle Black library, see, for example, *DD*, 112–17.
27   See Charles Donahue, Jr., 'The Legal Professions of Fourteenth-Century England: Serjeants of the Common Bench and Advocates of the Court of Arches', in *Laws, Lawyers, and Texts: Studies in Medieval Legal History in Honour of Paul Brand*, ed. Susanne Jenks, Jonathan Rose, and Christopher Wittick (Leiden: Brill, 2012), 227–31.
28   The autopsy was performed by Bartolomeo da Varignana, a doctor and lecturer at the city's university, a physician, Giacomo di Rolandino, and three surgeons; see Tommaso Duranti, 'Reading the Corpse in the Late Middle Ages (Bologna, Mid-13th Century–Early 16th Century)', in *The Body of Evidence: Corpses and Proofs in Early Modern European Medicine*, ed. Francesco Paulo de Ceglia (Boston: Brill, 2020), 71–2.
29   George R. R. Martin, 'The Real History Behind *Game of Thrones*', *Game of Thrones: The Complete Fifth Season*, [TV programme] HBO (2016).
30   Brian Cowlishaw, 'What Maesters Knew: Narrating Knowing', in *Mastering the Game of Thrones: Essays on George R. R. Martin's A Song of Ice and Fire*, ed. Jes Battis and Susan Johnston (Jefferson: McFarland, 2015), 61.
31   Ibid., 62.
32   Carolyne Larrington, *All Men Must Die: Power and Passion in Game of Thrones* (London: Bloomsbury Academic, 2021), 107.
33   Ibid.
34   Pycelle is less clearly guilty of conspiracy in the TV show.
35   For example, the chapter written from the perspective of Areo Hotah, Dornish Captain of Guards, in *FC*, 33–50.

Chapter 4

1   Mikal Gilmore, http://www.rollingstone.com/tv/news/george-r-r-martin-the-rolling-stone-interview-20140423.

2 For the classical definition, see Marc Bloch, *Feudal Society* (Chicago: University of Chicago Press, 1961). For an essential reframing, see Susan Reynolds, *Fiefs and Vassals: The Medieval Evidence Reinterpreted* (Oxford: Oxford University Press, 1994).
3 Alastair Dunn, *The Great Rising of 1381: The Peasants' Revolt and England's Failed Revolution* (Stroud: Tempus, 2002), 14.
4 See Rosamond Faith, 'The "Great Rumour" of 1377 and Peasant Ideology', in *The English Rising of 1381*, ed. Rodney Hilton and T. H. Alton (Cambridge: Cambridge University Press, 1987), 43–73; Christopher Dyer, *Making a Living in the Middle Ages: The People of Britain 850–1520* (New Haven: Yale University Press, 2009), 282.
5 Frederic Lane and Reinhold C. Mueller, *Money and Banking in Medieval and Renaissance Venice, Volume I: Coins and Moneys of Account* (Baltimore: Johns Hopkins University Press, 1985), 7–13.
6 Compare the intertwined racial and class politics of America in the antebellum and Reconstruction periods; see for example Keri Leigh Merritt, *Masterless Men: Poor Whites and Slavery in the Antebellum South* (Cambridge: Cambridge University Press, 2017).
7 Raymond de Roover, *Money, Banking and Credit in Mediaeval Bruges: Italian Merchant Bankers, Lombards and Money-Changers, A Study in the Origins of Banking* (Cambridge: Medieval Academy of America, 1948), 10.
8 Ibid., 40–1.
9 Carolyne Larrington, 'Game of Loans', *The Economist*, 20 April 2016, https://www.economist.com/1843/2016/04/20/game-of-loans. See also Larrington's chapter in this volume.
10 Lane and Mueller, *Money and Banking*, 73; Edwin Hunt, *The Medieval Super-Companies: A Study of the Peruzzi Company of Florence* (Cambridge: Cambridge University Press, 1994), 43.
11 Hunt, *The Medieval Super-Companies*, 39.
12 Lane and Mueller, *Money and Banking*, 70.
13 de Roover, *Money, Banking, and Credit*, 89, 99; Lane and Mueller, *Money and Banking*, 70.
14 Lane and Mueller, *Money and Banking*, 83.
15 John H. Munro, 'The Medieval Origins of the Financial Revolution: Usury, Rentes, and Negotiability', *International History Review*, 25 (2003): 505–62 at 506–12.
16 Hunt, *The Medieval Super-Companies*, 48–9, 61.
17 Munro, 'The Medieval Origins', 514; Hunt, *The Medieval Super-Companies*, 42–3.
18 de Roover, *Money, Banking, and Credit*, 84.
19 Hunt, *The Medieval Super-Companies*, 61.
20 Ibid., 190–1.
21 Zeynep Tufekci, https://blogs.scientificamerican.com/observations/the-real-reason-fans-hate-the-last-season-of-game-of-thrones/ (2019).
22 See https://awoiaf.westeros.org/index.php/Meereenese_knot.
23 Carolyne Larrington, '"(No More) Reaving, Roving, Raiding or Raping": The Iron-Born in George R. R. Martin's *A Song of Ice and Fire* and HBO's *Game of Thrones*', in *The Vikings Reimagined: Reception, Recovery, Engagement*, ed. Tom Birkett and Roderick Dale, Northern Medieval World (Kalamazoo: Medieval Institute Press, 2020), 162–78.
24 See, for example, *Egils saga Skallagrímssonar*, ed. Sigurður Nordal, Íslenzk fornrit 2 (Reykjavík: Hið Íslenzka fornritafélag, 1933); *Laxdæla saga*, ed. Einar Ól. Sveinsson, Íslenzk fornrit 5 (Reykjavík: Hið Íslenzka fornritafélag, 1934).

25 Larrington, '(No More) Reaving', 166; Søren M. Sindbæk, 'Networks and Nodal Points: The Emergence of Towns in Early Viking Age Scandinavia', *Antiquity*, 81 (2007): 119–32.
26 Enerelt Enkhbold, 'The Role of the *Ortoq* in the Mongol Empire in Forming Business Partnerships', *Central Asian Survey*, 38 (2019): 531–47; Thomas T. Allsen, 'Mongolian Princes and Their Merchant Partners, 1200–1260', *Asia Major*, 2 (1989): 83–126.
27 Tufekci, https://blogs.scientificamerican.com/observations/the-real-reason-fans-hate-the-last-season-of-game-of-thrones/.

Chapter 5

1 I would like to thank Sophie Hintersdorf, Evelyn Koch and Franz A. Klug for their suggestions and corrections of earlier drafts of this chapter.
2 Martin, as author and sub-creator, possesses the prerogative to invent or adapt names and concepts. He often does so with great skill and the idea of a 'sworn shield' has the ring of authenticity for most readers.
3 A selection of such helmets can be found at http://www.oobject.com/category/armored-face-masks/ and https://io9.gizmodo.com/the-weirdest-and-fiercest-helmets-from-the-age-of-armor-510686611.
4 This differentiation is maintained even when one and the same speaker is talking. Thus Joffrey uses 'Hound' when talking about Clegane to Sansa, yet 'dog' when addressing him directly immediately afterwards: '"If you won't rise and dress yourself, my Hound will do it for you," Joffrey said. "I beg of you, my prince . . ." "I'm king now. Dog, get her out of bed."' (*GT*, 743).
5 See, for example, the stories about faithful dogs from antiquity and later times in the relevant chapters of the bestiaries, such as in *The Book of Beasts: Being a Translation from a Latin Bestiary of the Twelfth Century*, ed. and trans. Terence Hanbury White (Stroud: Alan Sutton, 1992), 62. For a general discussion of the origin and history of the domestic dog, see James Serpell (ed.), *The Domestic Dog: Its Evolution, Behavior and Interactions with People* (Cambridge: Cambridge University Press, 2017). Lions, symbolizing valour in battle, were more popular with knights. It was usually the ladies who had a dog, the symbol of faithfulness, at their feet.
6 See http://www.animaliter.uni-mainz.de/hund/ for an overview of the medieval tradition(s) of the dog in different types of text. Almost every animal, with the possible exception of the lamb, could be interpreted *in bonam et in malam partem* (positively and negatively). The lion, for example, could be the noble king of animals and a symbol for Christ ('the Lion of the tribe of Judah', Revelation 5:5). It could also stand for the devil ('Your enemy the devil prowls around like a roaring lion looking for someone to devour', 1 Pet. 5.8).
7 For a short overview of the use of dogs in warfare, see Mike Homan, *A Complete History of Fighting Dogs* (Lydney, Gloucs: Ringpress Books, 1999), 9–13.
8 Since Sandor Clegane is not a POV character in Martin's books, we cannot know for certain about his potential doubts and misgivings concerning his master. However, Joffrey seems to have an instinctive awareness of how far he can tax the Hound's obedience and refrains from giving orders that Clegane would most likely refuse (e.g. beating Sansa).

9 See the books by Shiloh Carroll, *Medievalism in A Song of Ice and Fire and Game of Thrones* (Cambridge: D.S. Brewer, 2018), Carolyne Larrington, *Winter is Coming: The Medieval World of Game of Thrones* (London and New York: I.B. Tauris, 2016), and Ayelet Haimson Lushkov, *You Win or You Die: The Ancient World of Game of Thrones* (London and New York: I.B. Tauris, 2017), respectively.

10 Septon Meribald's dog 'Dog' (*FC*, 525), for example, is both pet and bodyguard (see Maria Błaszkiewicz, this volume); Ramsay's pack consists only of bitches and goes by the name 'the Bastard's girls'.

11 Cf. the slaves in Slaver's Bay, the Sparrows in King's Landing (and possibly elsewhere in Westeros) and the 'Brotherhood without Banners'.

12 See J. R. R. Tolkien, *The Silmarillion* (London: HarperCollins, 1994), 208. Huan was 'chief of the wolfhounds that followed Celegorm', and he followed his master into exile 'and was faithful' (Tolkien, *Silmarillion*, 207). However, when Celegorm betrays Lúthien and keeps her prisoner, he turns against his master because 'Huan the hound was true of heart, and the love of Lúthien had fallen upon him in the first hour of their meeting' (Tolkien, *Silmarillion*, 208). He helps Lúthien to escape and even defends Beren (and Lúthien) later on against the attack of Celegorm (Tolkien, *Silmarillion*, 213), thus openly breaking with his master. Partial parallels to Sandor Clegane's fate are obvious.

13 Eddard, reporting hearsay and tales about Ser Gregor, is the first to introduce the unmistakably Gothic horror element connected with Ser Gregor – who emerges from his first description as a kind of Bluebeard: 'He watched him with disquiet. Ned seldom put much stock in gossip, but the things said of Ser Gregor were more than ominous. He was soon to be married for the third time, and one heard dark whisperings about the deaths of his first two wives. It was said that his keep was a grim place where servants disappeared unaccountably and even the dogs were afraid to enter the hall. And there had been a sister who had died young under queer circumstances, and the fire that had disfigured his brother, and the hunting accident that had killed their father' (*GT*, 313–14).

14 Martin uses the term 'sigil' for coats of arms and badges. In our world 'sigil' refers to the 'sigillum' (i.e. seal) and is not used in real-world heraldry, but most readers will grasp what Martin means by this term. Neither is a second, much rarer meaning of the word as 'a sign, word, or device held to have occult power in astrology or magic' (*Merriam-Webster*, s.v. *sigil*) relevant to Martin's use. See the publications by Georg Scheibelreiter, *Heraldik* (Vienna: Oldenbourg, 2006), and 'Tiersymbolik und Wappen im Mittelalter', in *Tier und Religion*, ed. Thomas Honegger and W. Günther Rohr (Leipzig: Akademie Verlag, 2007), 9–23, for an in-depth discussion of medieval heraldry, and Gillian Polack, 'Setting up Westeros: The Medievalesque World of Game of Thrones', in *Game of Thrones versus History: Written in Blood*, ed. Brian A. Pavlac (Hoboken: Wiley Blackwell, 2017), 251–60, for an analysis of the sigils in Martin's epic. Polack (253) writes: 'Martin distinguishes each family through distinctive insignia. Each dynasty has its own form of medieval heraldry, which includes a kind of coat of arms called a "sigil".' See also Sophie Hintersdorf, 'A Feast for Beasts – The Role of Animals in George R. R. Martin's *A Song of Ice and Fire*' (MA thesis, Friedrich-Schiller-University, Jena, Germany, 2017).

15 See Łukasz Neubauer, '"Dark Wings" and "Grey Furs": The Old Germanic Roots of Carrion-Eating Beasts in *A Song of Ice and Fire*', in *George R. R. Martin's A Song of Ice and Fire and the Medieval Literary Tradition*, ed. Bartłomiej Błaszkiewicz (Warsaw: WUW, 2014), 181–209, and Hintersdorf, 'A Feast for Beasts'.

16 See Clegane's answer to Ser Beric Dondarrion: 'A knight's a sword with a horse. The rest, the vows and the sacred oils and the lady's favors, they're silk ribbons tied round the sword. Maybe the sword's prettier with ribbons hanging off it, but it will kill you just as dead. Well, bugger your ribbons, and shove your swords up your arses. I'm the same as you. The only difference is, I don't lie about what I am' (*SS*, 465).

17 The members of the clergy as the professional interpreters of the *liber naturae* (i.e. God's creation, our world) do not tire of reminding their audiences of the omnipresence of the spiritual element even in the most insignificant parts of creation. The famous anecdote about Saint Anselm and the hare may illustrate this attitude. In the summer of 1097 CE Anselm left the court and rode with his retinue towards his manor at Hayes. When they encountered a hare on the road, the boys of his household chased it with their dogs and the frightened animal sought refuge between the legs of Anselm's horse. His companions laughed at the terrified hare that did not dare to leave the relative safety of the horse's legs. Yet Anselm was moved to tears and rebuked them for making fun of the unhappy beast with the following words: 'You laugh, do you? But there is no laughing, no merry-making, for this unhappy beast. His enemies stand round about him, and in fear of his life he flees to us asking for help. So it is with the soul of man: when it leaves the body, its enemies – the evil spirits which have haunted it along all the crooked ways of vice while it was in the body – stand round without mercy, ready to seize it and hurry it off to everlasting death. Then indeed it looks round everywhere in great alarm, and with inexpressible desire longs for some helping and protecting hand to be held out to it, which might defend it. But the demons on the other hand laugh and rejoice exceedingly if they find that the soul is bereft of every support' (Eadmer, *Vita Sancti Anselmi (The Life of St Anselm, Archbishop of Canterbury)*, ed. and trans. R. W. Southern (London: Nelson, 1962), 89–90).

18 See cynic, adj. and n. *OED Online*, Oxford University Press, June 2021, www.oed.com/view/Entry/46638 (accessed 8 June 2021).

19 http://www.etymonline.com/index.php?term=cynic

20 Sandor Clegane's cynical view of chivalry is balanced by Brienne's idealism. See Iain A. MacInnes, '"All I Ever Wanted Was to Fight for a Lord I Believed in. But the Good Lords Are Dead and the Rest Are Monsters"': Brienne of Tarth, Jaime Lannister, and the Chivalric "Other"', in *Queenship and the Women of Westeros*, ed. Rohr and Benz, 77–102, for a detailed discussion of Brienne of Tarth and chivalry.

21 The death of the (at that moment still nameless) young knight of the Vale (later identified as Ser Hugh of the Vale) is later interpreted as a possibly intentional silencing of an important witness to Lord Arryn's death (see *GT*, 305–6). That Ser Gregor killed the young knight intentionally is also Sandor Clegane's opinion, as he points out to Sansa: 'That gorget wasn't fastened proper. You think Gregor didn't notice that? You think *Ser* Gregor's lance rode up by chance, do you? . . . Gregor's lance goes where Gregor wants it to go' (*GT*, 302). The only one to explicitly disapprove of Loras's trick is Ser Barristan Selmy: '"There is small honor in tricks," the old man said stiffly' (*GT*, 316). This 'trick' may be seen as a first indication that not all is as it seems with the Knight of the Flowers.

22 Sandor Clegane, who is somewhat drunk, tells Sansa about how he acquired his horrible scars: '"My father told everyone my bedding had caught fire, and our maester gave me ointments. *Ointments!* Gregor got his ointments too. Four years later, they anointed him with the seven oils and he recited his knightly vows and Rhaegar

Targaryen tapped him on the shoulder and said, 'Arise, Ser Gregor.'" Sansa is truly shocked about Gregor's cruel and brutal behaviour and objects: "'He was no true knight,'" she whispered to him. The Hound threw back his head and roared. . . . "No," he growled at her, "no, little bird, he was no true knight"' (*GT*, 303–4).

23 See Jaime's observation to Catelyn Stark: 'So many vows . . . they make you swear and swear. Defend the king. Obey the king. Keep his secrets. Do his bidding. Your life for his. But obey your father. Love your sister. Protect the innocent. Defend the weak. Respect the gods. Obey the laws. It's too much. No matter what you do, you're forsaking one vow or the other' (*CK*, 796). C. Stephen Jaeger provides an excellent discussion of the 'process of chivalrisation' of the medieval warrior caste in *The Origins of Courtliness – Civilizing Trends and the Formation of Courtly Ideals 939–1210* (Philadelphia: University of Pennsylvania Press, 1985). Martin exemplifies the more 'archaic' warriors in the men of the North, who are, for cultural and religious reasons, very rarely members of the chivalric caste.

24 For a discussion of chivalry and knights in Martin, see Corinna Dörrich, '"A Knight's a Sword with a Horse." Bilder von Ritterschaft und die Waffen der Frauen in *ASOIAF*', in *Die Welt von Games of Thrones*, ed. Markus May, Michael Baumann, Robert Baumgartner, and Tobias Eder (Bielefeld: transcript, 2016), 173–92; Steven Muhlberger, 'Chivalry in Westeros', in *Game of Thrones versus History: Written in Blood*, ed. Brian A. Pavlac (Hoboken: Wiley Blackwell, 2017), 47–55; and, most recently, Carol Parrish Jamison, *Chivalry in Westeros: The Knightly Code of A Song of Ice and Fire* (Jefferson: McFarland, 2018).

25 Lars Koch sums up his perceptive analysis of the state of knighthood in Westeros as follows: 'Als Repräsentant des sozialen und normativen Zentrums wird er [i.e. the knight] in seinen unterschiedlichen Stadien des Verfalls inszeniert. Ritter-Figuren wie der brutale Schlächter Ser Gregor Clegane (Hafþór Júlíus Björnsson), der Säufer Ser Dontos Hollard (Tony Way) oder der galante Turnier-Reiter Ser Loras Tyrell (Finn Jones) führen vor Augen, dass das alte normative Rollenmodell heroischer Männlichkeit nicht mehr trägt.' (As a representative of the social and normative centre, [the knight] is depicted in different stages of decline. Knight-figures like the brutal butcher Ser Gregor Clegane (Hafþór Júlíus Björnsson), the drunkard Ser Dontos Hollard (Tony Way) or the gallant tournament-rider Ser Loras Tyrell (Finn Jones) demonstrate that the old normative role models of heroic masculinity are no longer effective.) See Lars Koch, '"Power Resides Where Men Believe it Resides." Die brüchige Welt von *Game of Thrones*', in *Vom Game of Thrones bis House of Cards: Politische Perspektiven in Fernsehserien*, ed. Anja Besand (Wiesbaden: Springer, 2018), 139.

26 I have omitted Podrick Payne ('Pod'), who starts out as a kind of Sancho Panza to his Don Quixote (Brienne) and often functions as comic relief, yet who ends up as a Knight of the Kingsguard. Neither can I discuss Beric Dondarrion, whose career is reminiscent of Robin Hood and his Merry Men.

27 By June 2021, *A Song of Ice and Fire* still comprises five volumes, the last of which is *A Dance with Dragons*. The sixth volume, *Winds of Winter*, has not yet been published. The HBO show, in contrast, has concluded and I will base some of my concluding comments on the plot as outlined there.

28 See 'Sir Gowther', in *Middle English Breton Lays*, ed. Anne Laskaya and Eve Salisbury (Kalamazoo: Medieval Institute Publications, 1995). The famous wizard Merlin is said to have a similar parentage, which is why the narrator calls Gowther 'Merlin's half-brother' (l. 98).

29 This is, of course, also Theon Greyjoy's development. His Reek persona is very much reminiscent of Gowther during his time of penance. As compensation for killing Culann's guard dog in self-defence, the Irish hero Cúchulainn has to take over its role and becomes thus 'Culann's Hound'.
30 All quotations taken from: Jacobus de Voragine, 'S. Christopher', in *The Golden Legend. Lives of the Saints*, trans. William Caxton, ed. George V. O'Neill (Cambridge: Cambridge University Press, 1914), 48–55.
31 See especially the episode 'A Knight of the Seven Kingdoms' (8.2), where Arya and Sandor talk on the battlements of Winterfell. She asks him what he is doing up here and points out that, so far, he has not served anyone but himself. Now he serves others, like Saint Christopher.
32 I have limited my discussion to the most central motifs. Others, such as the possible influence of one of Saint Dominic's attributes, a dog with a torch in its mouth, may provide inspiration for further exploration. During their visit to the Quiet Isle (*FC*, 656–73), Brienne and her companions come across Clegane's horse Stranger in the stables and meet 'a brother bigger than Brienne [who] was struggling to dig a grave. From the way he moved, it was plain to see that he was lame' (*FC*, 661). It is very likely that this mysterious lame brother is Sandor Clegane, recovering from his wounds and doing penance for his past deeds. The situation shows parallels to the Old Norse *Þiðrekssaga*, where one of Þiðrekr's companions (Heime) also enters a monastery (at least temporarily). See the discussion of the Heime episode by Hermann Reichert, 'Heime in Wilten und in der Thidrekssaga', in *Studien zum Altgermanischen: Festschrift für Heinrich Beck*, ed. Heiko Uecker (Berlin and New York: Walter de Gruyter, 1994), 503–12.
33 The motif of sibling rivalry goes, of course, back to the biblical Cain and Abel, where we also have the first fratricide.

Chapter 6

1 Michael W. Blastic, 'Francis and his Hagiographical Tradition', in *The Cambridge Companion to Francis of Assisi*, ed. Michael J. P. Robson (Cambridge: Cambridge University Press, 2012), 70.
2 Ibid., 71.
3 Patricia Appelbaum, *St. Francis of America: How a Thirteenth-Century Friar Became America's Most Popular Saint* (Chapel Hill: University of North Carolina Press 2015), 141.
4 G. K. Chesterton, *St. Francis of Assisi* (London: Hodder and Stoughton, 1923), 8.
5 Appelbaum, *St. Francis of America*, 14–17.
6 This scene also has its counterpart in the modern popular reception of St Francis. A Marvel comic book not only presents Francis (and presumably Christ) as a superhero but even features the reception of the stigmata. This is clearly modelled on Giotto but is also invested with the typically pulp masculine aura characteristic of the series. One can only hope that this particular superhero will not join the Marvel movies team. See Appelbaum, *St. Francis of America*, 141.
7 Shiloh Carroll, *Medievalism in A Song of Ice and Fire and Game of Thrones* (Cambridge: D.S. Brewer, 2018), 2–8.
8 Michael Murrin, *History and Warfare in Renaissance Epic* (Chicago and London: University of Chicago Press, 1997), 58.

9   Ibid., 57.
10 Ibid.
11 Mark J. P. Wolf, *Building Imaginary Worlds: The Theory and History of Subcreation* (New York: Routledge, 2012), 106–10.
12 J. R. R. Tolkien, 'On Fairy Stories', in *The Monsters and the Critics and Other Essays*, ed. Christopher Tolkien (London: HarperCollins, 2006), 132.
13 Martin seems to have realized this; however, his attempts to fill the gaps in *The World of Ice and Fire* and *Fire and Blood* only worsen the situation. The more significant political role of the Church of the Seven in the early decades of Targaryen rule, the destructive fanaticism of the masses or the pathological zeal of Baelor the Blessed still lack the spiritual background of a normal, everyday piety on which such extremes might try to capitalize, and which could have balanced the picture. The revival of the Church Militant in the last part of *A Dance with Dragons* seems unconvincing, an abrupt sprouting of something unexpected and incongruous. Moreover, instead of contributing to the richness and fullness of the secondary world, the representation of the role of religion in *Fire and Blood* is almost grotesque, extremely powerful and destructive outbursts are separated by long intervals when faith becomes practically unimportant and almost invisible. Instead of an important constituent of the secondary creation, faith is reduced to a mere device used when needed and discarded whenever it seems no longer immediately useful. See Elio M. Garcia, George R. R. Martin, and Linda Antonsson, *The World of Ice and Fire* (New York: Bantam Books, 2014); George R. R. Martin, *Fire and Blood: 300 Hundred Years Before a Game of Thrones (A Targaryen History)* (London: HarperCollins, 2018).
14 Interestingly, in *Fire and Blood* there is the figure of a Lord Confessor, a court official, mentioned occasionally. However, when more is finally said about this position, it transpires that it amounts to nothing more than a glorified torturer. Such is Lord Graceford, Lord Confessor to young king Aegon III; the nature of the post leaves no further doubt when the next regent appoints Graceford's successor: 'A man who knows how to ease pain will also know how to inflict it' (*FB*, 701).
15 Carolyne Larrington, *Winter is Coming: The Medieval World of Game of Thrones* (London and New York: I.B. Tauris, 2016), 134.
16 Although the particular order of Chaucer's Friar is not specified and it is feasible to read this figure as a collective representative of all four mendicant orders, for the present study his possible Franciscan provenance will be explored.
17 The theological dispute about the nature of the Seven is a part of Meribald's only attempt at a sermon, yet, regardless of its potential, this is never elaborated as having specific importance in *A Song of Ice and Fire*.
18 Michael J. Robson, 'The Writings of Francis', in *The Cambridge Companion to Francis of Assisi*, 34–49 (34).
19 Appelbaum, *St. Francis of America*, 136–57.
20 The bond between an animal and a warg is no exception.

Chapter 7

1   George R. R. Martin, *A Game of Thrones* (1996; New York: Bantam, 2011); all references to *A Game of Thrones* refer to this edition.

2 '"Bet he killed them all himself, he did," Gared told the barracks over wine, "twisted their little heads off, our mighty warrior."' (*GT*, 3).
3 Geoffroi de Charny, *A Knight's Own Book of Chivalry*, trans. Elspeth Kennedy (Philadelphia: University of Pennsylvania Press, 2005), 104.
4 In an earlier chapter, I have elaborated on the neomedieval character of Martin's fictitious world, which not only alludes to mediated aspects of the Middle Ages (in Europe, most notably England) but also reflects critically on historiography and ideas of 'historical truth' through various narrative strategies. See Anja Müller, 'Die neomediävalen Ritter von Westeros und der Prozess der Zivilisation', in *Die Literatur des Mittelalters im Fantasyroman*, ed. Nathanael Busch and Hans Rudolf Velten (Heidelberg: Winter, 2018), 30–3.
5 Richard W. Kaeuper, *Medieval Chivalry* (Cambridge: Cambridge University Press, 2016), 9, 10.
6 Maurice Keen, *Chivalry* (New Haven: Yale University Press, 2005), 252–3.
7 Aldo Scaglione, *Knights at Court: Courtliness, Chivalry and Courtesy From Ottonian Germany to the Italian Renaissance* (Berkeley: University of California Press, 1991), 11.
8 Beverly Kennedy, *Knighthood in The Morte Darthur*, Arthurian Studies XI (Cambridge: D. S. Brewer, 1985), 6.
9 Ibid.
10 Ibid.
11 Steven Muhlberger suggests yet another triad, distinguishing between vassal knights (characterized by prowess), noble knights ('identified with nobility') and courteous knights ('the knight of song and story'). As the distinction, however, operates on three completely different levels and the chapter otherwise betrays only a superficial knowledge and awareness of research on knighthood in medieval studies, I do not regard it as relevant for ensuing consideration. Steven Muhlberger, 'Chivalry in Westeros', in *Game of Thrones versus History: Written in Blood*, ed. Brian A. Pavlac (Hoboken: Wiley and Sons, 2017), 48 (on vassal and noble knights) and 49 (on courteous knights).
12 Elias elucidates this in detail in the last two chapters of the first part in Norbert Elias, *Über den Prozess der Zivilisation: Soziogenetische und psychogenetische Untersuchungen. Vol. II: Wandlungen der Gesellschaft. Entwurf zu einer Theorie der Zivilisation* (Frankfurt am Main: Suhrkamp, 1997), 84–131.
13 Alfred Schopf, 'Die Gestalt Gawains bei Chrétien, Wolfram von Eschenbach und in Sir Gawain and the Green Knight', in *Spätmittelalterliche Artusliteratur*, ed. Karl-Heinz Göller (Paderborn: Schöningh, 1984), 85, fn. 14.
14 Kaeuper, *Medieval Chivalry*, 23.
15 For the sake of brevity, I am going to focus on Westeros only. An investigation of Essos might yield different results.
16 George R. R. Martin, *The World of Ice and Fire: The Untold History of Westeros and the Game of Thrones* (New York: Bantam, 2014), 10.
17 Ibid.
18 On the achievements of Jaehaerys I see Martin, *The World of Ice and Fire*, 60–5.
19 Martin, *The World of Ice and Fire*, 76.
20 Elias, *Über den Prozess der Zivilisation*, 248.
21 Charles Hackney, '"Silk Ribbons Tied Around a Sword": Knighthood and the Chivalric Virtues in Westeros', in *Mastering the Game of Thrones: Essays on George R. R. Martin's A Song of Ice and Fire*, ed. Jes Battis and Susan Johnston (Jefferson: McFarland, 2015), 132.

22 Corinna Dörrich, '"A Knight's a Sword with a Horse": Bilder von Ritterschaft und die Waffen der Frauen in ASOIAF', in *Die Welt von ‚Game of Thrones': Kulturwissenschaftliche Perspektiven auf George R. R. Martins 'A Song of Ice and Fire'*, ed. Markus May, Michael Baumann, Robert Baumgartner and Tobias Eder (Bielefeld: transcript, 2016), esp. 180–4.
23 See the essays by Renée L. Curtis, 'The Perception of the Chivalric Ideal in Chrétien de Troyes's Yvain', *Arthurian Interpretations*, 3, no. 2 (1989): 1–22; Jane H. M. Taylor, 'The Parrot, the Knight and the Decline of Chivalry', in *Conjunctures*, ed. Keith Busby and Norris Lacy (Amsterdam: Rodopi, 1994), 529–54, or Lisa Robeson, 'Noble Knights and 'Mischievous War': The Rhetoric of War in Malory's *Le Morte Darthur*', *Arthuriana*, 13, no. 3 (2003): 10–35. Richard Kaeuper remarks on the ambivalence of chivalry: 'Chivalry was one of the problems in medieval Europe, not just one of its creative solutions to problems' (Richard W. Kaeuper, 'Chivalry: Fantasy and Fear', in *Writing and Fantasy*, ed. Ceri Sullivan and Barbara White (Harlow: Longman, 1999): 62–73, 63.
24 See Kaeuper, 'Chivalry', 63.
25 'It was Visenya, not Aegon, who decided the nature of the Kingsguard. Seven champions for the Lord of the Seven Kingdoms, who would all be knights. She modeled their vows upon those of the Night's Watch, so that they would forfeit all things save their duty to the king. And when Aegon spoke of a grand tourney to choose the first Kingsguard, Visenya dissuaded him, saying he needed more than skill in arms to protect him; he also needed unwavering loyalty'; Martin, *The World of Ice and Fire*, 50.
26 In fact, the only cases of veritable courtly love in *A Song of Ice and Fire* are highly problematic: Rhaegar's devotion to Lyanna humiliated his wife and ended in a war. Jaime's notorious worship of Cersei breaks the incest taboo.
27 This duty of Westerosi knights resorts to popular ideas of the Middle Ages and serves as a moral yardstick to identify 'good' knights in Martin's novels. Whereas a knight's duty of protection mainly referred to the liege lord in medieval chivalrous codes, Martin highlights the problematic ethical choices knights might have to make between the protection of those who cannot protect themselves and the protection of the lord; see, for instance, Ramon Llull, *The Book of the Order of Chivalry* (Woodbridge: Boydell, 2013), V.11, 68.
28 I would argue that this also applies to the conclusion of the TV show. The nomination of Bran as King of Westeros, resting on the claim that he is the keeper of its cultural memory, is in no way consistent with the discourses of legitimation that had hitherto surfaced in that world. This inconsistency is aggravated as Jon Snow's legitimate genealogical claim to the throne, which had been built up during the final two to three seasons, suddenly appears to be of no further significance.
29 In Kaeuper's third phase in the chronological transformation of chivalry, such an 'expansion of a less formal knighthood' is one major constituent, coinciding – almost paradoxically – with a more restricted access to formal knightly status; see Kaeuper, *Medieval Chivalry*, 122ff.
30 As Davos first offers his loyalty to Stannis Baratheon and, after Stannis's death, to Jon Snow, Davos staunchly supports the conservative principle of legitimation by birth.
31 The sociological concept of habitus has been defined and explained by Pierre Bourdieu, who sees habitus as a matrix generating social practices which are experienced as natural, because the historical (material) conditions that have once produced the habitus have come to be obliterated and forgotten, while the practices

themselves are constantly repeated as if in a self-confirming feedback loop. Thus, habitus creates the appearance of an objective 'common sense world', in which certain practices are foreseeable within a particular social group. See Pierre Bourdieu, *Outline of a Theory of Practice*, trans. Richard Nice (Cambridge: Cambridge University Press, 1977), esp. 72–3 and 78–81.

32 George Martin's novellas about Ser Duncan, 'The Hedge Knight' (1998), 'The Sworn Sword' (2004) and 'The Mystery Knight' (2010) have been republished in one volume, titled *A Knight of the Seven Kingdoms* (London: HarperCollins, 2015).

33 By choosing the title 'A Knight of the Seven Kingdoms' for the episode in which Brienne of Tarth is at last knighted by Ser Jaime (8.2), the TV show not only pays homage to Ser Duncan the Tall but also appears to corroborate the fan theory according to which Brienne is a descendant of Ser Duncan. The title definitely implies an analogy between the two model knights – Ser Duncan and Ser Brienne – who both prove to be worthy knights despite origins that normally disqualify them from this rank for reasons of class or gender.

34 According to Maurice Keen, knighthood was individually conferred at first; only from the thirteenth century on, he perceives a 'shift of emphasis away from knighthood toward the hereditary capacity to receive knighthood'; Keen, *Chivalry*, 145.

35 George R. R. Martin, *A Clash of Kings* (1999; New York: Bantam, 2011); all references to *A Clash of Kings* refer to this edition.

36 Both the TV show and the novels leave no doubt about Brienne's chivalrous merits, as she basically fulfils all medieval chivalrous virtues. In numerous fights (including a melée), she proves her prowess and her extraordinary fighting skills. She endures and survives hardships and shows generosity (most obviously to her squire Podrick). Her devotion to Renly Baratheon and Ser Jaime Lannister is one of the few examples of (transformed or reversed, as it were) courtly love in Martin's novels: in both cases, Brienne's adoration of a man incites her to perform deeds and go on quests. Last but not least, Brienne is loyal to a fault.

37 *Game of Thrones*, 'A Knight of the Seven Kingdoms', 8.2, dir. David Nutter, writ. Bryan Cogman, HBO, April 2019.

38 Brienne's displaced nature may also reverberate in readers' reactions; they find Brienne's POV chapters boring and her character uninteresting not only because she is so full of scruples but also because she is obsessed with her quest and her righteous performance of the habitus of knighthood.

39 Whereas such an exclusion would comply with the prerogatives Ramon Llull proposed in his thirteenth-century *Book of the Order of Chivalry*, in which men are explicitly said to be 'more disposed than woman to have noble courage and be good', Carolyne Larrington cites examples of female warriors and knights in medieval romance, such as Britomart in Spenser's *Faerie Queene* and Bradamante in *Orlando Innamorato* and *Orlando Furioso*. Llull, *Order*, 41; Carolyne Larrington, *Winter is Coming: The Medieval World of Game of Thrones* (London: I.B. Tauris, 2016), 32.

40 John H. Cameron sees in her 'not simply a wonderfully nuanced and complex female hero, but a human being, with all the good and bad that that entails. […S]he is a hero […] regardless of what happens later, and her negotiation of knighthood has shown that she is as good "as any man could have, and better than most"'; Valerie Estelle Frankel views Brienne more critically from a feminist POV: 'Her character is very strong and certainly female, but her dislike for her own sex, like Arya's makes her a problematic feminist icon'; Yvonne Tasker and Lindsay Steenberg acknowledge Brienne's exceptionality, which is 'not bought at the expense of the

other women of Westeros', yet they also remark that the character is embedded 'within an intractable system of patriarchal domination and violence'. See John H. Cameron, 'A New Kind of Hero: A Song of Ice and Fire's Brienne of Tarth', in *A Quest of Her Own: Essays on the Female Hero in Modern Fantasy*, ed. Lori M. Campbell (Jefferson: McFarland, 2014), 203; Valerie Estelle Frankel, *Women in Game of Thrones: Power, Conformity and Resistance* (Jefferson: McFarland, 2014), 54; Yvonne Tasker and Lindsay Steenberg, 'Women Warriors from Chivalry to Vengeance', in *Women of Ice and Fire: Gender, Game of Thrones, and Multiple Media Engagements*, ed. Anne Gjelsvik and Rikke Schubart (London: Bloomsbury, 2016), 177.

41 Audrey Moyce therefore suggests perceiving the relationship between Brienne and Jaime as queer, because it very obviously plays with and challenges gender stereotypes of medieval romance. Dörrich also hints at Brienne's ambiguous gender, which, she maintains, is expressed in the 'destruction of her female body', as is revealed by the novel's repeated comments on her 'disturbing appearance' (my translation, A.M.). See Audrey Moyce, 'Brienne and Jaime's Queer Intimacy', in *Vying for the Iron Throne: Essays on Power, Gender, Death and Performance in HBO's Game of Throne*, ed. Lindsey Mantoan and Sara Brady (Jefferson: McFarland, 2018), 59–68; Dörrich, 'A Knight's a Sword with a Horse', 186.

42 George R. R. Martin, *A Feast for Crows* (2005; New York: Bantham: 2011), 914–16; all references to *A Feast for Crows* refer to this edition.

43 Elias, *Über den Prozess der Zivilisation*, 341.

44 *Game of Thrones*, 'The Iron Throne', 8.6, dir. and writ. David Benioff and D.B. Weiss, HBO, May 2019.

45 Contrary to Jaime's professed reluctance in the novels to have any share in the everyday political manoeuvres and intrigues at court and in the Small Council, the TV show presents Jaime on various occasions as a willing participant in Cersei's power plays, whether by participating in the Small Council, by his open confrontation of the Sparrows in King's Landing, or by recruiting Lord Tarly to Cersei's war against the Tyrells. The novels, in contrast, especially *A Feast for Crows*, have established Jaime's POV as a sober, rational counterpart to the paranoid chapters of power-hungry Cersei.

46 According to Tyrion, Jaime 'never untied a knot if he could slash it in two with his sword' (*GT*, 415).

47 Elias, *Über den Prozess der Zivilisation*, 332.

48 In this respect, it is also interesting to note that he no longer addresses Brienne as 'wench' in the Jaime POV chapter in *A Dance with Dragons* but as 'my Lady'. George R. R. Martin, *A Dance with Dragons* (New York: Bantam, 2011), 707.

49 Elias, *Über den Prozess der Zivilisation*, 341.

Chapter 8

1 Placing 'The Hedge Knight' in Westeros's equivalent of the late medieval period is mainly based on the analysis of the armour and tournament games depicted in the story. This conclusion is discussed at a greater length below.

2 In George R. R. Martin's stories, the notion of a hedge knight is highly reminiscent of the idea of knight-errant, or a wandering knight, from chivalric romances. Hedge

knights are usually impoverished knights with no inheritance who wander the land in search of employment and adventures.
3. Arguably, the similarities reach even further. Reportedly William Marshal found himself without a horse before his first tournament and was forced to sell his clothes to buy one. See Charles Phillips, *The Complete Illustrated History of Knights & the Golden Age of Chivalry* (London: Hermes House, 2010), 104. Dunk also lacks a key component before his tournament debut and needs to sell his master's gear to pay the armourer for his work.
4. Robert Jones, *Knight: The Warrior and World of Chivalry* (Oxford: Osprey Publishing, 2011), 86.
5. Phillips, *The Complete Illustrated History of Knights*, 90.
6. One such entry comes from a record from 1110 by Geoffrey of Malaterra who claimed that in 1062, during a siege in the war between Robert Guiscard and his brother Roger, warriors from both armies organized a joust. Even if Malaterra's account is fictitious, which it most probably is, it demonstrates that tournaments were being held in his lifetime.
7. *Ivanhoe*'s tournament strongly resembles those of the fourteenth and fifteenth centuries. It is true that tournament jousts existed in the twelfth century but they were not given much attention in that period.
8. Jones, *Knight*, 86.
9. Because of the dangerous and often lethal nature of mêlée such tournament events were consistently criticized by the clergy. Starting with Pope Innocent II's ban of 1130, followed by similar prohibitions in 1139 and 1179, tournaments were repeatedly outlawed, albeit with little success. The best illustration of the extent of the clergy's antagonism towards tournaments is the fact that those knights who were killed during the mêlée were denied a church burial.
10. The mêlée at Last Hearth is said to have taken place in 170 AC, while *A Game of Thrones*, and thus the whole book series, begins in 297 AC. If one compares the mêlée at Last Hearth to the Hand's tourney, it is clear that Westeros's martial games undergo the same evolutionary mechanisms as their historic, medieval counterparts. Martin prefaces the information on mêlée in *WIF* with the information that 'knighthood is rare in the North', and so are knightly tourneys; this might also suggest that the northern regions have developed more slowly than the South and thus they enjoy older, more outdated martial games. In fact, the Northmen are said to seldom tilt for sport, which directly points to their lack of interest, and possibly skill, in what is the dominant tournament game by the time of the events of *A Song of Ice and Fire*. See *WIF*, 136.
11. Jones, *Knight*, 87.
12. Ibid., 88.
13. Phillips, *The Complete Illustrated History*, 108.
14. Jones, *Knight*, 85.
15. Christopher Gravett, *Knights at Tournament* (Oxford: Osprey, 2002), 11.
16. A caricature of this practice can be seen during the Hand's tourney when Ser Gregor Clegane, having been unhorsed, attacks Ser Loras Tyrell with a sword. Martin presents the situation as an example of Clegane's savagery, but in the Middle Ages both parties would have been prepared to continue fighting on foot after the initial run with lances. A much better representation of the transition from joust to single combat with weapons can be seen in the descriptions of the tourney at Ashford Meadow where a number of knights duel with swords and axes after the initial pass with lances.

17 David Edge and John M. Paddock, *Arms and Armor of the Medieval Knight* (New York: Crescent Books, 1988), 69.
18 Richard Barber, *Edward, Prince of Wales and Aquitaine: A Biography of the Black Prince* (Woodbridge: The Boydell Press, 2002), 43.
19 Striking the shield of peace meant that one wanted to compete using blunted tournament weapons while the shield of war represented regular, sharp weaponry; Jean Froissart, *Chronicles*, trans. Geoffrey Brereton (London: Penguin Books, 1978), 373.
20 Gravett, *Knights at Tournament*, 19.
21 Jones, *Knight*, 83.
22 In England the practice of trial by combat is believed to have been introduced after the Norman invasion of 1066. The rules and regulations concerning the appointment of champions for judicial duels changed and evolved throughout the period. Initially, to become a champion one had to be a material witness to the case. See James B. Thayer, 'The Older Modes of Trial', *Harvard Law Review*, 5, no. 2 (1891): 66. Interestingly, in Normandy there were no such restrictions and one could legally hire a champion. Finally, in 1275 English law abandoned the requirement that the champion be a witness (Thayer, 'The Older Modes', 68). Champions would usually be employed by women, clerics, the old and the sick or crippled as judicial duels were perceived as *iudicium Dei*, a trial through which God could provide a verdict that humans could not, and thus it was believed that any attempts at swaying the outcome, 'whether by pitting unequally matched men or through magical intervention', would invoke 'divine wrath'. See Jacqueline Stuhmiller, '"Iudicium Dei, iudicium fortunae": Trial by Combat in Malory's "Le Morte Darthur"', *Speculum*, 81, no. 2 (2006): 428. Thus, in the medieval context, Tyrion's use of a champion in a judicial duel would not only be very typical for his condition but also completely justified from a legal perspective.
23 Gravett, *Knights at Tournament*, 22.
24 Ibid.
25 Interestingly enough, the TV series fixes the problem by removing the shield from the scene depicting the duel. In 'The Mountain and the Viper' (4.8), Ser Gregor wields his greatsword two-handed from the very beginning of the duel.
26 Chaucer's 'The Knight's Tale' is entirely devoted to the notion of two competing knights; it illustrates the conventions of a knightly trial by combat through a scene in which Arcite provides Palamon with a harness and weapons matching those he himself uses in order to ensure the fairness of their duel.

Chapter 9

1 I follow the critical approach developed in Thomas Honegger, '(Heroic) Fantasy and the Middle Ages – Strange Bedfellows or an Ideal Cast?', *Itinéraires* (2010–13): 61–70. On the work of George R. R. Martin in this context see Carolyne Larrington, *Winter is Coming. The Medieval World of Game of Thrones* (London and New York: I.B. Tauris, 2016), 13–53, Shiloh Carroll, *Medievalism in A Song of Ice and Fire and Game of Thrones* (Cambridge: D.S. Brewer, 2018), 1–22, and Carol Parrish Jamison, *Chivalry in Westeros: The Knightly Code of A Song of Ice and Fire* (Jefferson: McFarland, 2018), 1–18.
2 See the categorizations in Steven F. Kruger, *Dreaming in the Middle Ages* (Cambridge: Cambridge University Press, 2005), 17–32, and A. H. M. Kessels, 'Ancient Systems of Dream-Classification', *Mnemosyne*, 4, no. 22 (1969): 396–414.

3   Augustine, *De Genesi Ad Litteram*, XII, 6.15; 7. 16; translations based on Kruger, *Dreaming in the Middle Ages*, 37. Original text at https://www.augustinus.it/latino/genesi_lettera/index2.htm.
4   Aristotle, *Parva Naturalia, De Divinatione per somnum*, 39–40, trans. J. I. Beare and G. R. T. Ross, quoted from https://www.documentacatholicaomnia.eu.
5   Ibid., 39–40.
6   Cf. Kruger, *Dreaming in the Middle Ages*, 83–98.
7   Aquinas, *Summa Theologiae*, II, b, q. 95, art. 6. All references to *Summa Theologiae*, http://www.logicmuseum.com/wiki/Authors/Thomas_Aquinas/Summa_Theologiae/Part_IIb/Q95#q95a6co.
8   A more extensive discussion of Aquinas's dialogue with the Aristotelian tradition in the context of the categorization of dreams is provided by Harm Goris, 'Thomas Aquinas on Dreams', in *Dreams as Divine Communication in Christianity: From Hermas to Aquinas*, ed. Bart Koet (Leuven: Peeters, 2012), 1–19.
9   Aquinas, *Summa Theologiae*, I, 78, art. 4.
10 See the extensive discussion of the function of *imaginatio* in Jozef Matula, 'Thomas Aquinas and the Influence of Imaginatio/Phantasia on Human Being', *Acta Universitatis Palackianae Olomucensis Facultas Philosophica Philosophica*, 5 (2002): 169–75. See also Clive Staples Lewis, *The Discarded Image. An Introduction to Medieval and Renaissance Literature* (Cambridge: Cambridge University Press, 1964), 152–74; Aquinas, *Summa Theologiae*, I, q. 84, art. 7.
11 Aquinas, *Summa Theologiae*, II b, q. 95, art. 6.
12 Ibid., II b, q. 95, art. 6.
13 Ibid., I, q. 84, art. 7; *Summa Theologiae*, I, q. 111, art. 1.
14 Ibid., I, q. 111, art. 3–4; *Summa Theologiae*, I, q. 111, 3–4.
15 Ibid., I, q. 111, art. 3/4.
16 See Corinne Saunders, *Magic and the Supernatural in Medieval English Romance* (Cambridge: D.S. Brewer, 2010), 117–51; 208–16.
17 On the genre's relation with the era's philosophical and psychological context see also Kathryn L. Lynch, *The High Medieval Dream Vision. Poetry, Philosophy, and Literary Form* (Stanford: Stanford University Press, 1988), 34–40, 49–76.
18 A more extensive discussion of the motif outside the context of dreams is developed in Henry Jacoby, 'Wargs, Wights, and Wolves that are Dire: Mind and Metaphysics, Westeros Style', in *Game of Thrones and Philosophy: Logic Cuts Deeper than Swords*, ed. Henry Jacoby (Hoboken: John Wiley & Sons, 2012), 115–25. On the theme of prophecy in relation to skin-changing compare Andrew Zimmerman Jones, 'Of Direwolves and Gods', in *Behind the Wall: Exploring George R. R. Martin's A Song of Ice and Fire*, ed. James Lowder (Dallas: BenBella Books, 2012), 107–22.
19 Aquinas, *Summa Theologiae*, questions 75, 76.

Chapter 10

1   Edward James and Farah Mendlesohn, 'Introduction', in *The Cambridge Companion to Fantasy Literature*, ed. Edward James and Farah Mendlesohn (Cambridge: Cambridge University Press, 2012), 1.
2   This is the type of medievalism that David Matthews terms the Middle Ages 'as it never was', in contrast to the Middle Ages 'as it was' and the Middle Ages 'as it might

have been'; also Tison Pugh and Angela Jane Weisl call the image of the Middle Ages in the later epochs 'a fantasy'; David Matthews, *Medievalism: A Critical History* (Cambridge: D. S. Brewer, 2015), 37–8; *Medievalisms: Making the Past in the Present*, ed. Tison Pugh and Angela Jane Weisl (London and New York: Routledge, 2013), 1.

3   For more on circulation of emotions see Katie Barclay, 'The Emotions of Household Economics', in *The Routledge History of Emotions in Europe 1100 – 1700*, ed. Andrew Lynch and Susan Broomhall (London and New York: Routledge, 2019), 186.

4   Barbara H. Rosenwein, 'Introduction', in *Anger's Past: The Social Uses of an Emotion in the Middle Ages*, ed. Barbara H. Rosenwein (Ithaca and London: Cornell University Press, 1998), 1.

5   For a discussion of medieval emotions see, for example, Carolyne Larrington, 'The Psychology of Emotion and the Study of Medieval Period', *Early Medieval Europe*, 10, no. 2 (2001): 251–6; *Politiques des émotions au Moyen Age*, ed. Damien Boquet and Piroska Nagy (Firenze: Sismel and Editioni del Galuzzo, 2010); *Emotions in Medieval Arthurian Literature: Body, Mind, Voice*, ed. Frank Brandsma, Corinne Saunders, and Carolyne Larrington (Cambridge: D. S. Brewer, 2015); *Understanding Emotions in Early Europe*, ed. Michael Champion and Andrew Lynch (Turnhout: Brepols, 2015); *Tears, Sighs and Laughter: Expression of Emotions in the Middle Ages*, ed. Per Förnegård, Erika Kihlman, and Mia Åkestam, Gunnell Engwall, Vitterhets Historie och Antikvitets Akademien, Konferenser 92 (Stockholm: KVHAA, 2017); Damien Boquet and Piroska Nagy, *Medieval Sensibilities: A History of Emotions in the Middle Ages* (London: Polity, 2018); *Performing Emotions in Early Europe*, ed. Philippa Maddern, Joanne McEwan, and Anne M. Scott (Turnhout: Brepols, 2018); *The Routledge History of Emotions in Europe 1100 – 1700*, ed. Lynch and Broomhall.

6   Carolyne Larrington, 'Mediating Medieval(ized) Emotion in *Game of Thrones*', in *Authenticity, Medievalism, Music*, ed. Karl Fugelso, Studies in Medievalism 27 (Cambridge: D. S. Brewer, 2018), 37.

7   Thomas Dixon maintains that the terms 'passions', 'affections' and 'sentiments' were used rather than the term 'emotions' up till the nineteenth century; Thomas Dixon, *From Passions to Emotions: The Creation of a Secular Psychological Category* (Cambridge: Cambridge University Press, 2003), 11–12.

8   St Augustine and Aquinas are going to be referred to here as philosophers and not as theologians; otherwise a lot of critical space could be devoted to emotions in religious devotionality, as it has already been done, for example, by Sarah McNamer or Barbara H. Rosenwein, while the topic of medieval and early modern religious feeling and its present-day reception has recently been summarized by Paul Megna; see Sarah McNamer, *Religious Meditation and the Invention of Medieval Compassion* (Philadelphia: University of Pennsylvania Press, 2010); Barbara H. Rosenwein, 'Periodization? An Answer from the History of Emotions', in *The Routledge History of Emotions in Europe 1100 – 1700*, ed. Lynch and Broomhall, 15–29; Paul Megna, 'Dreadful Emotion', in *The Routledge History of Emotions in Europe 1100 – 1700*, ed. Lynch and Broomhall, 72–85.

9   The two approaches to emotions, the basic emotions theory and Frevert's constructivist approach are introduced, for instance, by Barbara H. Rosenwein; see Rosenwein, 'Periodization? An Answer from the History of Emotions', 15–16.

10 This is also the view that Peter and Carol Stearns famously advocated, since they noted that emotions felt should be distinguished from what they called 'standards of emotional expression'; see Peter N. Stearns and Carol Z. Stearns 'Emotionology:

Clarifying the History of Emotions and Emotional Standards', *American Historical Review*, 90, no. 4 (1985): 813-36.
11 Ute Frevert, *Emotions in History – Lost and Found* (Budapest and New York: Central European University Press, 2011), 7.
12 Barbara H. Rosenwein emphasizes the constructivist idea of medieval emotions when she criticizes 'the easy notion that emotions in the Middle Ages were the same as – if more loudly expressed than – our own'; Barbara H. Rosenwein, 'Controlling Paradigms', in *Anger's Past*, ed. Rosenwein, 242.
13 Johann Huizinga, *Waning of the Middle Ages*, trans. Francis Hopman (Garden City: Doubleday Anchor Books, 1954), 9.
14 On the other hand, while such critics as Stephen D. White noticed that Huizinga, like Marc Bloch and others afterwards, treated the history of medieval emotions 'as an interesting story of impulsive, emotionally intense people', White does not argue that the people experienced emotion intensely, but rather that this refers to their impulsive expression of emotions; see Stephen D. White, 'The Politics of Anger', in *Anger's Past*, ed. Rosenwein, 127-52 at 151.
15 To use Barbara H. Rosenwein's famous theory, emotional communities were formed in this manner; see Barbara H. Rosenwein, *Emotional Communities in the Early Middle Ages* (New York: Cornell University Press, 2007).
16 Tomasz Z. Majkowski, *W cieniu białego drzewa. Powieść fantasy w XX wieku* [*In the Shadow of a White Tree: the Fantasy Novel in the Twentieth Century*] (Kraków: Wydawnictwo Naukowe Uniwersytetu Jagiellońskiego, 2013), 299.
17 Ibid; the translation into English is mine.
18 Michael Champion and Andrew Lynch, 'Understanding Emotions: "The Things They Left Behind"', in *Understanding Emotions in Early Europe*, ed. Michael Champion and Andrew Lynch (Turnhout: Brepols, 2015), x.
19 Ute Frevert, 'Defining Emotions: Concepts and Debates over Three Centuries', in *Emotional Lexicons: Continuity and Change in the Vocabulary of Feeling 1700-2000*, ed. Ute Frevert et al. (Oxford: Oxford University Press, 2014), 17.
20 Ibid.
21 Ibid., 18.
22 Heribertus Dwi Kristano, *The Praiseworthy Passion of Shame: A Historical and Philosophical Elucidation of Aquinas's Thought on the Nature and Role of Shame in the Moral Life* (Rome: Gregorian and Biblical Press, 2019), 176.
23 This is how Aquinas discusses anger: 'The formal definition of anger is that is the desire for revenge and its material definition is that it is the boiling of the blood around the heart'; Aquinas, *Questiones disputate de veritate*, quoted in: Kristano, *The Praiseworthy Passion of Shame*, 176.
24 Monique Scheer, 'Topographies of Emotion', in *Emotional Lexicons*, ed. Frevert et al., 32-61 at 39.
25 Larrington, 'Mediating Medieval(ized) Emotion in *Game of Thrones*', 39.
26 Shannon Wells-Lassagne, 'Adapting Desire: Wives, Prostitutes, and Smallfolk', in *Women of Ice and Fire: Gender, Game of Thrones, and Multiple Media Engagements*, ed. Anne Gjelsvik and Rikke Schubart (New York and London: Bloomsbury, 2015), 29.
27 Mariah Larsson, 'Adapting Sex: Cultural Conceptions of Sexuality in Words and Images', in *Women of Ice and Fire: Gender*, ed. Gjelsvik and Schubart, 17-37 at 29.
28 William J. Bouwsma, *A Usable Past: Essays in European Cultural History* (Berkeley: University of California Press, 1990), 47.
29 Frevert, 'Defining Emotions', 19.

30. Rikke Schubart and Anne Gjelsvik, 'Introduction', in *Women of Ice and Fire: Gender*, ed. Gjelsvik and Schubart, 1–16 at 7.
31. For a discussion of Catelyn as a peace-weaver see: Kris Swank, 'The Peaceweavers of Winterfell', in *Queenship and the Women of Westeros: Female Agency and Advice in 'Game of Thrones' and 'A Song of Ice and Fire'*, ed. Zita Eva Rohr and Lisa Benz (Cham: Palgrave Macmillan, 2020), 109 *et passim*.
32. For a discussion of what political plans initially stood behind Catelyn's marriage see: Carolyne Larrington, 'Foreword', in *Queenship and the Women of Westeros*, ed. Rohr and Benz, vii–xviii at xi.
33. The original study in which these six basic emotions were identified was Paul Ekman and W. V. Friesen, 'Constants Across Cultures in the Face and Emotion', *Journal of Personality and Social Psychology*, 17 (1971): 124–9.
34. Frevert, *Emotions in History – Lost and Found*, 10.
35. Ibid., 41.
36. Monique Scheer, 'Are Emotions a Kind of Practice (And Is That What Makes Them Have a History)? A Bourdieuian Approach to Understanding Emotion', *History and Theory*, 52 (2012): 193–220.
37. Jorgensen, 'Introduction', in *Anglo-Saxon Emotions*, 1–17 at 3.
38. Ibid., 6.
39. Antonio Damasio, *The Feeling of What Happens: Body and Emotion in the Making of Consciousness* (New York and London: Mariner Books, 2000), 51.
40. 'It is arguable that Brienne influences the behaviour and ideals of another of Westeros's knightly fraternity – Jaime Lannister'; Iain A. MacInnes, '"All I Ever Wanted Was to Fight for a Lord I Believed in. But the Good Lords Are Dead and the Rest Are Monsters": Brienne of Tarth, Jaime Lannister, and the Chivalric "Other"', in *Queenship in Westeros*, 78.
41. Kristano, *The Praiseworthy Passion of Shame*, 93.
42. Ibid., 200.
43. Ibid., 191–231.
44. Pascal J. Massie and Lauryn S. Mayer, 'Bringing Elsewhere Home: *A Song of Ice and Fire*'s Ethics of Disability', in *Ethics and Medievalism*, ed. Karl Fugelso, Studies in Medievalism 23 (Cambridge: D. S. Brewer, 2014), 46.
45. Frevert, *Emotions in History – Lost and Found*, 21.
46. See Larrington, 'Mediating Medieval(ized) Emotion in *Game of Thrones*', 35.
47. Schubart and Gjelsvik, 'Introduction', in *Women of Ice and Fire: Gender*, ed. Gjelsvik and Schubart, 6.
48. Gail Kern Paster, *Humouring the Body: Emotions and the Shakespearean Stage* (Chicago and London: University of Chicago Press, 2004), 77.
49. See: Sylwia Borowska-Szerszun, 'Westerosi Queens: Medievalist Portrayal of Female Power and Authority in *A Song of Ice and Fire*', in *Queenship and the Women of Westeros*, ed. Rohr and Benz, 53–76.
50. See: Kavita Mudan Finn, 'Queen of Sad Mischance: Medievalism, "Realism," and the Case of Cersei Lannister', in *Queenship and the Women of Westeros*, ed. Rohr and Benz, 29–52 at 31.
51. Kavita Mudan Finn, 'High and Mighty Queens of Westeros', in *Game of Thrones versus History: Written in Blood*, ed. Brian A. Pavlac (Hoboken: Wiley-Blackwell, 2017), 17–31 at 20.
52. See Virgil, *The Aeneid*, trans. John Jackson (Ware: Wordsworth Classics, 1995).
53. Władysław Witalisz, *The Trojan Mirror: Middle English Narratives of Troy as Books of Princely Advice* (Frankfurt am Main: Peter Lang, 2011), 124–7.

Chapter 11

1. Tom Holland, 'Game of Thrones is More Brutally Realistic Than Most Historical Novels', *The Guardian*, 24 March 2012, https://www.theguardian.com/tv-and-radio/2013/mar/24/game-of-thrones-realistic-history (accessed 29 November 2019).
2. Kavita Mudan Finn, 'Queen of Sad Mischance: Medievalism, "Realism," and the Case of Cersei Lannister', in *Queenship and the Women of Westeros: Female Agency and Advice in Game of Thrones and A Song of Ice and Fire*, ed. Zita E. Rohr and Lisa Benz (Cham: Springer, 2020), 30.
3. Shiloh Carroll, *Medievalism in A Song of Ice and Fire and Game of Thrones* (Cambridge: D.S. Brewer, 2018), 16–17.
4. Ibid., 89.
5. Ibid.
6. Mariah Larsson, 'Adapting Sex: Cultural Conceptions of Sexuality in Words and Images', in *Women of Ice and Fire: Gender, Game of Thrones, and Multiple Media Engagements*, ed. Anne Gjelsvik and Rikke Schubart (London and New York: Bloomsbury, 2016), 21.
7. Ibid.
8. Valerie Estelle Frankel, *Women in Game of Thrones: Power, Conformity and Resistance* (Jefferson: McFarland, 2014); Mariah Larsson, 'Adapting Sex'; Rikke Schubart, 'Woman with Dragons: Daenerys, Pride, and Postfeminist Possibilities', in *Women of Ice and Fire*, ed. Gjelsvik and Schubart, 105–29. Shiloh Carroll also notes the development of the relationship in *Medievalism*, 93.
9. Frankel, *Women in Game of Thrones*, 12.
10. Glenn Richardson, 'A Cardboard Crown: Kingship in *The Tudors*', in *History, Fiction, and The Tudors: Sex, Politics, Power, and Artistic License in the Showtime Television Series*, ed. William B. Robison (New York: Palgrave Macmillan, 2016) 188.
11. Larsson, 'Adapting Sex', 23.
12. Ibid., 23, 25.
13. Kavita Mudan Finn, 'High and Mighty Queens of Westeros', in *Game of Thrones versus History: Written in Blood*, ed. Brian A. Pavlac (Hoboken: Wiley, 2017), 22.
14. Debra Ferreday, '*Game of Thrones*, Rape Culture and Feminist Fandom', *Australian Feminist Studies*, 30, no. 83 (2015): 24.
15. Frankel, *Women in Game of Thrones*, 24.
16. Larsson, 'Adapting Sex', 25.
17. Schubart, 'Woman with Dragons', 115.
18. Ibid.
19. Larsson, 'Adapting Sex', 25–6.
20. Frankel, *Women in Game of Thrones*, 1. Angela Watercutter, 'Yes, Women Really Do Like Game of Thrones (We Have Proof)', *Wired*, 3 June 2013, https://www.wired.com/2013/06/women-game-of-thrones/ (accessed 24 March 2021).
21. H. Tankovska, 'Distribution of Game of Thrones Social Media Mentions in the United States During Season 7 in 2017, by Gender', *Statistica*, 28 January 2021, https://www.statista.com/statistics/737521/game-of-thrones-social-media-gender/ (accessed 24 March 2021).
22. Ginia Bellafante, 'A Fantasy World of Strange Feuding Kingdoms', *The New York Times*, 14 April 2011, https://www.nytimes.com/2011/04/15/arts/television/game-of-thrones-begins-sunday-on-hbo-review.html (accessed 16 June 2021).
23. Carolyne Larrington, *All Men Must Die: Power and Passion in Game of Thrones* (London: Bloomsbury, 2021), 183–4.

24 Larsson, 'Adapting Sex', 17.
25 Ibid., 18.
26 James Hibbert, 'George R. R. Martin explains why there's violence against women on "Game of Thrones"', *Entertainment*, 3 June 2015, https://ew.com/article/2015/06/03/george-rr-martin-thrones-violence-women/ (accessed 16 June 2021).
27 Ibid.
28 Jarrod Bock and Melissa Burkley, 'On the Prowl: Examining the Impact of Men-as-Predators and Women-as-Prey Metaphors on Attitudes that Perpetuate Sexual Violence', *Sex Roles*, 80 (2019): 262–76 (abstract); Michael D. Robinson, Jessica L. Bair, Tianwei Liu, Matthew J. Scott, Ian B. Penzel, 'Of Tooth and Claw: Predator Self-Identifications Mediate Gender Differences in Interpersonal Arrogance', *Sex Roles*, 77 (2017): 272–86.
29 Bock and Burkley, 'On the Prowl', 268.
30 Larsson, 'Adapting Sex', 18.
31 Ibid.
32 Frankel, *Women in Game of Thrones*, 13.

Chapter 12

1 Amy S. Kaufman, 'Muscular Medievalism', *The Year's Work in Medievalism*, 31 (2016): 58.
2 For a discussion of representation of rape in *A Song of Ice And Fire,* see Sylwia Borowska-Szerszun, 'Representation of Rape in George R. R. Martin's *A Song of Ice and Fire* and Robin Hobb's *Liveship Traders*', *Extrapolation*, 60, no. 1 (2019): 4–11.
3 The scope of diverse reactions to female characters in the transmedial *GoT* universe is well reflected in a recent collection of essays devoted to the depiction of women in both the cycle of novels and the TV series. Like the readers and the viewers, the contributors to the volume differ in their perception of female characters, who can be read as either feminist or anti-feminist, subversive or repressive, empowered or objectified. See Rikke Schubart and Anne Gjelsvik, 'Introduction', in *Women of Ice and Fire*, ed. Anne Gjelsvik and Rikke Schubart (New York: Bloomsbury Academic, 2016), 1–10. Similarly, upon examining the responses of feminist fandom to the issue of rape in the TV series, Debra Ferreday notes that paradoxically in fan communities the discourses of rape culture are both reproduced and challenged, which once again highlights the ambiguity of the narrative. See Debra Ferreday, 'Game of Thrones, Rape Culture and Feminist Fandom', *Australian Feminist Studies*, 30, no. 83 (2015): 21–36.
4 John Hodgman and George R. R. Martin, 'John Hodgman Interviews George R. R. Martin', *Public Radio International*, 21 September 2011, https://www.pri.org/stories/2011-09-21/john-hodgman-interviews-george-rr-martin (accessed 20 November 2019).
5 David Matthews, *Medievalism: A Critical History* (Cambridge: D.S. Brewer, 2015), 21.
6 These widespread negative connotations with the term 'medieval' are evident in Marsellus Wallace's line from Quentin Tarantino's *Pulp Fiction*, where he threatens his rapist that he is going to 'get medieval on [his] ass' – an expression that has become widespread in American culture. In the scene the phrase is clearly associated with pain, torture, violence and sadism, but 'the medieval' remains strikingly ahistorical and atemporal. As Carolyn Dinshaw notes, the realm of the medieval in the movie is

not 'exactly another *time*' but rather 'the space of the rejects – really, the abjects – of this world'. See Carolyn Dinshaw, *Getting Medieval: Sexualities and Communities, Pre- and Postmodern* (Durham: Duke University Press, 1999), 185–6.
7   For a valuable discussion of the two streaks, the 'romantic' and the 'grotesque', in the changing perception of the Middle Ages, see Matthews, *Medievalism: A Critical History*, 13–35; and Tison Pugh and Angela Jane Weisl, *Medievalism: Making the Past in the Present* (London: Routledge, 2013), 1–11.
8   Mikal Gilmore and George R. R. Martin, 'George R. R. Martin: The Rolling Stone Interview', *Rolling Stone*, 23 April 2014, https://www.rollingstone.com/culture/culture-news/george-r-r-martin-the-rolling-stone-interview-242487/ (accessed 10 January 2020).
9   Anna Czarnowus, 'The Other Worlds of George R. R. Martin's *A Song of Ice and Fire*', in *George R. R. Martin's 'A Song of Ice and Fire' and the Medieval Literary Tradition*, ed. Bartłomiej Błaszkiewicz (Warszawa: Wydawnictwa Uniwersytetu Warszawskiego, 2014), 99.
10 Carolyne Larrington, *Winter is Coming: The Medieval World of Game of Thrones* (London and New York: I.B. Tauris, 2016), 1.
11 Brian A. Pavlac, 'Introduction: The Winter of Our Discontent', in *Game of Thrones Versus History: Written in Blood*, ed. Brian A. Pavlac (Hoboken: Wiley Blackwell, 2017), 11.
12 David W. Marshall, 'Neomedievalism, Identification, and the Haze of Medievalisms', *Studies in Medievalism: Defining Neomedievalism(s) II*, 20 (2011): 22. It is crucial to note here that the question of whether neomedievalism is separate from medievalism, or whether it is just one of many medievalisms, is a hotly debated topic in academia (for varying views on this, see, for instance the 2010 and 2011 issues of *Studies in Medievalism*). I have decided to choose neomedievalism as a conceptual framework of this article for two reasons: firstly, it emphasizes the diversion of Martin's narrative from more traditional or nostalgic types of medievalism, and secondly, it reflects Martin's eclectic use of the medieval motifs and topoi that are then supplemented with contemporary meanings.
13 Pugh and Weisl, *Medievalism: Making the Past*, 6.
14 I raise some points related to this discussion, although in a less detailed way, elsewhere. For a discussion of Cersei Lannister's rulership against the tactics employed by other queens of Martin's narrative, that is, Margaery Tyrell and Daenerys Targaryen, see Sylwia Borowska-Szerszun, 'Westerosi Queens: Medievalist Portrayal of Female Power and Authority in *A Song of Ice and Fire*', in *Queenship and the Women of Westeros: Female Agency and Advice in 'Game of Thrones' and 'A Song of Ice and Fire'*, ed. Zita Eva Rohr and Lisa Benz (Cham: Palgrave Macmillan, 2020), 55–9.
15 The term is used after Alcuin Blamires, who scrutinizes the body of medieval texts that attempt to construe a more positive view on femininity by responding to misogynistic accusations 'according to the cultural ideology of their period', not later ones. Such 'defences' of women cannot be really seen as 'feminist', Blamires argues, as the female virtues listed by medieval writers could be interpreted as negative stereotyping of women by contemporary feminists. See Alcuin Blamires, *The Case for Women in Medieval Culture* (Oxford: Oxford University Press, 1998), 13.
16 Howard R. Bloch, 'Medieval Misogyny', in *Misogyny, Misandry, and Misanthropy*, ed. Howard R. Bloch and Frances Ferguson (Berkeley: University of California Press, 1989), 1.
17 Ibid., 11.

18 In Aristotle's physiology, influential from the late twelfth century onwards, the perception of a male principle (soul, form) as superior to a female one (body, matter) results in conceptualizing a woman as a 'deformed' or 'defective' man. In Galen's medical tract on physiology and anatomy, *De Usu Partium* ('On the Usefulness of the Body'), female imperfection is further explained by an imbalance of humours and a tendency towards coldness, which blocks the exteriorization of her genitals, making them deficient and imperfect. For relevant passages, see *Woman Defamed and Woman Defended: An Anthology of Medieval Texts*, ed. Alcuin Blamires (Oxford: Oxford University Press, 1992), 1, 41–2.
19 Ruth Mazo Karras, *Common Women: Prostitution and Sexuality in Medieval England* (New York: Oxford University Press, 1998), 107.
20 *Against Marrying (De coniuge non ducenda)*, in Blamires, *Woman Defamed*, 127.
21 Karras, *Common Women*, 108.
22 Elizabeth Archibald, *Incest and the Medieval Imagination* (Oxford: Oxford University Press, 2001), 192.
23 Carolyne Larrington, *Brothers and Sisters in Medieval European Literature* (Suffolk: The University of York, York Medieval Press, 2015), 170.
24 Elizabeth Beaton, 'Female Machiavellians in Westeros', in *Women of Ice and Fire*, ed. Gjelsvik and Schubart, 199–204.
25 C. Patel, 'Expelling a Monstrous Matriarchy: Casting Cersei Lannister as Abject in *A Song of Ice and Fire*', *Journal of European Popular Culture*, 5, no. 2 (2014): 142.
26 Shiloh R. Carroll, '"You Ought to be in Skirts and Me in Mail": Gender and History in George R. R. Martin's *A Song of Ice and Fire*', in *George R. R. Martin's 'A Song of Ice and Fire'*, ed. Błaszkiewicz, 255.
27 'No One' (6.8).
28 Sam Haysom, 'Game of Thrones' Star Lena Headey Hints Cersei Is Headed to an Even Darker Place', *Mashable*, 12 December 2016, https://mashable.com/2016/12/12/lena-headey-cersei-season-7/?europe=true (accessed 24 January 2020).
29 Anne Campbell, *Men, Women, and Aggression* (New York: Basic Books, 1993), 1.
30 While we cannot be sure how the narrative of Daenerys continues in Martin's novels, the TV show featured her quick and poorly motivated descent into madness, making the stories of Cersei and Daenerys strikingly similar in the end. While the depiction of Cersei as a villain has been consistent from the very beginning, the portrayal of Daenerys has made her one of the most popular characters of the series and a serious candidate for the throne. That both of these powerful women, despite different characterization throughout the show, are eventually eliminated from the narrative seems to imply that the creators of *Game of Thrones* could see no place for a female leader at the very top of Westerosi power structures.
31 For a detailed discussion of the theory related to the 'wandering womb' and hysteria in early medical texts devoted to gynaecology, see Helen King, 'Once upon a Text: Hysteria from Hippocrates', in *Hysteria Beyond Freud*, ed. Sander L. Gilman et al. (Berkeley: University of California Press, 1993), 3–64.
32 Laurinda S. Dixon, *Perilous Chastity: Women and Illness in Pre-Enlightenment Art and Medicine* (Ithaca: Cornell University Press, 1995), 22.
33 Geoffrey Chaucer, 'The Canterbury Tales', in *The Riverside Chaucer*, ed. Larry Dean Benson (Oxford: Oxford University Press, 2008), 240.
34 Michael Camille, *Mirror in Parchment: The Luttrell Psalter and the Making of Medieval England* (London: Reaktion Books, 1998), 313.
35 Chaucer, 'The Canterbury Tales', 119.

36 See 'Noah and His Sons', in *The Towneley Plays*, ed. Martin Stevens and A. C. Cawley (Oxford: Oxford University Press, 1994), ll. 487–606.
37 Sigmund Freud, 'New Introductory Lectures on Psycho-analysis', in *The Standard Edition of the Complete Psychological Works of Sigmund Freud*, 24 vols, ed. and trans. J. Strachey (London: Hogarth Press, 1953–74), vol. 22 (1964), 125–6.
38 Siegfried Zepf and Dietmar Seel, 'Penis Envy and the Female Oedipus Complex: A Plea to Reawaken an Ineffectual Debate', *The Psychoanalytic Review*, 103, no. 3 (2016): 397.
39 Hilary M. Lips, *Sex and Gender: An Introduction*, 6th edn (Long Grove: Waveland Press, 2017), 63.
40 Mari Ruti, *Penis Envy and Other Bad Feelings: The Emotional Costs of Everyday Life* (New York: Columbia University Press, 2018), 1.
41 Kavita Mudan Finn, 'Queen of Sad Mischance: Medievalism, "Realism," and the Case of Cersei Lannister', in *Queenship and the Women of Westeros*, ed. Rohr and Benz (Cham: Palgrave Macmillan, 2020), 41.

Bibliography

Manuscripts

London, British Library, Additional MS 5832

Primary texts

Abélard, Pierre. *Historia Calamitatum*, translated by Henry Adams Bellows. Fordham University Medieval Sourcebook. New York: Macmillan, 1972. https://sourcebooks.fordham.edu/basis/abelard-histcal.asp.
Aristotle. *Parva Naturalis*. http://www.documentacatholicaomnia.eu/03d/-384_-322,_Aristoteles,_07_Parva_Naturalia,_EN.pdf (accessed 14 March 2020).
Armstrong, Regis J., O. F. M. Cap, Wayne Hellmann, O. F. M. Conv and William J. Short, ed. *Francis of Assisi: Early Documents: Vol. 1 The Saint; Vol. 2: The Founder; Vol. 3: The Prophet*. New York, London, Manila: New City Press, 2002.
Aquinas, St. Thomas. *Summa Theologiae*. http://www.logicmuseum.com/authors/aquinas/Summa-index.htm and https://www.corpusthomisticum.org/iopera.html (accessed 21 March 2020).
Augustine. *De Genesi Ad Litteram*. https://www.augustinus.it/latino/genesi_lettera/index2.htm.
The Bible. King James Version. https://www.biblegateway.com/ (accessed 2 April 2020).
Chaucer, Geoffrey. 'The Knight's Tale'. In *The Riverside Chaucer*.
Chaucer, Geoffrey. 'The Canterbury Tales'. In *The Riverside Chaucer: Third Edition*, edited by Larry D. Benson, 23–328. Oxford: Oxford University Press, 2008.
de Charny, Geoffroi. *A Knight's Own Book of Chivalry*, translated by Elspeth Kennedy. Philadelphia: University of Pennsylvania Press, 2005.
de Voragine, Jacobus. 'S. Christopher'. In *The Golden Legend. Lives of the Saints*, translated by William Caxton from the Latin of Jacobus de Voragine, sel. and edited by George V. O'Neill, 48, 55. Cambridge: Cambridge University Press, 1914.
Druon, Maurice. *Le Roi de Fer*. Paris: Editions mondiales, 1955.
Druon, Maurice. *La Reine étranglée*. Paris: Editions mondiales, 1955.
Druon, Maurice. *Les Poisons de la couronne*. Paris: Editions mondiales, 1956.
Druon, Maurice. *La Loi des mâles*. Paris: Editions mondiales, 1957.
Druon, Maurice. *Le Louve de France*. Paris: Editions mondiales, 1959.
Druon, Maurice. *Le Lis et le Lion*. Paris: Editions mondiales, 1957.
Druon, Maurice. *Quand un roi perd la France*. Paris: Plon et Éditions Del Duca, 1977.
Druon, Maurice. *The Accursed Kings*, translated by Humphrey Hare. London: Harper Collins, 1956–61/2013–14.
Druon, Maurice. *The Iron King*, translated by Humphrey Hare. London: Harper Collins,1956/2013.

Druon, Maurice. *The Strangled Queen*, translated by Humphrey Hare. London: Harper Collins, 1956/2013.
Druon, Maurice. *The Poisoned Crown*, translated by Humphrey Hare. London: Harper Collins, 1957/2013.
Druon, Maurice. *The Royal Succession*, translated by Humphrey Hare. London: Harper Collins, 1958/2014.
Druon, Maurice. *The She-Wolf*, translated by Humphrey Hare. London: Harper Collins, 1960/2014.
Druon, Maurice. *The Lily and the Lion*, translated by Humphrey Hare. London: Harper Collins, 1961/2014.
Druon, Maurice. *Les Rois Maudits* (édition integrale). Paris: Plon, 2014.
Druon, Maurice. *The King Without a Kingdom*, translated by Alan Simpkin. London: Harper Collins, 2015.
Eadmer. *Vita Sancti Anselmi (The Life of St Anselm, Archbishop of Canterbury)*, edited and translated by R. W. Southern. London: Nelson, 1962.
Egils saga Skallagrímssonar, edited by Sigurður Nordal. Íslenzk fornrit 2. Reykjavík: Hið Íslenzka fornritafélag, 1933.
Froissart, Jean. *Chronicles*, translated by Geoffrey Brereton. London: Penguin Books, 1978.
Ingulf, Peter. *Ingulf's Chronicle of the Abbey of Croyland*, edited and translated Henry T. Riley. London: Henry G. Bohn, 1854.
Laskaya, Anne and Eve Salisbury, ed. *Middle English Breton Lays*. Kalamazoo: Medieval Institute Publications, 1995. http://d.lib.rochester.edu/teams/text/laskaya-and-salisbury-middle-english-breton-lays-sir-gowther.
Laxdœla saga, edited by Einar Ól. Sveinsson. Íslenzk fornrit 5. Reykjavík: Hið Íslenzka fornritafélag, 1934.
Llull, Ramon. *The Book of the Order of Chivalry*, translated by Noel Fallows. Woodbridge: Boydell, 2013.
Malory, Sir Thomas. *Le Morte Darthur*, edited by P. J. C. Field. Cambridge: D. S. Brewer, 2017.
Martin, George R. R. *A Game of Thrones*. London: Harper Collins, 1996; New York: Bantam, 2011.
Martin, George R. R. *A Clash of Kings*. London: Harper Collins, 1998; New York: Bantam, 2011.
Martin, George R. R. *A Storm of Swords*. London: Harper Collins, 2000; New York: Bantam, 2011.
Martin, George R. R. *A Feast for Crows*. London: Harper Collins, 2005; New York: Bantam, 2011.
Martin, George R. R. *A Dance with Dragons*. London: Harper Collins, 201; New York: Bantam, 2011.
Martin, George R. R. *The World of Ice & Fire*, London: Harper Voyager, 2014.
Martin, George R. R. *A Knight of the Seven Kingdoms*. London: HarperCollins, 2015.
Martin, George R. R. *Fire and Blood: A History of the Targaryen Kings from Aegon the Conqueror to Aegon III*. London: HarperCollins, 2018.
Scott, Sir Walter. *Ivanhoe*. London: Penguin Classics, 2000.
Stevens, Martin and A. C. Cawley, ed. *The Towneley Plays*. Early English Text Society SS13. Oxford: Oxford University Press, 1994.
Tolkien, John Ronald Reuel. *The Silmarillion*, edited by Christopher Tolkien. London: HarperCollins, 1977/1994.
Virgil. *The Aeneid*, translated by John Jackson. Ware: Wordsworth Classics, 1995.

White, Terence Hanbury, ed. and trans. *The Book of Beasts. Being a Translation from a Latin Bestiary of the Twelfth Century*. Stroud: Alan Sutton, 1992.

Secondary texts

Allsen, Thomas T. 'Mongolian Princes and Their Merchant Partners, 1200–1260'. *Asia Major*, 2 (1989): 83–126.
Appelbaum, Patricia. *St. Francis of America: How a Thirteenth-Century Friar Became America's Most Popular Saint*. Chapel Hill: The University of North Carolina Press, 2015.
Archibald, Elizabeth. *Incest and the Medieval Imagination*. Oxford: Oxford University Press, 2001.
Barber, Richard. *Edward, Prince of Wales and Aquitaine: A Biography of the Black Prince*. Woodbridge: The Boydell Press, 2002[1978].
Bărbuceanu, Costina Denisa. 'Athena Rising? Mentoring in Higher Education'. *Revue des Sciences Politiques*, 62 (2019): 45–54.
Barclay, Katie. 'The Emotions of Household Economics'. In *The Routledge History of Emotions in Europe 1100 – 1700*, edited by Andrew Lynch and Susan Broomhall, 185–200.
Barker, Juliet. *The Tournament in England 1100–1400*. Woodbridge: The Boydell Press, 2003.
Barrow, Julia. 'Churches, Education, and Literacy in Towns 600–1300'. In *The Cambridge Urban History of Britain*, edited by D. M. Palliser, 127–52. Cambridge: Cambridge University Press, 2000.
Battis, Jes and Susan Johnston, ed. *Mastering the Game of Thrones: Essays on George R. R. Martin's A Song of Ice and Fire*. Jefferson: McFarland, 2015.
Beaton, Elizabeth. 'Female Machiavellians in Westeros'. In *Women of Ice and Fire*, edited by Anne Gjelsvik and Rikke Schubart, 193–218.
Blamires, Alcuin, ed. *Woman Defamed and Women Defended: An Anthology of Medieval Texts*. Oxford: Oxford University Press, 1992.
Blamires, Alcuin. *The Case for Women in Medieval Culture*. Oxford: Oxford University Press, 1998.
Blastic, Michael W. 'Francis and his Hagiographical Tradition'. In *The Cambridge Companion to Francis of Assisi*, edited by Michael J. P. Robson, 68–83. Cambridge: Cambridge University Press, 2012.
Błaszkiewicz, Bartłomiej, ed. *George R. R. Martin's "A Song of Ice and Fire" and the Medieval Literary Tradition*. Warszawa: Wydawnictwa Uniwersytetu Warszawskiego, 2014.
Bloch, Howard R. 'Medieval Misogyny'. In *Misogyny, Misandry, and Misanthropy*, edited by Howard R. Bloch and Frances Ferguson, 1–24. Berkeley: University of California Press, 1989.
Bloch, Marc. *Feudal Society*. Chicago: University of Chicago Press, 1961.
Bock, Jarrod and Melissa Burkley. 'On the Prowl: Examining the Impact of Men-as-Predators and Women-as-Prey Metaphors on Attitudes that Perpetuate Sexual Violence'. *Sex Roles*, 80 (2019): 262–76.
Boquet, Damien and Piroska Nagy, ed. *Politiques des émotions au Moyen Age*. Firenze: Sismel and Editioni del Galuzzo, 2010.

Boquet, Damien and Piroska Nagy. *Medieval Sensibilities: A History of Emotions in the Middle Ages*. London: Polity, 2018.

Borowska-Szerszun, Sylwia. 'Representation of Rape in George R. R. Martin's *A Song of Ice and Fire* and Robin Hobb's *Liveship Traders*'. *Extrapolation*, 60, no. 1 (2019): 1–22.

Borowska-Szerszun, Sylwia. 'Westerosi Queens: Medievalist Portrayal of Female Power and Authority in *A Song of Ice and Fire*'. In *Queenship and the Women of Westeros*, edited by Zita Rohr and Lisa Benz, 53–76.

Bourdieu, Pierre. *Outline of a Theory of Practice*, translated by Richard Nice. Cambridge: Cambridge University Press, 1977.

Bouwsma, William J. *A Usable Past: Essays in European Cultural History*. Berkeley: University of California Press, 1990.

Brandsma, Frank, Corinne Saunders and Carolyne Larrington. *Emotions in Medieval Arthurian Literature: Body, Mind, Voice*. Cambridge: D.S. Brewer, 2015.

Cameron, John H. 'A New Kind of Hero: A Song of Ice and Fire's Brienne of Tarth'. In *A Quest of Her Own: Essays on the Female Hero in Modern Fantasy*, edited by Lori M. Campbell, 188–206. Jefferson: McFarland, 2014.

Camille, Michael. *Mirror in Parchment: The Luttrell Psalter and the Making of Medieval England*. London: Reaktion Books, 1998.

Campbell, Anne. *Men, Women, and Aggression*. New York: Basic Books, 1993.

Carroll, Shiloh R. '"You Ought to be in Skirts and Me in Mail": Gender and History in George R. R. Martin's *A Song of Ice and Fire*'. In *George R. R. Martin's "A Song of Ice and Fire"*, edited by Bartłomiej Błaszkiewicz, 247–59.

Carroll, Shiloh R. 'Rewriting the Fantasy Archetype: George R. R. Martin, Neomedievalist Fantasy, and the Quest for Realism'. In *Fantasy and Science Fiction Medievalisms: From Isaac Asimov to A Game of Thrones*, edited by Helen Young, 59–73. Amherst: Cambria Press, 2015.

Carroll, Shiloh R. *Medievalism in A Song of Ice and Fire and Game of Thrones*. Cambridge: D. S. Brewer, 2018.

Champion, Michael and Andrew Lynch. 'Understanding Emotions: "The Things They Left Behind"'. In *Understanding Emotions in Early Europe*, edited by Michael Champion and Andrew Lynch, ix–xxxiv.

Champion, Michael and Andrew Lynch, ed. *Understanding Emotions in Early Europe*. Turnhout: Brepols, 2015.

Chesterton, Gilbert Keith. *St. Francis of Assisi*. London: Hodder and Stoughton, 1923.

Chewning, Susannah Mary. 'Hildegard of Bingen'. In *The Oxford Encyclopedia of Women in World History, Volume I*, edited by Bonnie G. Smith, 452–53.

Clasby, Daniel J. 'Coexistence and Conflict in the Religions of Game of Thrones'. In *Game of Thrones versus History*, edited by Brian A. Pavlac and Elizabeth Lott, 195–208.

Cowlishaw, Brian. 'What Maesters Knew: Narrating Knowing'. In *Mastering the Game of Thrones*, edited by Jes Battis and Susan Johnston, 57–69.

Curtis, Renée L. 'The Perception of the Chivalric Ideal in Chrétien de Troyes's Yvain'. *Arthurian Interpretations*, 3, no. 2 (1989): 1–22.

Czarnowus, Anna. 'The Other Worlds of George R. R. Martin's *A Song of Ice and Fire*'. In *George R. R. Martin's "A Song of Ice and Fire"*, edited by Bartłomiej Błaszkiewicz, 95–114.

Damasio, Antonio. *The Feeling of What Happens: Body and Emotion in the Making of Consciousness*. New York, San Diego and London: Mariner Books, 2000.

Debosscher, Adam. '#ForTheThrone: A Study of the Emphasis on the Medievalism in the Paratext of G. R. R. Martin's *A Song of Ice and Fire* in HBO's *Game of Thrones*'. *The Year's Work in Medievalism*, 33 (2018): 78–92.

de Ridder-Symoens, Hilde. *A History of the University in Europe*, 4 vols. Cambridge: Cambridge University Press, 1992.

de Roover, Raymond. *Money, Banking and Credit in Mediaeval Bruges: Italian Merchant Bankers, Lombards and Money-Changers, A Study in the Origins of Banking*. Cambridge: Medieval Academy of America, 1948.

Dinshaw, Carolyn. *Getting Medieval: Sexualities and Communities, Pre- and Postmodern*. Durham: Duke University Press, 1999.

Dixon, Laurinda S. *Perilous Chastity: Women and Illness in Pre-Enlightenment Art and Medicine*. Ithaca: Cornell University Press, 1995.

Dixon, Thomas. *From Passions to Emotions: The Creation of a Secular Psychological Category*. Cambridge: Cambridge University Press, 2003.

Donahue, Charles, Jr. 'The Legal Professions of Fourteenth-Century England: Serjeants of the Common Bench and Advocates of the Court of Arches'. In *Laws, Lawyers, and Texts: Studies in Medieval Legal History in Honour of Paul Brand*, edited by Susanne Jenks, Jonathan Rose and Christopher Wittick, 227–51. Leiden: Brill, 2012.

Dörrich, Corinna. '"A Knight's a Sword with a Horse": Bilder von Ritterschaft und die Waffen der Frauen in ASOIAF'. In *Die Welt von 'Game of Thrones': Kulturwissenschaftliche Perspektiven auf George R. R. Martins 'A Song of Ice and Fire'*, edited by Markus May, Michael Baumann, Robert Baumgartner and Tobias Eder, 173–92. Bielefeld: transcript, 2016.

Dunn, Alastair. *The Great Rising of 1381: The Peasants' Revolt and England's Failed Revolution*. Stroud: Tempus, 2002.

Duranti, Tommaso. 'Reading the Corpse in the Late Middle Ages (Bologna, Mid-13th Century– Early 16th Century)'. In *The Body of Evidence: Corpses and Proofs in Early Modern European Medicine*, edited by Francesco Paulo de Ceglia, 71–104. Boston: Brill, 2020.

Dyer, Christopher. *Making a Living in the Middle Ages: the People of Britain 850–1520*. New Haven: Yale University Press, 2009.

Edge, David and John M. Paddock. *Arms and Armor of the Medieval Knight*, New York: Crescent Books, 1988.

Ekman, Paul and W. V. Friesen. 'Constants Across Cultures in the Face and Emotion'. *Journal of Personality and Social Psychology*, 17 (1971): 124–9.

Elias, Norbert. *Über den Prozess der Zivilisation: Soziogenetische und psychogenetische Untersuchungen. Vol.II: Wandlungen der Gesellschaft. Entwurf zu einer Theorie der Zivilisation*. Frankfurt/M.: Suhrkamp, 1997.

Enkhbold, Enerelt. 'The Role of the *Ortoq* in the Mongol Empire in Forming Business Partnerships'. *Central Asian Survey*, 38 (2019): 531–47.

Faith, Rosamund. 'The "Great Rumour" of 1377 and Peasant Ideology'. In *The English Rising of 1381*, edited by Rodney Hilton and T. H. Alton, 43–73. Cambridge: Cambridge University Press, 1987.

Ferreday, Debra. '*Game of Thrones*, Rape Culture and Feminist Fandom'. *Australian Feminist Studies*, 30 (2015): 21–36.

Finn, Kavita Mudan. 'High and Mighty Queens of Westeros'. In *Game of Thrones versus History*, edited by Brian A. Pavlac and Elizabeth Lott, 17–31.

Finn, Kavita Mudan. 'Queen of Sad Mischance: Medievalism, "Realism" and the Case of Cersei Lannister'. In *Queenship and the Women of Westeros*, edited by Zita Rohr and Lisa Benz, 29–52.

Förnegård, Per, Erika Kihlman and Mia Åkestam ed. *Tears, Sighs and Laughter: Expression of Emotions in the Middle Ages*. Gunnell Engwall Vitterhets Historie och Antikvitets Akademien Konferenser 92. Stockholm: KVHAA, 2017.

Frankel, Valerie Estelle. *Women in Game of Thrones: Power, Conformity and Resistance*. Jefferson: McFarland, 2014.
Freud, Sigmund. 'New Introductory Lectures on Psycho-Analysis'. In *The Standard Edition of the Complete Psychological Works of Sigmund Freud*, 24 vols., edited and translated by James Strachey. London: Hogarth Press, 1953–1974; Vol. 22 (1933): 1–182.
Frevert, Ute. *Emotions in History – Lost and Found*. Budapest and New York: Central European University Press, 2011.
Frevert, Ute. 'Defining Emotions: Concepts and Debates over Three Centuries'. In *Emotional Lexicons: Continuity and Change in the Vocabulary of Feeling 1700–2000*, edited by Ute Frevert et al., 1–31. Oxford: Oxford University Press, 2014.
Garcia, Elio M., George R. R. Martin and Linda Antonsson. *The World of Ice and Fire*. New York: Bantam Books, 2014.
Gilman Sander L., Helen King, Roy Porter, G. S. Rousseau and Elaine Showalter. *Hysteria Beyond Freud*. Berkeley: University of California Press, 1993.
Gjelsvik, Anne and Rikke Schubart. *Women of Ice and Fire: Gender, Game of Thrones, and Multiple Media Engagements*. New York and London: Bloomsbury, 2016.
Goris, Harm. 'Thomas Aquinas on dreams'. In *Dreams as Divine Communication in Christianity. From Hermas to Aquinas*, edited by Bart Koet, 1–19. Leuven: Peeters, 2012.
Gravett, Christopher. *Knights at Tournaments*. Oxford: Osprey, 2002.
Hackney, Charles. '"Silk Ribbons Tied Around a Sword": Knighthood and the Chivalric Virtues in Westeros'. In *Mastering the Game of Thrones*, edited by Jes Battis and Susan Johnston, 132–49.
Harbus, Antonina. 'Affective Poetics: The Cognitive Basis of Emotion in Old English Poetry'. In *Anglo-Saxon Emotions*, edited by Alice Jorgensen, Frances McCormack and Jonathan Wilcox, 19–34. Farnham: Ashgate, 2015.
Haskins, Charles Homer. *The Rise of Universities*. London: Cornell University Press, 1957.
Hintersdorf, Sophie. 'A Feast for Beasts – The Role of Animals in George R. R. Martin's *A Song of Ice and Fire*'. Staatsexamensarbeit (State Examination Thesis), Department of English, Friedrich-Schiller-University, Jena (Germany), 2017.
Homan, Mike. *A Complete History of Fighting Dogs*. Lydney, Glos: Ringpress Books, 1999.
Honegger, Thomas. '(Heroic) Fantasy and the Middle Ages – Strange Bedfellows or an Ideal Cast?' *Itinéraires [Online]*, 2010-13. 61–71. http://journals.openedition.org/itineraires/1817 DOI: 10.4000/itineraires.1817 (accessed 24 March 2020).
Huizinga, Johann. *The Waning of the Middle Ages*, translated by Francis Hopan. Garden City: Doubleday Anchor Books, 1954.
Hunt, Edwin. *The Medieval Super-Companies: A Study of the Peruzzi Company of Florence*. Cambridge: Cambridge University Press, 1994.
Hunter, Mikayla. '"All Men Must Die, but We Are Not Men": Eastern Faith and Feminine Power in A Song of Ice and Fire and HBO's Game of Thrones'. In *Queenship and the Women of Westeros*, edited by Zita Rohr and Lisa Benz, 145–68.
Jacoby, Henry. 'Wargs, Wights, and Wolves that are Dire: Mind and Metaphysics, Westeros Style'. In *Game of Thrones and Philosophy. Logic Cuts Deeper than Swords*, edited by Henry Jacoby, 115–28. Hoboken: John Wiley, 2012.
Jaeger, C. Stephen. *The Origins of Courtliness – Civilizing Trends and the Formation of Courtly Ideals 939–1210*. Philadelphia: University of Pennsylvania Press, 1985.

James, Edward and Farah Mendlesohn. 'Introduction'. In *The Cambridge Companion to Fantasy Literature*, edited by Edward James and Farah Mendlesohn, 1–4. Cambridge: Cambridge University Press, 2012.

Jamison, Carol Parrish. *Chivalry in Westeros: The Knightly Code of A Song of Ice and Fire*. Jefferson: McFarland, 2018.

Jones, Andrew Zimmerman. 'Of Direwolves and Gods'. In *Behind the Wall. Exploring George R. R. Martin's A Song of Ice and Fire*, edited by James Lowder, 107–22. Dallas: BenBella Books, 2012.

Jones, Robert. *Knight: The Warrior and World of Chivalry*. Oxford: Osprey Publishing, 2011.

Jorgensen, Alice. 'Introduction'. In *Anglo-Saxon Emotions*, edited by Alice Jorgensen, Frances McCormack and Jonathan Wilcox, 1–17. Farnham: Ashgate, 2015.

Kaeuper, Richard W. 'Chivalry: Fantasy and Fear'. In *Writing and Fantasy*, edited by Ceri Sullivan and Barbara White, 62–73. Harlow: Longman, 1999.

Kaeuper, Richard W. *Medieval Chivalry*. Cambridge: Cambridge University Press, 2016.

Karras, Ruth Mazo. *Common Women: Prostitution and Sexuality in Medieval England*. New York: Oxford University Press, 1998.

Kaufman, Amy S. 'Muscular Medievalism'. *The Year's Work in Medievalism*, 31 (2016): 56–66.

Keen, Maurice. *Chivalry*. 1984. New Haven: Yale University Press, 2005.

Kelly, Douglas. *The Art of Medieval French Romance*. Madison: University of Wisconsin Press, 1992.

Kelly, A. Keith, ed. *Power and Subversion in Game of Thrones: Critical Essays on the HBO Series*. Jefferson: McFarland, 2022.

Kennedy, Beverly. *Knighthood in The Morte D'arthur*. Arthurian Studies XI. Cambridge: D.S. Brewer, 1985.

Kenney, Jeffrey T. and Ebrahim Moosa. *Islam in the Modern World*. New York: Routledge, 2015.

Kersey, Shirley. 'Medieval Education of Girls and Women'. *Educational Horizons*, 58, no. 4 (1980): 188–92.

Kessels, A. H. M. 'Ancient Systems of Dream-Classification'. *Mnemosyne ser. 4*, 22, no. 4 (1969): 389–424.

Koch, Lars. '"Power Resides Where Men Believe it Resides". Die brüchige Welt von Game of Thrones'. In *Vom Game of Thrones bis House of Cards. Politische Perspektiven in Fernsehserien*, edited by Anja Besand, 129–52. Wiesbaden: Springer VS, 2018.

Kristano, Heribertus Dwi. *The Praiseworthy Passion of Shame: A Historical and Philosophical Elucidation of Aquinas's Thought on the Nature and Role of Shame in the Moral Life*. Rome: Gregorian and Biblical Press, 2019.

Kruger, Steven F. *Dreaming in the Middle Ages*. Cambridge: Cambridge University Press, 2005.

Lambert, Charles. 'A Tender Spot in My Heart: Disability in *A Song of Ice and Fire*'. *Critical Quarterly*, 51, no. 1 (2015): 20–31.

Lane, Frederic and Reinhold C. Mueller. *Money and Banking in Medieval and Renaissance Venice, Volume I: Coins and Moneys of Account*. Baltimore: Johns Hopkins University Press, 1985.

Larrington, Carolyne. 'The Psychology of Emotion and the Study of Medieval Period'. *Early Medieval Europe*, 10, no. 2 (2001): 251–6.

Larrington, Carolyne. *Brothers and Sisters in Medieval European Literature*. Woodbridge: York Medieval Press, 2015.

Larrington, Carolyne. *Winter is Coming: The Medieval World of Game of Thrones*. London: I. B. Tauris, 2015.
Larrington, Carolyne. 'Game of Loans'. 2016. https://www.1843magazine.com/culture/the-daily/game-of-loans.
Larrington, Carolyne. 'Mediating Medieval(ized) Emotion in *Game of Thrones*'. In *Studies in Medievalism XXVII, Authenticity, Medievalism, Music*, edited by Karl Fugelso, 251–56. Cambridge: D. S. Brewer, 2018.
Larrington, Carolyne. '(No More) "Reaving, Roving, Raiding, or Raping": The Ironborn in George R. R. Martin's A Song of Ice and Fire and HBO's Game of Thrones'. In *The Vikings Reimagined*, edited by Tom Birkett and Roderick Dale, 162–79. Boston: Medieval Institute Publications, 2019.
Larrington, Carolyne. 'Foreword'. In *Queenship and the Women of Westeros*, edited by Zita Rohr and Lisa Benz, vii–xviii.
Larrington, Carolyne. *All Men Must Die: Power and Passion in Game of Thrones*. London: Bloomsbury, 2021.
Larsson, Mariah. 'Adapting Sex: Cultural Conceptions of Sexuality in Words and Images'. In *Women of Ice and Fire*, edited by Anne Gjelsvik and Rikke Schubart, 17–37.
Lewis, Clive Staples. *The Discarded Image. An Introduction to Medieval and Renaissance Literature*. Cambridge: Cambridge University Press, 1964.
Lips, Hilary M. *Sex and Gender: An Introduction*. 6th edn. Long Grove: Waveland Press, 2017.
Lushkov, Ayelet Haimson. *You Win or You Die*. London: I. B. Tauris, 2017.
Lynch, Andrew and Susan Broomhall, ed. *The Routledge History of Emotions in Europe 1100 – 1700*. London and New York: Routledge, 2019.
Lynch, Kathryn L. *The High Medieval Dream Vision. Poetry, Philosophy, and Literary Form*. Stanford: Stanford University Press, 1988
MacInnes, Iain A. "'All I Ever Wanted Was to Fight for a Lord I Believed in. But the Good Lords Are Dead and the Rest Are Monsters": Brienne of Tarth, Jaime Lannister, and the Chivalric "Other"'. In *Queenship and the Women of Westeros*, edited by Zita Rohr and Lisa Benz, 77–102.
McKisack, May. *The Fourteenth Century 1307–1399*. Oxford: Oxford University Press, 1959.
McNamara, Rebecca F. 'The Emotional Body in Religious Belief and Practice'. In *Routledge History of Emotions in Europe*, edited by Andrew Lynch and Susan Broomhall, 105–18.
McNamer, Sarah. *Religious Meditation and the Invention of Medieval Compassion*. Philadelphia: University of Pennsylvania Press, 2010.
MacNeil, William P. 'Machiavellian Fantasy and the Game of Laws'. *Critical Quarterly*, 51, no. 1 (2015): 34–48.
Maddern, Philippa, Joanne McEwan and Anne M. Scott, ed. *Performing Emotions in Early Europe*. Turnhout: Brepols, 2018.
Majkowski, Tomasz Z. *W cieniu białego drzewa. Powieść fantasy w XX wieku [In the Shadow of a White Tree: Fantasy Novel in the Twentieth Century]*. Kraków: Wydawnictwo Naukowe Uniwersytetu Jagiellońskiego, 2013.
Marshall, David W. 'Neomedievalism, Identification, and the Haze of Medievalisms'. *Studies in Medievalism: Defining Neomedievalism(s) II*, 20 (2011): 21–34.
Martin, George R. R. et al. *The World of Ice and Fire: The Untold History of Westeros and the Game of Thrones*. New York: Bantam, 2014.
Massie Pascal J. and Lauryn S. Mayer. 'Bringing Elsewhere Home: *A Song of Ice and Fire*'s Ethics of Disability'. In *Studies in Medievalism XXIII, Ethics and Medievalism*, edited by Karl Fugelso, 45–60. Cambridge: D.S. Brewer, 2014.

Mathews, Richard. *Fantasy: The Liberation of Imagination*. New York: Routledge, 2002.
Matthews, David. *Medievalism: A Critical History*. Cambridge: D.S. Brewer, 2015.
Matula, Jozef. 'Thomas Aquinas and the Influence of Imaginatio/ Phantasia on Human Being'. *Acta Universitatis Palackianae Olomoucensis Facultas Philosophica Philosophica*, 5 (2002): 169–83.
Megna, Paul. 'Dreadful Emotion'. In *Routledge History of Emotions in Europe*, edited by Andrew Lynch and Susan Broomhall, 72–85.
Merritt, Keri Leigh. *Masterless Men: Poor Whites and Slavery in the Antebellum South*. Cambridge: Cambridge University Press, 2017.
Mitchell, Lynsey. 'Re-affirming and Rejecting the Rescue Narrative as an Impetus for War: To War for a Woman in *A Song of Ice and Fire*'. *Law and Humanities*, 12, no. 2 (2018): 229–50.
Mondschein, Ken. *Game of Thrones and the Medieval Art of War*. Jefferson: MacFarland, 2017.
Moyce, Audrey. 'Brienne and Jaime's Queer Intimacy'. In *Vying for the Iron Thrones: Essays on Power, Gender, Death and Performance in HBO's Game of Thrones*, edited by Lindsey Mantoan and Sara Brady. Jefferson: McFarland, 2018, 59–68.
Müller, Anja. 'Die neomediävalen Ritter von Westeros und der Prozess der Zivilisation'. In *Die Literatur des Mittelalters im Fantasyroman*, edited by Nathanael Busch and Hans Rudolf Velten, 29–44. Heidelberg: Winter, 2018.
Muhlberger, Steven. 'Chivalry in Westeros'. In *Game of Thrones versus History*, edited by Brian A. Pavlac and Elizabeth Lott, 47–56. Hoboken: Wiley and Sons, 2017.
Munro, John H. 'The Medieval Origins of the Financial Revolution: Usury, Rentes, and Negotiability'. *International History Review*, 25 (2003): 505–62.
Murrin, Michael. *History and Warfare in Renaissance Epic*. Chicago and London: The University of Chicago Press, 1997.
Neubauer, Łukasz. '"Dark Wings" and "Grey Furs": The Old Germanic Roots of Carrion-Eating Beasts in *A Song of Ice and Fire*'. In *George R. R. Martin's A Song of Ice and Fire*, edited by Bartłomiej Błaszkiewicz, 181–209.
Orme, Nicholas. *Education and Society in Medieval and Renaissance England*. London: Hambledon Press, 1989.
Paster, Gail Kern. *Humouring the Body: Emotions and the Shakespearean Stage*. Chicago and London: The University of Chicago Press, 2004.
Patel, C. 'Expelling a Monstrous Matriarchy: Casting Cersei Lannister as Abject in *A Song of Ice and Fire*'. *Journal of European Popular Culture*, 5, no. 2 (2014): 135–47.
Pavlac, Brian A. 'Introduction: The Winter of Our Discontent Brian'. In *Game of Thrones Versus History*, edited by Brian A. Pavlac and Elizabeth Lott, 1–15.
Pavlac, Brian A. and Elizabeth Lott, ed. *Game of Thrones versus History: Written in Blood*. Hoboken: Wiley Blackwell, 2017.
Phillips, Charles. *The Complete Illustrated History of Knights and the Golden Age of Chivalry*. London: Hermes House, 2010.
Polack, Gillian. 'Setting up Westeros: The Medievalesque World of Game of Thrones'. In *Game of Thrones versus History*, edited by Brian A. Pavlac and Elizabeth Lott, 251–60.
Prendergast, Thomas A. and Stephanie Trigg. *Affective Medievalism: Love, Abjection, and Discontent*. Manchester: Manchester University Press, 2018.
Pugh, Tison and Angela Jane Weisl, ed. *Medievalisms: Making the Past in the Present*. London and New York: Routledge, 2013.
Rajani, M. B. 'The Expanse of Archaeological Remains at Nalanda: A Study Using Remote Sensing and GIS'. *Archives of Asian Art*, 66, no. 1 (2016): 1–23.

Rashdall, Hastings. *The Universities of Europe in the Middle Ages*, 2 vols. Oxford: Clarendon Press, 1945.

Reichert, Hermann. 'Heime in Wilten und in der Thidrekssaga'. In *Studien zum Altgermanischen. Festschrift für Heinrich Beck*, edited by Heiko Uecker, 503–12. Berlin and New York: Walter de Gruyter, 1994.

Reynolds, Susan. *Fiefs and Vassals: The Medieval Evidence Reinterpreted*. Oxford: Oxford University Press, 1994.

Robeson, Lisa. 'Noble Knights and "Mischievous War": The Rhetoric of War in Malory's *Le Morte D'arthur*'. *Arthuriana*, 13, no. 3 (2003): 10–35.

Robinson, Carol L. and Pamela Clements. 'Living with Neomedievalism'. *Studies in Medievalism*, 18 (2009): 55–75.

Robinson, Michael D., Jessica L. Bair, Tianwei Liu, Matthew J. Scott, Ian B. Penzel. 'Of Tooth and Claw: Predator Self-Identifications Mediate Gender Differences in Interpersonal Arrogance'. *Sex Roles*, 77 (2017): 272–86.

Robson, Michael J. 'The Writings of Francis'. In *The Cambridge Companion to Francis of Assisi*, edited by Michael J. P. Robson, 34–49. Cambridge: Cambridge University Press, 2012.

Rohr, Zita and Lisa Benz, ed. *Queenship and the Women of Westeros: Female Agency and Advice in Game of Thrones and A Song of Ice and Fire*. London and New York: Palgrave Macmillan, 2019.

Rosenwein, Barbara H., ed. *Anger's Past: The Social Uses of an Emotion in the Middle Ages*. Ithaca and London: Cornell University Press, 1998.

Rosenwein, Barbara H. 'Introduction'. In *Anger's Past*, edited by Barbara H. Rosenwein, 1–8. Ithaca.

Rosenwein, Barbara H. 'Controlling Paradigms'. In *Anger's Past*, edited by Barbara H. Rosenwein, 233–47.

Rosenwein, Barbara H. 'Periodization? An Answer from the History of Emotions'. In *Routledge History of Emotions*, edited by Andrew Lynch and Susan Broomhall, 15–29.

Ruti, Mari. *Penis Envy and Other Bad Feelings: The Emotional Costs of Everyday Life*. New York: Columbia University Press, 2018.

Ruys, Juanita Feros. 'Heloise'. In *The Oxford Encyclopedia of Women in World History, Volume I*, edited by Bonnie G. Smith, 445.

Salih, Sarah. 'Cinematic Authenticity Effects and Medieval Art: A Paradox'. In *Medieval Film*, edited by Anke Bernau and Bettina Bildhauer, 20–39. Manchester: Manchester University Press, 2009.

Saunders, Corinne. *Magic and the Supernatural in Medieval English Romance*. Cambridge: D. S. Brewer, 2010.

Scaglione, Aldo. *Knights at Court: Courtliness, Chivalry, & Courtesy from Ottonian Germany to The Italian Renaissance*. Berkeley: University of California Press, 1991.

Scheibelreiter, Georg. *Heraldik*. Vienna: Oldenbourg, 2006.

Scheibelreiter, Georg. 'Tiersymbolik und Wappen im Mittelalter'. In *Tier und Religion*, edited by Thomas Honegger and W. Günther Rohr. Leipzig: Akademie Verlag, 2007, 9–23.

Scheer, Monique. 'Are Emotions a Kind of Practice (And Is That What Makes Them Have a History)? A Bourdieuian Approach to Understanding Emotion'. *History and Theory*, 52 (2012): 193–220.

Scheer, Monique. 'Topographies of Emotion'. In *Emotional Lexicons: Continuity and Change in the Vocabulary of Feeling 1700–2000*, edited by Ute Frevert et al., 32–61.

Schmitt, Jean-Claude. *The Holy Greyhound: Guinefort, Healer of Children since the Thirteenth Century*. Cambridge: Cambridge University Press, 1983.

Schopf, Alfred. 'Die Gestalt Gawains bei Chrétien, Wolfram von Eschenbach und in Sir Gawain and the Green Knight'. In *Spätmittelalterliche Artusliteratur*, edited by Karl-Heinz Göller, 85–104. Paderborn: Schöningh, 1984.

Schubart, Rikke. 'Woman with Dragons: Daenerys, Pride, and Postfeminist Possibilities'. In *Women of Ice and Fire*, edited by Anne Gjelsvik and Rikke Schubart, 105–29.

Schubart, Rikke and Anne Gjelsvik. 'Introduction'. In *Women of Ice and Fire*, edited by Anne Gjelsvik and Rikke Schubart, 1–16.

Serpell, James, ed. *The Domestic Dog: Its Evolution, Behaviour and Interactions with People*. Second edition. Cambridge: Cambridge University Press, 2017.

Sindbæk, Søren M. 'Networks and Nodal Points: The Emergence of Towns in Early Viking Age Scandinavia'. *Antiquity*, 81 (2007): 119–32.

Smith, Bonnie G., ed. *The Oxford Encyclopedia of Women in World History, Volume I*. Oxford: Oxford University Press, 2008.

Spector, Caroline. 'Power and Feminism in Westeros'. In *Beyond the Wall: Exploring George R. R. Martin's A Song of Ice and Fire*, edited by James Lowder. Dallas: Smart Pop, 2012.

Stearns, Peter N. and Carol Z. Stearns. 'Emotionology: Clarifying the History of Emotions and Emotional Standards'. *American Historical Review*, 90, no. 4 (1985): 813–36.

Stuhmiller, Jacqueline. '"Iudicium Dei, iudicium fortunae": Trial by Combat in Malory's "Le Morte Darthur" '. *Speculum*, 81, no. 2 (2006): 427–62.

Swank, Kris. 'The Peaceweavers of Winterfell'. In *Queenship and the Women of Westeros*, edited by Zita Rohr and Lisa Benz, 105–28.

Tasker, Yvonne and Lindsay Steenberg. 'Women Warriors from Chivalry to Vengeance'. In *Women of Ice and Fire*, edited by Anne Gjelsvik and Rikke Schubart, 171–92.

Taylor, Jane H. M. 'The Parrot, the Knight and the Decline of Chivalry'. In *Conjunctures: Medieval Studies in Honor of Douglas Kelly*, edited by Keith Busby and Norris Lacy, 529–44. Amsterdam and Atlanta: Rodopi, 1994.

Thayer, James B. 'The Older Modes of Trial'. *Harvard Law Review*, 5, no. 2 (1891): 45–70.

Tolkien, John Ronald Ruel. 'On Fairy Stories'. In *The Monsters and the Critics and Other Essays*, edited by Christopher Tolkien, 109–61. London: Harper Collins, 2006.

Tufekci, Zeynep. https://blogs.scientificamerican.com/observations/the-real-reason-fans-hate-the-last-season-of-game-of-thrones/. 2019.

Walker-Meikle, Kathleen. *Medieval Dogs*. London: The British Library, 2013.

Wells-Lassagne, Shannon. 'Adapting Desire: Wives, Prostitutes, and Smallfolk'. In *Women of Ice and Fire*, edited by Anne Gjelsvik and Rikke Schubart, 39–56.

White, Stephen D. 'The Politics of Anger'. In *Anger's Past*, edited by Barbara H. Rosenwein, 127–52.

Witalisz, Władysław. *The Trojan Mirror: Middle English Narratives of Troy as Books of Princely Advice*. Frankfurt am Main: Peter Lang, 2011.

Wolf, Mark J. P. *Building Imaginary Worlds: The Theory and History of Subcreation*. New York: Routledge, 2012.

Woloch, Alex. *The One vs. the Many: Minor Characters and the Space of the Protagonist in the Novel*. Princeton and Oxford: Princeton University, 2003.

Workman, Leslie J. 'Editorial'. *Studies in Medievalism*, 7 (1995): 2.

Young, Helen. *Race and Popular Fantasy Literature: Habits of Whiteness*. New York and London: Routledge, 2016.

Zepf, Siegfried and Dietmar Seel. 'Penis Envy and the Female Oedipus Complex: A Plea to Reawaken an Ineffectual Debate'. *The Psychoanalytic Review*, 103, no. 3 (2016): 397–421.

Film and TV Shows

Martin, George R. R. 'The Real History Behind Game of Thrones'. *Game of Thrones: The Complete Fifth Season*. 2016, HBO.

Websites

Collins, Sean T. 'Game of Thrones' Recap: For Whom the Bell Tolls'. *Rolling Stone*, 13 May 2019. https://www.rollingstone.com/tv/tv-recaps/game-of-thrones-recap-season-8-episode-5-the-bells-832998/

Drezner, Daniel W. https://www.washingtonpost.com/outlook/2019/05/20/minutes-iron-banks-board-directors-meeting-one-act-play/?noredirect=on&utm_term=.0242aa94400a. 2019.

Gendler, Alex. https://www.ted.com/talks/alex_gendler_the_wars_that_inspired_game_of_thrones?language=en. 2015.

Gilmore, Mikal. https://www.rollingstone.com/culture/culture-news/george-r-r-martin-the-rolling-stone-interview-242487/. 2014.

Hibberd, James. https://ew.com/article/2015/06/03/george-rr-martin-thrones-violence-women/. 2015. (accessed 20 January 2021).

Haysom, Sam. '"Game of Thrones" Star Lena Headey hints Cersei is headed to an even darker place'. *Mashable*, 12 December 2016. https://mashable.com/2016/12/12/lena-headey-cersei-season-7/?europe=true (accessed 24 January 2020).

Hodgman, John and George R. R. Martin. 'John Hodgman Interviews George R. R. Martin'. *Public Radio International*, 21 September 2011. https://www.pri.org/stories/2011-09-21/john-hodgman-interviews-george-rr-martin (accessed 20 November 2019).

Holland, Tom. https://www.theguardian.com/tv-and-radio/2013/mar/24/game-of-thrones-realistic-history. 2012. (accessed 29 November 2019).

Larrington, Carolyne. https://www.1843magazine.com/culture/the-daily/game-of-loans. 2016.

Martin, George R. R. www.theguardian.com/books/2013/apr/05/maurice-druon-george-rr-martin. 2013.

Martin, George R. R. www.georgerrmartin.com/maurice-druons-the-iron-king/. 2013.

https://www.statista.com/statistics/737521/game-of-thrones-social-media-gender/ (accessed 24 March 2021).

University of Oxford. 'Introduction and History'. 2014. https://www.ox.ac.uk/about/organisation/history (accessed 10 August 2020).

Watercutter, Angela. 'Wired'. 6 March 2013. https://www.wired.com/2013/06/women-game-of-thrones/ (accessed 24 March 2021).

www.asoiaf.westeros.org/index.php?/topic/87914-the-accursed-kings-characters-in-asoiaf-ak-spoilers/

Index

Abélard, Pierre (Peter) 39
Acciaiuouli, the 54
Adam 164
Alcalá 41
Alebelly 132
Anjou 16
Anjou, Queen Margaret of 15
Antisthenes 74
Appelbaum, Patricia 81
Aquinas, Saint Thomas
   dreams 120–3, 125, 130
   emotions 138, 140–1, 144
Aragorn 4, 12, 50
Archambaud 21
Archmaester Ebrose 49
Archmaester Marwyn 124
Aretaeus of Cappadocia 168
Aristotle 120–3, 164
Arryn, Jon 16, 37, 46, 168
   Lysa 20, 168
Artois, Mahaut of 13, 16, 19, 20
   Robert of 13, 16–17, 20, 21
Ashford, Lord 113
Ashford Meadow 7, 108–9, 111, 113
Astapor 59–60, 63
Athens 74
Augustine, Saint 120, 121, 138, 141, 146
Avignon 14, 16, 20

Baelish, Petyr (Littlefinger) 20, 48
   death 63
   emotions 144–5
   finances 46, 52, 56, 63–4, 168
   and Sansa Stark 42, 144
   and Tyrion Lannister 46
Baelor, Great Sept of 39, 96, 114, 129, 167
Baglioni, Giannino 20
   Guccio 13, 17, 19, 22
Banbridge, Northern Ireland 173

Baratheon, Joffrey 48, 58, 75, 99, 139
   abuse of Sansa 28
   cruelty of 24
   fathering of 144
   Louis IX 14
   poisoning of 16, 38
   rule of 98
   Sandor Clegane 67–9, 71
   Myrcella 21
   Renly 16, 47, 102, 128, 174
   Robert 30, 47, 67, 72, 98, 145
      Cersei 165, 168–9, 171
      children of 28, 144
      Lyanna Stark 102
      and money 54, 56
      murder of 46, 166
      and Robert d'Artois 20, 22
      rebellion of (*see* Robert's Rebellion)
      treason 143
   Selyse 17
   Shireen 42, 44, 45, 47
   Stannis 17–18, 28, 58
      dreams 128
      and Maester Cressen 47
      and Ser Davos 104
      siege of King's Landing 26
   Tommen 21, 58, 99, 105, 164
      and Cersei 8, 165
      conversion 41
      rule 18, 98
      suicide 167
Bardi, the 54–5
Basilisk Isles, the 59
Batten, Caroline R. 7
Battis, Jes and Susan Johnston 5
Battle of the Bastards 25, 31–2, 42, 71
Battle of Blackwater Bay 21, 48
Battle of Winterfell 31
Benioff, David and Daniel Weiss [D. B. Weiss] 45, 96, 107
   and plot development 1, 64

sensibilities   38
vision   173
Berkeley Castle   20
Bingen, Hildegard von   42
Blacktyde, House   38
Błaszkiewicz, Bartłomiej   5, 7
   Maria   6
Bloch, Howard R.   163–4
Boccaccio, Giovanni   17
Bock, Jarrod and Melissa Burkley   159
Boiardo   82
Bologna   39, 41, 43
Bolton, Ramsay (Snow)   42, 64, 71
   Roose   32, 71
Bonaventure, Saint   81
Boniscambi, Ugolino   81
Bourdieu, Pierre   143
Bouville, Chamberlain   19, 22
Bouwsma, William J.   141
Braavos   52
   Iron Bank of   7, 18, 53–9
Brabant, Duke of   21
Broken Men, the   88, 90
Brother Ray   31, 89–91
Brotherhood without Banners, the   24, 31, 40, 125
Bruges   54
Burgundy, Marguerite of, Queen of France   13, 16, 20

Calcidius   120, 129, 133
Cambridge   38
Campbell, Anne   167
Capets, the   11
Carroll, Shiloh R.   2, 5, 82, 150, 165
Cassell, Ser Rodrick   99
Casterly Rock   27, 97, 169
Castle Black   38, 43, 47, 48, 125
Caxton, William   76
Celano, Thomas of   80–1, 86, 87
Champion, Michael and Andrew Lynch   139
Charlemagne, Emperor   82
Charles the Bald, King   109
Chaucer, Geoffrey   85, 113, 134, 164, 169
Chesterton, Gilbert Keith   81
Children of the Forest, the   123, 135
Christopher, Saint   76, 78–9

Cicero   119
Citadel, the   7, 37, 49, 83
Clegane, Ser Gregor [the Mountain]   16, 74, 101, 109, 167
   and Cersei   45
   death of Prince Oberyn   7
   resurrection of   37, 43
   sigil of   71
   weapon of   115
   Sandor [the Hound]   6, 26, 31, 90–1
   and Brienne   89
   as cynic   67–79
Clement, Pope   13
Cowlishaw, Brian   45
Crécy, Battle of   21
Cressay, brothers   13
   Marie de   19
Criseyde   134
Cromwell, Thomas   149
Crone, the   87, 161
Czarnowus, Anna   7, 162

Damasio, Antonio   143
Dance of Dragons, the   18, 98
d'Argenteuil, Héloïse   39, 42
d'Aunay, Philippe   20
Dayne, Ser Arthur   27, 128, 135
de Charny, Geoffroi   95, 96, 101
Descartes, Réné   140
Dido   146
Dimittis, Noho   57
Diogenes   74
Diomede   134
Dixon, Laurinda S.   168
Dog   86–8
Dondarrion, Beric   31, 45
Dörrich, Corinna   98
Dorne   21, 52, 128
Dothraki   7, 53, 59, 62–3, 153–5
Douglas, Kirk   2
Dragonstone   58, 98, 129
Draper, Henry   80, 81
Drogo, Khal   8, 45, 63, 127, 149–61
Drogon   34
Drowned God, the   17, 83
Druon, Maurice   6, 11–23
Duncan, Ser the Tall (Dunk)   74, 99–101, 109–12, 114
Dustin, Lady   38, 47

Edward II, King   13, 15–17, 20
Edward III, King   11, 15–16, 18, 21, 55, 112
Edward IV, King   11
Eisenstein, Phyllis   22
Elias, Norbert   95–107
Essos   24, 33, 34, 39, 163, 173
   economy   50–4, 59–61, 64
Eve   164
Eyrie, the   20, 125, 128

Faith Militant   41, 57, 167
Faith of the Seven   14, 39, 41, 83, 86, 124
   divine aspects of   131
   and economy   55, 57
Fennesz   60
Ferreday, Debra   156
Finn, Kavita Mudan   150, 156, 171
Fioretti, the   7, 81–2, 87–8, 91
Flanders   18, 110
Flea Bottom   52, 101
Flemings, the   18
Florence   54
Forel, Syrio   42
France   11–23, 55
Francis of Assisi, Saint   7, 80–91
Frankel, Valerie Estelle   151, 154, 156–7, 160
Frankenstein, Dr   44
Frankenstein's monster   71
Free Cities, the   18, 52–3
Freud, Sigmund   170
Frevert, Ute   138, 140, 143
Frey, Lord Emmon   129
   Walder   42, 141
Froissart, Jean   112

Galen   44, 168
Gared   95
Gendler, Alex   11
Gendry   14, 32, 33, 40
Germany   3
Gilly   42, 47, 125
Gjelsvik, Anne and Rikke Schubart   5, 142, 144
Gowther, Sir   75–6
Gozzadini, Bettisia   41
Górniak, Przemysław Grabowski   7, 108–16

Grand Maester Pycelle   37, 44, 46, 57
Great Britain   3
Great Grass Sea   62–3
Gregorius, Legend of   75
Gregory IX, Pope   80
Greyjoy, Asha/Yara   47, 161, 173, 174
   Balon   61, 64, 132, 173
   Euron   63
   Theon [Reek]   47, 61, 128, 132
Greywater   132
Grey Worm   33, 34, 173
Gubbio   81, 87–8

Hackney, Charles   98
Hainault, Duke of   18
   Philippa of   18
Hand of the King   27, 28, 46
Hand of the Queen   43
Hare, Humphrey   12–13
Harrenhal   7, 108, 113, 128, 129, 174
Hart-Davis, Rupert   12
Harvey, William   44
Headey, Lena   167
Hedge knights   100–1, 108–9, 111–12, 114
Henry V, King   11
Henry VI, King   11, 15
Heywood, John   164
High Sparrow   14, 57, 164, 167
Highgarden   18, 58, 63
Hightower, Ser Gerold   128
Hildebrand, Kristina   139, 149–60
Hirson, Beatrice   13, 16–17
Hizdahr zo Loraq   59
Hoat, Vargo   27, 143
Hob   76
Hobbes, Thomas   140
Hodgman, John   162
Hodor   135
Holland, Tom   149
Hollard, Ser Dontos   83
Holy Roman Emperor, the   76
Hot Pie   40
Huan, hound   71
Huizinga, Johann   139, 145
Hungary, Clémence of   19
Hunt, Edwin   55
Hunt, Ser Hyle   84, 100, 104
Hunter, Mikayla   7, 83

Iceland   61–2
Innocent VI   20
Iron Islands, the   38, 61–3
Iron Throne, the   32, 37, 46, 63, 129, 160
  competition for   19, 21, 24, 37, 98
  at end of show   34, 160, 167
  and Robert Baratheon   72
  symbol   98
Ironborn, the   2
  economy of   7, 61–3
  religion of   17
Isabella of France, Queen   13, 15–16, 18, 20
Italy   18, 19, 55

James, Edward and Farah Mendlesohn   137
Jamison, Carol Parrish   5
Jordayne   38

Kaeuper, Richard W.   96, 97
Karras, Ruth Mazo   164
Karstark, House   38
Kaufman, Amy S.   8, 161
Keen, Maurice   96, 101
Kelly, A. Keith   5
Kenilworth Castle   20
Kennedy, Beverly   101
Kettleblack brothers   99
  Osney   166
King's Landing   34, 52, 98, 105, 128, 139
  during Battle of the Blackwater   71
  court at   19, 39, 104
  economy of   7, 56–8, 62–4
  Jaime's return to   96
  Massacre of   1
  middle class in   40
  Ned Stark in   56
  purge of   31, 34
  Riot of   127
  Sansa Stark in   26, 144
  Sept at   39
  siege of   26, 28, 126
Kingsguard   26, 27, 75, 79, 99–102, 104–7, 128–9, 139
  chivalric order of   98
  sole survivor of   99
Kraznys mo Nakloz   59–60
Kristano, Heribertus Dwi   140

Lady Stoneheart   25, 31, 45, 104
Lambert, Charles   25, 27
Lannisport, Golden Bank of   57
Lannister, Cersei   8
  dreams of   126, 128
  emotion   145–6
  and Iron Bank   53–8, 62
  and Isabella of France   14–15, 18–22
  and Jaime   105–7, 129–30, 140–4
  misogyny   162–72
  queenship of   8, 99, 102
  and Qyburn   43–6, 71
Jaime
  chivalry   71, 75, 96, 102–7
  disability   24–8
  dreams   125–6, 128–31, 135
  emotions   140–5
  education   41, 48
  incest   165–9
Joanna   130–1
Kevan   18
Lancel   166
Tyrion   1, 20, 21, 105
  disability   24, 26–8, 173
  dreams   126–7
  education   40, 46, 48–9
  and the Hound   67–8, 71, 73
  as politician   19, 33–4, 56
  and Sansa   16, 125
  trial by combat   114
Tytos   72
Tywin   18, 41, 46, 48, 120–31
  and Cersei   53, 56, 169, 173
  death of   73, 128
  and the Hound   71
Lannisters, the   11, 21, 24, 28, 56–8, 143
Larrington, Carolyne   6, 41, 46, 61, 83, 150, 163, 165
  and emotions   138, 141
Larsson, Mariah   141, 150–1, 155–60
Last Hearth, mêlée at   110
Le Guin, Ursula   4
Leibniz, Gottfried Wilhelm   140
Leonardo da Vinci   44
Lewis, C. S.   162
Lips, Hilary M.   170
Llull, Ramon   96, 100
Lombards   17–18

Lommy 40
Lord of Light, *see* R'hllor
Louis IX 'le Hutin', King of France 14, 16, 19–20
Louis the German, King 109
Lucian 74
Lys 16, 56

Macmillan, John 174
Macrobius 119, 124, 129
McShane, Ian 89
Maegor's Holdfast 72
Maester Aemon 38, 46, 47
Maester Cressen 37, 39, 47
Maester Luwin 41–2, 46, 122–4
Maester Pycelle, *see* Grand Maester Pycelle
Maesters, Order of 7, 37–49, 98
Maggy the Frog 39
Magnificent Seven, The 32
Maiden, the 87, 124, 161
Maidenpool 83–4
Majkowski, Tomasz Z. 139
Malory, Sir Thomas 26, 31, 97, 99
Manichaeism 17, 20
Mantel, Hilary 149
Marco Polo 77–8
Marillion 126
Martell, Arianne 21
    Elia 42
    Lewyn 128
    Oberyn 7, 14, 38, 43, 108, 115
Marvel Comic Universe 4, 174
Massie, Pascal J. and Lauryn S. Mayer 144
Master of Coin 52, 56–7
Matthews, David 2–3
Meereen 7, 50, 125
    economy 59–63
Melisandre 16–17, 40, 45
Michelangelo 44
Milton, John 127, 134
Mirri Maz Duur 58
Missandei 33, 48, 173
Modena 39
Momoa, Jason 155
Mondschein, Ken 5
Mongol Empire 7, 62
Moon Door, the 20

Mopatis, Illyrio 21, 52
Morgagni, Giovanni 44
Mormont, House 38
Mormont, Ser Jorah 32, 40, 48, 59, 75, 102, 125
    cure for greyscale 43–5
Morris, William 162
Mortimer, Roger 13, 15–16, 18, 20
Mother, the 87, 161
Mountains of the Moon 126
Müller, Anja 7
Murrin, Michael 82
Myr 18, 52, 171
    Thoros of 32

Naharis, Daario 59, 125
Navarre, Queen Jeanne of 20
Nestoris, Tycho 18, 54, 57–8, 63
Neubauer, Łukasz 6
Newman, John Henry 81
Night King, the 25, 33, 45, 167
Night's Watch, the 45, 47, 95, 99, 102, 125
Nogaret, Guillaume de 13, 16
North, the 32, 34, 63, 64, 163, 167
    education 40, 46
    martial customs 109–10
Notre Dame de Paris 39
Nymeria 87, 88

Oathkeeper (sword) 27
Old Nan 124
Oldtown 37–9, 124
Onesti, Azzolino 43
Order of Templars 11, 13, 16–17
    Grand Master of (Jacques de Molay) 13, 17
Osha 131
Others 37, 49, *see also* White Walkers
Oxford 38, 39

Paris 12, 13, 16–19, 29, 39
Paster, Gail Kern 145
Payne, Ser Ilyn 128
    Ser Podrick 79, 87
Peasants' Uprising, the 51
Peck 106
Penny 28
Pentos 18, 21

Philip (Philippe) IV 'le bel', King   13–14, 17–18, 20
Philip (Philippe) V, King   16, 19
Philip (Philippe) VI, King   21
Pia   106
Pliny   78
Poole, Jeyne   25
Pope, the   54, 75–6
  Clement   13
  Gregory IX   80
Prendergast, Thomas A. and Stephanie Trigg   3
Pugh, Tison and Angela Jane Weisl   2
Purple Wedding, the   16

Qarth   52, 59
Quiet Isle, the   83, 85, 88–9, 91
Quixote, Don   103
Qyburn   37, 43–5

Red Comet   39
Red Keep   43, 46, 48, 127, 129, 167
Red Woman, *see* Melisandre
Reed, Jojen   123, 131
Reeds, the   123
Reprobus   76–8
R'hllor   17, 32, 45, 83
Richard I, King   111
Riverlands, the   83–4, 86
Riverrun   89, 125, 129
Rivers, Ser Brynden   131, 134
Robert le diable   75
Robert's Rebellion   30, 46, 75, 129, 135
Robinson, Carol L. and Pamela Clements   2
Rochester Bestiary, the   69, 70
Rohr, Zita and Lisa Benz   5
Rosby, Lord Gyles   57
Rosenwein, Barbara   137
Rouse, Robert and Cory Rushton   6
Royce, Ser Waymar   95, 101
Ruti, Mari   170

Salamanca   41
Salic law   20
Scaglione, Aldo   97
Scandinavia   61–2
Scheer, Monique   141, 143
Schopf, Alfred   97

Schubart, Rikke   5, 142, 144, 151, 156
Scott, Sir Walter   7, 108
Seaworth, Ser Davos   13, 25, 32, 128
  and Iron Bank   18, 58
  social mobility   33, 40, 52, 75, 100–4, 173
secondary world
  absence of religious faith in   80, 83, 85, 91
  dreams in   119, 122, 124, 129, 131, 133–6
  medievalized   1, 50, 108, 109, 119, 171
Selmy, Ser Barristan   48, 56, 60
  epitome of chivalry   26, 75, 99
Sens   39
Septa Mordane   38, 40, 41
Septon Chayle   39
Septon Meribald   80, 83–91
Seven Kingdoms, the   25–6, 34, 167, 173–4
  chivalry in   97–8, 101
  economic system of   51
  educational system of   37–8, 47–8
  spirituality in   83–6, 88
Seven Samurai, The   32
Shepherds' Crusade, the   14
Simpkin, Andrew   12
Six Kingdoms, the   1
Sky-Cells, the   20
Slaver's Bay   28, 33, 173
  economy   52, 59
Small Council, the   22, 34, 41, 43, 46, 49
Smaug   4
Snow, Jon   32, 42, 73, 104, 144
  and dreams   125, 132, 133
  education of   47–8
  as leader   38, 57, 63
  murder of Daenerys   33, 160
  resurrection of   45
  true ancestry   19, 135, 142
Sons of the Harpy   59
Sopranos, The   25
Spector, Caroline   30, 31
Speyer, Julian of   80
Spinoza, Baruch   140
Stark, Arya   21, 33, 89, 139, 161
  dreams   125, 126, 132
  education   40–1, 47

Bran   19, 72, 126, 154
  disability   24, 27–8, 34, 48, 143–4, 173
  king   1, 33, 79
  idealism   7, 26–8
  injury by Jaime   27–8, 105, 122, 140
  visions of   33, 48, 49, 122–4, 131–4
Catelyn   27, 31, 33, 106, 154, 161
  dreams of   125–6
  marriage   142, 144
Eddard (Ned)   19, 67, 72, 105, 142
  dreams   126, 128–9
  death of   14, 24, 58, 139
  father   34, 42
  Hand   53, 56, 58
  husband   142, 144–5
  past of   135
Lyanna   37, 42, 102, 113, 129, 135
Rickon   19, 122–3, 126
Robb   14, 21, 32, 47, 126
  marriage of   42, 58, 141–2
Sansa   99, 144, 165, 170, 173
  Brienne's quest for   83
  dreams   126, 127, 132
  and the Hound   72–4
  and Ramsay Bolton   64, 71
Starks, the   11, 19, 24, 34, 64, 123, 131
Starry Sept of Oldtown   39
Stone Men   44
Storm, Edric   14
Storm-God, the   17
Strickland, Harry   18
Strong, Ser Robert   71

Taena   171
Talhoffer, Hans   114, 115
Talisa   42, 141
Targaryen, Aegon I, King   63, 98–9
  Aegon the Unworthy   172
  Aenys I, King   98
  Aerys II, King (the Mad King)   99, 102, 105–6, 172
    killing of   105, 128–9, 141, 143
  Baelor   114
    Great Sept of   39, 96, 129, 167
  Daenerys   16, 42, 45, 58, 102, 161
    Battle of Gold-road   18
    dragons   8, 42, 167, 172

    dreams   125, 127
    and Jon Snow   19
    in Meereen   50, 53, 59–64
    rulership of   7, 32–4, 45
    sexual violence   8, 151–7, 160
  Jaehaerys I, King   98
  Maegor I, King   41, 98, 172
  Rhaegar   102, 113, 129
    marriage of   37, 42
  Rhaenys   98
  Visenya, Queen   99
  Viserys   63, 127, 152, 154
  Viserys I, King   98
Targaryens, the   28, 30, 72, 110, 165
Tarly, Dickon   47
  Randyll   47
  Samwell   38, 42–3, 79, 124–5, 192
Tarth, Brienne of   27, 33, 47, 49, 126, 161, 173
  chivalry   75, 79, 96, 103–7, 143, 150
  dreams   125
  and Septon Meribald   83–9
  House of   38
Thersites   30
Three-Eyed Raven/Crow   48, 49, 122, 133–4
Tolkien, J. R. R.   3–5, 12, 50, 71, 82–3, 150, 162
Tolomei, Spinello   17–18
Tormund Giantsbane   32, 103
Tourney, at Ashford Meadow   108–13
  of the Hand   7, 101, 108, 113
  at Harrenhal   7, 108, 113
Toussaint, Steve   174
Tower of Joy   129, 135
Trial of Seven, the   7, 108, 114
Troilus   134
Troyes, Chrétien de   98–9
Tufekci, Zeynep   64
Tully, Brynden   28
  Edmure   33
Tullys, the   24
Tyrell, Loras   28, 47, 74–5, 101–2, 174
  Mace   18, 22, 58
  Margaery   42, 57, 128, 161, 166
  Olenna   16, 42

Unsullied, the   34, 59–60

Vaes Dothrak   63
Vale, Ser Hugh of the   74
Vale, the   64
Valyria   27, 37, 40, 123, 174
Varys   19, 21, 43, 44, 128
   and Petyr Baelish   46, 48–9, 63
Velaryon, Corlys   174
   Laenor   174
Venice   54
Vikings   2, 38, 61–2
Vikings, The   2
Voragine, Jacobus de   76

Walk of Shame, the   166
Wall, the   18, 30–2, 45, 48–9, 125, 131, 163, 173
War of the Five Kings   4, 15, 26, 57
Wars of the Roses   4, 11, 15, 22, 26
Weir, Peter   89
Wells-Lassagne, Shannon   141
Westerling, Jeyne   42, 58, 141
Whent, Ser Oswell   128

White Cloaks   27
White Walkers   37, 49, 173
Will   95
William IX, Duke of Aquitaine   15
William Marshal   109–11
Windsor   112, 113
Winterfell   27, 31, 32, 67, 72, 97, 113, 135
   dreams   122, 124–5, 128, 132
Wolf of Gubbio   81, 87, 88
Woloch, Alex   28–30
Workman, Leslie   2
Wun-Wun   30

Xaro Xhoan Daxos   59, 60

Ygritte   48
Yoren   125
Young, Helen   2, 150
Yunkai   59, 60

Zepf, Siegfried, and Dietmar Seel   170
Zoroastrianism   17

www.ingramcontent.com/pod-product-compliance
Lightning Source LLC
Chambersburg PA
CBHW062217300426
44115CB00012BA/2101